the American Lady

ALSO BY PETRA DURST-BENNING

The Glassblower
The Paradise of Glass (forthcoming)

A the American Lady

The Glassblower Trilogy

PETRA DURST-BENNING

Translated by Samuel Willcocks

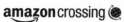

Text copyright © 2002 by Petra Durst-Benning
English translation copyright © 2015 by Samuel Willcocks

The American Lady was first published in 2002 by Ullstein in Berlin as *Die Amerikanerin*. Translated from German by Samuel Willcocks. Published in English by AmazonCrossing in 2015.

Published by AmazonCrossing.

Cover design by Marc Cohen

www.apub.com

ISBN-13: 9781477826584
ISBN-10: 1477826580

Library of Congress Control Number: 2014910547

For Mimi—
this one's for you!

PROLOGUE

Lauscha in the Thuringian Forest, March 1910

*The dance whirls round as the world turns round
and I yearn for a joy I had forgot.
A promise, a passion, a taste on my tongue,
a sweetness lost that can still be found,
a sparkling glass filled with—what?*

Marie sat at her workbench late into the night. To her right was a crate of glass rods, and to her left was a board studded with nails. She put the globes there to cool before they were taken to another bench in the workshop to be coated with silver and then painted. Marie was weary, but she nonetheless felt a gentle swell of pride in her work as she concentrated on the task before her. It wasn't the same surge she had felt some nineteen years ago when at the age of seventeen, she, Marie Steinmann, had been the first woman to blow glass in Lauscha, snatching the privilege from the men of the village. But it was pride all the same, and it warmed her heart every time she saw her niece Anna sit down at the workbench and lean forward to turn the gas tap as though it were the most natural thing in the world.

The idea of a woman blowing glass was nothing new in Lauscha these days, when the boys and girls at the glassblowers' trade school sat together in the same classroom, all intent on the same task. Marie smiled. Nineteen years might be just the blink of history's eye anywhere else, but here in Lauscha it was light-years.

Tshhhh . . . it was such a comforting, familiar sound. "The flame has to sing if it's to take the glass." She could still hear her father's voice as he spoke the words. And once more she wondered what Joost would say if he could see them now: she was a glass-blower, Johanna was a businesswoman, and together, they'd made and sold thousands upon thousands of Christmas baubles over the years.

Marie stretched, then turned off the flame and got up from her stool. It was time to go to bed.

There was no warning at all. Suddenly someone behind her shoved something down over her head. It slammed her nose on the way down and squashed her right ear painfully. She turned her head from side to side but felt trapped in a narrow space.

"What's going on?" she called out, startled. The words sounded strangely muffled, as though she were a little girl again, talking into a saucepan to hear the echo. But this wasn't a pan on her head now—whatever it was, it was made of glass. A huge bell jar, already turning milky pale with her breath.

Was this some kind of silly joke? Weren't Johannes and Anna far too old for such pranks? The twins were sixteen, for heaven's sake.

Irritated, Marie tried to remove whatever it was from her head, but the palms of her hands were damp and kept slipping on the smooth curved glass. The sides of the jar were perfectly rounded—a globe rather than a bell—and it was warm, as though it had just come from the flame.

Marie could feel her own breath hot on her face, trapped in the glass.

It was a globe! The opening at the base was just large enough to fit over her head. The edges were smooth and rounded, but the whole thing was so heavy that she could feel it beginning to dig into the flesh at the base of her neck. She tried to wedge two fingers into the gap, but the globe clung tight to her like a suction cup, and her flesh was already swelling up around the rim.

Marie felt a wave of panic. This wasn't a joke; this was a matter of life or death! She was gasping for breath now, panting out little damp clouds that clung to the glass. The more she tried to shake off the globe, the less air there was. The fear was metallic on her tongue. She tried to lick her lips and found that her mouth was completely dry.

"Help! Why won't any of you help me?" she heard her own voice cry from far off.

A moment later, Marie was back outside the globe. She was just about to breathe a sigh of relief when she found herself back inside again. Inside? Out? She was still trapped—her eyes were staring out from behind the glass like a frog's and her cheeks were puffed up like the gills of a fish. It was ludicrous. Wretched. Pitiful. Cold sweat ran down her clammy forehead and trickled down her neck, pooling along the inner rim of the globe.

She had to breathe; she needed air! A loud humming buzzed round and round her head, growing louder all the time. She tried to put her hands over her ears, but could only touch the glass.

Suddenly she knew that she would suffocate here.

She started to scream . . .

She sat up. Her nightgown was drenched in sweat, and Magnus's arms were around her, his voice in her ear, reassuring her.

A dream. It had all been just a dream. But all the same, it was a long time before Marie's breath was back to normal and she could take her hands from her neck. She still felt as though she were choking.

It was five o'clock in the morning.

Exhausted, she lay back down, not even sure that she wanted to go back to sleep.

Magnus looked at her with worry showing in his face.

Marie closed her eyes so that she wouldn't have to talk. What a way to start a birthday!

◆ ◆ ◆

"Marie! I hadn't thought I would see you here today," Alois Sawatzky said, bowing before her. "Allow me to wish you all the very best on this happy day." He helped her out of her coat and hung it on a rickety hook behind the door.

"It's very kind of you to remember . . ." She wiped a few rain-drops from her forehead. There were damp patches on her sleeve where the rain had soaked through her overcoat, but they didn't seem to bother her.

Sawatzky had never known her to visit his bookshop and bring an umbrella along. Apparently Marie Steinmann thought that carry-ing an umbrella was more trouble than getting wet.

"What a great shame that the weather is so poor on your birth-day. Is there anything worse than March rain, day after day?"

"Unfortunately that's not the only thing that spoiled my birth-day mood," Marie said with a sigh. "I'd better tell you straight out: I'm in a terrible temper today."

Sawatzky raised his eyebrows questioningly. She didn't say any-thing more, though, so he asked, "What about a cup of tea? I've just brewed a fresh pot."

"It certainly won't hurt." Without further ado Marie flopped down into one of the shabby old leather armchairs that the book-seller had set out for his clients. Sawatzky smiled to himself as he noticed that even on her birthday, she was wearing her usual work clothes. Marie Steinmann wore pants and had done so for years; she could put any of those daring young things in the Berlin or Munich art world into the shade—but oddly enough, people here-abouts seemed to care even less about what she wore than where she worked. Or perhaps it was just that nobody was surprised at anything Marie Steinmann did anymore.

With a practiced hand he carried two cups of tea through the narrow confines of his shop, never once brushing up against the piles of books that reared up on all sides, as high as he was tall. He put one of the cups down on the low table in front of Marie and then sat down across from her and sighed. His arthritis had been giving him such trouble in the morning that he had toyed with the idea of keeping the shop closed today, but now he was glad that he hadn't succumbed to that moment of weakness. Marie was more than just a loyal customer. They had known one another for nineteen years now, and she had become something like the little sister he never had.

He stirred his tea thoughtfully and Marie did the same. For a moment there wasn't a sound aside from the gentle chime of candy sugar against the sides of the cups.

A customer could sit and browse or read an entire book in this cozy part of the shop. This was where his most passionate customers met to rediscover the classics, or to indulge in heated debates about the works of the latest writers. Alois Sawatzky's little circle of intellectuals was well-known far beyond the town of Sonneberg. As was his bookshop, which stocked such a range of high-quality titles that it rivaled any of the big city shops.

"You look rather tired," he said as he sipped his tea. "Did you begin celebrating your birthday last night already? Isn't that supposed to be bad luck?"

Marie waved away the suggestion. "I would even welcome a bit of bad luck if it would shake things up a little. Apart from the fact that Johanna and the others insisted that I take the day off, it's been a day just like any other."

Once again he was surprised at how serious this young woman was about everything. He would have loved to see Marie Steinmann really make a day of it. She should put her hair up, put on a pretty dress, and let her sweetheart take her out somewhere, instead of sitting here with an old man.

"We shall have to do something about that!" He stood up and vanished into the depths of his shop. He came back a moment later with a bottle and two glasses. "It's early in the afternoon, but may I nevertheless invite you to a glass of sherry?"

He didn't wait for Marie's answer but poured two fingers of the rich, golden-brown liquid into each glass. He knew that where tea was no help, sherry usually did the trick.

"To your health!"

She took the glass from him. "And to yours," she replied.

He leaned forward in his chair. "Well then. Now you must tell me what's on your mind. And don't try to pretend that everything's fine."

Marie grimaced. "Everything really is fine, though. I mean, it's ridiculous really, but . . ." She hesitated for a moment and then told him about her dream.

"I really thought I was going to suffocate," she said when she had finished. She was still badly shaken. "Poor Magnus was scared almost out of his wits when I screamed!" She heaved a great sigh. "Thank God it really *was* a dream. I still feel awful just thinking about it."

Sawatzky scratched his head. "Sigmund Freud would love to hear about a dream like that," he said dryly.

Marie looked askance at him. "Don't get started with Mr. Freud and his theories of the subconscious! I have to wonder why he can't discover something useful instead." Her voice was dripping with scorn. When Sawatzky didn't reply, she went on, "Something that makes people's lives easier. Machines or some such thing . . ."

Not for the first time, the bookseller thought how strange it was that Marie always reacted so strongly to any mention of psychoanalysis and its founder. In other matters she was quite happy to hear about new ideas.

"As far as we can tell, knowledge of the subconscious has great potential to make people's lives easier," he replied rather pedantically. "But let's not argue on your birthday. Or if we do, let's at least have an argument that leads somewhere."

He put down his glass. "Do you know what? You go ahead and find a book that you like and that can be your present!" If he didn't manage to bring a smile to her face today, his name wasn't Alois Sawatzky. Seeing her hesitate, he added, "It could even be one of those expensive illustrated volumes you like so much." He raised his hands when he saw Marie open her mouth to speak. "No, I won't hear a word of protest!"

She stood up hesitantly. But she had not even looked through the first shelf of books when she turned back to Sawatzky. "There's no point." She shook her head and went back to her chair, fighting back the tears as she sat down. "I don't know what's wrong with me. Now I'm spoiling your fun . . ."

He didn't say a word.

Marie lifted her head at last, almost in despair. "It wasn't so long ago that I believed I would find the whole world in these books. I read every line devoutly, and I spent hours studying the pictures. Sometimes I felt a real connection with all those painters and artists. But what good did it do me? I wanted to better myself. To make something of my artistic gifts. Hah!"

He had been expecting just such an outburst for some time now. Any fool could see that Marie Steinmann wasn't happy. All the same, he was shocked by the bitterness in her voice.

"So much for discovering the world! There are others who can do that. Your Sigmund Freud has discovered the subconscious, Franz Marc paints his blue horses, and just last week you were telling me about Alfred Döblin and his story 'The Murder of a

Buttercup'—now how in the world does anyone get an idea like that?" She looked over at Sawatzky almost accusingly. "Meanwhile, I paint stars and posies and bells and baubles for Christmas trees. Just the way I always have." She swallowed hard. "And I don't even paint well anymore." Marie gazed into space.

Marie Steinmann. The youngest of the Steinmann sisters. The first woman who had ever dared to sit down at the lamp to blow glass. While the other women of Lauscha had been content to paint the finished wares as they had done for centuries in the glass workshops and to marry the men who blew the glass, Marie had sat down at her dead father's lamp when she was just a young girl and practiced and practiced, in secret and at dead of night, until she had mastered the craft. And gradually she had begun making the loveliest Christmas tree decorations that Lauscha had ever seen. Glass baubles so beautiful, so imaginative, and so finely crafted that they made even the humblest home a palace when the holidays came around. There had been envy and gossip, of course, but success as well; it had started as a family business, with Marie as glassblower and her sisters, Johanna and Ruth, doing the rest of the jobs, but now they employed more than twenty workers. The Steinmann-Maienbaum workshop sold tens of thousands of baubles every year worldwide. Most glassblowers in Lauscha grumbled about the state of the economy and their waning orders, but with Johanna keeping the books and Marie bubbling over with new ideas, the Steinmann sisters were doing brisk enough business to expand. Even their critics had to concede that they had not done badly for themselves—especially for a business in which the women ruled the roost. And Ruth, the middle sister, who had followed her heart and left Lauscha years ago to be with the man she loved in America, also did her bit to help the business by taking care of their partners and purchasers stateside.

The children of many families in Lauscha had to leave for the big city to earn a living in the factories that were springing up like mushrooms after rain. Johanna and her husband, Peter Maienbaum, however, had no such worries for their twins, who would take over the family business when the time came.

Marie spoke up again, as though she had been reading Sawatzky's thoughts. "Of course I'm happy that our Christmas baubles are still selling as well as ever. Especially these days . . . But it's just a matter of time until the others notice that I've run out of ideas. I always feel so tired and empty! I just find everything dreadfully dull. Whenever I have to come up with a new design, I feel that I've painted it all before. I'd like to throw all my dreary little sketches in the trash, but we have to publish a catalog every year, don't we! And the inquiries from America about new designs keep coming. Woolworth's the worst; he won't leave us alone. . . Do you think I might have used up all my ideas? Have I designed everything I have in me?" Her eyes were suddenly wide with fear, as though this were the first time she had dared to speak such thoughts aloud.

Sawatzky looked at her. Her shoulders were drawn together, her nose seemed almost sharp, and a thousand sparks seemed to be fading away unnoticed in her dark-gray eyes.

All of a sudden he pictured another Marie in his mind's eye. She had been eighteen years old back then, slim as a willow, with a high forehead and narrow cheeks—and eyes that any man would gladly have drowned in if only she had let him. But Marie had no time to think of anything but her art back then, and she had let nothing and no one distract her. He smiled at the memory. The first time he had shown her where the art and design books were shelved, she hadn't been able to believe that so many people shared her passion.

"Are these all books about art?"

She had been so eager back then. She had spent all the money she had earned with her first commission on the books she loved.

It had been hours before she left the shop with a big stack of books under her arm, with Magnus faithfully following. She had been so devoted to her art that she had never even noticed how smitten he was with her.

Marie hardly looked any different now. She still had the figure of a girl and even her face was unchanged, with large eyes and high cheekbones. Sawatzky chewed thoughtfully on his lip. It was nothing new for an artist to go through a fallow period. But for a booklover like her to turn down the offer of books was more than worrying.

Suddenly he felt a powerful urge to get to his feet and shake Marie by the shoulders. Instead he said, "What you need is a new source of inspiration. You've just been here in the forests for too long, that's all. You've spent years studying the chickadees and the finches, looking at their feathers. And I must admit I'm amazed you managed to get decades of inspiration out of pinecones—speaking for myself, I've never found nature studies terribly interesting."

Marie frowned.

"What you need, my dear Marie, is inspiration from elsewhere—from other art, from other artists. Nobody can work for years on end with only themselves for company—not even the great glassblower Marie Steinmann!" He winked as he said it so that she knew he was not mocking her.

Struck by an idea, he reached for a shabby little volume buried in the pile of books behind him. The poet Else Lasker-Schüler had written a book in memory of her friend Peter Hille when he died, and he had been meaning to give Marie some of Else's poetry for some time. Lasker-Schüler did with language exactly what Marie was trying to do with glass; her poems and stories pushed words to the limits, putting them to new use.

He leafed through it for a moment until he found the poem he was looking for. All the same, he hesitated. Marie was in a bleak mood—would she be able to see the symbolism at work here? The poem was not an easy one to understand. But she had surprised him often enough in the past with how readily she could find her way into difficult texts. Well, it was certainly worth a try, he decided, and held the open book out to her.

"Would you be so good as to read aloud for both of us?"

Reluctantly, she did as he asked. *"I fled from the city and sank down exhausted before a cliff, and I rested for one drop of a lifetime, deeper than a thousand years . . ."*

Sawatzky shut his eyes and listened to Marie's voice as she puzzled her way through the poet's strange choice of words.

"And a voice tore itself free from the peak of the cliff and called out, 'You are so miserly with your self-substance!' And I cast my eyes upward and I blossomed forth, and a happiness took hold of my heart that had chosen me alone."

With every word, Marie's voice melted ever more closely together with the story and her yearning became part of the poetry. Sawatzky's heart beat more quickly.

". . . And a man climbed out of the rocks of the earth, the hair on his head and the hair of his beard was hard, but his eyes were velvet mounds . . ."

Sawatzky watched Marie closely. Would she think that it was all too much when Else compared her friend Peter with Petrus, the rock? The mythic resonances had led to much debate and discussion in intellectual circles, but Marie kept right on reading without comment.

". . . the night had swept away my tracks, nor could I remember my name, for the howling, hungry North had torn it to shreds. And the man whose name was rock called me Tino. And I kissed the gleam of his chiseled hand and I walked by his side."

Sawatzky shut his eyes again. When he opened them once more, he saw tears running down Marie's cheeks. And he knew that he had chosen the right text.

"Why are you doing this to me? Why are you torturing me like this?"

There was despair in Marie's eyes. She snuffled noisily.

"To be able to feel like that! To forget *where* you are, *who* you are . . . *nor could I remember my name, for the howling, hungry North had torn it to shreds*," she read again, moved to tears. "And at the same time to know that you've been chosen, that you can't waste your time on others!" Her eyes were shining. "*A happiness took hold of my heart that had chosen me alone*—she can really count herself a happy woman." Marie was quiet for a moment. Then she spoke again. "But what does all this have to do with me? I have no friend to stand by me and take a fatherly interest—well, other than you— nobody to inspire me like that. And I don't live in a big city or have an exciting life. Who or what do you suppose will give me my artistic inspiration? I sit here in my little village with Magnus by my side and my whole family depending on me and my designs."

"But that's entirely your own choice," Sawatzky said with more than a touch of impatience. And he couldn't resist adding rather harshly, "Even Else had to break free of her family home and run away to the city, as you've just read."

Marie looked up, irritated. "I know, I know, everyone has their own road to follow. And next thing you're going to tell me all over again about that painter who preferred to die in obscurity rather than follow the fashion of the times. What was her name again— Paula Modersohn-Becker?" She held a finger to her forehead as though concentrating hard. "Or you'll tell me about some poet or other who may not have had any food on her table but wrote uncompromising poems all the same."

"Sarcasm doesn't suit you," Sawatzky declared, looking down at his shoes. "I . . ."

She grasped hold of his hand before he could say anything more. "I apologize. It didn't come out the way I meant it, and you know that quite well. I'm being a silly cow today, that's all. And ungrateful to boot." She bit her lip.

He looked up again, half won over. "You never did care much for role models, did you?"

Marie shrugged. "What good do they do me? I've never found one in Lauscha, that's for sure. After all, I *have* broken free of the lives our forefathers led! And I really don't see what I did as being so revolutionary, not anymore. What do you think I have in common with all those women out in the big wide world? Why do you mention them so often?"

"For one thing, you have the world in common," he said, waving his hand in the air.

Marie laughed. "The way you say that! As though the world were a slice of cake and all we have to do is help ourselves with a fork."

Sawatzky laughed. The image was completely Marie. He sighed. "It's not quite so simple, no—and thank God for that. But don't you think it's time to leave Lauscha for a bit? To see a little more of the world?" He wanted to remind her of her dream and the meaning that lay beneath it, but instead he said, "Look at it this way—every bauble you blow travels farther than you ever have—isn't that rather a frightening thought?"

PART ONE

NEW YORK,
THREE MONTHS LATER

*And when the night became day
and the day became a dream,
all my questions fell
into glittering dust.*

1

Dittmer's was the best delicatessen in the city. Those who didn't have the money to step inside the magnificent doors could at least lust after the wonderful window displays, which were so artfully assembled that they put some art galleries to shame. The shop's cleaning women went out at least a dozen times a day to wipe away the fingerprints and marks left by greedy passersby pressing their noses up against the glass. And of those who could afford the prices, hardly anyone had the willpower to walk on past and ignore the wonderful scents wafting through the revolving door . . . Just a quick look, just to buy one little treat. Don't you deserve it, after a long day at work? A bit of cheese? Or three chocolate truffles? Or a handful of those dark-purple plums, gleaming and juicy? Such resolutions generally vanished as soon as customers stepped inside the store and saw everything that was for sale—more delicacies than any other store in the world—and they left with light-blue Dittmer's bags bulging with treats.

Fruit, vegetables, sausage, salami, cheese, prepared dishes—Dittmer's had virtually any delicacy a person could desire. The bakery counter was lined with baskets full of long, thin baguettes and platters piled high with southern Italian biscotti. Next to them, deep-black pumpernickel loaves were stacked up like bricks. At the cheese counter a customer could choose from eighty varieties, and the next counter over displayed oysters from Blue Point, Chesapeake Bay, and Pine Island. To make the choice a little easier, the store offered half a dozen oysters for tasting on the spot—with salt and lemon juice on the side. Or customers could opt for a dish of Dittmer's incomparable oyster stew with butter, cream, and rosemary. A customer could sit down to a plate of oysters and admire the cold counter across the way: with almost ten yards of canapés, it was a feast for the eyes. Whether she was giving an intimate dinner for eight or a banquet for thirty, there wasn't a hostess in town who could afford *not* to include at least one course from Dittmer's, whose dishes were as much part of a society meal as handwoven linen napkins or Tiffany flatware.

Whoever had the money could order the entire meal from Dittmer's expert cooks. No order was too large and no dish too refined for the kitchen. Three dozen Polish pirogis, filled with Russian caviar? No problem, *madame*! A banquet for one hundred and thirty guests, to be served five hours from now? Something of a challenge, but you can rely on us! Such orders unleashed a flurry of activity that the customer would never see. Cooks jostled for space on the gas rings, while kitchen hands scrubbed vegetables and plucked grapes as though they were trying to set a record. And when the goods were delivered, everything had been prepared with such loving care that you'd have thought the cooks had spent the whole week doing nothing else.

This perfectionism fascinated Wanda. She glowed with pride at the thought that she was part of this perfectly tuned machine, that her work helped create such marvels.

Of course her mother had turned up her nose at the news that Wanda was going to start work as a counter girl at Dittmer's.

"Why is there anything dishonorable about selling groceries?" Wanda had asked before Ruth could even say a word. Perhaps she hadn't been about to say anything. Perhaps now that Wanda was eighteen she didn't care how she spent her days. But Wanda preferred to think that her mother was upset by her choice.

"There is nothing at all dishonorable about selling groceries. And there's nothing dishonorable about preparing food," Ruth had declared. "I'm just wondering why you didn't go all the way and become a chef."

"I haven't yet, but there's still time," Wanda had shot back, somewhat annoyed that her mother hadn't been as shocked by her new job as she had imagined.

She straightened her gleaming, starched apron one more time—she had made a point of putting it on at home instead of waiting until she got to work, as all the other counter girls did—and looked expectantly at the door.

Wanda had been working at Dittmer's for two and a half weeks now. So far, every day had brought fresh surprises. And best of all was that Mason Dittmer seemed happy with her work. Granted, he hadn't actually said anything yet, but every time he came past her counter he gave her a friendly nod—though he never so much as glanced at the rest of the girls. Was that because she coped with stress better than most people? Because even amid all the hustle and bustle she kept a cool head? Because even in her first days on the job she had never made a mistake taking an order or writing up the check? Or better yet—perhaps it was because some of the customers had praised her work? After all, she was Wanda Miles; she was from one of the best families in all Manhattan, and that had to help when she was advising customers about their orders. Didn't it? Her mother was one of the most fashionable hostesses in town and an important customer for Dittmer's, which had to mean that Wanda knew what others would want as well. Who better to deal with the whims and wishes of high-society ladies than someone who had grown up in their world? That had been Wanda's argument when Mr. Dittmer had wondered out loud whether the society ladies might not perhaps feel uncomfortable giving orders to her. In the end he had been won over by Wanda's enthusiasm.

"All the parties are such a bore this season! There's no spark anymore! Nobody has any new ideas! Everybody's just chewing over the same old recipes that have already been served up everywhere else!" said Monique Desmoines, wife of Charles Desmoines—one of the most influential brokers at the Stanley Finch Bank—as she fanned herself ostentatiously. She glanced around the counters with an expression approaching disgust.

Wanda took a clean cloth and wiped an invisible splash from the rim of a platter of deviled eggs. "But Mrs. Desmoines, I'm sure you're never short of ideas!"

Monique looked up from contemplating her perfectly manicured nails. Was she imagining it, or was Wanda's smile just a little less subservient than she expected from the service at Dittmer's? Was there even a hint of sarcasm in it?

"No more than your mother is," she replied, frowning slightly, and then she sighed. She still hadn't quite gotten used to the idea that the Miles girl was working at Dittmer's. Thank God her own daughter Minnie would sooner drop dead than stand on her feet for a ten-hour shift. But Ruth Miles herself was a little eccentric—no matter how legendary her hospitality was. Well, the girl was no better than her mother . . . She sighed again, then remembered what she had actually come for.

"Your mother could certainly tell you a tale or two about that; too many parties, too many guests, and nobody these days really knows how to appreciate the lengths a hostess has to go to." She waved a hand dismissively. "But there's no use complaining, I always say. Deeds, not words! Deeds, indeed!"

If that's the worst of your troubles, you should count yourself lucky, Wanda found herself thinking. Out loud she said, "The talent to be a true hostess is something you must be born with." She squared her shoulders. "Do you have something in particular in mind for your next event? Perhaps you have it all planned out already? As you know, we at Dittmer's are here to help make whatever you intend go smoothly." *We at Dittmer's*—wonderful!

Monique Desmoines sat up straighter. The Miles girl knew what she was doing after all. Ruth had probably told her what wonderful parties Monique threw. She made a mental note to invite Wanda's parents to the dinner she was currently planning, then remembered that she had waited in vain for an invitation to Ruth's most recent event. She struck Steven and Ruth off the list in her head.

"Do I have a plan?" she said triumphantly. "I have more than just something in mind. I have it all written out!"

Monique began to root around in the depths of her handbag. A few moments later she looked up and sighed impatiently. She was holding a sheaf of folded notepaper in her hand.

"What I have in mind will light a fuse under my guests. I'll be the first to admit it: I want to shock them!" She pursed her lips as though she were expecting Wanda to object. When nothing of the kind happened, she leafed through her bundle of notes.

Wanda waited patiently.

"Of course I want to spoil my guests, but more than anything else I want them to realize just how spoiled we all are—myself included, my dear! Who can still enjoy a dish when we all have so much more than we need? Who can still appreciate food as God's gift to mankind?"

She swept her hand around in a gesture that included all the counters in Dittmer's.

"You might say that what I am planning is a culinary allegory, a description in food, a gastronomic depiction of how we were driven from Eden." Monique raised her eyes piously, as though she were expecting heavenly approval for her idea right then and there.

"A culinary allegory, I see," Wanda said, nodding earnestly. "That will certainly impress your guests." *Goodness gracious—even for Monique Desmoines, this is going a bit far!*

"Here it is," Monique said. She smiled triumphantly as she handed a folded sheet of notepaper across the counter. But before Wanda could reach out and take it, she snatched it away again.

"Just so that we understand one another . . . I expect absolute discretion. For this party of all parties, nobody must know what to expect. You'll understand exactly what I mean when you see what I have in mind . . ." Monique glanced hurriedly over her shoulder as though she feared that a pack of hyenas were skulking somewhere, just waiting to steal her party ideas.

Wanda put her fingers to her lips. "I shall be as silent as the grave. And I'll do more than that; an important event like this calls for uncommon measures on our part." She beckoned Monique to lean a little closer. "I'll take your order directly to the kitchen department without going through catering as we usually do. I will also personally guarantee that nobody catches sight of the dishes when they are ready to be delivered. There are spies everywhere after all . . ." she whispered. *Ha, if Mr. Dittmer only knew what trouble I am taking over one of his most important customers.* She took the folded sheet of notepaper and put it into the pocket of her apron as though she didn't dare look at Monique's order herself. Then she buttoned the pocket closed.

"Your guests will have a surprise they will never forget!"

◆ ◆ ◆

At the other end of town, at the harbor, where thousands of crates from all over the world were unloaded every day of the year, two people were sealing a deal.

The shorter of the two, a nervous little man, shoved an envelope into his jacket pocket as the taller man snapped his briefcase shut with a flourish.

"I'm very pleased with your work, Mr. Sojorno," the tall man said. "You have been a great help to us, preparing the way like this. Not every warehouse supervisor would be so . . . cooperative. My father and I assume we may rely on your help in the future as well."

Cooperative—who is he trying to kid? Sojorno thought. They had him over a barrel and they damn well knew it! Sure, they paid him well for what he did, but what good would that money do him behind bars? He wiped the sweat from his brow and said a quick prayer to Santa Lucia to ask that he never end up in jail. Then he looked around nervously.

"Part of the shipment was already a little . . . well, let's say it had . . . suffered from the journey," Sojorno whispered. "I worry about what might have happened if there hadn't been enough air."

Franco de Lucca frowned deeply. "Well, shipping certain kinds of goods over such a distance is a tricky business, we all know that. And . . . special shipments like these need constant temperatures and good airflow. But please don't worry, Mr. Sojorno. Our man in Genoa is a master of his craft. As long as nobody interferes with the crates on the crossing, there's plenty of air inside."

The other man nodded. He found Franco de Lucca's words reassuring. "When can we expect the next delivery?"

"First thing next week," de Lucca answered, leafing through his pocket diary.

"So soon? I thought that *signore* would go back to Genoa first—"

"I do not pay you to think, Mr. Sojorno! If you have any trouble with this, you must let me know," de Lucca interrupted. He fixed his ice-blue eyes on Sojorno until the man began to shift uncomfortably from foot to foot. Like a dog submitting to the pack leader, he hunched his shoulders and made himself look as small as he could. He simply shook his head in response.

De Lucca's gaze became a little easier to bear. "I knew that we could rely on you," he said, and even smiled.

Why does the dear Lord hand out his gifts so unfairly? Sojorno wondered. The mere fact that the other man had smiled at him made him feel like one of the chosen few. The young aristocrat had everything that he did not, everything that he wished for; he had a physique that made Roman sculpture look clumsy, olive-brown skin that bristled with manly stubble even at this early hour, and eyes that could glow like hot stones—or glitter cold as ice, as they had just now. Finally, there was a tenderness and sensitivity in the shape of his mouth and chin that could make women swoon. *Madonna mia!*

"I will be in New York all summer. Since we have so many shipments arriving, my father felt it could do no harm to have one of us here looking after things in person," the young de Lucca said as he put his diary away.

Sojorno found it hard to take his eyes off the other man. Franco de Lucca didn't owe him any explanations. The fact that he gave them all the same was a special sign of favor.

"Would I be right to assume that the next few shipments will also be, ah, special deliveries?" He put a touch of sarcasm into his voice as he used de Lucca's words, but a moment later, he felt a hard hand press his Adam's apple against his windpipe.

"Just so we understand one another, Sojorno—we ship Italian red wine. Nothing more!"

2

Marie spent the first two days aboard the ship in her cabin. Not because she was suffering from seasickness like so many of the other passengers, but rather because she spent hours at a time reading the English dictionary that Sawatzky had given her. She went to the dining room at mealtimes but left before the last guests had put down their flatware. She justified her solitary habits by telling herself that if she worked hard at learning the vocabulary, then at least she would be able to understand a little of what was being said around her when she reached New York. Even though she was also—or, mostly—making this journey to meet new people, right at the moment she didn't feel like it. In fact, she didn't feel like doing anything much, and she had to admit that she deeply regretted her decision to go visit her sister Ruth in America. *What am I doing here?* she wondered as she hurried through the narrow corridors below decks, her head down. She would much rather be sitting at her lamp, blowing glass. Or trying to at least . . .

Back in early April she had mentioned that she might like to travel to America one day. No sooner were the words out of her mouth than she realized that she had set an avalanche in motion that she could not stop. Rather than objecting—as she had expected them to—Johanna and Peter had said it was a wonderful idea. She deserved a reward for all her hard work, and a change would do her good. Marie had protested, asking who would do all her work, but Johanna had just waved a hand dismissively; they could get by without her for a while, especially if she traveled during the summer when there was less work. It would be quite enough if she came back in the fall, since they didn't need to have the new catalog ready until the following February. When Marie had tried to say that the journey would cost too much, Peter just frowned and asked whether she planned to take her savings to the grave. Besides which, he added, she would be staying with Ruth and wouldn't need to spend anything on room and board.

And so Marie had had no choice but to get used to the idea of leaving Lauscha for a while. Magnus had kept quiet, as he usually did. He may have been silently hoping that Marie would ask him to come along, but if so he hid his disappointment well when she did no such thing.

If Marie were honest with herself, the idea of getting away from his dogged devotion for a bit was at least as tempting as sightseeing in New York and the thrills of the big city. And so she set out on her own to the county hall in Sonneberg to apply for her passport.

But now that she was all on her own in the narrow little cabin, Marie couldn't understand how she could have been so mean. She felt as though she had turned around and suddenly discovered that her shadow was missing.

She tucked her dictionary under her arm and went off to one of the second-class passenger lounges. She picked out a sofa in the far corner of the room and sat down, her face to the wall. Perhaps she'd feel a little less homesick here.

She was just learning how to say, "Excuse me, sir, but I've lost my way," when she heard the rustle of linen and felt a jolt through the sofa cushions as someone sat down next to her.

What kind of ruffian would just take a seat without asking . . . ?

Marie looked up, irritated, and found herself looking into a beaming round face.

A plump white hand reached out to shake hers.

"Do excuse my manners—I haven't even introduced myself! My name's Georgina Schatzmann, but you can call me Georgie—everybody does. I'm on my way to my sister's wedding, and unless I'm quite wrong, you and I are the only ladies on board traveling on our own. So I thought it would be nice if we got to know one another a little better. I've been keeping my eyes open for you"—she giggled—"and now I've found you, haven't I?"

Sadly so! thought Marie. She was just trying to think of a polite but firm way to give this woman the brush-off when Georgie prattled on.

"You'll probably think me very forward, but I've been all aflutter about the trip, you know! The crossing, the wedding, New York—I feel I might burst from all the excitement!"

When Marie looked at her neighbor's roly-poly features, she decided this wasn't at all unlikely; Georgina Schatzmann's eyes were practically popping out of her face and her eyelids were indeed aflutter. Her cheeks were shot through with a network of fine veins and they rose and fell as Georgie chewed on her prominent lower lip. Her teeth were off-white. All in all, it was a tragicomic sight.

"I'm Marie Steinmann, and I'm on my way to visit my own sister. Although she's been married for quite a long time now," she heard herself reply.

"Well whoever would believe it! Steinmann and Schatzmann—we've even got the same name, almost!" Georgie shook her head. "That must mean something . . ."

What it means is that I'll never learn English on this crossing!

From that moment on Georgina Schatzmann clung to her like a lapdog who had found a new mistress. At mealtimes she waited in front of Marie's cabin so that Marie had no choice but to go into the dining room with her, and between meals Georgie managed to track Marie down again and again in one or another of the lounges. On the third day, Marie simply gave in to her persistence; if she couldn't have a bit of peace and quiet, then she would make the best of the company she had. Since it turned out that Georgie was a teacher by profession, she asked whether she would be willing to help her learn vocabulary. "Of course," Georgie replied.

Georgie was good at thinking up funny images to help Marie remember the difficult words, and soon her knowledge of English was coming along by leaps and bounds. The language barrier had been her biggest worry before the trip, but it seemed that she might have a knack for speaking English. At least that's what Georgie said.

Marie was flattered by the compliment and soon they began to talk of more personal matters. When Georgie found out that Marie was a glassblower and that she made Christmas baubles, her excitement knew no bounds.

"Steinmann glass—I should have realized right away! We have your baubles hanging on our tree every year! I love your pinecones and the little nuts, but my mother prefers the larger figures, like Santa Claus and the angels. So we always argue a little about which piece to hang where." She laughed her cheerful laugh and her eyes grew even rounder. "Every year we go into Nuremberg, right after the first Sunday of Advent, and we go to the big department store by city hall and see what's new from the Steinmann line. And of course we buy a few pieces every time. But tell me, how in the world do you get all those lovely ideas?"

Marie smiled. "Most of the time the ideas just fall right in my lap," she admitted. "All I have to do is go for a walk in the woods or along the banks of the Lauscha—that's a creek near our house—and then I'll see a flower and notice that the blossom has a particular shape and there you have it, I already want to capture it in glass."

"The way you say that . . ." Georgie's eyes shone with admiration. "It's as though you're a magician."

Marie gave a thin smile. "But I lost my magic powers long ago."

When she saw Georgie frown, she added hastily, "But that's enough about home! Why don't you show me the clothes you bought for the trip to the big city?"

She didn't want to talk about glassblowing, indeed she couldn't talk about it. She didn't even want to think of the last few weeks at her workbench, when she had felt like a mere beginner again. She had sat there looking at the rod of raw glass in her hand as though it were something from another universe. All her movements had felt clumsy and unnatural, and she hadn't created any new shapes. She had blown a few standard globes just to have something to do but had felt the panic rise inside her until she fled from the room. Unable to bring herself to tell the others that she couldn't bear her own shortcomings a moment longer, she simply said that the soup from supper the night before had given her indigestion.

She feigned interest as Georgie showed off her new dresses. Try as she might, however, she couldn't find anything to like about the shapeless, mouse-gray tent of a garment that Georgie wanted to wear for her sister's wedding. She had an idea and looked into her handbag, then fetched out a necklace of glass beads that she had made herself. She held it up to the neckline.

"Just look at that! The cloth seems to shine all of a sudden with your beads next to it. That's magic!" Georgie said, reaching out and touching the necklace, awestruck.

"No, it's just glass," Marie replied, smiling. "It's for you. A present!"

Georgie flung her arms around Marie gratefully.

Then Marie asked why Georgie was making the trip, rather than either of the two older brothers she had already heard about, or even Georgie's parents.

Georgie grinned. "Mother certainly wanted to . . . but Father decided that the ironmongery business wouldn't last a day without him. And Mother didn't want to send my brothers. She was probably afraid that if she asked them afterward what America was like they'd just grunt 'very nice' and leave it at that. By sending me, she can be sure I'll spend a week telling her all about everything."

"A week? Will that be long enough?" Marie raised her eyebrow skeptically.

Georgie didn't take offense at the joke but spluttered with laughter. Marie was surprised to find herself thinking that Georgie was actually a lot of fun.

"It sounds like your family is very nice," she said.

"Oh, they are," Georgina replied. "All the same I'm happy to be away from them for a while. They give me such sorrowful looks just because I haven't a husband in sight! Is it my fault that the dear Lord made me broad in the beam?" She lifted her plump little fists and let them fall on her wide thighs. "If I were as slim and pretty as you are, I'd have been married long ago as well," she sighed.

"But I'm not married," Marie protested.

"Aren't you? I thought that you and Magnus . . ."

"Well yes, we live together, but we're not married. I know that must sound strange, and I suppose it is," she added, seeing the confusion on Georgie's face. "But somehow we never got around to marrying. I . . . never felt the need to marry Magnus."

Georgie looked even more startled. "I've never heard of such a thing! Your neighbors must have a thing or two to say about that, don't they? Well, if I had a man who wanted to—I'd say yes before he could count to three! But who knows, maybe I'll find someone in America who loves me." She shut her eyes for a moment, and for that moment her face was calm and still. "Do you know what I'm looking forward to most? For once I won't be fat Georgina Schatzmann, who can't get a man. I'll walk along the streets of New York, and I'll be just a woman out having fun! A woman like any other."

Marie looked at her new friend thoughtfully. Georgie knew exactly what she wanted from her journey. If only she could say the same.

Soon the voyage was almost over. "I will bet the whole of New York Harbor will be covered in fog," Georgie had said on the evening before they docked, but in fact the morning of June 15 was as clear as if someone had polished the sky with a soft, clean cloth. They were already out on deck together before breakfast, each with a blanket around her shoulders against the morning chill. They were surprised to find a good number of passengers up there before them—everybody wanted to be first to catch sight of the big city.

Marie felt strange. All of a sudden she wished the crossing would last a little longer. When the first dark silhouettes began to show on the horizon, she was glad to have Georgie at her side, beaming as always.

"*. . . just a woman out having fun.*"
Could I do the same myself?

People stood shoulder-to-shoulder down on the steerage deck as well. The immigrants had been herded together like livestock down in the belly of the ship for twelve days—with no fresh air and not enough food—and their new country was coming closer, moment by moment. They were headed for a new beginning and for an ending as well. They would say farewell, and they would arrive. Anticipation thrummed in the cold morning air.

All of a sudden there was a stir in the crowd.

"There she is! There she is!"

"Look over to the left there, everybody!"

"Quick, come over here or you'll miss her!"

They responded with excited cries and waving hands, fingers all pointing the same way, as though toward someone they all knew well, someone they wanted to greet. Inside of a minute they had all rushed over to the railing on the left side.

"It's Lady Liberty! Look at her raising her golden torch to greet us!" Georgie dug her elbow into Marie's ribs in excitement, never once taking her eyes off the most famous statue in the world. Her outline shone in the morning air, the spikes of her crown dark against the bright sky. Her own eyes were turned back to the Old World as she stood there with her torch of freedom raised to light the way to the New World.

When Marie didn't react, Georgie turned to face her. "What is it? Why are you crying?"

Marie shook her head. She didn't know whether she could speak if she tried.

"You stop that right now, you moping minnie! Or I'll start as well," Georgie threatened, only half in jest. She poked Marie in the ribs several times. "Enjoy this moment! We don't get a greeting like this every day, you know!"

"Oh, I know," Marie sniffed. "I feel I've never seen anything so beautiful in my life."

Georgie put an arm around Marie's shoulders. She grinned impishly. "Just you wait. This is only the beginning!"

3

Just a few steps from where New York made—and lost—its money was the Brooklyn Bar. The clientele was mostly bankers and brokers in their shirtsleeves. Sometimes one of them would invite his secretary to join him, but there were generally few female customers. The bar's owner, Mickey Johnson, set great store by the fact. "Where can a man have a few drinks in peace and quiet these days? There's nowhere safe from women, I'm tellin' ya!" he often lamented. If he saw a woman come through the doors he usually gave her a frosty welcome indeed.

Whether they'd made money that day or lost it, in the evening the customers crowded about Mickey's counter in such numbers that the beer pumps never rested for a moment. Full glasses were simply passed back through the crowd as the barmaid could never have kept up on her own. And whether it had been a good day or bad, Mickey's bar was always astonishingly loud. Huge quantities of alcohol were consumed and the tobacco smoke was thicker than the morning mist on the Hudson River. A chance passerby, who was drawn in by the crowds and chose to drop in for a beer, would never have been able to guess what kind of day it had been on the New York Stock Exchange. Mickey himself boasted that he could tell just from the smell of the men's sweat; good cheer and excitement smelled quite different from dogged determination, and different again from panic and fear.

Harold Stein had just taken his first sip of scotch when he saw Wanda come through the door. They had made it a habit to meet here every Wednesday after work, though most of the time he was there an hour before she was.

Her head held high, her eyes fixed dead ahead, she made her way through the press of wildly gesticulating men. The expression on her face was icier than an approaching storm, yet every man in the room looked at her in awe all the same—Mickey included. As soon as he spotted Wanda hurrying past his counter, he left the beer glasses unattended and reached up for the bottle of aniseed liqueur. He poured it into a tall, slim glass, which he handed to the nearest customer. "Pass it through! This one's for the lady!" he barked, then watched keenly as the glass made its way through the crowd.

How does Wanda manage to win people over like that without having to do a thing? Harold wondered, not for the first time. Charm alone was not enough, no more than beauty—though Wanda had plenty of both, to be sure. Was it her unmistakable laugh, so free and easy that everybody in the room turned their heads to look when they heard it? The enthusiasm she brought to everything she did, even the smallest daily task? Harold had never been quite able to say just what her gift was, but he knew that he sometimes envied it—especially when he had to deal with a difficult client. Wanda would probably have found it the easiest thing in the world to persuade that Oregon hog baron to invest in Silver International—but, despite his best efforts, he had to let the stubborn old goat leave without signing a thing.

Harold noticed the admiring looks the other men gave Wanda as she sat down across from him on the narrow bench. How they would have liked to touch her light-blonde hair! To inhale that smell of peaches and young skin! To put an arm around her slender, supple waist or run a finger along the smooth line of her neck. All of a sudden the air in Mickey's bar, the haunt of hard-bitten profit hunters, tingled with quite another appetite.

Wanda's drink had reached the table just before she did, and she picked it up and took a sip the moment she sat down. She wore a grim look on her face.

Harold noticed right away that she was not carrying that silly white apron over her arm. Hadn't she come straight from work, though? It wasn't hard to figure out what had happened. Well, he knew he wouldn't hear that charming laugh today.

"What was it this time?" he asked. "Am I right to assume that you're finished with Dittmer's?"

Wanda frowned. "How did you . . ." But instead of finishing her question, she sighed. "It was Monique Desmoines's pig trotters!"

"Her *what*?"

"I got the order wrong. Actually, no I didn't. If Monique hadn't made such a song and dance about her dinner party and—" Wanda waved her hand dismissively. "Then the way she reacted—it was ludicrous! All because of a little misunderstanding."

She was putting on a brave face, but she couldn't hide the fact that she had been deeply humiliated—the pain was visible in her eyes and her mouth was drawn tight.

Harold raised an eyebrow. The last job that Wanda had lost had been at Arts and Artists, a chic, modern gallery. As he recalled, she had been fired there because of a "misunderstanding" as well. She had only been on the job two weeks when she spotted a shabby-looking fellow packing sculptures away into his bag, and she had raised an alarm. Two cops who happened to be walking past the gallery just then had duly taken the man, loudly protesting, down to the station house. That had been the end for Wanda; the supposed thief turned out to be a well-known sculptor who had come to take some of his pieces back and put out new ones for sale, all with the gallery owner's permission.

Wanda's eyes were glittering, though Harold couldn't tell whether this was because she was furious or fighting back tears.

"Oh, Harry, it's so awful!" she snorted. "Mason Dittmer never even bothered to listen to my side of the story! I'll tell you one thing; that's the last they'll ever see of me. I'd rather starve than buy so much as a slice of cake from there!" To lend force to her words, she drank down the liqueur in one gulp.

"Mixing up an order is hardly a reason to fire you," Harold said, trying to downplay the whole episode. Then he looked at her skeptically. "What did you do, send ham instead of salami? But didn't you say something about pig's trotters?"

"Well, perhaps it wasn't such a simple story after all," Wanda said slowly. She looked down into her empty glass, absorbed by whatever she saw there. A moment later she giggled quietly, deep in her throat. Then she told Harold all about the huge fuss that Monique had made about keeping her secrets and about the sheet of notepaper that Wanda had passed on directly to the cooks. And she told him how they had duly prepared a platter of pig's trotters, a dish of stewing steak, and a tureen of tripe soup. She also told him how she had decorated the casseroles and dishes herself so that nobody could spoil the surprise.

"I can't believe it!" Harold said, leaning across the table to Wanda. "Tell me you're pulling my leg! You must have noticed that something wasn't quite right!"

She was taken aback. "Of course I thought it was odd!" she said defensively. "But after Monique had blathered on about the Fall of Man and culinary allegories, I thought that pig's trotters sounded like just the thing. And apart from that, how was I supposed to know that the notepaper she gave me was her weekly order for the down-and-out shelter? I never even saw the menu for her party! It turns out the dishes were all supposed to be dyed black with squid ink." She giggled nervously. "I would have loved to see the look on the guests' faces."

Harold couldn't make himself laugh along. "You're impossible! Why didn't you go straight to Dittmer if you had the slightest doubt?"

"I never even thought of that," she admitted and shrugged. "If you knew Monique and her crowd as well as I do, you wouldn't even ask the question. There's no end to their foolish ideas!"

He shook his head. On the one hand, Wanda liked to pretend that she couldn't care less about being one of the upper class. On the other, she exploited her privilege shamelessly when it suited her. Rather than simply doing what was asked, she acted of her own accord, and never even thought about the consequences. This sort of behavior could be quite charming in a woman—but it was right out of place at Dittmer's deli, or in any other job.

Wanda heaved a long sigh. "Oh, Harold, it's so unfair! Why do these things always happen to me? I wanted nothing more than for it to work, this time." She slumped in her seat. All her nonchalance had vanished and she looked young and vulnerable.

"Mason Dittmer can go to the devil! He's a lout, and he doesn't deserve you," Harold heard himself say vehemently. *Why do I always let her wind me around her little finger like this?* he wondered, as he took Wanda's hand and uttered soothing words.

They had met at the Spring Ball that his employer—the Stanley Finch Bank—threw for the company's most important clients every year. Steven Miles had brought his family. When he saw how Wanda spoke to her parents, Harold had realized that she clearly did as she liked and got away with it, with no regard for the rules, thanks to her beauty and charm. He had resolved to be stricter with Wanda than everybody else was; if he wanted to make an impression on her, he had to play tough. It wasn't an easy resolution to keep, however, for every time he looked at her lovely face he felt an urge to lay the world at her feet. But even he could do nothing to change the fact that this was the fourth job in a row she'd lost.

"Perhaps it just wasn't meant to be," he said. "Perhaps you're not cut out for that sort of work." He shook her arm gently. "Any one of your colleagues would have shown the order to Mr. Dittmer, but you went right ahead and did things on your own. As you always do. And that was your downfall. Not for the first time, I might add. Let me just remind you of Arts and Artists, and how you—"

"All right, all right. You don't need to list my failures," she cut in icily. "I hate it when you sound like my father."

For Harold, this was almost a compliment. There were few men he admired as much as Steven Miles. He made no secret of his ambition to be just as rich and influential one day.

Ignoring Wanda's sulky expression, he told her, "Your parents certainly won't be angry if you give up the idea of working once and for all. And when we're married, I'll earn enough for both of us anyway. My darling—there are so many other ways a woman can keep busy! Especially a woman as charming and clever as you." He nodded encouragingly.

She withdrew her hand. "I know you'd like it if I were like my mother and found one hundred and one ways to do nothing all day long. But I have to disappoint you there. I want to do something meaningful with my life," she said loudly.

A few heads turned to look at them.

"Why shouldn't I be able to do what thousands of seamstresses, chambermaids, and governesses do every day of their lives? Why shouldn't I hold down a job? Am I not as clever as them, perhaps?"

"Nobody's saying that. But why don't you mention the real difference between yourself and these other women?"

"And what would that be?" she asked suspiciously.

Harold shrugged. "They *have* to work, but you don't!" *They've never known any other life*—he could have added—*they've worked from morning till night ever since they were small.* But one look at her downcast face told him it was better not to say anything more.

"But I can't spend all my time sitting about at home!"

"For my part, I really wouldn't mind being a gentleman of leisure," he answered with a grin. Once he saw her frown again, he hastily changed the topic. "By the way, am I mistaken or wasn't your aunt supposed to be arriving from Germany today?"

"Six o'clock this evening. You're mistaken, though, if you think I'm going to help with taking our small-town relative around New York. Mother can show her sister the city—I won't be in any hurry to help, that's for sure. From everything I hear about Aunt Marie, she's a real oddball." Wanda frowned. "What else could you call someone who's never left her hometown in her life?"

Harold laughed. "I can see that you've already made up your mind about your German aunt."

Wanda waved his remark away. "I won't have time for her anyway; after all, I have to look for another job."

She looked at her watch and put a hand to her mouth. "I'm already late! I was supposed to be at the hairdresser's a quarter of an hour ago." No sooner had she spoken than she was on her feet, stooping over to give Harold a good-bye kiss on the cheek.

"The hairdresser? Don't they expect you to be home when your aunt arrives?" Harold asked, surprised.

Wanda made a face. "So what if they do? I'm sure some gossip has already told my mother about what happened at Dittmer's—it could even have been Monique herself," she remarked mockingly. "Since I'm sure to get a good scolding for that, a second one hardly matters . . ." She shrugged. "Thank you for listening so patiently."

And she was off.

4

"I still can't believe you're really here!" Ruth squeezed Marie's arm as the two of them waited for the taxi driver to stow the luggage away behind the passenger bench.

"Nor can I," Marie said, glancing around nervously at the harbor, her ship, the *Mauretania*, on its way to Ellis Island, the skyscrapers, which were so much taller from close up . . . and the taxi, and Ruth. Above all Ruth. It was all so strange.

"You look wonderful," Marie said spontaneously. She reached out almost reverently and stroked the silk sleeve of Ruth's navy-blue suit.

At first she had hardly even recognized her sister. They had sent photographs to one another over the years, of course, but no picture in the world could have prepared her for Ruth's elegance at thirty-eight years old. Her outfit was modest but of the finest quality—there was no longer any hint of the girl she had been in her youth, when she had always put on another string of beads rather than take one off.

"And I feel wonderful as well." Even the way Ruth laughed was elegant. "But don't you worry. Starting tomorrow, we'll spend all our time looking after you and your happiness." She frowned as she plucked at Marie's dress. "The first thing we'll do is get you some new clothes—we can't have you running around in these old things. I suppose I should consider myself lucky that you didn't turn up wearing those famous pants of yours!"

Marie felt a twinge of shame as she climbed into the car behind her sister. She resolved not to tell anyone that she had bought this dress especially for the trip to New York. Now it seemed that had been money down the drain.

The taxi moved off slowly, and Marie gazed out the window. "I'm in New York—isn't that crazy?" She laughed joyfully.

"And you could have been here long before. I wrote letter after letter trying to get one or the other of you to come visit me here, but what good did it do?" Ruth was only half pretending to be upset.

Marie didn't want to let go of Ruth's hand ever again. "My goodness, how long has it been since we saw one another?"

"Wanda had just turned one, or . . . drat it . . . I'm so excited I can't even think straight," Ruth squeaked, wiping a tear from the corner of her eye. "It's been seventeen years, can you imagine? I feel as though we're talking about another life."

Marie felt tears prickling at her eyes as well.

"You know how it is at home—always too much to do and never enough hands for all the work," she sniffled. "But I'm here now. And I'm so glad!" New York blurred before her eyes.

Nothing had prepared her for what she was feeling at this moment. Strange though it may sound, Marie was surprised at how happy she felt to see her sister again. Of course she loved her, but as girls, they had simply been too different to feel anything more than the usual family fondness—Ruth had gone one way and Marie had gone another, as far as such a thing was possible in the narrow little house they shared.

"That aside, *you* could have visited *us*, you know!" she said once she had dried her tears. Then she shrank back into her seat, startled, as another car came toward them and missed them by a hair's breadth.

For the briefest of moments Ruth's face clouded over. "You know it was never as easy as that. But not a day has passed that I didn't think of you all. Now tell me—how was the crossing?"

Marie told her about Georgie, and how she wanted to visit her while they were both in New York.

Ruth didn't seem especially interested in hearing more about her new friend. "And you had no trouble on arrival?"

Marie shook her head. "The border guards looked rather fierce. One of them even went through my handbag, but that was all. Then they let me on through." She laughed briefly. "You should have seen how excited the immigrants were! We had hardly gotten past the Statue of Liberty when the whole lot of them started staring into one another's eyes. Georgie told me that they were deathly afraid of having some sort of eye infection. 'Trachoma,' I think she said—anyone who's sick with it gets sent straight back. Have you heard of such a thing?"

Ruth nodded. "I think it's quite right that they check very carefully who they let into the country. We can't cope with infectious disease. Just imagine, more than eleven thousand people arrive here every day! They have nothing but a bundle of old clothes under an arm, and every single one of them thinks the streets are paved with gold! But this whole business with immigration is simple, really. Four or five hours and then they're through, and the New World awaits!"

"Did you have to come through Ellis Island back then?" Marie asked curiously. She suddenly realized that she knew next to nothing about how Ruth had left Germany.

"Good heavens, no!" Ruth waved a hand. "For one thing, there weren't as many people arriving back then. And for another I had my papers in order . . ." She instinctively dropped her voice to a whisper, though it was most unlikely that the taxi driver understood German.

Marie giggled. "Baroness Ruthwicka von Lausche—you must have had the fright of your life, didn't you, when you saw that Steven had gotten hold of forged papers that gave you a noble title?"

Ruth grinned. For a moment Marie thought her sister looked just like the daring young girl who had left Lauscha, and her husband, in the dead of night all those years ago.

To this day, Marie didn't quite know why Ruth's marriage to Thomas Heimer had failed. He was the son of one of the most prosperous glassblowers in the village, and at least at first, Ruth had been head over heels in love. But then one day she had turned up back home with all her worldly goods and her three-month-old daughter, Wanda. "I'm never going back to him," was all she said—not a word of explanation otherwise. Johanna and Marie had had no choice but to accept it.

"Having a title certainly did me no harm," Ruth said now. "You can hardly imagine the way people bent over backward to help. Of course that was also because I arrived with Steven. All the same . . ." She looked thoughtful. "I never felt comfortable about those forged papers. That first year was very hard. Whenever the doorbell rang, I thought, well that's it, they're coming to get me." She sighed. "When Thomas finally agreed to the divorce and Steven and I could get married, a weight fell from my shoulders! I've felt like a new woman ever since I became Steven's wife."

"It's odd—at the time I hardly noticed what was going on, somehow," Marie replied, embarrassed.

Ruth just laughed. "And you think that's odd? You had nothing but those baubles of yours on your mind, day and night!" Then she pointed out the window. "Look, we're just crossing the Avenue of the Americas now. It won't be long before we arrive." She gave

Marie a quick explanation of the city's grid layout, with its streets and avenues that imposed some order on the chaos of Manhattan.

Marie was astonished when the taxi stopped among the soaring buildings. "You live *here*?"

"We have the top apartment," Ruth replied proudly, pointing vaguely up to the top of the slim skyscraper before them. "Don't tell me you never heard about our move a year ago!"

"Well, quite, but I thought someone as wealthy as Steven would live in his own house . . ."

"Not at all!" Ruth said triumphantly. "Anyone who can afford it is moving to Fifth Avenue these days. I can hardly imagine ever having lived anywhere else. Steven and I were among the first to recognize the advantages of living right in the middle of town: you need fewer staff to run an apartment, you're much closer to the shops and the opera, you don't have all the bother of a garden . . . Let me tell you, it won't be long before they *all* leave their old houses! Fifth Avenue is already called Millionaire's Row, I'll have you know." She snapped her fingers and the taxi driver followed her through the elegant front door with Marie's luggage. Marie followed—and then stopped, thunderstruck.

"I don't believe it!" She looked around, astonished.

Over a hundred square yards of red marble stretched out before her, with gilded benches of black granite lining the edges and vast palms growing in pots by the walls. The whole back wall of the lobby was one vast aquarium in which fish in every color of the rainbow swam among coral and strange-looking plants. Just as Marie was expecting a parrot to fly out and land on her shoulder, a uniformed page boy opened the elevator door. Marie followed her sister hesitantly into the elevator cage, a gleaming chamber of bronze and glass, which began to glide upward.

"Well, this is living, isn't it?" Ruth said, her eyes gleaming with amusement. "You won't see anything like this in London or Paris.

This style of apartment house is a New York invention. I can hardly wait to show you my little kingdom."

Marie felt vaguely dizzy, but she figured it was from the unaccustomed speed of the elevator.

Ruth and Steven's apartment was no less luxurious than the imposing lobby downstairs. Long hallways to the left and right led to a multitude of vast rooms, all lavishly outfitted with mahogany furniture, Chinese carpets, and heavy silk curtains. Marie was shown to the guest suite she would occupy, complete with its own bathroom, which was decorated in pastel green from floor to ceiling. There was a brand-new set of a hairbrush, comb, and mirror laid out for her on the dresser and, alongside that, an arsenal of little pots and jars with creams and lotions that made Marie nervous just to look at. She sat down on the enormous bed to test it and then spotted a selection of ladies' magazines on her bedside table. They had been fanned out so artfully that she could hardly imagine picking one out to read. Goodness gracious—who did Ruth imagine was coming to visit here? An opera diva?

Marie washed her hands and face quickly and left it at that— Ruth had already told her that a maid would unpack all her luggage—then set out in search of her sister.

As she walked soundlessly across the plush carpets that covered the whole length of the hallway, she found herself thinking how Ruth used to polish the stairs in their childhood home, scouring away with the block of beeswax until the wood came to a high shine. After their mother had died so young, the three sisters had divided up the housework and all the jobs in the workshop. Ruth had taken care of the cooking and most of the housework and was rarely to be seen without a cleaning cloth in her hand, or a knife for peeling potatoes. She had never complained about all the hard work, but even as a young girl she had dreamt of meeting a prince someday who would carry her off to his castle. Johanna and Marie had thought this was all empty talk and daydreaming. Marie smiled at the memory. Whoever would have thought that Ruth's castle would be here on Fifth Avenue in New York?

Marie peered cautiously through the next door on the right. It appeared to be another parlor, this one decked out in shades of red, but just like the three other rooms she had looked into, this one was dark and deserted. She was relieved to hear the rattle of dishes from somewhere next door, and she thought she could smell coffee too. Ruth's drawing room at last! But when Marie opened the next door, she found herself in a tiny kitchen where a red-cheeked cook was watching over several pots simmering away on the stove.

"Hello, my name is Lou-Ann. Can I help you?" she asked, heaving a large pot from the stove as she spoke and setting it down to cool on the marble kitchen counter. Without missing a beat, she went over to a window and opened it to let the smell of soup out of the room. Then she opened the oven and took out the tray of cookies that Marie had smelled from next door. Soup and broth, coffee and cookies—the smells seemed so comforting to Marie that she suddenly wanted nothing more than to sit down right there with Lou-Ann with a cookie in one hand and a glass of milk in the other.

But Ruth was waiting impatiently for her at the end of the corridor with tea and cakes.

"There you are! I thought you must be so bone-tired you'd fallen asleep. Don't worry, you can go to bed soon enough. Steven promised to come home from work early today so that we can take an early supper. He can hardly wait to see you!"

"I'm looking forward to seeing him—your Steven is such a fine fellow," Marie replied. "The last time I saw him was when we inaugurated the new warehouse in Sonneberg."

Unlike Ruth, Steven had come to Thuringia every year in the early days, back when he was still working for Frank Woolworth.

Once he began working for his father's firm again, however, he didn't come as often. Whenever he did, he made sure to look in on Ruth's sisters, even if their business relationship didn't strictly call for it. Steinmann-Maienbaum still made Christmas decorations for Woolworth's stores as well as for Miles Enterprises, the Miles family's wholesale business.

"But most of all I'm looking forward to seeing Wanda! I can hardly believe that little scrap of a girl has grown into a young woman by now. Where's she hiding?"

Ruth sighed. "Heaven only knows where the girl is. She's not at work; that much is certain. Her boss . . . oh, forget about it. Why don't you tell me what you think of the apartment?" She swept her arm all around.

"It's wonderful, of course! Everything I've seen so far has been . . . beautiful. I can hardly wait for you to give me the grand tour! You could fit a whole street of Lauscha houses in here," Marie replied. It was odd, she thought as she spoke, that Ruth didn't want to talk more about her daughter. When she had first become a mother, she had talked about little else. Marie hadn't quite understood how anyone could talk for hours about a babe in arms, and had found the whole thing rather tiresome back then.

"Your drawing room is especially elegant. It's so different!" Marie swept her hand around at the sleek black furniture, decorated only with modest inlay work. Dotted about the room were a bust of a pensive girl, a nude marble figure with long hair cascading down her back, and a bronze sylph.

"You were probably expecting me to make myself a doll's house of a room, full of flounces and lace curtains," Ruth replied, feigning indignation. "Come here, I'll show you something I'm really proud of." She walked over to a glass-topped table. Under the pane was a recessed tray, lined with black velvet, holding a whole swarm of butterflies and dragonflies, an array of brooches showing ladies' profiles, and peacock feathers.

"These are my treasures. Of course Steven would buy me jewels with precious stones anytime I asked, but I prefer this kind of costume jewelry. I think they're so much more original than the same old string of pearls or diamond necklace." She laughed. "You really ought to see my friends craning their necks and peering to see whether these are real insects or just jewelry." She picked out a gleaming, dark-gray hornet and held it up. "Doesn't it look like it is real? It's by René Lalique. And this snake here, I find there's something very erotic about it. It's from a workshop that . . ."

Marie felt ever more uncomfortable as Ruth picked up one jewel after another and told her about each piece, prattling on about artists whose names Marie only knew from Sawatzky's books. She had never realized until that moment that there were actual people who could afford such artworks—and that her own sister was one of them. Ruth suddenly seemed a stranger to her. And the apartment she was so proud of looked more like a museum than a family home—though of course she would never say as much to Ruth.

What would Georgie make of all this? Marie wondered, and knew the answer right away: Georgie would most likely have gobbled down a whole tray of cookies by now, rather than nibbling daintily at one as Ruth was doing.

"Hallo, is there anybody there? Mother, Aunt Marie . . . Are you home?" The voice came from the hallway.

The door to Ruth's drawing room opened wide and a tall, slim young woman stood in the doorway, whose hair . . . a grin flitted across Marie's face.

"Wanda!" Ruth cried, putting her hand to her mouth, her eyes wide with shock. "For heaven's sake, what have you done?"

All her poise and refinement were gone. She spoke—no, shrieked—in a hoarse voice.

Wanda raised her eyebrows and smiled at her mother.

"Do you mean my new hairstyle?" She pointed at her silver-blonde hair, which fell to just below her ears. "Didn't it turn out well? So chic, and just in time for summer! You'll all be hot and bothered while I'll be able to enjoy the summer breezes!"

Only then did she seem to notice the guest. She turned to Marie.

"Aunt Marie, I'm so pleased to meet you," she said with exaggerated good manners. She held out her hand awkwardly.

Marie put out her own hand in reply, calloused and tough from hours at the workbench, and grasped hold of Wanda's. The girl's skin was smooth and soft.

Their eyes met. Wanda's eyes were blue and clear as water and they sparkled with amusement, as though she were laughing over some secret joke.

The little minx! Marie shook hands much harder than she usually did.

"Don't worry; I only rarely bite."

5

Why hadn't he managed to get to the Casa Verde an hour earlier! Franco looked over irritably at the bar, where customers were already crowded three deep. As usual at this hour, the restaurant was packed to the rafters—the shifts had just changed at the nearby garment factories. Though all the tables were full, the stream of customers coming in the door never stopped. Italian tailors and factory hands, just off from their ten-hour shifts, the last three hours dreamt away in visions of a plate of steaming pasta and a glass of wine. And maybe a smile from Giuseppa, the owner's daughter. Well, at least he had been given a table right away.

Franco leaned back, resigned. Given the crowd, it didn't look as though Paolo would have any time for him in the next half hour.

There was loud talk and laughter from the next table, where a fresh batch of customers had taken their seats amid much shuffling of chairs. As Franco looked across, he realized that the diners were all restaurant owners from the neighborhood. And they were all customers of the de Lucca family company too. So this must be some sort of regular get-together. Meaning it wouldn't be long before someone came to him with the next complaint—as if he hadn't had enough of those already today. And he had at least another three restaurants to visit after this one!

Franco put a surly look on his face. Then, all of a sudden, a gust of garlic wafted up to his nose and a moment later, Giuseppa set a plate of pasta down in front of him. He wasn't in the least bit hungry but dug his fork in all the same so that nobody would disturb him.

Giuseppa took several jugs of wine over to the next table, where they were greeted with whoops of glee.

Fine, then. As long as they were busy getting drunk, they would leave him in peace.

Franco put his fork down. He was tired. None of his previous visits to New York had been such hard work. But this time, wherever he went there was nothing but trouble, day in and day out. And everybody expected him to conjure up the answer to whatever problem they had.

It had started with the very first restaurant he had visited that morning; the owner, Silvester Forza, had refused to take on two of the five kitchen hands he'd been sent, claiming that they were too old. Franco had demanded that he call the men and see for himself that they were barely into their thirties. So what did Silvester want? Children? Franco had said sharply that his father would hardly be pleased to hear that Silvester was acting as coy as a virgin on her wedding night. Was there anyone else, Franco asked, who could get hold of cheaper labor for him? Of course not, Silvester was forced to reply.

The next piece of bad news had come not long afterward. Michele Garello, who owned five of the best restaurants around, reported angrily that three of the kitchen hands he'd taken on had run out on him after just a week. He gave an ultimatum; either he got another three men from the next shipment, he said, or he wanted his money back, adding, "You tell your father that if I have to, I'll find my own workers over here. I may have to pay them a few more dollars in wages but it won't bankrupt me."

Damn it! He would never have said such a thing to the old count in person.

Franco's next customers hadn't been all smiles either. One of them had complained that he didn't need to buy as much wine at one time since his clientele mostly drank beer anyway. Of course he was just angling for a discount, because as soon as Franco mentioned the possibility, the beer drinkers were no longer an issue. The next restaurateur was having trouble with his liquor license. Perhaps Franco could put in a good word for him . . . Franco waved the idea away. "Pay your taxes, and they'll restore your license. Besides, what makes you think that I have any pull with City Hall in these matters? I'm a foreigner!" Just because he was a nobleman, these people believed that his word was law.

Franco was clutching the fork so tightly that his knuckles had turned white. Tomorrow he would have his weekly telephone call with his father. He already knew what he would hear: *Don't let these people get away with anything! Show them that they mustn't mess with the de Luccas* . . . Disgusted, Franco pushed the plate away. As though playing the tough guy would fix every problem!

"What's wrong? Don't you like Mama's spaghetti?" Giuseppa asked, sitting down in the chair across from him and frowning.

"Your mother is one of the best cooks in the whole city," Franco said, eating a hearty forkful of pasta to show her he meant it. Giuseppa and her mother were not to blame for his troubles after all.

"I could bring you something else . . ."

Why was she looking at him so fearfully? Had he ever done anything to her? Franco frowned and shook his head. "Please don't bother."

He had already visited half a dozen customers before Paolo. Everywhere he went, they had given him something to eat—the *padrones* probably thought they'd have an easier time making their case if they softened him up with a plate of tuna, a slice of pizza, or a dish of zabaglione.

Giuseppa stood up. "I'll get going then. Papa wanted me to tell you that he'll be with you in a few minutes. I could bring you a glass of wine in the meantime."

"Thank you, no, I still have some." He pointed to his half-full glass.

"Maybe he's just fed up with drinking his own wine! You should offer the count a glass of Chianti! I bet he wouldn't say no to that!" one of the men at the next table called over to Giuseppa. Another man elbowed him in the ribs to keep quiet.

There was laughter around the table, but it had a nervous undertone.

Franco glared at the group and saw that the man who had spoken was Solverino Mauro. He was a customer too, but not a good one. Only two days earlier, Franco had needed to pay a call on Solverino with four of his bruisers to collect some money he still owed from the last wine shipment.

The other diners were all looking over at Franco now like animals that had caught wind of something interesting. Some looked nervous, others awestruck, a few of them skeptical—there was hardly anybody in the neighborhood who didn't know him. Everybody wanted to know how the powerful Count de Lucca's son would react to such a provocation.

Franco looked coolly at Solverino. "I wouldn't talk so loud if I were you. Or have you forgotten our little conversation a couple of days ago?" Solverino had only agreed to pay once one of Franco's men had started to get a little rough.

The man lifted his hands in apology and gave an embarrassed grin.

"Solverino doesn't know the first thing about wine!" another man called over to Franco. "Or he'd know that the de Lucca Rossese di Dolceacqua really lives up to its name . . ." He looked around to make sure that everyone was listening before unleashing his punch line. "It has no more flavor than the water it's named after!"

The table erupted with raucous laughter.

"What's going on? Haven't you got anything better to do than bother my guests with your idle chatter?" Paolo interrupted. "Maybe I should come eat at your place and do the same."

He heaved a sigh as he sat down in the chair his daughter had occupied a few moments earlier. "What a rabble! As soon as they've had a few drinks they start to behave like silly schoolboys. Is there anything worse than having your competitors in as customers?"

Silly schoolboys! Not at all. Franco gritted his teeth. "Let's talk about your next order. I have other calls to make today."

When Franco got back to his apartment that night, he felt as though he'd spent a week working in a Sicilian quarry. His back ached and the muscles in his cheeks were so tense he could not relax his face at all.

It was a warm night. Tired though he was, he didn't feel the need to go to bed yet. Instead he lit a cigarette and went out onto the balcony. Although he was almost at the top of an eighteen-story block, with only one apartment above him, there was nothing special about the view; to the right was a strip of the harbor and to the left the back wall of a print works whose chimney belched out stinking smoke day and night. Franco supposed it had to belong to one of the daily papers, though not one of the important ones.

He stared at the glowing tip of his cigarette.

Back home in Genoa the crickets would have begun their nightly symphony at this hour, the chirring call carried along on warm winds from the sea that reached into every last corner of the palazzo. The green marble floor of the courtyard would be shining silver in the light of the sickle moon.

The cigarette smoke had turned stale. Franco tasted a flat, musty flavor on his tongue like that of a rotten lemon.

Nobody had ever criticized his family's wine before, not on any of his previous trips to New York. He would never have believed that anyone would dare.

He tossed his cigarette from the balcony and watched it arc away into the darkness. Something had to be done. He could not allow centuries of tradition—or his family's good name—to be harmed.

He could well imagine what his father would say in this situation:

You have to be tougher. You have to shut up loudmouths like that before they can even say Mamma mia! *If all our ancestors had been good-natured chumps like my son is, our family would never have lasted four hundred years. Do you want to be the first Count de Lucca to drag our name through the mud?*

And so on and so forth.

Franco laughed bitterly at the thought. His father would never consider the possibility that one way to secure the family's good name might be to make good wine. No, the old count had his own methods. Franco hated to admit it but he had to concede that—in their own way—they worked. Liguria was not by nature a fine wine region like Lombardy, for instance, or the Veneto, but there wasn't a family in Italy who exported more wine to America. This was because the count bought up all the grape juice he could find on the market—and he didn't care about the quality as long as the price was right.

All of a sudden Franco could hear his grandmother Graziella's voice in his ear. *"Wine only comes out right if the Lord God blesses it with just enough sun and rain."* He smiled at the memory of the elegant old lady. She had always taken him along with her to the vineyards when he was a little boy. He had held her hand, and in the last years of her life, when she was no longer so steady on her feet, she had held his. She clasped hold of his arm with her right hand and held the walking stick in her left, its silvered handle shaped like a bunch of grapes.

His father may not have passed on a love of winemaking—but grandmother Graziella certainly had.

"Just enough sun and rain, and if the Lord God is feeling especially kind then he will bless you with a woman who knows the vines, whose love will make them grow stronger than any of your modern breeding techniques. A woman's love can make even the tenderest green shoots flourish. Nothing is stronger than that, my child."

A woman's love . . .

Franco felt a fist clench around his heart.

If you lost a woman's love, then whatever life was within you died away.

And all at once he was far away, lost in the distant past.

It had been many years ago. Franco was in his early twenties and had just finished his degree in economics in Rome when she had crossed his path—quite literally. He was leaving the university administration offices where he had just completed the final formalities for his degree when he had bumped straight into Serena Val'Dobbio. She was one of the first women ever admitted to study in the university's hallowed halls, and she was on her way to register for courses. After only a few minutes in Serena's company, Franco was hopelessly smitten, and he knew that he wanted to spend the rest of his life with her. She seemed to like him too, and they met whenever her seminars would allow it. He told her of his plans to plant a new kind of grape in the vineyards when he was done with his studies, and about his attempts at hybridization. She listened closely and confessed that she knew nothing about wine but that she was in charge of the vegetable garden at home. She told him that the villagers said her tomatoes grew as well as they did because she always had a song on her lips when she worked in the garden. Franco's heart leapt. He could see wonderful pictures in his mind's eye, promises of happiness . . . himself and Serena, hand in hand among the vineyards. *"A woman's love can make even the tenderest green shoots flourish."*

And then it was time for him to go back to Genoa. They swore a thousand oaths of loyalty as they parted, promising to meet again when Serena was on vacation from the university.

Their letters sped from Genoa to Rome and back. They numbered every letter they wrote, worried that the Italian postal service might lose one. By day Franco was the hard-driving businessman his father had always wanted, shelving his plans to plant new vines because there was a longshoremen's strike to deal with, and in the evenings he sat in his room in his parents' palazzo, writing poems to Serena. He wrote to her about love—all-consuming and painful—and of his plans to make their family land at Lucca into the best wine estate of all time, with her help.

But the count had not approved of his son's infatuation with a complete stranger. A woman who was not of their class. The daughter of a master baker from Palermo. He had acted as he had seen fit.

And Franco had been young and obedient . . .

Try as he might to recall Serena's face to his mind's eye, it had faded. It no longer hurt to remember her.

No other woman had managed to conquer his heart since then. He had had affairs, but these were only to satisfy his physical needs.

Franco felt a flash of bitterness. Whatever had become of the young man who had tried to capture the moonlight over Genoa and put it down in words? The man who had spent hours poring over volumes of botany to find out how to cross the old-established vines with other varieties to bear more fruit, to add depth of flavor to the white Cinque Terre and Colli di Luni wines his family had made since time immemorial?

Was he even living his own life anymore?

Or was he just an extension of his father's will?

6

Marie felt she had been caught up in a whirlwind and no longer knew which way was up. Over the last few days, she and Ruth had been constantly on the go, barely ever stopping for a rest.

"You didn't come here to sit around our parlor. If I know you, you want to go back to Lauscha with a whole suitcase full of sketches and ideas to use in your glassblowing. And then next year, with any luck, we'll be able to look forward to the New York Collection!"

Marie had almost forgotten what it felt like to hold a gas tap in her hand. All the same she nodded, embarrassed.

"Let's hope you're right," she said halfheartedly. So far nothing had inspired her.

She only rarely saw her niece.

Once Wanda had wanted to go shopping with them, but Ruth had refused to take her daughter unless she hid her short hair under a hat, while Wanda had refused just as firmly to "spoil" her new hairstyle, so nothing came of it. Marie didn't know whether she really felt sorry about that.

A few days later, however, the three of them did go shopping. Ruth seemed to have made peace with the idea of Wanda walking around without a hat. But the truce proved short-lived as soon as the time came to decide which shops to visit; whatever Ruth thought was chic, Wanda declared as hopelessly old-fashioned. Once inside, the squabbling continued, since there was hardly an article of clothing that mother and daughter could agree on. Marie kept out of these arguments entirely—not that she was asked for her opinion. When she said that she wanted to go into the menswear department—she couldn't wear the same old pair of Father's pants forever—they looked at her in horror.

Though Wanda was reserved toward her aunt and cheeky to her mother, she was charming and gracious with strangers. The salesgirls fought for the privilege of serving her, bringing dozens of garments, box after box of shoes, and all sorts of other wares for her approval. It seemed to Marie that Wanda wanted to prove something to Ruth and her: *Just look how nice I can be when it suits me.* She had the feeling that there was more to Wanda's stubbornness than the younger generation's typical love of making things difficult for their elders. But Ruth had packed their days so full that Marie had not yet found an opportunity to get Wanda alone and find out why her niece thought she always had to strike the first blow.

When they were not out shopping—which Marie found very hard work—Ruth showed Marie the town. She learned soon enough that in New York, the two activities went hand in hand: there were hundreds of shops all along Fifth Avenue; the theaters on Times Square stood one next to the other, each with their brightly lit billboards; and just a little to the south was the world's largest department store, Macy's. A couple of miles north was the Metropolitan Museum of Art. They had gone past the impressive building a few times, and Ruth assured Marie that there would be plenty of time to visit it later.

While her sister always marched into the shops at top speed, Marie could have spent the whole day standing outside and gazing up at the skyscrapers that soared above.

"You know," she confessed to Ruth one day, "I actually thought it was rather odd how you kept going on about the skyscrapers in the first few letters you wrote to us. I wondered what could be so special about a building, no matter how tall. But I understand now! These things are really incredible." She waved her hand at the whole street. "Just imagine: there haven't been buildings like this since the great age of the Gothic cathedral eight hundred years ago!"

As Marie gazed up into the heights, her eyes gleaming, Ruth told her that each skyscraper hid a whole town behind its soaring façade, with its own post office, lawyers, shops, shoemakers, and everything else one might need in life.

Of course they went into a Woolworth's store as well—after all, the chain had been the first customer to bring Marie's baubles to America. Marie wouldn't rest until she had sat down at one of the famous lunch counters and eaten an ice-cream sundae while shoppers thronged all around her. Ruth, however, turned up her nose at this sort of entertainment—it was all much too low-class for her. Marie teasingly reminded her that she had only met her husband Steven through Woolworth himself, so there was nothing low-class about the man. Ruth agreed, laughing.

"Who knows—perhaps we'll find another Steven here, for you!" she said, her eyes twinkling. Marie just waved the idea away. She had come all this way partly to be free of Magnus for a few weeks—she wasn't going to let her sister start choosing men for her!

Ruth told her that at Christmas there were tables full of Lauscha glass all around the ground floor of the shop. Globes, angels, and Santa Claus figures were all set out neatly on red velvet, just waiting for customers to pick them up and take them home.

"Just imagine: they tell me that last year fistfights almost broke out at the tables over your silver angels! There were even reports in the newspapers. With photographs!" Ruth said, laughing at the memory. "They just didn't have enough angels for everyone. Johanna had even made a point of telling Mr. Woolworth he needed to order more. Well, sometimes even a business genius like him can get his numbers wrong."

Despite Ruth's detailed descriptions, Marie had trouble imagining her Christmas baubles here; she couldn't draw the connection between her daily work at the bench back home and the hustle and bustle around her.

Sometimes they met Steven for lunch in restaurants with melodious names—Delmonico's and Mamma Leone's. Marie had to get used to the idea of going out to eat in a restaurant even though they were just a few steps from home. And she had to get used to the food as well: crabs, lobster, poached chicken breast, and all sorts of strange fare that didn't fill her up. She would much rather have stayed home and eaten a few eggs or a plate of potatoes with Ruth at the kitchen table—simple home cooking, the kind of thing that Lou-Ann made for herself and the two maids. They could have talked about old times as they ate. And about the new times too. But they only ever got to do that in the evenings when they returned to the apartment with all their packages and bags. Even then they didn't sit down in the kitchen, where Ruth rarely went, but in the drawing room just as they had the first evening, drinking tea and nibbling at biscuits.

Most of the time Ruth asked questions and Marie answered at length. Ruth was mostly interested in Johanna and Peter and the twins, of course.

"Anna looks terribly solemn in all the photographs Johanna sends me—is she really like that?" Ruth wanted to know.

"Solemn? I don't know . . ." Marie shrugged. "I don't think I would call her solemn. Obstinate perhaps. In fact Anna's even more obstinate than I was as a girl—if that's possible. Sometimes I'll come into the workshop in the morning and find her sitting there after she's worked all night on one of her designs!"

Ruth looked rather taken aback; she had never really understood anyone who poured herself into her work like that. Then she asked after Magnus. Did he still follow Marie around like a faithful dog? Ruth had never had a very high opinion of the man in Marie's life. She also wanted to know who did which jobs in the workshop, how they all approached their work, whether the new warehouse in Sonneberg was really such a great step forward, and so on and so forth. "Do you remember our first commission for Woolworth? The whole house was full of boxes stacked up to the ceiling! We could hardly move." She laughed.

Marie answered all the questions as well as she could, but she sometimes had to admit that she simply didn't know—whether the question was about actual business matters or just village gossip.

"You're still my little sister Marie. Nothing in your head but glassblowing," Ruth said, smiling sadly at her sister. Then she reached out and stroked Marie's hair in a gesture of rare tenderness. "Which makes me even happier that you've come to visit. I had expected that Johanna might come someday. But you . . ."

"I haven't been feeling myself lately," Marie murmured. "I needed a change of scenery, as they say."

She could see the question in Ruth's eyes but said nothing more about it. What could she have said? That she felt dried up, like a fruit that had withered on the vine? That she was scared even to think of her workbench back home? Her sister was one of her greatest admirers, but they had never been able to talk about glassblowing and artistic matters.

Instead she said, "By the way, your ex-father-in-law isn't doing too well. They say he's on his deathbed."

Ruth's face clouded over for a moment.

"Are you even a little bit interested in how Thomas and his family are?" Marie asked after a while, when the silence had stretched out too long.

"If you really must know, no I'm not," Ruth said, standing up suddenly. "To tell you the truth I would rather that you never mention them again. As far as I'm concerned the whole pack of them could up and die tomorrow—I couldn't care less!"

Marie looked up in confusion. "But Ruth—they're a part of your life as well! And Thomas is Wanda's father."

Ruth grabbed her wrist hard. "Even if that's true a thousand times over, you will never say that again, do you hear me? Especially not when Wanda is anywhere near. Steven is the only father Wanda has."

"All right, all right . . ." Marie waved a hand. "I'll make sure I never mention the past again," she said, stung.

"Don't misunderstand me," Ruth pleaded. "It's only the Heimers I don't want to hear about. It may have been a long time ago, but I can't forget the pain they caused me. You do understand that, don't you?"

Marie didn't want to make it too easy for her sister. "Well, all right—but I have to say I find it odd that you never told Wanda who her father really is. She has a right to know where she comes from, doesn't she? It's not as though she would love Steven any less because of it."

If *she* were in Wanda's shoes, she would want to know that she was the daughter of one of the best glassblowers in all of Lauscha!

"Or are you still ashamed of the divorce? Getting divorced is really not that uncommon these days. Even the Baroness of Thuringia . . ."

Ruth shook her head vehemently. "It's not about that. If Wanda knew that Steven wasn't her biological father that would just make everything more complicated than it already is, believe me. Never you mind having a right to know—that would all be grist to Wanda's mill!" She heaved a deep sigh. "Sometimes I just don't know what to do with her. My daughter insists fiercely on what she sees as her rights, but woe betide me if I ever ask her to recognize that she has duties as well! She won't even hear of it! She's a great deal like her father in that respect, if nothing else."

"Aha—now you're the one mentioning Thomas!" Marie said triumphantly.

"And I'd rather cut my tongue out than ever mention him again!" Ruth replied, grinning. "As for Wanda, perhaps she'll become a little easier to deal with once she and Harold are married." She bit her lip. "If only they already were . . . I'm sure the two of them have hardly done more than kiss—not that I want Wanda to do more than that, don't misunderstand me—but I am a little surprised that they are so much like brother and sister. When I remember how I felt back then with . . . Thomas . . . I could hardly wait to lie in his arms. And then once Wanda was on the way we couldn't get married fast enough . . ." She smiled at the thought.

"Perhaps Harold just isn't the man of her dreams," Marie said, thinking of Magnus. She had never been swept away by emotion when he took her in his arms, and when they made love it was more for his sake than for her pleasure. "Perhaps some women simply don't have as great an erotic appetite as others."

Ruth looked at Marie skeptically. "Be that as it may, I hope Harold proposes to Wanda soon. Steven says that he has to get ahead in his career first. But the way I see it, she couldn't hope to find a better man."

"Ruth!" Marie said, outraged. "You sound as though you can hardly wait to get rid of your daughter. Wanda is only eighteen—isn't that rather young to marry?"

"What should she be waiting for?" Ruth replied. "To meet the wrong man and then make the same mistake I did? Or to find some job that takes up all her time and energy, and then become a bitter old maid? Just imagine, in the spring she even came up with the idea of becoming a nurse! I thought my ears were deceiving me. My Wanda, in a bloodsmeared surgical gown? Thank heavens a friend of mine found her a job in a gallery not long after that." She shook her head, appalled. "A nurse—as though any man would ever be interested in marrying her after she'd seen such things and worked herself half to death!"

"But if she wants to help people, shouldn't you be happy about that? Once she's spent some time emptying bedpans and changing soiled bandages, I daresay the work would lose a little of its charm. The way you keep forbidding Wanda from pursuing her dreams just makes her all the more determined."

"What nonsense! Nobody wants to stop her from helping the needy. I go to the hospital once a week myself and read to the patients. I've asked her often enough whether she wants to come with me. But that hardly means that she should make a career of it."

"If your daughter has even the slightest trace of your own stubbornness, you'll have a hard time making her into the compliant little miss you seem to want," Marie said. She gave Ruth a gentle dig in the ribs. "And now it's time for you to test me on yesterday's vocabulary. I want to have a go at the next chapter in my English textbook later this evening."

Ruth groaned. "Not again! Can't we skip class just for once? You already speak wonderful English."

"But I want to understand as well. I still have trouble with that," Marie answered stoically as she opened her phrase book.

◆ ◆ ◆

She had been pounding the pavement all day. There was a secretarial opening not far from Harold's bank—and Wanda fondly imagined how they would meet for lunch each day. And another job at the Municipal School Board, where she would be in charge of handing out free textbooks to needy children. And a position as receptionist at the Waldorf Astoria hotel. All her efforts were in vain. The men in gray suits who interviewed her needed only a moment to spot the link between her name and Miles Enterprises and then suddenly decided that she was too young for the post. Or it was already taken. Only the man at the Waldorf Astoria had told her straight out that they had been disappointed already by "young ladies of your background" who spent most of their time flirting with the guests rather than getting to work. Wanda hadn't bothered to reply that she would take her work very seriously if only somebody would give her a job!

It had been a long and frustrating day, and now her ankles were swollen, her legs ached, and a dull anger gnawed at her belly. She wanted nothing more than to creep into her room for the rest of the evening. On the other hand, given the way her mother monopolized Marie's every waking moment, she had hardly gotten to see her aunt. And she was hungry too. So despite her bad mood, she sat down for dinner with her parents and Aunt Marie. Lou-Ann's eyes shone with pride as she dished up a potato gratin that Marie had specifically requested. Her mother eyed the crispy cheese crust suspiciously and held her hand over her plate to stop Lou-Ann from serving her more than a mere spoonful, but Wanda asked for a double helping. It was time to see what kind of food her country cousins in Thuringia ate.

"Look what I bought myself today. A New York guidebook! In English!" Marie took the book proudly from her pants pocket and passed it to Steven.

Wanda was still amazed that Marie had managed to ignore Ruth's attempts to dress her respectably. But she'd done it somehow, and at least here at home she wore pants and a selection of tight-waisted blouses that were cut like men's shirts, with ruffles down the front and at the cuffs. Marie looked so daring in her getup that Wanda found herself thinking of the Three Musketeers. She would like to try it herself sometime . . . but Mother would never allow that.

"What a good idea! In fact you should have had a city guide all along," her father said, looking fondly at his wife. "Ruth knows all there is to know about the best shoe stores and boutiques. But if you ask her what year a building dates from or who the architect was, my dear wife is usually stumped for an answer, aren't you, my love?"

Ruth shrugged indifferently. Wanda knew her mother didn't care about that sort of thing.

"Well, I think that the authors just copy off one another. Most of them have never set foot in the city," Wanda said. But she felt a twinge of annoyance that she hadn't thought to give her aunt a guidebook herself. Perhaps the two of them could have taken one of the walking tours described in its pages.

Marie looked at her curiously. "Do you think so? I find it very informative. Especially the section about New York's bridges—that was the first thing I read, right through! Look, I'll show you something."

Everyone around the table smiled—Marie's fascination with New York's bridges was well-known by now.

"Look, this is how they built the Brooklyn Bridge," Marie said, pointing to a photograph of a dozen workers grinning as they struck poses in a nest of steel cables. "It says here that they used fourteen thousand miles of steel cable. By the time it was done, it had cost three times as much as they expected."

"Does the book say how many workers died building the bridge?" Wanda asked with a hint of concern in her voice as she bent over the page. "Or that thousands of poor immigrants worked on the site for decades, sweating their guts out for two dollars a day?"

"Wanda!" Ruth chided her.

"What do you mean, *Wanda*? Aren't you the one who always says there are two sides to every question? Light and shade, remember.

Where there's wealth, there's poverty too. And that's especially true of New York. You only show Marie the side of the city you think she should see. How is she supposed to form her own impression?"

"Oh heavens, there you go again with your views on the social question. I hardly think Marie came all this way so that she could go visit the slums," Ruth said icily.

"That's not what I'm talking about," Wanda shot back. "Aunt Marie is an artist. That means she wants to see more than Broadway and the temples of commerce. Or the grand events at Madison Square Garden. That's not where art really happens these days—true art moved on long ago. Pandora says—"

"Kindly spare us your dance teacher's opinions in such matters. The woman's mad," Steven interrupted gruffly. Then he turned back to Marie.

"Wanda's right about one thing, though," he said, glancing over at his daughter with a frown. "New York is a work of art in its own right. There are no new worlds to discover in this day and age, but this world-class city is the work of human hands. A work in progress. And each and every one of us should feel grateful to be a part of it."

"I never knew you could be such a poet," Marie said, giving Steven a gentle dig in the ribs. "Go on, it's fun hearing you talk like this."

Why couldn't her aunt talk to her, just once in a while? Wanda turned back to her food in a huff. The potatoes tasted very good, even if they looked like mush.

Steven pointed out the window. "Out there the buildings are so tall that some streets don't get to see the moon and stars at all. It's like living in a canyon, but each canyon offers thousands of opportunities every day. Win or lose—everyone holds their future in their own hands. That's the real beauty of this city, for me."

"Opportunities!" Wanda spat out, before Marie's face could cloud over again with that dreamy look of hers. "You mustn't believe everything that Father says. If you happen to be young, and a woman, there are next to no opportunities. All you ever hear is what you're not allowed to do."

Marie looked at her, baffled. "Whatever do you mean?"

"She probably means she's looking for another job," Steven said, then turned to his daughter. "Must you really bore our guest with all that?" he asked her in a much sharper tone than usual.

Ruth couldn't help but add, "Just how often does your father have to offer you a job at Miles Enterprises? It's getting a little tiresome how muleheaded you can be."

"And just how often do I have to tell you that I don't want to let Daddy give me a job in the family firm?" Wanda asked right back, imitating her mother's tone. Switching back to her normal voice, she added, "After all, when Father was my age he went to work for Mr. Woolworth. He didn't ask his own father for a job."

"Harold isn't altogether happy about your wild ideas either," Ruth announced as though Wanda had never spoken. "He's already complaining that he hardly gets to see you."

"You and Harold are all cut from the same cloth, it seems!"

The argument went on, back and forth across the table. Sometimes the tone grew harsh, sometimes a little less so. Then all of a sudden, after a particularly bitter exchange, Ruth burst into tears.

"Ruth, my darling, don't cry!" Steven reached out tenderly and brushed the tears from his wife's cheeks.

She raised her face toward him.

"What did we do wrong? She's always had everything she ever needs, hasn't she?" she whispered, her voice thick with tears.

Wanda swallowed hard. They were talking as though she weren't there—again! Even Aunt Marie was ignoring her.

"That's how young people are at that age. At least nowadays. I'm quite sure that Wanda will apologize, as she knows she should, and . . ." Steven spoke to his wife in soothing tones.

All at once Marie pushed her chair back and stood up.

"That's enough! I am sure you will excuse me if I leave the table. Nobody can put up with this kind of palaver."

"Marie, please stay!" Ruth said, jumping to her feet. "I can't let Wanda drive you away too."

"What do you mean, Wanda? You two are the ones who are acting as though she were the first woman who ever wanted to work!" Marie stood in the door for a moment, shaking her head. "I just don't know what your problem is," she told Steven. "First you tell me that New York is the city of a thousand opportunities, but as soon as your daughter tries to seize one of them, you both scream blue murder! Good gracious—she isn't planning to steal the moon from the sky! All she wants is to go to work somewhere nearby."

Wanda stared at her, astonished—she had never heard her German aunt talk this way!

Ruth frowned. "It's not as simple as all that. There are certain conventions we have to . . ."

Marie laughed out loud. "Conventions! Oh, and didn't we care about those when we were Wanda's age?" she asked, her voice dripping with sarcasm. "You've obviously forgotten that we were young once too . . ."

Shaking her head, she walked out of the room.

7

"Stop, stop, that's enough, girls. We're taking a break!" Pandora Wilkens clapped her hands and shooed her dance class over to a corner where a table stood with a carafe of water.

"You have to drink!" she called out. "Water is the elixir of life. Water and air, air and water, never forget that!"

Marie held her sides. "I can't go on, I've got the most dreadful stitch," she gasped. Exhausted, she lay down on the parquet floor, which had been worn smooth by the tread of countless dancing feet. Wanda passed her a glass of water and she took it, her hands trembling, and put it beside her.

When Wanda had asked her that morning whether she wanted to come to her weekly dance class, she hadn't wanted to pour cold water on the idea. It was the first time that her niece had come to her with any such suggestion. So the two of them had set out together to walk to the southernmost point of Manhattan Island. Marie had been a little surprised when Wanda stopped in front of a shabby-looking brownstone building with three steep iron staircases zigzagging across the front.

A dance class? Here? How on earth did they squeeze a ballet studio in here? Would there be wall-length mirrors? Velvet ropes and gilded pillars? Then they went into the dressing room, which was no bigger than a broom cupboard, and Marie realized that Pandora Wilkens's dance classes would be nothing like what she had imagined. She had been expecting a genteel pastime for young ladies.

Now she wiped the sweat from her brow with the back of her hand.

"This is the first time we've gone out together—why did you pick something that's such hard work?" she groaned as she tried to get back to her feet.

Wanda laughed. "You're breathing wrong, that's the problem."

"How can I be breathing wrong?" Marie panted. "I'm just glad I'm still breathing at all!" *What am I doing here?* she wondered as she sipped at the stale, flat water. She felt horribly out of place. The "girls," as Pandora called her dance students, were all at least ten years younger than Marie. And none of them were wheezing like an old woman. She felt that she was on her last legs. And speaking of legs—everyone in the room was bare-legged. Wanda's teacher had insisted that everyone take off their stockings and their corsets as well. She clearly had her own ideas of what to wear for dancing. Marie glanced over at her. She was nothing much to look at—short and almost plump—but beneath that unprepossessing exterior lay a real artistic temperament. With her doll-like face and curling blonde locks, Pandora Wilkens looked as though she would never dance anything more strenuous than a sedate minuet. So much for first impressions. Right at the beginning of class she had shown them all what she was made of—she told the girls to stand around in a circle and then kneel down. Then she smiled graciously, walked to the center of the circle, and gave a sign to the piano player in the corner of the room, a Russian man named Ivo.

"I call this dance *Escapade*," Pandora had announced, and then she and Ivo had hurled themselves into a frenzy of wild sound and astonishing movement. Marie had never even known that the human body could make such shapes. The poses she struck were so shockingly strange they were almost indecent. Marie had sat there without daring to move a muscle, watching as Pandora danced and danced and finally flung herself full-length to the floor as though struck down by an arrow.

Wanda raised her glass of water to her lips and drank it down.

"You really should pay more attention to how you breathe," she told Marie, and then held her empty glass up as though it were a trophy. "What we did just now was only a warm-up. After the break Pandora will tell us the theme for today's class."

Marie heaved a sigh. "I'm beginning to think your father was not far wrong when he said your dance teacher was mad."

"Imagine it's the depths of winter," Pandora told the class once they were back in a circle. "You're freezing cold, perhaps you're hungry too and you have nowhere to go to get warm. How does that make you feel? I want to see these feelings as you dance. Now, shut your eyes and freeze!"

The girls groaned.

"Why does it have to be winter?" one of them asked.

Pandora looked over at her scornfully. "I would hardly need you to use your imaginations if I asked you to sweat, now, would I?" she said, wiping the sweat from her own brow with a dramatic gesture.

Marie laughed like all the others, but it didn't feel right. The whole thing was just so embarrassing.

But when Ivo struck up a sad, slow tune, the winter did not seem so far away after all. As Ivo played a melody that conjured up Russia and the cold wind blowing across the endless steppe, a shiver ran down Marie's spine. But she couldn't move for the life of her.

"Shut your eyes," Pandora whispered as she went past.

When she closed her eyes, suddenly Marie could see. Frost flowers, showing their fine fronds as if through a microscope. A windowpane with a weathered wooden frame, fingers tracing lines on the cold glass. Marie lifted her right hand almost without knowing she did so, and then her left. Then she leaned forward a little.

Snowflakes!

Each one more beautiful than the last. Each a tiny world that fell apart when she touched it.

As if in a trance, Marie began to bend this way and that.

If only she could catch hold of one, just one!

Her fingers grasped the air, seeking, questing.

Faster, she had to move faster than the snow could fall, she had to turn, turn . . .

Suddenly the music stopped and Pandora was clapping her hands.

"Very good, girls! Now breathe deeply and swing your arms," she ordered.

Startled, Marie opened her eyes.

Pandora asked one of the girls what she had seen.

"I imagined I was walking through town with my mother on a January day and I'd forgotten my coat. Brrr, that was cold!"

The others laughed.

Pandora nodded to the next in line.

"I thought of the polar bears in the city zoo. And how they always have to have cold water around them."

"And what did our visitor see?" the teacher asked, turning abruptly to Marie.

"I . . ." She was confused, and took a step backward.

"Don't worry, this is what we always do," Wanda whispered.

Marie hesitated for a moment longer. Well, why not?

"I remembered something that I haven't thought of for a long time. And I felt wonderful!" She shook her head, still bewildered.

"It was just before Christmas, and I was racking my brain over what I could give my sisters, something really special. I couldn't think of anything—we were poor, we didn't have money for presents," she added. "Then one night I was standing by the windows, they were frozen over, and as I was looking out I saw the frost flowers that had formed on the pane. They were shining, so cold and so beautiful!"

She smiled dreamily.

"That night I sat down to blow glass for the first time. I blew my first Christmas baubles, and then I painted them with frost flowers. I wanted to capture the essence of winter."

"Aunt Marie is very well-known for her glass," Wanda added proudly. "Her ornaments are sold all over the world. You probably hang them on your own trees."

At that, the girls all looked at Marie, their eyes shining.

"How romantic!"

"And what happened next?"

"What did your sisters say? They must have been surprised!"

Marie answered their questions, smiling, while Pandora stood next to her and frowned in thought.

"And what was my mother doing back then?" Wanda asked, her eyes shining even more brightly than the other girls'.

Marie's cheerful mood suddenly vanished. *Your mother was heavily pregnant with you—by a man whose name we don't even speak out loud these days where she can hear it.*

"Ruth was . . ." she began, struggling for an answer, when Pandora suddenly clapped her hands.

"Enough of Christmas and baubles and all these stories!" She shooed the girls away until they were scattered around the room again. "We're here to dance, after all! Which is why I want to dance a piece for you now. Make another circle, please, come along now, get moving!"

As they walked home afterward, Marie felt better than she had for a long time. The dance lesson had broken up a huge block of ice somewhere inside her. She had been frozen inside, motionless, but now all that was over and done with. She wanted to hug the whole world! Instead she linked arms with Wanda.

"Your Pandora is a real artist!"

From then on Marie went out with Wanda more often. They went for walks in the park or drank coffee or visited the library, where they would borrow great big picture books about America, using Wanda's card. Once Wanda took her to a specialized art supply store, but Marie was deeply downcast by the time they left. There were hundreds of shades of paint and thousands of pencils, but not even the sight of all those made her want to pick up her own brush or sketchpad. Quite the opposite in fact—she was relieved she didn't have to paint here. Wanda had clearly meant for the trip to the shop to be a special treat, so Marie didn't breathe a word of her misgivings, but she felt shaken to the core nonetheless.

Ruth watched their outings jealously. She would have preferred to have Marie all to herself. But once it became clear that that wasn't going to happen, she tried to turn the new situation to her advantage.

"Please try to talk Wanda out of looking for a job—she's making herself look ridiculous. Do it for my sake," she begged Marie. "We had to work, back in the old days, but she doesn't have to. At least, she doesn't have to work for money. She could work for a good cause—now that would be quite another matter. But the way Wanda carries on, anyone might think we were struggling to make ends meet! People must have started talking behind our backs by now. Please suggest that she do some charity work. Steven's niece Dorothy, for instance . . ."

"If I get the chance, I'll see what I can do," Marie replied vaguely. She was hanged if she was going to join in on Ruth's side, with all her ideas about what was proper and what wasn't. When all was said and done, she wasn't even part of this world, was she? On top of which it was hardly as though she and Wanda had suddenly become best of friends—Wanda hadn't even introduced her to her fiancé yet. They went on the odd jaunt together but they were a long way from baring their souls to one another.

Marie went along with Wanda to the next dance class as if it were the most natural thing in the world. She had enjoyed the dance, the games, Ivo's piano playing—why not have another go?

At first she thought she would never be able to tackle this week's exercise. Pandora read them a poem about a panther in a cage, and then told them to dance what they felt. But then Ivo started playing the music and Marie felt as though she were inside the great black cat, felt all its imprisoned helplessness. Her heart began to beat faster; her arms and legs moved quite without conscious command. When the music ended, she was happy to be back in her own skin.

Later, after they had changed and dressed, Wanda took Marie to talk to the dance teacher. Pandora was busy counting the money she had taken from the class for that week's lesson when Wanda cleared her throat.

"It's like this . . . Marie, my aunt, she's come to visit us . . . from Germany."

Marie raised her eyebrows in surprise. What was the girl up to now?

"Yes, so?" Pandora put the bundle of paper money into a little box in front of her on the table, then began counting coins.

"Well, you said once that your people are from Germany and that you speak pretty good German yourself," Wanda went on. "So I thought the three of us could go out and do something together.

Maybe go get a coffee, or some ice cream . . . Then you could talk about Germany as well . . ."

Marie felt herself blush. "Wanda!" she said, embarrassed. "I hardly think that's a good idea . . ."

"Why ever not? Of course we can," Pandora broke in, smiling. She took a little key and poked it into the lock on her moneybox, then fished out some money. "I haven't had anything to eat all day, and I'm ravenous! Why don't you join me? But I warn you—I have no idea where we may end up or what I feel like eating!"

She took a crimson shawl and threw it over her shoulders with a dramatic gesture, then marched off without even turning around to glance at Marie and Wanda.

They had no choice but to follow her.

"Does she have to do that? Now I feel like a dog being taken out for a walk," Marie hissed to her niece. Wanda just grinned.

What came next was a tour of a part of New York that Marie had never seen before, a journey of discovery through food. First Pandora took them to the Lower East Side. More than forty thousand Jews lived here, and Pandora's family as well, though she had no intention of visiting them. Instead she went into a tiny little restaurant with no more than three tables and ordered gefilte fish, coarse rye bread, and something she called a "schmear," which she spread on the bread and which tasted of mustard.

Marie was hungry as well, and helped herself—there had been nothing for lunch at Ruth's but salad, again. The food here was unfamiliar, but tasted good. She wasn't bothered by the fact that they were the only women in the place, nor by the way all the men around them were wearing braided earlocks and little caps on their heads. Pandora explained between mouthfuls that the Lower East Side was the most densely populated place on the planet. "At least that's what those clever men with their statistics manuals say." She shrugged. "All I know is that it's fearfully crowded behind those high housefronts. You'll often find more than twenty people living in one room—can you imagine? I'm just glad I don't have to live here myself anymore."

"It's not much different back home in Lauscha. There are plenty of families who eat, sleep, and work in one small room," Marie said. "The ones like us who make Christmas ornaments are always walking around with glitter powder on our skin and clothes. It's very finely ground glass, and it gets absolutely everywhere."

Pandora nodded knowingly. "I know all about that, it's the same with the garment workers here. They end up with cotton threads in their soup and needles in their bed. They say that there are more than a million Jews in New York City, and most of them come from Europe like my family," she said.

When the waiter came and asked if they wanted more, Marie was ready for another plate of fish. But Pandora said no. "That was just the appetizer," she said mysteriously, and paid up. Then she leapt to her feet and was out on the street in an instant.

Marie and Wanda looked at one another and laughed. Then they hurried out after Pandora.

"Just a woman out having fun . . ." All at once Marie could hear Georgie's words from back on the ship. Having fun was easy, she discovered.

They ate sticky rice from tiny bowls in Chinatown, spicy goulash in a Hungarian restaurant, and spaghetti with clams in Little Italy. One of them said that they might be up half the night with indigestion and worse—and the idea seemed so funny that all at once they were crying with laughter.

Pandora was recognized everywhere they went. Like a peacock displaying her tail, she was always the center of attention. The owner came to shake her hand in every restaurant, and she invariably got an extra glass of wine or a basket of rolls on the house. Everybody was happy to have her visit, and Marie wasn't surprised; Pandora had a way of spreading good cheer wherever she went. Marie also liked the fact that she could say whatever she wanted to Pandora, since they could speak in German.

"I had no idea there were so many cozy little places in New York," she said between two forkfuls of spaghetti. "This restaurant is hardly bigger than the village tavern back home. And everybody knows everybody else."

As they laughed over their glasses of red wine, they didn't see the men at the bar turn and look at them.

◆　◆　◆

"Who are those three?" Franco de Lucca asked, gazing across the room at Marie, spellbound. Her hair had come loose from its knot during dance class, and now it fell down over her shoulders like a cape. With her high cheekbones, gray eyes gleaming with their own inner light, and trim figure, she looked more aristocratic than any of the Italian countesses his mother had ever arranged for him to meet or tried to marry him off to.

Somehow she reminded him of Serena. Her carefree, almost childlike laughter, utterly unaffected and bubbling over with happiness. Happiness . . . the very idea was almost strange. Franco felt a pang in his chest. He couldn't remember the last time he had laughed that way.

The restaurant owner replied, "The one with the red shawl is Pandora, the dancer. She's mad. The other two gals must be dancers as well, or painters or something like that. Shall I ask them to come over?" He was already halfway out from behind the counter, eager to get into Franco's good books.

Franco shook his head, almost imperceptibly.

"Not now, I don't have time. I have to be getting to my next meeting. She doesn't look American," he said thoughtfully, still staring at Marie.

The other man went back behind the bar, disappointed, and returned to washing glasses.

"If you ever change your mind, all you have to do is go to one of those artist cafés in Greenwich Village. You'll find Pandora and her gang there anytime."

Franco waved his hand dismissively, as if to say *what do I care for those three!* All the same he took careful note of what the other man said.

◆ ◆ ◆

Every district Pandora led them through was like a little world unto itself. The faces on the street changed, the clothing, even the languages they heard. Uptown, where Ruth and Steven lived, the avenues were shaded by tall trees and fringed with flowerbeds, but here the streets were crowded with peddlers and their pushcarts. There were fewer motor cars but the subway could be heard underfoot, making an infernal racket. And there were people everywhere.

At first the crowds made Marie nervous or even afraid, but she soon realized that everyone around them considered it perfectly normal. She was fascinated. New York was a cocktail, a city like no other, and she was already a little drunk.

It was after seven in the evening when the three women sank onto a bench down by the harbor, exhausted. Marie knew Ruth must be worried about her and Wanda as well.

Marie's feet ached so much that it was hard to resist the urge to take her shoes off. Her eyes were red, her throat was dry, and her muscles were sore. But none of that mattered compared to the fun she'd had.

"Do you know that I've seen more of the city today than I have in all the weeks I've been here?"

"Well, you just have to go out with the right people," Wanda said, pleased with herself. "I think Pandora knows more about New York than all the guidebooks put together."

"You're right," Marie agreed fervently. "But tell me—how do you know it so well?"

"New York is like a village—and if you've spent your whole life here . . ." Pandora said offhandedly. She seemed pleased with the compliment nevertheless. "I have to say that I enjoyed our little outing as well. It was almost like seeing everything for the first time again. I say we do this again next week after class."

Wanda's face glowed when she heard that.

For a while they just sat and watched the bustle of the harbor. Two fishing boats and a ferry went past, then a string of barges. Farther out on the water, a gleaming silver ocean liner was making its stately way into port.

"How can one city have so many different faces?" Marie asked in amazement. "I've read in my guidebook that they call New York a melting pot, and it's true, isn't it? What is it—why are you laughing?" she asked Pandora.

"I just think it's funny that the guidebooks have taken up that term. A friend of mine was the first to use it—Israel Zangwill," she declared proudly. "He wrote a play two years ago about a Russian musician whose dearest wish is to write a symphony showing every facet of New York. Israel has the young Russian standing up on top of a high-rise and looking down at the city."

Pandora stood up, climbed onto the bench, and struck a dramatic pose.

"There she lies, the great Melting Pot—listen! Can't you hear the roaring and the bubbling? There gapes her mouth—the harbor where a thousand mammoth feeders come from the ends of the world to pour in their human freight."

She climbed down from the bench, ignoring the startled looks from passersby.

"Israel has the young Russian hero say that," she said, making a face. "It was just his bad luck that the *New York Times* gave the play a bad review, though. They thought it was a romantic potboiler. And it was my bad luck too: I was working for him as a stagehand at the time—I was very short of cash, as it happened." She sighed. "When I think about it . . . I've actually had quite a lot of different jobs. But all that was before I managed to get the money together for my dance studio," she added.

"I was wondering how you managed to learn whole speeches from a play by heart!" Marie said. "All the same—you're beginning to scare me, just a little."

The three of them got up from the bench, laughing, and Pandora linked arms with Wanda and Marie.

"If it's any consolation: I have my weak spots too. One of them is that I don't know how to handle money, meaning that I can't even pay the rent this month, and I'm always having to scrimp and save. Which is why I suggest that we stop somewhere for a glass of white wine on our way home, and *you* can pay!"

8

It was early July. Marie could hardly believe that she had arrived in New York only a few weeks ago. She had settled so easily into her New York routine that it was as though she had never lived anywhere else.

Most days she and Ruth breakfasted late and then went shopping. They didn't always buy something significant like a dress or a hat. Ruth was quite capable of spending hours choosing one of ten different hatbands. Or trying on dozens of silk flower corsages, and then settling for a simple rose of pale-gray tulle. Marie simply couldn't understand how anyone could spend so much time on things they didn't really need, but then she remembered that even when they were girls Ruth could spend hours on end in front of the big shard of mirror that hung in the laundry shed at the back of the house. Even back when she had had little more than a couple of lace collars, some bead necklaces she had strung herself, and a few hairbands, she had spent ages making herself look nice. It had made Marie and Johanna furious!

Once a week Ruth had a morning appointment at the hairdresser, and she insisted that Marie come along and have her hair styled too. At first Marie dug her heels in and protested. She would never have considered going to the hairdresser back in Lauscha, even if the village had had a hairdresser—which it didn't—so she would have had to walk to Sonneberg. But in the end she gave in and even had to admit that all the salves and lotions they used at the salon really worked, and smelled wonderful to boot. Her hair had never shone so brightly in her life. It was usually a rather faded brown, but now it had a warm glow, like coffee with a drop of cream. And then there was the powder they put on at the end, so that she carried the scent around with her all day like a breath of spring.

Ruth usually spent her afternoons planning the menu and table decorations for her dinner parties. Most of the time the dinner guests were important clients for Miles Enterprises who were passing through town. Steven was firmly convinced that there was no better way to network than to sit down to an elegant dinner. Ruth was a born hostess and eagerly embraced the idea. Whether it was a small gathering or a banquet for twenty guests, she tackled every task with the same enthusiasm.

So in the afternoons Marie had time to do as she pleased. Ruth undoubtedly would have been shocked to learn that her sister sometimes did nothing more than wander the streets and breathe in the city scents. Or that she could spend hours sitting on a bench in Central Park, watching the world go by, enjoying the sunshine and the shimmering haze on the black asphalt paths, listening to the birdsong echo down from the tops of the shady chestnut trees.

For the first time in her life, Marie did not have to spend her days following the strict timetable of a glassblower's workshop: mornings at the bench and lamp, afternoons designing new baubles or drawing pictures for the samples catalog. Now that she didn't have to concentrate on working the glass in front of her, she found her thoughts wandering all over the place like paper boats drifting on a pond. It was a strange feeling, and she didn't quite know whether she even liked it. But she let it happen, just as she let all the other experiences wash over her, and welcomed the new impressions. She still hoped in vain that all these new sights and sounds would reawaken her imagination and bring it back to life.

But so far . . . nothing.

Sometimes she found herself remembering the terrible nightmare that had led, as much as anything, to her trip to America: how she had been trapped inside a bauble like a glass prison. *Did I bring my prison here with me?* she wondered.

Whenever another day had passed without her picking up a pencil to sketch, she was happy when Wanda suggested some outing for the next afternoon. Or announced that it was time for them to go to Pandora's dance class. On days like those she could forget for a while her feeling of imprisonment.

After their first successful outing, Marie, Wanda, and Pandora had decided to go out for coffee after every class.

One of their favorite cafés was in Central Park, where Pandora knew one of the waiters. If his boss wasn't watching, he always slipped them an extra scoop of ice cream or refilled their coffee cups for free. On top of which, the café had a fine terrace with sunshades and cast-iron furniture and a view over half the park. What could be better than sitting there on a summer's day, enjoying a treat in the open air?

One day, as they were sitting there under a striped umbrella, Wanda proudly announced, "Starting next week I'm afraid you'll have to do without my company. I've found a job!"

She beamed as the other two congratulated her and then explained what the new job was.

"Supervisor in an overcoat factory?" Pandora frowned and put down her sundae spoon. "But darling—you can't be serious!"

"Oh but I am!" Wanda said, laughing. "I know it's not the most exciting work, but I'm glad to have found anything really. And don't we always say you have to make the best of what you've got?" She put a hand to her head and tucked her hair behind her ear with a carefree gesture.

She had been expecting Pandora to turn up her nose at the news. "Why don't you come and work for me?" her teacher had asked recently. "You could be my assistant." Both of them knew, however, that it was utterly impractical, however kindly meant; Pandora barely had enough money to cover the rent, never mind to pay an assistant's wages.

"Make the best of it?" Pandora said now excitably. "Make the best of a job as a slave driver? Don't you know what it's like in those factories? Those poor women have to work hundreds of hours a week, and they're only paid a pittance. The sewing machines are deafeningly loud, and they have to sew the heavy cloth so fast that they're always getting their fingers in the machines. Stitched right through. The windows and doors are barred so that they can't even look outside or take their mind off their work for a moment." She was counting off her points on the fingers of her left hand as she spoke.

"Not *all* factories can be so awful, can they?" Marie asked, disturbed by what she heard.

"That's what I read last November in the newspapers. There was a special report. Fifteen thousand seamstresses went on strike over poor working conditions. It was the biggest women-only strike ever. The factory owners were so riled up they hired squads of bruisers to keep the strikers in line. But the women refused to back down. They spent three weeks picketing the factory gates, standing out in the snow and ice and slush. They didn't do that just for fun, believe you me. You must have read about it." Pandora shook her head and turned to Wanda.

"Well, yes," Wanda said slowly, then leaned forward on the bench. "But they say that things have gotten better since then, in lots of ways. And if I'm a supervisor I can make sure that the improved working conditions really are observed."

Pandora shook her head. "Well even if that's the case—which I very much doubt!—I refuse to have anything to do with those slave drivers. If one of those factory owners offered me a hundred dollars to dance, I'd refuse!"

Wanda heaved a deep sigh. "All the same, I don't see that I have any choice but to give it a try. Who knows? Perhaps I can even help the women who work there? In any case, I've made up my mind to do everything right this time."

Everything would be all right; it *had* to be. Why had she let Pandora's remarks get to her like that? Not that Harold's reaction had been much better: he had asked her whether she had switched sides and joined the proletariat now. What a stupid thing to say!

As they were talking, the ice cream in the silver bowls in front of them had melted to a pink puddle. Wanda began to scoop it up with fresh enthusiasm.

"In all the jobs I've had so far, there's always been some string of ghastly coincidences that ended up in me getting fired. But my bad luck can't last forever, can it?"

She saw Marie nodding in agreement, which made her feel a little better. Pandora just frowned.

"This time it'll all work out, I can feel it!"

◆　◆　◆

Whereas Marie always felt that Wanda was keeping something back, she was convinced that she knew what Pandora was thinking. The dancer never bothered to conceal anything but lit up the whole world with her good cheer. Marie had never met anyone who took life so lightly. Wanda had charm and could win over strangers whenever she chose, but Pandora was an absolute master of this art.

She hardly ever had any money, but she never let that spoil her fun. She could always find someone—including Marie and Wanda—who was happy to pick up her share of the tab.

And so Marie thought it the most natural thing in the world that she should pay for their tickets to the Metropolitan Museum of Art, especially since she had to work hard to persuade Pandora to come along in the first place. The dancer had declared that she cared only for the works of the younger generation of artists, the wild and the free.

But as soon as they entered the hall where the Dutch Old Masters hung, she couldn't pretend to be bored any longer. Rembrandt, Bruegel, Jan Steen, Vermeer—Pandora darted like a butterfly from one painting to the next, sipping, tasting, drinking them in. She dived into the sea of color, the golden glow of the sunbeams, the dark shadows and luminous outlines. Her eyes glazed over as if she had drunk too much red wine, and she gave little cries of joy.

Marie, by contrast, stood reverently in front of the pictures. She knew these paintings of course, but only as reproductions in her art books. She looked up, startled, as she realized that Pandora was beginning to sway back and forth before a portrait of a woman by Peter Paul Rubens. She wasn't going to start dancing here, was she?

"Just look at that back! It's just like she was drenched in gold. And the blonde hair! A bit thin, perhaps, given that she's so young, but there's so much . . . *joy* in the brushwork! As if he loved every hair on her head. He painted everything just exactly as he saw it, every wrinkle, every fold. It's incredible! It makes me want to reach out and touch it . . . that soft, creamy skin. And look at the backside on her—now that's erotic, don't you agree?" She laughed. "She's got quite a pair of hips as well! But then there are some men who like exactly that sort of thing."

"I think the fuller figure was in fashion back then," Marie said, smiling. So Rubens was a dirty old man? Whatever would Alois

Sawatzky say if he could hear Pandora's opinions? Marie stepped closer and looked at the bronze plate that hung under the painting. "It says here that he painted this after he had traveled to Spain and Italy, where he was influenced by—"

"Oh, who cares about all that?" Pandora interrupted. "All that happened three hundred some years ago. All I care about is what I feel, here and now." She spun around on her toes. "Don't be so shocked!" she said, noticing the look on Marie's face. "All right, I admit it, I never expected these old paintings to inspire me so. But that doesn't mean I have to kneel down and pray here, does it?"

Marie was still skeptical. "Since you ask, I have to say that's exactly what I want to do: kneel down and pray."

Pandora patted her on the arm. "Too much respect is never a good thing. Look at me: whether it's music, poetry, painting, I can only be as good as I am when I take my inspiration from the real masters of every art," she said happily. "If I didn't have that, I'd still be dancing pointe, doing *Swan Lake* for the umpteenth time, and torturing young girls with old-fashioned ballet. Inspiration and an open mind are sisters in art—you need both to create anything really new."

They made their way arm in arm toward the museum café. When the waiter had brought them each a glass of white wine, Marie suddenly leaned forward. Before she could stop to think about what she was doing, she told Pandora everything. She had clutched these terrible thoughts to herself for too long. She had to talk about it—about how helpless she felt, useless, as empty as a drained pond.

Pandora listened, her face expressionless, sipping now and then at her wine.

"Ever since I got here I've been waiting for the touch of the muse's wings! The city, all these people, so many new impressions— damn it all, it has to have some effect on me, sometime!" Marie threw her hands in the air. "But no! I don't even want to think of my workshop back home. It's gotten so bad that even any talk of home makes me see red. I panic whenever I think that once the trip is over I have to go back to my bench and lamp and pick up where I left off." Pandora still said nothing, so Marie went on talking, and even told her about her nightmare. Finally, exhausted and downcast, she leaned back in her chair. "What is it? Have I disappointed you so much you can't think of anything to say?"

"Nonsense! You don't need to say another word!" Pandora replied. "I know exactly how you feel. Or rather, I don't actually know since I've been lucky enough never to experience a mental block like that. I would die if I couldn't dance!" She was talking so loud by now that the other guests in the café turned their heads to look at her, and she beamed back at them. "But I know too many artists who have had to go through the same valley of tears: poets, painters, musicians, actors—you name it!" As always when she spoke, she gestured excitably with her hands. "I'll tell you one thing, though: it won't help if you try to hold your nose to the grindstone and concentrate on nothing but work. You have to go out, have fun, meet interesting people. And above all . . ."—she raised a finger—"above all, you have to talk to people who have sacrificed everything for their art. Good God, those blowhards who strut the boards in the Times Square theaters don't count as artists no matter what your dear sister thinks! Same goes for the painters in the Fifth Avenue galleries. That's commerce, and nothing more." She waved a hand dismissively. "You're lucky, you know that? This afternoon my best friend Sherlain is giving a reading. She's one of the greatest poets this country has ever seen. I've used some of her poems in a dance piece already. Although I have to admit that her work is a little too . . . dark for my tastes. But the poems are heartfelt; there's no doubt about that. The best thing we could do is go and listen." She leapt to her feet. "Sitting about moping has never helped anyone. So what are you waiting for?"

"Now? A poetry reading? I don't know . . . in fact, my sister was going to . . ."

Ruth had suggested that they look through some old photographs that afternoon. She had dug out some albums the evening before, so many that Marie could hardly believe that they were all pictures from Lauscha. Johanna always hired a photographer to come to all the important family occasions, be it the twins' birthday or the opening of the new warehouse in Sonneberg, and of course she always sent a few pictures to America. She had even insisted, once, that the photographer take a portrait of Marie sitting at her lamp. He'd grumbled quite a bit when he saw what the gas flame did to his light-exposure levels, but in the end the picture had come out all right. To Marie's eternal embarrassment Johanna had insisted on putting it at the end of the catalog with the caption "*A woman's hands create the finest artworks in glass.*" The customers seemed to like it, though—the orders had come flooding in that year.

Marie smiled. She'd been looking forward to rummaging about in the memory box. But if Pandora was kind enough to invite her . . .

She took her jacket. The photograph albums weren't going to run away, after all.

"Let's go and hear how it's done!"

◆   ◆   ◆

It was a little after one o'clock by the time Wanda finally found the front door of the overcoat factory. She was supposed to have been there at one o'clock sharp—at least that's what her future boss, Mr. Helmstedt, had told her. But she had turned a corner one block too early, and then had to retrace her steps. When she had finally found the right area, she couldn't quite remember where the factory was and had wandered around for a while trying to spot an address on the buildings. She was hot and thirsty by the time she recognized the huge building on the corner of the block that housed the factory. Clamping her handbag under her arm, she ran toward it.

I do hope Mr. Helmstedt won't mind my being a little late, she thought as she ran. As she approached the building, she wondered why there were so many other women standing around the factory gates. Surely they couldn't all have one o'clock appointments?

"On strike?" Wanda looked from one face to the next, startled. "But this is supposed to be my first day at work!"

The women standing near her laughed.

"You can forget about that!" one of them said, standing in front of the gate with her arms crossed. She was obviously the leader, and she had such a strong accent that Wanda had trouble understanding her.

"We are the League of German Socialist Women Workers, and we're organizing this strike. And we won't accept defeat like last time!" she shouted. She was screaming in Wanda's face as though the defeat were all her fault.

Wanda took an involuntary step back, then several hands shoved her forward again.

It couldn't be true!

It took her a little while to understand what the locked gate and the mob of shouting women meant: her future boss would be waiting for her in vain, as there was no way she could get inside the building.

She was so agitated that she clutched at the brown linen cloth of her simple dress. She had spent ages choosing exactly what to wear. She hadn't wanted to look too fancy, but she also wanted to make sure she didn't look too much like the workers—if she was to be a supervisor, they had to have some respect for her.

But now? It seemed that it had been wasted effort. Another dress that Mother could give away to the poor and needy! Off to the rag bag!

The idea suddenly seemed so funny that she had to laugh. Her laugher sounded shrill, hysterical.

The strike leader stared at her, furious. "Women like you are to blame when we workers don't get the rights we're fighting for. You don't take anything seriously!" She raised a finger and jabbed Wanda hard in the chest before she had a chance to dodge.

But Wanda wasn't even listening. There were tears running down her face, and she couldn't stop laughing. When Harold heard about this . . . he'd think she'd made the whole thing up.

Some of the women standing around began to laugh as well. It was the laughter of despair, not merriment, but it was infectious all the same. All of them had families at home, children to feed, and they had no idea how they would put food on the table in the coming weeks. Who could blame them if they were beginning to wonder what they had done?

"Go on, laugh!" their leader yelled. "Can anyone tell me what's so funny? We're on strike, remember! But if you're ready to betray the cause, go on then, enjoy life! Go see a film, why don't you? Go spend your money on cheap trinkets. Go find a man to whisper sweet nothings in your ear!"

The other women grew uncertain at these remarks, almost frightened. What was wrong with going out and having a little fun at the end of a fourteen-hour shift?

Wanda saw the look on their faces out of the corner of her eye. For a moment she felt a mixture of respect for their bravery and sympathy for their cause. But she was so upset about her own situation that the feelings died away as quickly as they had come.

Meanwhile the strike leader was still speechifying. "If you're serious about the struggle, learn solidarity!"

Small drops of spittle flew through the air and landed on Wanda's face and dress.

"Listen to me: attend the Socialist Women Workers' meetings. Don't waste your time with lollipops and dance floors when you could be reading Tolstoy!"

A few of the women clapped.

The leader turned to look at Wanda. She was clearly spoiling for a fight.

"What are you doing here?" she asked quietly. "This is no place for the likes of you."

Wanda wiped away the last of her tears. The fit of laughter was gone now, as were her dreams of earning her own money and taking responsibility for her own life.

"I admit it: I don't know all the details of what you're striking for, and perhaps you're right that I don't belong here," she said. She felt a dull pang of pain as she thought, *So where do I belong?* "But I know one thing for sure: You won't win an inch of ground if you go about it like this, all dour and joyless. You can't forbid these women to laugh—you may as well forbid them to breathe!"

She looked at the woman disdainfully.

The others standing around them began to mutter quietly.

Wanda was happy to see that the strike leader didn't know what to say next.

She began again. "The way you're bossing them about, you're no better than the ones you're fighting against! That's what I think, anyway. Make it more positive, even fun, and you'll have a lot more people join in, don't you think?"

She turned abruptly and walked off through the crowd, her head held high.

"So why don't you take her place if you're so much better at it?" called a voice from the back.

"Yeah, come on, why don't you join us? We can always use someone with a big mouth. And we can use a bit of fun too."

Wanda's mouth went dry. Her tongue was glued to the roof of her mouth. *Should I . . . ?* But she had no idea what the strike was even about—she didn't know the first thing about workers' rights.

"Leave the poor baby alone; I can see from here that she'd give up at the first hurdle!" one of the older women called.

And Wanda slunk off with her tail between her legs.

Another hope dead and buried.

9

As they walked over the rubble, Marie had to lift the hem of her skirt several times to avoid snagging it on a particularly big stone. *I wouldn't have all this trouble if I were in trousers,* she thought as she picked her way after Pandora, who had hurried on ahead. The air smelled of smoke and engine oil, and seagulls wheeled in the sky above, so she knew they must be somewhere near the harbor. There were no shops or restaurants, no tenement blocks or children's playgrounds, just an endless sprawl of huge warehouses. They had been walking between the vast buildings for half an hour now.

"Are you quite sure the reading is happening here? It's the back of beyond!" Marie said at last. She would never find her way home on her own, that much was certain.

Pandora turned and looked at her. "Have you already lost the taste for adventure, darling?" She marched on, undismayed. "Listen, anyone can stand up with a book in their hand at a reading in a café. But never mind, we'll be there soon."

Marie raised her eyebrows. All of a sudden she wished Wanda had been able to come along. But her niece had to supervise the garment workers. She smiled at the thought. Wanda was probably feeling just as uncertain as Marie, but she would never admit it.

It was even hotter in the warehouse than it had been outside in the blazing July sun. The building was roofed with sheet steel, and the trapped air was baking hot. Marie's hair stuck to the nape of her neck as soon as they walked in.

She looked around while Pandora bustled off to find a drink.

The venue was nothing more than a vast lumber room; over to one side was a huge stack of old chairs and tables, suggesting that the place had been used previously for meetings. On the other side was a heap of folded cardboard boxes, tin canisters, and rusty iron bars. Marie had no idea what they were for. The floor was covered with pigeon droppings, and the birds fluttered about in the rafters every time the door opened. Marie figured there must be fifty people there already, and more were arriving every minute.

"Wherever have I ended up?" she muttered when she saw Pandora coming back toward her. She pointed in surprise at the glasses the dancer was carrying. "Where did you conjure those from?"

Pandora smiled. "Let's not waste our breath talking about this dive. You'll see soon enough that the venue is all part of Sherlain's art. And as you can see, it's not quite so uncivilized as all that."

Marie sipped her wine while Pandora told her more about the poet. If Marie still believed that Pandora was eccentric, she was soon corrected. Compared to Sherlain, Pandora was as mild as a lamb!

Sherlain had left her husband and their seven-year-old son when she was twenty-four years old, and broken off ties with her whole extended Irish family. She raged against the Irish church, accusing it of stifling the life of its flock and of being the enemy of pleasure and a pack of hypocrites. It hadn't taken long for Sherlain's family to denounce her in turn; her father had forbidden anyone, mother, cousin, or uncle, to speak to Sherlain ever again. Even her son was not allowed to talk to her. They were forbidden to so much as mention her name. It was as though she had never existed.

"That's all a bit much, isn't it?" Marie asked, frowning. "How does your friend manage on her own?"

"She gets by," Pandora answered with a shrug, then continued.

Once she had left respectable society, it didn't take long for Sherlain to run into money trouble. She lived in a damp basement flat without a single window. Some weeks the poet was so weak with hunger that she couldn't even get out of bed. Friends brought her food, though she was loath to accept it.

"But why does she do all this? She could write poems even with a husband and child," Marie said in dismay.

Pandora just shook her head.

Sherlain believed that she was a kind of Celtic goddess. When she turned her back on the Irish church, she had taken up the old Celtic rites of her country. Heathen rites, Pandora explained.

"Of course it's just a way of breaking society's rules," she said in a matter-of-fact voice. "But Sherlain finds her salvation in words. Sometimes she'll stay up all night long writing, and by morning, she has a single poem. Just one."

Marie raised her eyebrows. "I don't want to say anything unkind about your friend . . . but do you really think I can learn anything from her that will help with the dry spell I'm going through?"

"You'll have to decide that for yourself," Pandora answered cheerfully.

There was a stir among the crowd at the front.

"It looks as though things are about to get started. Come on, let's go up to the front!"

Privately Marie had already packed Sherlain away in a box and pasted on a label with the word "Madwoman." But then a thought came to her: a lot of what Pandora said about her friend was very much like what Alois Sawatzky had told her about the German poet Else Lasker-Schüler. She lived in dire poverty too, had broken with conventional society, and lived her life according to some "cosmic laws" or whatnot. There must be something special about these madwomen after all . . .

Suddenly a drum pounded, breaking her train of thought.

Four young men, all cloaked in white robes, set out dozens of candles in a circle and lit them. All at once a tension filled the air, as though a thunderstorm were brewing. A shiver ran down Marie's spine.

The poet came into the hall, dressed in a billowing silk robe. Her rusty red hair glowed as though on fire and hung loosely down her back with not a clasp or hairpin anywhere. The drum pounded again, and the four young men bowed deeply.

Marie swallowed hard. She had been determined not to let this crazy poet impress her, but no sooner had Sherlain knelt down inside the circle of candles than Marie was utterly transported.

What a woman! What an aura she had! All of a sudden Marie found herself thinking, *She's a goddess.*

Sherlain lit a cigarette. Instead of inhaling, however, she spluttered in disgust and coughed it back out. Then she began to recite from a scrap of paper, without a word of greeting or introduction, between drags at the cigarette. At first she was quiet, so quiet that many at the back of the crowd couldn't hear her at all. Her voice grew louder, though, after the first few words.

> . . . seven summers, seven sins,
> hell above me, sweet haven below
> my memory lost in glorious mercy
> my shell empowered with lust . . .

Another shiver ran down Marie's back, an unsettling prickling feeling, as she listened to the poetry with her eyes closed. The sounds of American English were still strange to her but she heard the joy in the bright vowels, *i* and *e*, and the sadness in the dark *u*'s and *o*'s. Sherlain's voice changed from one moment to the next, sometimes soft, sometimes hard. She was a musician, coaxing her voice like an instrument, making sounds it had never been intended to create.

Although she couldn't understand every word and only had a rough idea of what the poem meant, Marie felt she had never heard anything so . . . melodious.

> . . . dazzle, moon, dazzle
> for me and for all
> to follow thee!

The poet swung a whip and cracked it to end the poem. The cigarette glowed next to her on the ground.

Marie stood there, her head spinning as though she had been turning in circles. Most of the rest of the audience seemed to be under the same spell; they stared straight ahead, their eyes unfocused, or shook their heads and rubbed their eyes as though they had just woken up. Then they began to applaud and shout "Bravo!"

"I was there when she wrote that poem—what a night that was!" Pandora shouted in Marie's ear. Her cheeks glowed red. "The seven summers are when Sherlain was a mother. Hell above her is the Catholic church and its oppression. And haven is a pun of course, with *heaven* as well, you see? It means the goddess, sensuality, joy . . ."

Marie waved her away, annoyed. She felt precisely the way Pandora had felt that afternoon in the museum; she didn't want explanations. She just wanted to . . . feel. By now she couldn't care less that the reading was taking place in a scrap heap—she realized that the contrast between the ugliness of the surroundings and the beauty of Sherlain's words was an integral part of the whole effect.

Marie wanted more.

More of this strange elixir that let her forget her own inadequacies, however briefly.

◆   ◆   ◆

It was sheer chance that Franco was anywhere near the warehouses that afternoon. Later he would say that the gods had led him there, some higher power or destiny—but in fact it was coincidence.

He didn't know anything about a poetry reading. None of his agents knew anything about it either, since nobody had asked the warehouse supervisor for permission, and nobody had officially rented the hall. It belonged to the de Lucca family business, just like half a dozen other warehouses in the New York docks. Unlike the others, however, this one wasn't used to warehouse the imported wine before the barrels were distributed to the Italian restaurants in the city, nor was it used for any other, darker purposes. It had been empty for a while now. At least, that's what Franco had assumed.

He was just haggling over the sale price with the owner of the warehouse next door, when they heard strange sounds coming from his own property.

Probably hobos, drinking and brawling, Franco's watchman declared grimly. He ran for reinforcements.

Franco and the other warehouse owner rallied three watchmen and armed themselves with clubs. They were just about to kick down the rear door and storm the warehouse when they heard a woman's voice from inside, hoarse but powerful.

I give you my blood
sweet lamb of mine
to still your thirst
to strengthen your spine . . .

Franco was startled. He gestured to his men to stay where they were. Poetry? Here? He went inside on his own, into the dark, following the bittersweet words.

No killing will follow
I promise you so
my love will be stronger
my love will come through . . .

The closer he got, the more strongly the words spoke to him. He fell under their spell. He didn't understand every word, but he knew that it was a love poem. That it spoke of the deepest love that one person could feel for another—true love—the kind of love for which a man could die. Love that could outlast the darkness . . .

Franco hastily wiped the sweat from his brow. He was feeling a little dizzy, but he didn't know whether from the heat or the foul air. He never even noticed the bohemian crowd standing around in his warehouse with wineglasses in their hands; he didn't remember his own men waiting outside for him to give them an order. He only heard this smoky, silvery voice.

Please help me, you devilish fawn
to get the night over
to make love last till dawn . . .

A moment later, applause broke out.
"Bravo!"
"Superb!"
"We love you!"
Franco joined in the applause and clapped till the palms of his hands stung.

The poet's words had stirred something inside him that he had thought had turned to stone long ago. Even if he had wanted to, he would not have been able to defend himself against this extraordinary feeling in his chest.

And then he saw her.

Not ten yards from him stood the unknown woman he had seen so often in his mind's eye these last few days. Ever since he had first spotted her in Bruni's trattoria, he had not stopped thinking about her. How beautiful she was. How graceful. How she smiled. More than once he had regretted not talking to her when he had the chance.

And here she was, here of all places!

Just like the last time, the dancer with the red shawl was by her side.

Franco went toward the woman as though sleepwalking.

Her cheeks were flushed, as though she had just woken from a long, restful sleep. Tears gleamed in her eyes.

How vulnerable she looked!

The crowd was still roaring their praise, but their shouts were nothing more than a gentle humming in Franco's ears.

She didn't notice him at first, since she was gesticulating wildly to where the poet stood. Then she took a step to one side—and trod on his foot.

"Oh my goodness!" She giggled and turned around. "I beg your pardon. I didn't mean to . . ."

Her eyelids fluttered nervously as their eyes met. She put her hand to her mouth, startled, almost frightened.

Their faces were just a handsbreadth apart. She was even more beautiful from close up. Not as young as Franco had thought at first, but her eyes were deeper than a mountain lake.

She still had her hand in front of her mouth, and her eyes were wide with surprise.

Franco reached for her hand and lifted it to his mouth. He kissed her little finger, then the next, then the next. He did not let her hand go until he had kissed every finger and then the palm.

"No need to apologize," he said, and he meant every word.

10

"Why can't you understand, darling, that it's just not meant to happen?" Ruth said, frowning as she looked up from her notepaper. "There's simply no work to be had in the summer months, everybody knows that. You won't change anything by wearing out the soles of your boots looking."

Wanda watched as Ruth shuffled name cards around on a large sheet of paper, trying new seating arrangements for a dinner party.

"And what will change when the fall comes? The weather's not to blame for the fact that I go from one disappointment to the next!"

Wanda had tried to look busy all morning, but in the end she had given up and joined her mother in the dining room. Marie was off goodness knows where, Harold was at the bank, and she didn't feel like going shopping—what else was left for her to do?

Ruth seemed happy with the way the names were placed on her sheet of paper. She smiled at her daughter. "Why not help me a little with planning the dinner party for Marie? I'm sure she'd be glad to know you had a hand in it."

Wanda made a face. "Oh, mother, we both know that nobody can plan these things as well as you do! I'm sure you've put down everything in those lists of yours already, from the table linens to the music."

She was pleased to see Ruth blush slightly. Her mother was feeling so sorry for her that she was even ready to let her play at helping out. It had gotten that bad.

"Besides, Marie doesn't much seem to care what we do this past week or so," she added cattily.

Ruth pursed her lips. "You're right there, unfortunately. Ever since she met that Italian count we can think ourselves lucky to see her at all."

"Ha! She'll end up not coming to her own party, just because Franco can't be there—perhaps you should put that into your seating chart as well," Wanda went on. She was enjoying this. Her mother had been most put out when Marie's new admirer had dared to turn down an invitation from the uncrowned queen of the New York dinner-party circuit.

Ruth's eyebrows shot up. "I invite a complete stranger to one of my parties—bending my rules for Marie's sake—and what thanks do I get?"

Wanda heaved a sigh of sympathy. "A man whose name doesn't appear on the A-list and who nobody seems to know the first thing about."

"You are quite right, my dear. This Franco could have spent an evening with the best people in town. But if his business affairs are that much more important, so be it!"

Wanda was grinning inside. Mother never even noticed when she was being teased about her snobbery. She decided to lay it on even thicker.

"Maybe he's not a nobleman at all, just a con man, and he's not coming to dinner because he's afraid he'll be found out."

"Please, Wanda! Don't make me worry more than I already am!" Ruth said. "The fact that none of our friends know any Count de Lucca doesn't mean anything in itself—we don't have very many Italians among our sort, after all. But I'll tell you one thing: I'm going to meet this Franco face-to-face one day. You see if I don't! He won't be able to plead *important* business every time we invite him, will he now?"

Just as Wanda was beginning to get bored by the whole conversation, her mother waved her to come closer. "Don't you ever breathe a word of what I'm about to tell you to anyone else," she said theatrically.

Wanda shook her head as she leaned forward.

"If this man really is who he claims to be, then I'm not sorry at all that Marie met him. I've never seen her so . . . relaxed or so happy in all her life! The look in her eyes when she talks about Franco, the way they shine—I don't think my dear sister has ever felt this way before! Is it any wonder, though? An Italian count . . ."

"He really is very handsome," Wanda had to admit. She had seen Franco once, briefly, when he had come to pick up Marie. If she were honest with herself, he had been so handsome that she had been quite startled for a moment and only just managed to stutter "Good evening." Granted, her aunt was not unattractive—she had fine, rather sharp features and long legs, which looked especially good in men's pants—but she was old! Wanda would never have thought that a man like that would be interested in someone like her.

"Franco de Lucca makes poor old Harold look like a wet blanket," she sighed.

"Wanda! One simply doesn't say such things," Ruth scolded her. "Let Marie have her handsome Italian! I always thought that Magnus wasn't the man for her. And Johanna did rather suggest something of the sort in her last few letters before Marie set off to join us." Ruth glanced hastily over her shoulder, as if to make quite sure that Marie hadn't suddenly appeared in the doorway.

"What did she say?" Wanda was intrigued. Her mother didn't often share such confidences.

Ruth sighed meaningfully. "She wrote that Marie was depressed but didn't know it. So of course the first question that popped into my mind was how dear Johanna managed to diagnose it. She thinks that anyone who doesn't work a twelve-hour day with a smile can't be right in the head. But now that I've seen Marie here with us, I have to admit that Johanna seemed to be right: my little sister didn't seem terribly happy when she arrived."

Wanda shrugged. "But she seemed happier even before she met Franco, don't you think?" She didn't want to say so, but she was quite sure that it had done Marie good to get out and about with Pandora and herself. What Marie had really needed was to meet other artists and talk to them about their ideas.

"Well I should think so! If she hadn't flourished under our tender loving care, there would have to have been something really wrong with her!" Ruth declared in mock outrage.

Wanda grinned. It was fun talking to her mother like this. She felt sorry now for having teased her earlier.

"A little love affair never hurt anyone. Although I'm surprised at how quickly she forgot Magnus. That's not like her," Ruth went on thoughtfully. "Marie was never much interested in the opposite sex. I remember the first May dance after our dear father died . . . how the boys all tried to get her onto the dance floor! But Marie brushed them all off. First I thought that she was just waiting for the right one to come along, but then I realized that she simply found the lot of them boring. Blowing glass was more exciting to her than spending time with boys. She never cared for clothes or jewelry, or how her hair looked, because she was never interested in looking good for the boys." Ruth was silent for a moment, lost in memory. "When I think about it . . . when she was a young girl, Marie was very much like you are today. After all, you don't take much trouble to make yourself look pretty for Harold. It's no wonder he hasn't proposed yet! When I think how things happened with your father all those years ago . . ." She sighed. "The way we flirted and gazed into one another's eyes and held hands under the table . . . Oh, and then I followed him halfway around the world, all for love!"

At first Wanda wanted to protest that what Ruth had said about Harold was unfair, but instead she asked, "Will you tell me again what it was like to set off from Lauscha in the dead of night, in secret and all on your own?" Wanda loved the story, and Ruth loved to tell it. She always worked herself up into such a pitch of enthusiasm that she could be talked around to anything afterward. But today she wouldn't let Wanda distract her.

"No, that's enough talk! I have to come up with the wine list. And I have an idea for you as well. Can you get a pen and paper, please?"

Wanda looked up, ready to take orders. "What would you like me to do?"

"You could write a letter to Aunt Johanna. It's weeks overdue now. Your cousin Anna writes me every six weeks, you know, even if it's just a few lines," Ruth added.

Wanda made a face. She was ready for any little task except writing to her country cousins in Thuringia. Why couldn't they get themselves a telephone?

"And I'll ask Marie to write something as well when she comes back today. She's been here nearly two months now and hasn't dropped them a line—it's simply shocking!" Ruth said emphatically.

Wanda stood up hurriedly. Her mother could quite easily work herself into a rage and end up forbidding Wanda to do this, that, or the other.

"I'm very sorry, but my dance class begins in thirty minutes. If I don't get moving, I'll miss the start!" She gathered her skirts and was halfway out the door before Ruth could protest. "Perhaps I will even see Marie at Pandora's studio! If I do, I'll remind her about the party tomorrow."

◆ ◆ ◆

"*What* didn't you do?" Wanda was almost shrieking.

"Pay the rent. I just forgot." Pandora waved away Wanda's fury. "You might say I had a minor cash-flow problem. These things happen! Not to you, of course, you have Daddy for that sort of trifling detail, don't you?"

Wanda did her best to ignore the jab. She pointed to the huge bundle of luggage that was piled up in the courtyard of the building where Pandora used to have her dance studio. "Now what?"

The dancer simply shrugged.

When Pandora had announced that the class would take place outside that day, Wanda hadn't suspected anything was wrong. It was one of Pandora's exercises, she thought; perhaps they were going to watch the children playing in the streets and then include that in their dance. She only had her doubts at the end of the lesson—which had been much more conventional than Pandora's usual style—when she and the others wanted to freshen up in the restroom, and Pandora told them that it was closed for repairs. *Repairs,* Wanda wondered, *in that fleapit?*

While the others had trotted off without washing, Wanda had taken out a handkerchief and wiped the sweat from her brow as best she could.

Now Pandora was sitting on the pile of luggage that was all she had left in the world, her shoulders drawn up in misery. Her haughtiness had vanished as though in a puff of smoke.

"Something's always turned up at the last minute, until now," she said in a weak voice. "I have so many friends!"

Wanda nodded. And when the moment came, none of them were there to help her!

She turned away and opened the clasp of her handbag discreetly to see how much money she had in her purse. Then she went over to Pandora.

"Get up, you lame duck! I may be just a little rich girl, but let me tell you what happens next! You need a three-stage plan, nothing else will do."

A faint flicker of hope gleamed in Pandora's eyes.

"The first thing we need to do is take everything back inside. It won't do your reputation any good to be seen out here looking like a common beggar." Wanda had already picked up a bundle.

"Don't you think I've already thought of that? I know how all these law-abiding citizens' minds work. They're wondering right now why they should take me seriously as a dancer if I can't even pay my rent! They simply don't understand that an artist lives at least partly in another world, so to speak," Pandora said as she gathered up a stack of hatboxes.

Wanda made a face. That sounded like the old Pandora!

"The next thing I'll do is talk to your landlord and give him the rent for this month and for August."

"I can't accept that!" Pandora protested, although she was already putting the hatboxes down on the first landing.

Wanda felt a flash of anger. She couldn't help but feel that Pandora had just been waiting for some well-meaning chump like her to turn up. Well, maybe so. Somebody had to take charge of this scatterbrained woman.

"And the third thing . . ." She paused dramatically. Pandora put down the leather suitcase she had in her hand and looked at her. "The third thing we'll do is organize a dance recital for you, so that you can put a little money back in your cashbox."

11

It was oppressively hot. The air shimmered in the streets and by midday the housefronts were as hot as a stovetop. The trees were in such dire need of water that they had begun losing their leaves early, as though fall had already come.

On a day like this there was only one place that held out even a hope of relief, Franco declared—the waterfront. And so he took Marie to Coney Island.

Just as he had hoped, Marie was enchanted from the moment she set foot in the Luna Park amusement park, which had its own special atmosphere. They spent hours there, riding the carousels, having their fortunes told by a palmist—"You have many happy days ahead of you," as if they hadn't known that already!—and then eating ice cream and strolling barefoot on the sand, hand-in-hand, surrounded by happy people with happy faces. But none of them were happier than Franco.

They made a lovely couple, and the other day-trippers kept glancing at them. Franco had never enjoyed being the center of attention so much. *Yes, look over here, all of you!* he wanted to call to each and every one of them. *Look here and be amazed! The most beautiful woman on God's earth. But keep your distance, for she's mine!*

When darkness arrived and the thousands upon thousands of lights in Luna Park came on, tears welled up in Marie's eyes. She leaned her head on Franco's chest, inhaling the scent of his tobacco, and told him about Lauscha, about how the flames of the glassblowers' lamps shone from the windows of their little homes every evening, like glowworms lighting up the dark. He heard a melancholy note in her voice and was jealous. What was it that made her sad? Was she thinking of someone back home? But then she kissed him and was his own beloved Marie again. He pulled her closer.

"There is a kind of magic that only comes from the place you call home. Back in Genoa we have a fireworks show in midsummer every year. It's at least as big as the New Year's show, and the fireworks are launched from ships anchored in the harbor. When thousands of new stars explode in the sky, the sea looks like something from a fairy tale. We have a wonderful view of the whole thing from our town house; you can see every star that falls." Franco waved his hand at the sea that lay before them now, its water shining black in the twilight. How much bluer, how much clearer was the sea that lapped the shore at home.

Marie smiled. "That sounds beautiful. Tell me more."

"When I was a little boy there was nothing I wanted more than to be big enough to stay up late and watch the fireworks launch. 'Am I big enough this year?' I would ask my mother every summer, to no avail. We have a family tradition of throwing a grand ball on that night—and she thought that a child would just get in the way. But my grandmother Graziella took pity on me. As she so often did!" He smiled at the memory. "She would always come into my room just before the fireworks launch to wake me up and then take me upstairs in secret to her own suite. We would stand together at the window and watch the stars shower down. Afterward she would take me back down to bed and give me a bonbon, then go back to the ball as though nothing had happened."

"Your grandmother must have been a very good, kind woman," Marie said.

"And she was clever as well!" Franco sighed. "What I wouldn't give to know everything she did about wine. She only needed to glance at a vine in spring and she could tell you whether it would give a good harvest that fall. When I was very little, I thought that she could make the vines blossom just by touching them. *Mamma mia*, she had winemaking in her blood, that woman!"

Marie gave him a little dig in the ribs. "I could say the same about you. I've never met anyone who can talk about wine with such enthusiasm."

"Am I boring you with my stories? If I am, you only have to tell me. I don't want to . . ."

"Shhh!" She kissed him. "I love your stories. When I listen to you, it's as though a whole new world opens up. And even though it's a world that's strange to me, I feel that I know it. The way that this . . . passion is passed down from one generation to the next— it's the same in my family. With us it's glassblowing, and with you it's winemaking." She laughed happily. "No wonder we get on so well!"

Franco joined in her laughter, but deep inside he felt a gnawing sense of unease. How he would have loved to share Marie's certainty that the two of them had so much in common! Yet when she spoke, he felt once again how far he had drifted from his original dreams, however hard he pretended otherwise to her. He had begun to feel a deep yearning, a new hope that grew stronger with every day he spent with Marie. The two of them would be together, their love so strong that it could move mountains—he held tight to the thought, convinced that it would be his salvation.

◆　◆　◆

Later that evening they sat in one of the many beachside restaurants, a plate of steaming mussels between them. Marie reached across the table and took Franco's hand.

"Thank you for such a wonderful day! I . . . I feel as though I'm in some wonderland that's far, far away from New York . . . and from the rest of the world. It's just like a fairy tale . . ." She raised her hands helplessly. How could she put her happiness into words?

"I thought New York was wonderland enough for you," he teased her.

"It is. But you have to admit it can be a fairly tiring city." Marie took a piece of bread and threw it to a seagull, which pounced on it.

Franco shrugged. "I find my work rather tiring, that's all. It doesn't leave me enough time for private pleasure, *mia cara*."

Marie groaned. "Must you say that? I already feel guilty that I'm out and about so much. My sister would say that I am being flighty! I really ought to spend an evening with Ruth and Steven." She sighed. "But whenever I've made up my mind to do just that, either Pandora or Sherlain drops by and suggests something that sounds tremendously exciting! And then I just can't say no. It's just so exhilarating meeting all these artists and talking to them! I would never in my wildest dreams have imagined that little Marie Steinmann from Lauscha would end up sitting in the artists' cafés of New York City discussing Expressionism! And now here I am sitting with you . . ."

Her heart almost burst with the love she felt for this man.

"Do you have to mention me in the same breath with all those crazies?" he grumbled. "I don't like the idea of you spending so much time in Greenwich Village. I worry that something might happen to you . . ."

"Whatever could happen to me there?" she asked, laughing. She knew that Franco simply found the artists' quarter too strange. It wasn't a neighborhood with just one smell or just one sort of people, like Little Italy or Chinatown. Voices speaking English, Yiddish, Russian, and German filled the air, and the whole neighborhood was crowded and shabby. But she found it easy to find her way around. She made an effort to sound reassuring.

"It's not called the Village for nothing, you know. Everyone knows everyone else, so I feel much happier and more comfortable there than I do in Ruth's apartment building. All those huge yawning lobbies and the long, lonely corridors!"

When he didn't answer, she added, "Besides which, you know quite well why I spend so much of my time with artists." She frowned. "Oh, Franco—whatever is wrong with me? I've never been so happy in my life as I am now—but why can't I put the feeling down on my sketchpad?"

"Don't be sad, *mia cara*. I can't bear to see you unhappy." He leaned across the table toward her. "Your friends drag you from one diversion to the next as though you were a convalescent. As though you had something wrong with your head, and your hands!"

His remark made her smile slightly.

"Pandora behaves as though she were in charge of your treatment, but you're not sick! When I think of that 'free speech evening' she made us go to last week—I still have no idea what that was supposed to be about." He rolled his eyes. "They switched topics so fast it was like watching a mountain goat leap from one cliff to the next. Women's emancipation, the revolution in Russia, Tolstoy, free love . . ."

"What do you have against free love?" Marie replied, smiling again. She reached out and brushed aside a lock of hair that clung to his forehead. She didn't want to argue with Franco.

"And then that excursion the week before with the photographer, Harrison—I still haven't forgiven Pandora for that," Franco said, clenching his fist.

"But why ever not? Don't you think it's interesting to see the dark side of the city once in a while? Not spend all our time living among the bright lights?"

"The dark side of the city? I don't need some high-minded photographer to show me that. And those dreadful pictures he takes! Do you really think that people who already live crammed together like animals in cages enjoy having him come to take their photograph? All that talk about artistic value—he's just using these poor people's misery to make money!" Franco was angry. He flapped his hands to shoo away a wheedling seagull that was trying to perch on the edge of their table. "You had nightmares for days after our trip to the slums. Are you going to tell me that's *artistically valuable* as well?"

"I won't forget seeing those poor people, not as long as I live," Marie said, looking away from his fierce, dark gaze. She didn't want to talk about it anymore, but she felt as if she had to explain. "Harrison says that men and women created those slums, so men and women must be the ones to do away with them! I do so hope that it happens."

"This Harrison takes himself mighty seriously—they all do. Everyone in that crowd thinks they're so important!" Franco said savagely.

"But isn't it good when people want to change things?"

"But what are they changing, *mia cara*? They sit there in their discussion groups, and the world keeps turning outside the door. Faster and faster. And none of them even notice!"

Marie gazed down at the heap of mussel shells on the plate. She felt hurt.

"Maybe in your eyes these people aren't doing anything very special or important. But speaking for myself, I've never seen anyone dance like Pandora. And I've never heard such heartfelt poetry as Sherlain writes. You said yourself that her work speaks to you!

The Greenwich Village crowd is like family to me; each of them has his own particular passion and we all have that one thing in common. Surely you understand!" she cried out, almost desperately. "And they accept that right at the moment I cannot make my art. Nobody looks askance at me. They all say that I simply have to gather enough inspiration, and it will start to happen again."

"Do you think that a vine bears more grapes if I sit down in front of it and plead for days on end? Isn't it better simply to leave it alone to grow?" Franco asked. He reached out and lifted her chin, but Marie didn't reply to his question. "When you seek and seek like this, you are going about it the wrong way, believe me! Why not just enjoy life? Like today. There are some things you cannot force, so you must simply let them take their course."

Marie tore up another piece of bread and threw it to the greedy gulls, which huddled together and squabbled over the crumbs. Maybe Franco was right. All the same something inside her refused to give in.

"I never had a close friend in my life. Back in Lauscha there was simply no time for friendship; all I ever did was work." She looked thoughtful. "And perhaps the other women in the village thought I was an odd bird." She laughed. A woman who sat at the lamp and flame from morning till night, like the men did—certainly they must have found it strange. "But here I have two close friends, three if you count Wanda. They like me, and I like them. And each of them, in their way, is at least as odd as I am. But nobody here seems to find it at all strange when a woman does her own thing. I am always the outsider in Lauscha, even if people have gotten used to my job by now."

Franco didn't answer. For a moment, they were each alone with their own thoughts.

How could she explain to him that he had no reason to be jealous of Pandora or anybody else? Nothing even came close to what she felt for him. She had never been in love like this. She felt like a girl again. She loved him so much that she never wanted to let go of his hand. She had to make an effort to do anything but gaze at him rapturously, her eyes wide. She wanted to kiss him again and again, his lips, his strong, manly mouth. She loved him so much . . .

◆　◆　◆

Franco was annoyed at himself. This wasn't the way to get through to her. He knew exactly what she needed to unleash the forces of her creativity once more: his love. His hands on her body, his kisses on her naked skin. Nights of passion when he could make a woman of her. But he had to keep his desires in check for now—Marie wasn't like Sherlain, or any of those other women who gave themselves to any man who came along. He knew that she wasn't a virgin, of course—she had told him about Magnus back home. But the man couldn't have meant very much to her, given the way she had spoken so indifferently about him. Franco had the impression that she had never truly loved anything or anyone but her art—until now. There was something innocent about Marie, something untouched . . .

Just as there had been about Serena.

He cleared his throat. "Pardon me if I have offended you. It's just that sometimes you seem to care more about these women than you do about me! What do you really know about me?" He raised his hands helplessly.

"Well, I know for instance that you are my handsome Italian. My jealous, handsome Italian." Marie kissed his pinkie teasingly, then the other fingers, one by one. "And I know that the de Lucca family wine arrives in crates here by the shipload. That you ship thousands of barrels every year from Genoa to America, and that you have to be here in charge of distribution even though you'd much rather be back home taking care of the vineyards." She was counting off the points on her fingers now, like a schoolmistress summing up a lesson. "And I know that I have never loved a man the way I love you," she finished up in a hoarse whisper.

For a moment they simply gazed into one another's eyes. Then a waiter came to the table and asked if he could bring them anything else. Franco asked for the check and the waiter hurried off to fetch it.

"Sending wine all this way—is it really worth it?" Marie asked. "I mean . . . the Americans make their own wine now, don't they?" It was only as she spoke and saw the expression on Franco's face that she realized he might take offense at the question.

"The Americans do, of course, but the Italians who live here don't," Franco answered as he reached for his billfold. "You have to be clever in the export business; you have to know exactly which market you're targeting. We only supply businesses run by Italians, you see," he explained. "Did you know that there are more Italians living here than there are in Rome? They even say there are more Italians in New York than there are in Genoa, Florence, and Venice put together!"

Marie frowned and was about to ask how that could be the case, but he went on.

"Italy is poor. Very few people live as well as my family does. You know yourself that there are hardly any factories in Europe. So how do people live? Anyone who isn't a landowner . . ." Franco shrugged. "Every Italian who arrives here has already made a great sacrifice. Many families save for years to be able to send even one of their sons to America. They all think that the streets here are paved with gold!" He shook his head. "Well, we both know that it isn't like that, but most Italians here live pretty well." Suddenly his face lit up. "Let me show you *my* New York, so that you can meet a few Italians! There's a big parade over on Mulberry Street this weekend, the festival of our patron saint, Saint Rocco—I could take you on Sunday afternoon."

"A parade for the patron saint, that does sound wonderful . . . I'd love to come! Ruth's dinner party will have come and gone by then, so I'll be able to do what I want with my time again." She made a face. "She wants to go shopping with me and Wanda tomorrow to buy me a *ball gown*! It'll take all day, I'm sure. You see that I never get a moment to relax!"

Franco laughed. "How can a beautiful woman like you be so utterly indifferent to how she looks? I'd tell your sister to buy you ten ball gowns! But each of them has to be fit for a queen." His eyes shone with pride and love as he reached out and stroked her hair. "This hair of yours is like finest Genoese silk. Please promise me you'll never have it cut the way your niece has. It would be a mortal sin!"

Marie felt herself blushing again. She still hadn't gotten used to all his compliments. She sighed.

"I really don't like it when Ruth makes such a fuss over me. If only you could be at the party with me. Can't you move this business meeting of yours to some other day?"

His face clouded over.

"You know how much I want to. But the *Malinka* puts in on Saturday evening, and I have to be there when it unloads. There's no way around it. Last time there was an incident that . . . my father . . ." He bit his lip. "There are some things it's not so easy to explain. Not to mention that—"

Marie took his hand. "You don't need to say any more. Work comes first, I understand of course. But then we'll have Sunday all to ourselves, won't we?" she said, struggling to keep her voice light. She didn't want him to feel guilty about having to spend time away from her. She had already changed their plans a few times to go to a reading or a show at a gallery or just to spend the evening with her friends.

When the waiter came back to the table and Franco paid the check, Marie felt a rush of relief. She couldn't explain why exactly, but the conversation had taken some wrong turns. First his complaints that she was spending too much time with her artist friends, and then her indiscreet questions about his family business . . . It was a bit strange, but despite that she had never felt such depths of passion for anyone else before.

She felt a rush of panic as she took Franco's arm and they walked toward the exit to the amusement park. She didn't want to go back to the city, back to the burning heat of the asphalt jungle. She wanted to be alone with Franco, far away from all the questions. She wanted to be with him—just the two of them and the passion they shared.

12

Despite all her misgivings about the grand party being thrown in her honor, Marie was having a wonderful time: Ruth's guests were all quite nice, if rather formal and distant with her; the music was lovely; and the ballroom that Ruth had rented on the top floor of the apartment building was magnificent.

Even getting ready for the evening had been enjoyable; Ruth had hired a French hairdresser for the occasion. He arrived at nine in the morning with his two assistants and spent hours showing Ruth, Wanda, and Marie how they looked with the latest French hairstyles. While Jacques and his assistants spent hours curling, combing, braiding, and piling up their hair, the ladies leafed through a stack of French fashion magazines. Even Marie was enchanted by French fashion, which looked to her a great deal simpler and more practical than the outfits in New York's department stores, which were all ruffles and billows. When Ruth happened to mention that there was a French couturier nearby, Marie resolved to visit it as soon as time allowed—she already knew that Franco liked to see her wearing the latest fashions.

Franco . . . perhaps she had bored Ruth and Wanda a little, she reflected, mentioning his name so much.

"Franco says that . . ."

"Franco thinks . . ."

"Only yesterday, Franco was telling me . . ."

In the end she felt quite silly—she couldn't speak two sentences in a row without mentioning his name! But Ruth and Wanda had been wonderfully patient with her.

The hairdresser was just finishing up when a parcel arrived for Marie, a little box wrapped in dark-blue silk. She shivered with delight when she saw Franco's name on it. The other two exclaimed as she unwrapped it and took out a diamond tiara.

She read out the message on the card that accompanied the gift. *"For the princess of this evening's ball—in deepest admiration, Franco."* Ruth insisted that Jacques start all over again with Marie's hair to show off Franco's present to best advantage.

That evening, while a waiter refilled her glass with champagne, Marie put her hand to her head and stroked her hair unobtrusively. She had never expected to wear a tiara in her life . . .

"No need to worry, you're wearing so many hairpins it won't slip out of place," Ruth whispered, noticing her gesture. She squeezed Marie's arm. "If only they could see you now in Lauscha!"

A shadow flitted across Marie's face. Did Ruth really have to remind her of home, tonight of all nights? She changed the subject hastily. "Your friends are all so pleasant and so . . . interested! I would love to know what you told them about me."

"Only that you're a famous artist, and that you work in glass," Ruth said, waving at someone across the room. "The Americans are always interested in anything to do with Europe."

"I've noticed that," Marie said. "The people I meet down in the Village all seem to think I must know Franz Marc personally. And this evening your friends have asked me about the palace of Versailles and the Botanical Garden in Munich! I may come from

Europe, but I'm not an expert on the whole continent!" she said, laughing. "Do they think that Europe's tiny?"

Ruth raised her eyebrows in reproach. Then she sighed. "What a shame your Franco can't be here," she said. "His present certainly shows that he's very generous. He must be a fine man."

Marie smiled to herself. That was so typical of Ruth! All at once she wanted to hug her sister.

"Thank you again for such a wonderful party! The flowers everywhere, all the fine food, the music—it's as though you'd spirited us away to a fairy-tale castle!" Marie waved her hand around in a gesture that encompassed the whole beautifully decorated ballroom.

"Were you really expecting us to host the event in our apartment?" Ruth giggled happily.

Marie shrugged. "How many parties like this do you think I've ever been to? I can't be expected to know how they—" She stopped as Wanda leaned across the table to speak to them both.

"The conductor's just given me the signal. If you agree, we can have Pandora's show now." She tugged excitedly at the ringlets Jacques had put into her hair.

Ruth opened the cover on her jeweled wristwatch. "Ten o'clock—well, she's right on time at least," she said, pleased. "I hired a soprano for Steven's last birthday, and he turned up ten minutes late, can you imagine?"

Marie made a suitably shocked noise, winking slyly at Wanda as she did so.

◆　◆　◆

Pandora had suggested dancing to Smetana's *Vltava*, justifying her choice by calling it "an homage to Marie's European roots." Ruth had agreed; it was just the sort of romantic, tuneful piece her guests would enjoy. Wanda had breathed a sigh of relief at that. Given that

Pandora was deeply committed to expression and feeling in her art, and Ruth was more concerned with the dos and don'ts of high society, she hadn't expected them to agree on a program so quickly. But now she even thought she detected something like a mutual respect between them. Granted, her mother hadn't actually gone so far as to seat Pandora at one of the tables in the ballroom, but she had made sure that the dancer was served every course in one of the side rooms. And Pandora seemed truly grateful for the chance to put her finances back on track after the debacle with her landlord, thanks to the very generous fee that Ruth had offered her. For once she hadn't launched into her usual tirade about the conservative tastes of New York's upper crust.

"Mother's very pleased to have you here," Wanda whispered to her friend. "She thinks that your performance will give the evening a certain Bohemian touch."

As the music struck up, Wanda congratulated herself on killing two birds with one stone; she had done her bit to make Marie's party a night to remember, and she had helped her dance teacher out of a hole.

Pandora came into the room wearing a shimmering silver gown. Or rather: she was just there, all of a sudden, so quiet on her bare feet that nobody had heard her come in. The guests had been told that there was to be a dance recital and greeted her with polite applause but without great interest. They were well fed from the eight-course banquet, and they had had their fill of art as well. Hardly a week went by when there wasn't some performance or recital or soiree.

Pandora bowed in front of Ruth's table. Then she removed two hairpins with a theatrical gesture, shook her hair free, smiled beatifically, and began to dance.

"Doesn't she look beautiful?" Wanda whispered to Marie with something approaching maternal pride. "Like a bird of paradise!"

"She does indeed, but I don't think she's wearing a corset underneath that gown. Or even a slip," Marie replied, grinning. "Does she think that's how we do it in Europe?"

Now Wanda noticed as well; every time the glittering gown swung open she could see Pandora's legs, all the way to her thighs. This would mean trouble. And there was worse to come: Was she imagining things, or had she seen a nipple?

Wanda glanced over to where her mother sat, but Ruth's expression revealed nothing. Either she didn't find Pandora's outfit so scandalous after all, or she was making an effort not to show her dismay.

The strains of the orchestra wafted through the room and Pandora swayed gently in time with the music. Wanda watched the other guests for their reaction. All eyes were on the dance floor now, the conversation had subsided, and cigars smoldered unattended in the ashtrays. Even Harold, who just a moment before had been absorbed in discussing financial matters with Steven, was staring dead ahead.

Wanda relaxed a little. Everything was fine. She didn't want any scandal or uproar. Not today.

Pandora danced as though in a trance. Soon the instruments could no longer keep up with her wild movements as she swung her legs ecstatically and her breasts bounced beneath the gown. The music sounded tame by comparison. But then, who was listening to the music by now?

Harold let out a short but shrill whistle. Wanda was horrified to hear some of the other men do the same.

"Is this really supposed to be a musical portrait of a river? It looks more like the Niagara Falls!" He reached for Wanda's hand and his fingers were hot and sweaty.

Angry, Wanda snatched her hand away. Whenever Pandora came near her table she tried to signal to her. Slower! Tone it down a little! Dear God in Heaven, help us please!

She suddenly had the feeling that she was watching an obscenity, but she wasn't sure exactly *whose* behavior was obscene—the dancer's, or the guests', who were gazing upon her with such lust in their eyes. Wanda felt a knot in her stomach that pressed up against her lungs. She found it hard to breathe.

By now Pandora had danced herself into a frenzy. It didn't seem as if she noticed the audience at all—not the lust on the men's faces or the expressions of utter shock on the ladies in the front row. And she didn't seem to see Ruth sitting there, stone-faced.

Pandora stopped dancing as suddenly as she had started. Then she nodded vaguely toward the audience and left the ballroom without so much as a bow or a curtsy.

The applause that followed was scattered and distracted, though Marie and Wanda did their best to keep it going. Most of the guests were looking over at Ruth and Steven as if to ask, *What do we do now?*

Ruth held out her champagne glass to Steven with a look of serene indifference on her face.

"Darling, I think that the waiter is neglecting us dreadfully. Would you be so good as to pour me another glass?"

The whole crowd seemed to exhale at once. They silently agreed to behave as though the dance performance had never even happened. Here and there guests discreetly wiped the sweat from their brows or fanned their cheeks.

Wanda couldn't stay in her seat any longer. She ran out of the room after Pandora.

It didn't take long to find her.

Pandora was leaning against the wall, trembling. She had a hand up to her chest as though her heart were giving her trouble. She had been crying, and her makeup had run so that there were dark splotches around her eyes. When she saw Wanda coming toward her she turned abruptly away.

"Pandora . . ." Wanda put a hand on her friend's shoulder, at a loss. "I'm sorry if people didn't . . . react the way your audiences usually do. My parents' friends are a little—"

"How could you expose me to treatment like that!" Pandora snarled at her. "You threw me to the lions! It was torture out there!"

Wanda ducked her head low. Then she saw Marie coming down the hall. If her aunt began to call her names as well . . .

"Well that didn't go down too well!" Marie groaned when she reached them. "Ruth is so angry she's ready to burst, and some of the guests still look as though they'd seen a pink elephant." She giggled.

Wanda breathed a sigh of relief. At least Marie wasn't going to rake her over the coals.

"Thank you for the comparison!" Pandora said, sniffing.

Marie nudged her in the side. "You know very well that's not what I meant. I just wanted to say that you've shocked pretty nearly everybody! If it's any comfort, though, I liked your dance a great deal."

"Some comfort! I felt like a Coney Island sideshow out there! The two-headed lady! The human snake! Throw a nickel in the bucket and take a look! These people don't realize that I am one with my art, that when I dance I let them into my life. They think it's all just something to gawk at!" She wiped the tears from her face. The black splotches were stripes down her cheeks now. "Fifth Avenue—I should have known! I'll tell you something: from now on I'll only dance for an audience I've chosen for myself, even if that means I'll never earn a red cent!" And with that, she hurried off, her head held high.

Taken aback, Marie and Wanda watched Pandora leave while waiters scurried by with more drinks for the guests and a waltz struck up in the ballroom.

By now Harold had joined them. He cleared his throat, embarrassed.

"Don't fret, Wanda! Pandora will calm down soon enough. As for her dance, I thought it was wonderful!"

"I noticed how much *you* were enjoying it, thank you very much!" Wanda spat back. But a moment later she slumped like a deflated balloon. "Oh hang it all! Now it's going to be all my fault again. Why does everything I try my hand at have to go wrong?"

Marie sighed. "Don't talk such nonsense, my dear. You don't want to hear this, I know, but I could have told you right away that your mother never would have liked anything Pandora did. But what's the point of standing here talking about it? I'll go back in and tell Ruth that I enjoyed the performance a great deal. That will calm her down."

"No, wait!" Wanda caught hold of Marie's sleeve, then took a deep breath. "I really don't want to go back into the lion's den. Why don't we just go down to the bar on the corner before I'm eaten alive? Come on, I'll buy you both a drink!"

She forced a smile and then linked arms with Marie and Harold, so that they had no choice but to go with her.

Harold squeezed her hand. "I warn you, my darling, if you order a glass of that dreadful aniseed muck you like so much, I'll give you the telling off you're hoping to avoid from your mother!"

"Don't worry, I'd much rather have a whiskey!" Wanda replied. In fact her throat was so dry that she wanted nothing more than a tall glass of water.

"A whiskey—listen to the girl!" Marie said. "We'll all end up drunk, and I shudder to think what your mother will have to say about that."

Wanda shrugged tersely. "Some things are easier to bear when you've had a stiff drink."

Marie giggled. "Now you sound just like your father. That's what he used to say when he and Ruth had squabbled."

"Father? What do you mean?" Wanda turned to look at her, frowning. "He never touches spirits . . ."

13

"I . . . I only meant that . . ." Marie looked down the hallway. She was horrified to see that Ruth was headed straight for them with a thunderous look on her face.

"The lion has ventured from its den," Wanda muttered. She let go of Marie's arm. "So, what did you mean just now?"

Wanda had always thought that attack was the best form of defense, and right now she seized on Marie's odd remark as a welcome distraction. She hoped that if she spent a little longer digging around here, perhaps the lion would forget to roar. "I can't remember my father ever taking a drink because he'd squabbled with Mother. The two of you agree on everything, isn't that right, Mother?"

"Would anybody like to tell me what is going on here?" Ruth asked. There was a tiny tremor beneath her right eye—a first sign that a migraine was coming on.

"Nothing at all," Marie reassured her desperately. "Would you like to come back inside with me? I'm dying for a glass of champagne and—"

"Now really, Aunt Marie! You can't call my father a drunkard and then just leave it at that!" Wanda looked the very picture of innocence. "Or is there perhaps something that I ought to know about my father?" She put an accusing note into the question.

"Marie?" Ruth's eyelids were fluttering now. She was clearly disconcerted, and her rouged cheeks had turned pale. "What . . . what have you told her?"

That was odd—Mother's voice sounded so thin and strange! She also seemed to have forgotten entirely that she was supposed to be angry at Wanda. A strange feeling knotted at the pit of Wanda's stomach.

Harold cleared his throat. "Wanda, my dear, I suggest we bring this conversation to a close. Shall we dance?" He offered her his arm gallantly. *Please don't make any more trouble,* his eyes pleaded.

Wanda glared at him. "Well really! I hope that I may expect an answer to a simple question. I'm becoming quite tired of your treating me like a fool. I may be young, but I'm not stupid!"

"Perhaps not, but you seem not to realize that one simply does not pry into one's parents' past indiscretions," Harold replied.

He had a cheerful grin on his face, which just irritated Wanda all the more. Don't cause a fuss; don't make trouble—that was so typical of Harold! He could take her side once in a while, just for a change. If not, she would just have to speak up for herself!

"Past indiscretions . . ." she said, trying out how the phrase sounded on her lips.

"Nonsense!" Marie laughed shrilly. "We had no time for indiscretions back in Lauscha; we had to grow up fast. Faster than we wanted to . . . isn't that right, Ruth?"

Wanda was horrified to see the look her mother shot Aunt Marie.

Leave it. Take Marie's arm and act as though she never said anything, said a voice inside her.

Why? asked another voice simultaneously. *If you act as though nothing has happened, you will be just like Mother!*

Wanda looked from her aunt to her mother. She felt as though she were watching a play onstage but also acting in the scene at the same time. And the drama was about to reach its climax. All the actors were in place and waiting for the next cue. Was it her line? Suddenly every word she spoke, every move, seemed fraught with huge significance.

Why did her mother look as though she'd been caught breaking into a safe?

Why did Aunt Marie look as though she wished the ground would swallow her up?

She had only wanted to distract their attention from the debacle of the failed dance recital . . .

Father, a drunkard? Never. There was something wrong here. Very wrong.

". . . *we had to grow up fast. Faster than we wanted to.*"

Wanda turned to face Marie slowly, excruciatingly slowly. She was as stiff as a marionette on strings. It was as though she wanted to put off the next moment as long as she could.

"Marie . . . perhaps you weren't actually talking about . . . Steven Miles?" Her voice failed her.

Nobody said anything.

Wanda felt her throat tighten. Her mouth was so dry that her tongue was stuck fast to the roof.

"Why . . . why are you behaving so strangely? Mother? Marie? What is it?"

Ruth's eyes were fixed somewhere far off in the distance, and Marie had frozen like a statue. Neither of them could say a word nor move a muscle.

Wanda felt dizzy. Why was it that all of a sudden she could read their thoughts so clearly?

"Steven isn't . . . my father? Mother, tell me that's not true!"

◆ ◆ ◆

"It's the heat, Signor de Lucca! The heat . . ." The man pointed outside as if accusing the summer air.

Franco was pacing up and down the length of the wooden shack that served as an office. Five paces from the desk to the shelves, five paces back.

"I can see for myself that it's hot!" he said, stopping abruptly. "Why didn't you call me? We could have begun unloading earlier!"

"But Signor de Lucca! You gave the order yourself that we were not to start unloading until the right men were on duty at customs . . ."

Franco began to pace again. Damn it all, the man was right!

"Everything worked out in the end, this time at least," he snarled. But it had been a close call, closer than last time. One of the boys was in poor shape. And as for the grandfather—he might not even last the night . . .

The other man cleared his throat. "Now that the cargo is taken care of . . . will there be anything else? Does the count have any particular wish?" He pushed aside the hair that hung down over his forehead and looked toward the door, waiting for his chance to get away.

Franco waved a hand impatiently and sent the man scurrying off. Enough talk. It was no good blaming the wrong man. They had made a mistake back in Genoa; there was no doubt about it. Too many barrels. If they had loaded ten or twenty fewer, there would have been more air for the men. They could have opened the hatches earlier as well; it was the height of summer after all!

Once the man had gone Franco locked up the warehouse. He was dead tired, but he knew that he wouldn't sleep easily tonight. Perhaps after a few glasses of wine . . .

But instead of setting off toward Mulberry Street, he sat down on one of the empty steel drums that his workers used as table and chair during their breaks, and he stared out at the water. A fishing fleet was just setting out to the open sea, the lights from the boats dancing gently on the waves.

Genoa to New York. It was a long way, especially if you spent the crossing below deck, crammed in between hundreds of barrels of wine, hardly able to catch a breath of air, with no water to wash in and just the bare minimum to eat and drink. This was why they had begun by taking only strong young men in their prime. If one of those young fellows had run into trouble with the law, who cared about that? The de Luccas certainly didn't, as long as he had money to pay for his crossing. Soon, though, they realized that there were many other men who wanted to cross the ocean this way, men who were not so young and not in such good health—men who would never have passed the official health checks at immigration. Though Franco had pleaded with his father to take more care choosing who to send, there were a few older men on board each time.

He lit a cigarette and sucked greedily at the smoke.

What if the old man had died during the crossing? Would the others have sat there quietly and waited? That was exactly what they had been told to do, of course, with bloodcurdling threats. But perhaps they would have forgotten all that with a dead man in their midst. Perhaps they would have drummed on the side of the wooden crate and made such a din that one of the crew noticed them. And then? What would the ship's officers say if they found a dozen stowaways hiding in the huge crates used for de Lucca wine? The risk was simply too great—though his father turned a deaf ear to all his protests. Franco felt a pang of bitterness at the thought. Why did the old man insist on weekly telephone reports if he wasn't going to pay any attention to his recommendations?

He flicked the cigarette, and it arced through the air, landing in a puddle.

At first he had believed what his father told him, believed that they were doing a good deed by making it possible for young Italians to enter America even if they had been refused their papers for whatever reason. Franco hadn't seen anything wrong with the fact that their families had to beggar themselves to pay for the crossing, or that the men themselves had to spend a year working for certain handpicked restaurant owners—all customers for de Lucca wine—until the rest of the cost was paid off. After all, his family had to be paid for the risk. He even thought it was rather heroic to help a few poor souls toward a better future by smuggling them in among the crates of red wine. Perhaps he might still think so today if his father hadn't sent him to New York with a few hundred dollars to make sure that the customs agents turned a blind eye at the right moment. For the first time he saw with his own eyes what it was like when the crates were unloaded, when the men crawled out on all fours, weak with thirst. And then his romantic ideas died, never to return. Franco realized that there was nothing heroic in buying and selling human beings.

For this was what it was.

He, Franco, was a slave trader.

14

It took some time for Ruth to wake up from her faint. She lay on the chaise longue, surrounded by her Art Nouveau treasures, pale and exhausted, with a damp cloth on her brow. As soon as she opened her eyes she called out, "Wanda . . . ? Where is my daughter? I have to go to her, I have to explain everything. I . . ." She sat up, swaying.

Marie held her tight by the arm. "Wanda has run off. She doesn't want to see anyone."

"Run off?" Ruth began to cry, putting her hands in front of her face like a child. "What have you done? I . . . I don't want to lose her."

Marie was struggling with tears as well. The good cheer from earlier in the evening had long since evaporated. She forgot about Pandora, about Franco, about how she had wanted to make him laugh by turning the dance fiasco into a humorous anecdote.

"I'm so sorry, so dreadfully sorry! It was a chance remark . . . I don't know myself how it happened. I promise you I'll make everything right!" She would have promised Ruth anything just then, but her sister's face remained buried in her hands.

"There are some things that cannot be made right," she muttered without looking at Marie.

After Steven had come to Ruth's side to take over for Marie, she left the apartment with Harold to look for Wanda again. While he walked along Fifth Avenue calling her name, Marie went to the small bar on the corner of Sixth Avenue. She paid no attention to the customers' high spirits on this Saturday evening, any more than she let the oppressive heat on the streets put her off.

"She's not in the apartment, and we've looked everywhere we can nearby. Where else shall we try?" Marie's voice was low and troubled when Harold met her at the bar. "She won't have gone to Pandora, will she?"

"I shouldn't think so." Harold seemed distracted. "There's somewhere we haven't tried, though. She told me once that she likes to go out on the roof. Because it brings her closer to the stars."

"My father was a glassblower in Lauscha . . ." Wanda was leaning against the chimney. Her face was gray, and her eyes were glazed. The wind was tugging at the thin fabric of her ball gown and her right foot was planted firmly in a slick puddle, but she seemed not to notice.

Marie looked around, distraught. Was this really Wanda's favorite hideaway? This horrible place? How lonely she must be if this was where she felt safe!

When they had found Wanda, Marie sent Harold away. She wanted to talk to her niece alone.

Wanda looked up. "My father was a violent man—is that really true?" Tears ran down her face.

Marie felt panic rise inside her. *I can't do this,* a voice inside her cried.

"I think everybody has their own different truth," she said. How hollow that sounded! Shuddering, she remembered how Ruth and Wanda's argument had ended.

"You want to know why I never told you anything about the man you call your *father*?" Ruth had asked, grabbing her daughter by the arms so that their faces were only inches apart. Hysteria and despair battled in Ruth's face, twisting her fine features. "I'll tell you why: because when you were just a babe in arms, he would have beaten you to death if I hadn't sheltered you with my own body! *That's* the truth about your father."

At that, Wanda had doubled over as though punched in the gut.

"I don't believe you. You're a liar!" she whispered, then ran away, her hands clasped over her ears.

"Ruth and Thomas were young. They were too young to know that they weren't really suited for one another," Marie began.

Wanda laughed. She sounded tired. "For eighteen years now I've been calling a man Father who isn't really my father at all—*that's* the truth!" She began to cry. "This can't be true! I . . ."

Marie was afraid that Wanda would shove her away as soon as she put her arm around her niece's shoulders, but Wanda simply nestled into her embrace.

"I just don't know what to do . . . Marie, help me!"

And so Marie told her about Lauscha. Wanda's head lay on her breast and her gown was wet with tears. She stumbled over the words at first, for the memories were rusty, but with every sentence she spoke the past came more vividly to life.

She told her about the three Steinmann sisters, about how they had lost their parents at such a young age. They had been left with nothing, knew nothing of how hard life could be, had nothing but their dreams. Johanna had dreamt of the big wide world. And so she had been the one to go to Sonneberg and work for one of the wholesalers. Marie hesitated again as she told her niece how the man had brutally raped her sister. Wanda straightened up and was just about to ask a question, but Marie put a finger to her lips. Times had been hard for three orphan girls. Then she told her about

Ruth, about how she had been so in love with Thomas Heimer, the son of one of the richest glassblowers in the whole village. At the time the three sisters had been hired hands in Wilhelm Heimer's busy glass workshop, which is where Ruth had met Thomas. They had been truly happy together, at least at first, and the wedding had been a grand occasion.

"Then you came along. He had wanted a son more than anything, and when you turned out to be a girl Thomas just couldn't forgive your mother. Some men are like that. He drank too much as well, and the marriage went downhill very quickly after that. And then, one night, there was Ruth—scared out of her wits and carrying her little girl and all her worldly goods, standing in front of our family home. Your mother is a very proud woman. She never told us what finally put an end to the marriage. She kept a firm lid on all her suffering. Then when Steven came into her life, he was the fairy-tale prince she'd always dreamt of. You were only a year old when he took the two of you off to America. He had forged papers for both of you, and Ruth was traveling as Baroness von Lausche. Two years later, Thomas Heimer finally agreed to a divorce." Marie sighed.

Wanda clamped her lips together and didn't say a word. She seemed amazed, as though she couldn't believe that what Marie was telling her had anything to do with her mother, the elegant New York society lady who was always so calm and collected.

"Ruth made a mistake by never telling you about him. Thomas isn't such a bad fellow, in his way," Marie added. "He never married again, by the way."

Wanda looked at her foot as though she had no idea what it was doing in that puddle.

"All these years . . ." she said. "I always wondered why I felt so out of place my whole life long! Now I know at last. They never wanted me here. I was always just in the way, spoiling their royal majesties' fun with my presence."

"Wanda, that isn't true! Ruth loves you more than her own life! When you were a baby, she always used to call you her own little princess." Marie's heart ached as she told Wanda how she and Johanna had always thought Ruth loved the little girl too much.

"Once"—Marie laughed without thinking—"she saved up all her hard-earned money to have a photograph taken of you. And God knows that wasn't something that just anyone did, back then! Believe me, no mother has ever been prouder of her baby than Ruth was. You meant the world to her. And nothing's changed since then."

As she spoke, thunder roared overhead. Lightning lit up the shapes of the skyscrapers all around, which seemed to reach toward them like clutching fingers. Black clouds raced across the sky. All at once it was cold.

Marie blinked as she felt a raindrop splash onto her dress. This was all she needed! With any luck, though, the storm would pass over quickly.

"But why did she lie to me for eighteen years?" Wanda said. "Nothing means anything anymore; everything's just a lie, even the least little thing she says! She's always talking about my cousins Claire and Dorothy, Steven's nieces, about how hard they work at school and how polite they are to their parents. But I'm not their cousin! I'm not related to them at all!" She sobbed from a mixture of despair and rage. "I was never elegant enough. She always says that I'm too lazy, too cheeky, too much I don't know what. Why is she always trying to make me into somebody else? Do I remind her of my father—is that it?"

Marie shook her head. "Your mother has entirely forgotten your father. I think she's suppressed the memory so entirely that he never existed as far as she's concerned—which is probably why she never told you about him. You aren't the least bit like him, believe me. You are who you are!"

"And who's that, then?" her niece shot back. "All my life I've believed I'm American, and now I suddenly find out I was born in Germany. In the back of beyond, in the middle of the forest."

"Now don't talk that way! You're still Wanda; you're an enchanting young lady with more charm than most other girls," Marie cried out. *Who am I, really?* The question kept coming up—it seemed she couldn't run away from it.

Now the skies had really opened. But Marie couldn't bring herself to suggest that they take cover somewhere. She wanted to finish the conversation up here, one way or another. As she huddled closer to the chimney, Wanda suddenly jumped to her feet and ran out into the middle of the roof.

She spread out her arms and raised her face to the sky.

"Maybe the best thing would be if I were struck by lightning right now! Then it would all be over!" She laughed hysterically as lightning flashed nearby. "Closer, please! One more try! Here I am!" She spun around wildly.

A moment later, Marie had wrestled her to the ground.

"Are you mad? You could have died!" She held her niece firmly in her arms, a trembling bundle of misery. "You're out of your mind!"

Wanda sobbed again. "Mother has Steven, Harold has his bank, Pandora has her dance, you have your glassblowing—everybody but me has something to live for! I'm nobody; I'm good for nothing. I feel as empty as a bird's nest in December. Useless, worthless. I can't go on like this."

Wanda's despair shook Marie to the core, more strongly even than the storm that raged around them. The thunder growled and echoed back from the skyscrapers, the rain lashed across her back and her arms, but for the first time in ages she felt a deep gratitude well up within her. She had her gift. All at once it was easy to answer the question of who she was. She was a glassblower, and she always would be!

"Everything will be all right, believe me. I'll tell you all about Lauscha; I'll tell you everything you want to know. I'll tell you about your father; I'll tell you about his brothers and about your grandfather. If you want I can describe every piece of glass they ever made, everything that came out of their workshop. You'll know where your roots are, I promise you that." Marie shook Wanda by the shoulders.

"And what good will all that do? What does that have to do with me, with my life here?"

Wanda's skepticism simply strengthened Marie's resolve. Yes, she wanted to give Wanda something she could call her own—that was the least she could do for her niece.

"Look at it this way—Steven will always be your father. But today you've found you have another father as well!"

"That's wonderful! If I'm such a lucky girl, why do I feel as though I'd just been run over by a streetcar?" Wanda made a face, but she smiled the ghost of a smile as well.

The two of them were soaked to the skin when they climbed back down the fire escape ladder a little later.

That night—after she had taken Wanda off to her room and sat by her bedside until she fell asleep—Marie picked up her sketchpad and got one of her drawing pencils from her luggage. She could have cried with relief at the feeling of holding the pencil again, the same dear old familiar feeling. How could she ever have forgotten this comfort! It felt so good to sit here with a fresh new sheet of paper in front of her.

She stayed up the rest of the night drawing. She started by sketching what seemed useless—ball gowns, the flower arrangements that had sat on every table—nothing that she could adapt for

Christmas baubles. But Marie didn't care. She felt her heart welling over with gratitude that her pencil was moving once more, gliding over the page as if of its own free will. She could still do it! She hadn't lost her gift!

She drew and shaded, adjusted her lines, corrected the shapes. Suddenly she saw the New York skyline take shape before her eyes, dark and sharp-edged. Then streetlamps below, lights in the windows, a moon casting a cold light over the silhouette of the Brooklyn Bridge.

Day was beginning to break when Marie finally put down her pencil. There wasn't a blank sheet left in the pad. She had leafed through the pages so often that they were soft and pliant now, and here and there the pencil had worn furrows in the paper or smudged it black. Now it was time to sort through what she'd drawn.

It was a miracle! Among the night's sketches were at least ten images, maybe twelve, that would be perfect for a new line of baubles. They only needed a little work . . .

Then Marie's smile faded. How could she be so happy when Wanda was doubtless in a flood of tears just a few doors down the hall?

But were joy and sorrow ever far apart? They were like day and night, light and shade . . .

The *Night & Day Collection*—if she ever managed to make anything from these sketches, then that was what she would call it. She would get to work on the fine detail first thing after a few hours of sleep. She wasn't the least bit worried that she might fail. Now that she had made a fresh start, she could feel her creative powers bubbling away within her like lava in a volcano, pushing to the surface.

Marie leafed through the pad once more. She especially liked the scene depicting the skyscrapers and the night sky above. And the one where the moon hung low over the harbor front. The globes would have to be silvered inside first; then the outlines could be painted in white enamel and the shapes filled in with glitter dust . . . yes, that would be lovely!

Enamel paint and glitter . . . the thought was hardly formed when she realized what it meant. These *Night & Day* designs were a return to her roots, to the first globes she had ever painted eighteen years ago when she had begun to blow glass in secret. All she had back then was black and white paint, since her father had never needed anything else in his workshop. She had made her own glitter powder by begging some broken bits of glass off old Wilhelm Heimer, then taking them home and crushing them as fine as dust. She hadn't had anything else to work with, and her first baubles had needed nothing else. The contrasts, the light and shade, did it all.

Marie felt that she saw some deeper message in this return to her roots. She had already decided to tell Wanda all about where she came from. Perhaps that was bringing her, too, back to where she had begun?

15

After the previous night's storm, the morning was bright and clear. When Marie finally rose, drew aside the silk curtain, and looked out the window, the sunlight was so strong that it brought tears to her eyes. She blinked.

This was just the weather for a saint's day!

She put on a dressing gown and went into the breakfast room. She was relieved to see that Ruth and Wanda were sitting at the table together. They were both pale—this was the first time since she'd arrived that Marie had seen Ruth without any makeup—and they both looked unhappy, but at least they were talking.

For a moment Marie was tempted to tell them about the miracle that had happened to her during the night. But she dropped the thought when Steven stood up and offered her a chair, his face somber.

Of course there was only one topic of conversation. Wanda still couldn't understand why her parents had never told her, in all these years. "Why? Why didn't you . . . ? How could you have . . . ?"

Ruth and Steven tried to explain, taking turns, patiently.

Marie took another roll from the basket, more to have something to do than because she was really hungry.

Ruth suddenly turned on her. "There you sit, gobbling down one roll after another as though nothing at all had happened!" Wanda was in tears, again. "Is it too much to ask that you join in the conversation?"

Marie put down her roll and the honey spoon. "I'm so sorry. I really don't know what to say. I . . ." Her eyes fell on the cabinet clock behind Steven. "Is it really so late?" She stood up sharply, her chair squeaking across the marble floor. She looked from face to face. "I truly am sorry . . . but if I don't hurry, I'll still be in my nightgown when Franco arrives!"

"Oh yes, you run off and have fun!" Ruth yelled after her. "While you're gone we can clear up the mess you've landed us in!"

Marie could hardly wait to get out of the house. She could hardly wait to see Franco. She felt a pang of guilt as she brushed her hair and put on eyeliner. She even applied a little rouge—today was a special day, after all. She plaited her hair into one simple braid and then wound it about the crown of her head. Ruth would call it a frightfully old-fashioned hairstyle, but Marie felt like being a little old-fashioned today.

She spent a little while choosing what to wear. There was only one color for a summer's day like this—white! Pure, gleaming white. With plenty of ruffles and lace.

When she crept out of the apartment like a thief at one o'clock and went down to the lobby to meet Franco, Marie felt just as romantic as she looked.

"You look like a bride," Franco whispered when he saw her. "No, even more beautiful than that," he said in the very next breath. "Like the Virgin Mary!"

More Mary than Virgin, she wanted to say, but she bit back the remark. Franco didn't like it when women made off-color jokes.

"Thank you so much for the wonderful tiara. It's far too lavish, though, you really shouldn't have," she said instead.

Franco pulled her close. "Too lavish? What else should I buy to grace the head of a queen?"

He kissed her, and she felt weak at the knees. She clung closer to him. How much could she love this man?

From the moment they met, Franco only needed to touch her, and she felt wonderful. He smelled so good, her handsome Italian! Marie found herself wondering again and again what it would be like to lie in his arms. Naked, passionate. Drat it all, she didn't want him thinking of her as a virgin! She wanted to make love to him with every fiber of her being. The only question was how she could talk him into it. She wasn't like Sherlain; she couldn't just drag a man off to bed when she liked the look of him. She couldn't tell him how much she yearned for him—couldn't even *hint* at it. How was she supposed to put it into words? Oh, if only she weren't so clumsy at these games, if only she knew the rules that men and women played by.

She could only hope that Franco would make the first move, and soon.

Little Italy was festooned with decorations that day, as though the neighborhood wanted to outshine the old homeland across the Atlantic. Mile upon mile of bunting was strung across the streets and thousands of tiny colorful flags fluttered in the breeze. Musicians stood at every street corner, practicing for their moment in the grand parade. Crowds gathered all along Mulberry Street to watch. Excited children wriggled through the barriers that kept spectators on the sidewalk and ran out into the street, and their mothers ran after them to fetch them back. *Mamma mia*, it didn't bear thinking about if their *bambini* ran under the wheels of one of the parade floats!

For a while Marie and Franco let the crowd carry them along, flitting from one distraction to another like butterflies. But the cheering and the throngs all around her began to get on Marie's nerves and soon she felt her temples throbbing painfully. If only she'd gotten more than a couple of hours' sleep! She didn't want to be here in the crowd—she wanted to be alone with Franco, to tell him all about last night, about her hours with the sketchpad.

They eventually sat down for a late lunch at one of the restaurants. Franco ordered a huge dish of spaghetti with meatballs and wine from one of his family estates. Now that they were out of the glaring sun, Marie's headache subsided and she felt a little better. She raised her glass to Franco and looked into his eyes.

People kept coming over to the table, locals who knew Franco and were curious about his beautiful companion. Marie smiled and shook hands every time. Everybody was so polite, almost reverential, that Marie wanted to return their friendly gestures. And so, to Franco's astonishment and the delight of the other guests, she sprinkled a few Italian phrases into her remarks in English.

"How on earth do you know my language? And why have you never let on before now? Do you have another admirer hidden away somewhere?" Franco asked jealously.

"Well if I did, I certainly wouldn't tell you!" Marie replied teasingly. Then she laughed and told him how the Italian migrant laborers had come to Lauscha twenty years ago to help build the railroad. "Two young fellows stayed behind and married village girls. Lugiana is the daughter of one of those families, and she comes by twice a week to help us with the housekeeping." She shrugged. "Over the years I've picked up a word or two from her. But to tell the truth, I didn't want to make a fool of myself speaking broken Italian to you."

"I'd hardly call it broken—you speak it very well!" Franco seemed offended that she had kept this a secret from him until now.

"The *signorina* is not just beautiful but clever as well! A woman like that is rarer than a Lombard truffle," said Stefano, the restaurant owner. He looked at Franco with respect. "May I pour the lady another glass?"

Marie shook her head. "Two glasses is enough, thank you. I know that I shouldn't refuse de Lucca wine, but I don't want to end up tipsy." She already felt a little light-headed. But before she could mention this to Franco, the next visitor came to the table. He was the owner of another nearby restaurant, and unlike the rest of the well-wishers he was rather reserved as he spoke to Franco in a low voice. Marie expected Franco to tell her what the man was saying, as he had with all the others, but she waited in vain.

She frowned. She had never seen Franco's eyes glow with that strange, cold light before.

"Is there anyone in this neighborhood who you don't know?" she asked, almost in annoyance, once the man had gone. She suddenly felt nauseous from the smell of cigarette smoke, garlic, and cooking odors.

Franco frowned. "It's more the other way around. The people here know *me*, or they know my father. I have trouble putting a name to every face."

He was still talking, but suddenly Marie couldn't hear his words. She felt ill. She swallowed hard.

"Marie, what is it? What's wrong, my darling? You're pale!"

Marie couldn't even answer. It took all her concentration just to keep breathing. She was so dizzy, her throat felt tight . . .

She mustn't faint . . .

The first thing that Marie noticed when she woke up was the smell of linen drying in the sunshine. It reminded her of home. For a moment she didn't know where she was. These walls, the beige curtains, the green striped wallpaper—all of it was strange. Her muscles tensed up as though in response to some hidden threat.

"*Mia cara . . .*" She was with Franco! The tension drained away at once.

"What happened? The festival . . ." She wanted to sit up, but Franco pushed her gently back down.

"You fainted. It was probably from the heat. Stefano and I carried you here to my apartment so that you can recover."

His apartment.

No more strangers around them.

No noisy crowds.

No more feast of Saint Rocco.

Marie sat up with some effort. Her dress clung to her back. She wanted to lift the cloth away from her skin, but the bodice was too tight.

"You still don't feel well? Should I call a doctor?"

Marie shook her head. "I need a little more air, that's all. I'm so hot." She pointed to the buttons that were hidden in the seam down her back. "Perhaps you could . . ."

Their eyes met. Marie saw a mixture of concern and desire in Franco's gaze, and it electrified her. A hot shudder ran through her body when she felt Franco's hands at the back of her neck. As the first button eased through its elaborately embroidered buttonhole, then the next, she had to make an effort not to cling to him. She felt the urge to tell him to go faster.

Then at last he was at the last button.

It was now or never. Marie wriggled out of the bodice and threw it down next to her without looking to see where it landed. The thought that soon she would feel Franco's hands on her naked skin almost drove her out of her mind.

She turned her face toward him and came closer to his mouth, opened her own mouth for his questing tongue. They kissed, tiny kisses as light as a feather. Franco's hands wandered up and down her back, his fingers fumbling with the satin strap that held her corset together. Soon this too fell to the floor.

"Come here," Marie whispered. Her hands trembled as she reached for the collar of his shirt to undo the first button. She could have screamed in frustration when it wouldn't come loose right away.

"Slowly, my love . . ."

At last they lay there, skin on naked skin. Her gentle curves nestled into his hard, muscular body. Marie caught fire beneath Franco's hands, and she yearned for the moment when he would take her. She thrust herself toward him like a young foal, wanting to wrap her long legs around him, but Franco stopped her. As he pushed her back down into the pillows with his left hand, he ran his right hand down her side.

His hand glided in wide, strong strokes from her calves up to her breasts and then back down to her belly. Although she thrust her mound toward him, he lifted his hand over it and resumed stroking her thighs. At first Marie could have screamed from the disappointment; she wanted more, more, more, and it had been so long since a man had touched her! But soon his long, powerful strokes calmed her, and she felt beautiful and slim and young. All of a sudden she felt his mouth on her right breast. She was overcome by dizziness. How many other women had he driven wild this way? She didn't know, but she knew she never wanted to share him again. She was shocked by the vehemence of her reaction.

He kissed her again on the mouth and then took her nipple between his teeth, sucking on it until a thousand bolts of lightning shot through her. She wanted to wriggle out from beneath him, but his left hand held her fast. He moved his mouth across to her other breast and had his way with her there too. Only after that did he release her. She shimmied toward him and pulled him to her. Her legs spread open like a flower in bloom, as though she were a blossom carried from a cool, dewy garden into the warmth of a house. When she felt how hard he had become, she groaned aloud. She wanted this man. Now. Right now. And forever after.

But again Franco stopped her at the threshold. He pressed his body down upon hers, but he put his hand on her soft opening instead. He moaned when he felt how wet she was, and the sound made her so happy she was even a bit frightened. She whimpered.

"I love you so much that it hurts," she whispered hoarsely, her voice torn to shreds by the passion she felt for Franco, the passion that grew with his every touch. Anything that Magnus had ever done to her was faded and forgotten now, meaningless, unimportant, not worth her memory.

"I love you! *Mia cara* . . ." Franco took her head between his hands, his thumbs pressed into her cheeks, and his eyes held her gaze as he thrust himself into her.

At last!

She was scared to give away all that she was feeling and wanted to shut her eyes, as though there were some way to disguise her innermost self. But she returned his gaze, more scared that she would hurt him if she did not. When he let go of her head and clasped his arms around her body, she buried her face in his shoulder and breathed in deeply. The aroma of tobacco, sweat, and cologne was unmistakably and uniquely his. *If I die tomorrow, I will die happy,* she thought and laughed out loud.

From then on they moved to the same rhythm. They were one flesh, one passion. It didn't take long for their desire to reach its climax—they had waited long enough for one another. They screamed aloud together, one voice, one triumph, as they conquered the last peak, clinging to each other, slick with sweat, trembling.

Marie did not want to let go of Franco. He tried to shift his weight off her, but she clung tight to him. *Never leave! Don't say a word. Don't even stroke me.* He understood. He stayed there with her, propping himself up very slightly on his elbows. Marie never wanted this feeling to end, never. She was complete now.

16

That summer New York was in love with itself and so was Marie. For the first time in her life she felt the need to make herself look pretty, to wear perfume and jewelry, and she did it all for Franco. Until now she had barely bothered with such frivolities, but the blazing sun of his adoration beamed down upon her and made her shine.

"You slept with him!" Pandora blurted out the first time she saw Marie after the festival.

Marie blushed more than just a little, then nodded. "How . . . do you know that?"

"There's a certain gleam in your eye that women only have after a night of love. A night of pleasure! What I wouldn't give to feel that way again." She sighed deeply. "But at the moment all the men I meet are either unappealing or more interested in their own sex. Would it help if you kissed me? Maybe happiness is infectious?"

They flung their arms around one another and giggled for a moment.

"Love is a strange beast," Pandora said, becoming serious again. "It attacks us poor women and—"

"Leaves us crazed with happiness!" Marie interrupted, laughing.

Pandora took Marie's hand and squeezed it as though trying to bring her back down to earth.

"I was going to say, and before we know what's happened we're flat on our backs. Be careful, Marie! They can talk all they like about free love and the emancipation of women—but in the end we women are the ones who are left with a bun in the oven and no husband to show for it."

Marie laughed. "Is this really you speaking? I would have expected something like that from my sisters. But never mind." She leaned in closer to Pandora. "I haven't exactly lived like a nun up till now, and I've never been pregnant yet. I might not even be able to have children!"

Magnus had been downcast about that, at least in the early years. "Why don't we have a little bundle of joy?" he would often ask when her period came again, as it always did. Marie always felt he wanted an explanation from her. But she didn't miss having a child. He eventually stopped saying anything but went around with a long-suffering look on his face.

Magnus . . . Marie found that she had almost forgotten him. She shook herself like a dog shaking burrs from her coat.

She would have to write to him, at some point, and explain everything.

"You might be surprised at what changes when you have a new lover," Pandora said dryly. "Anyway, tell me, what was it like?"

Marie swallowed. Should she really tell? She felt a sort of superstitious dread, as though simply talking about how much she loved Franco might make her love vanish into air. But she was so happy she couldn't keep quiet about it.

"It was wonderful! I've never felt anything like it. Franco and I . . . I felt the whole time that we belonged together all along and our moment had finally come. Does that make sense?"

"Whether it does or not, you've got it bad!" Pandora replied with a knowing look in her eyes.

Now that she was drawing again, Marie saw the people and the street scenes around her with new eyes. A paving slab laid in some unusual pattern, the fire-eaters at a street party, the silhouettes of the ships in the morning mist over the harbor—all at once she found herself surrounded by dozens of ideas, and all she had to do was pick out the finest images and put them down on paper.

"Haven't I always said that your talent will come back to life of its own accord?" Franco said triumphantly. He was quite convinced that it was his love that had awoken Marie's creativity. She didn't have the heart to tell him that she had started drawing again the night before they made love for the first time. She too liked the idea that Franco's love could work such a change.

When she sent her designs back to Lauscha, Johanna and the others were so delighted that they sent a telegram bubbling over with words of praise. Reading between the lines, she could see that they were all very pleased with themselves for having had the idea of sending Marie off to Ruth for new inspiration. None of them knew that it wasn't New York itself that made Marie so happy, but rather being in love. Nor did they know anything about the drama that had taken place in the Miles household. Ruth had decided it best not to mention it in the letter that accompanied the drawings.

Although Marie had apologized a dozen times over for her faux pas, Ruth hadn't forgiven her. The sisters were still cool and distant toward one another despite Steven's best efforts at reconciliation. Wanda, too, had gone back into her shell and rarely wanted to see anybody.

Not wanting to stay in the apartment amid such tension, Marie had no choice but to go out on her own.

"I'll walk along the streets of New York, and I'll be just a woman out having fun! A woman like any other." As she recalled Georgie's words from the ship more loudly than ever, she felt guilty that she still hadn't paid her a visit. But there was simply no time for that; there was so much to do each day.

When she wasn't with Franco, Marie usually headed to Greenwich Village. She was still convinced that she had to drink in every impression, that she mustn't miss anything. And she was finally beginning to understand all the connections that had passed her by before: the Naturalists and the Symbolists, the apostles of fin de siècle decadence who had traveled in Europe, Pandora's expressive dance and Sherlain's expressionist poetry, and even the Art Nouveau artists who made Ruth's costly jewelry—they were all pieces of a puzzle, part of something greater that still had no name. This was a new creation, made not by God's hand but by man, and there was no single style to it. Everything was allowed here, and styles flourished and multiplied. Though Marie had been in America for months, she still found this astonishing variety confusing, almost humbling. She wondered yet again where she fit into the daring leaps of thought, the protests, the new discoveries about the subconscious, the emancipation of women. She had to admit that her idea of art was rather more commercial than what people liked here, yet she was nonetheless part of the greater whole. The sketchbook she carried around with her, its pages bursting with images, was all the proof she needed. And there was further proof as well; the other artists all treated her with respect, especially after a conversation in which she could give as good as she got in discussing matters of art.

"You're from Germany? Then surely you know my friend Lyonel Feininger? He's been living in Germany for a while now," one painter had asked her almost the first time she had joined a group at one of the café tables. The whole group seemed to stop their chatter and await her answer. As chance would have it, Marie knew the name from Alois Sawatzky's weekly gatherings. She knew that he was a painter, that he had been born in America to a German family, and she even knew his themes.

"Where Cézanne found his lifelong inspiration in Mont Sainte-Victoire, your friend has found his in the village of Gelmeroda," she declared. "He paints the village church over and over again, as though he's looking obsessively for some deeper meaning hidden there. And although the Cubist elements in his paintings certainly prevail, I do believe that he's a Romantic at heart." Or so some of Sawatzky's guests had said, at least.

That had raised a few eyebrows and won her recognition. She had passed the test! She, a glassblower from Germany, could now join the circle of the select few. The next moment they switched the topic of conversation and began to discuss subjective perception. All of them agreed that "a man truly has to *want* to see!"

Whenever Marie was out and about with Pandora and Sherlain, they were surrounded by a cast of colorful characters who listened devotedly as the poet recited her works in her smoky voice, or who thundered out their own lines of verse. There was a crazy German everyone called Kristi, who claimed to be a count but who dressed as though he had raided a theatrical costume department. A fiery-eyed Communist, he was never to be seen without a glass of red wine in his hand and was always ready to share a bottle with anyone who sat down at his table. Marie always liked listening to his stories, even though he smelled more than somewhat. Once he mentioned scornfully that his blue-blooded family had tried its best to cure him of alcoholism. They had even sent him to a mountain called Monte Verità in Switzerland, he said, so that he could kick the bottle in a *salatorium* there.

"A salad what?" Marie asked. But Kristi had already moved on to the story of how he had won his crossing to America in a bet. So now here he was!

Pandora had been sitting at the table as well, and later she explained what the remark meant. "There's a sort of sanatorium in Switzerland, above Ascona, in the hills above Lake Maggiore. It's run by a collective of artists and freethinkers. I think they chose the name Mount Truth for the hill where they built their settlement because they hoped that Mother Nature would grant them some great revelation there. Apparently it's entirely vegetarian as well, no meat allowed."

Marie giggled. "So that's why he called it a *salatorium*! I can imagine Kristi having a hard time of it there!"

Pandora nodded. "You hear a lot of stories about Monte Verità. Apparently the artists' chosen lifestyle takes a certain amount of getting used to. Some seem to thrive on it—but not Kristi!"

"I wouldn't grumble about having to do without meat. When I was a child we were so poor we couldn't afford meat," Marie said.

"I don't think that's the most important aspect. It's more about the . . . How shall I put it? The atmosphere of the place. A friend of mine, Lukas Grauberg, went there last year. He was suffering from some sort of psychosis, hearing voices, that sort of thing . . ."

Pandora waved a hand as though hearing voices were quite normal.

"Lukas wrote to me at New Year's and was in raptures about Monte Verità and the people who live there. He told me that he'd begun writing a book about his visions and that he'd finally met people who understood him—as if we didn't!" she said indignantly. "Well, anyway, Lukas is feeling better, and if we are to believe him, it's all because of that magical place. He wrote me that the sun and the mountain air heal most of the complaints people have when they arrive at the mountain. And then at the end of the letter he was good enough to tell me that he wasn't coming back and that I should give away all his possessions to our friends here. Apparently he and some woman named Susanna were building their own wooden cabin in the colony, and he didn't want to clutter up his new life with memories of the old. A wooden cabin, can you imagine!" Pandora reached for the wine bottle that was doing the rounds and poured another glass for herself, then offered to do the same for Marie, who waved the bottle away, lost in thought.

A place where the sun shone and where everybody could do— or not do—whatever they chose? With a view of Lake Maggiore? She found the notion very tempting. She asked why the artists had chosen to build a sanatorium, and Pandora replied that it was just the means to an end.

"After all, they have to live off something, don't they? And this way at least they are helping the sick, rather than having to bow and scrape to commercial tastes—the way some of us have to," she added, still smarting over her recital at Ruth's party. "They recently built a very modern dance studio at Monte Verità—I'd love to see it one day!"

"It does sound magical," Marie said, realizing once again that the world was getting smaller all the time. The distances were shrinking. Apparently it was nothing strange to end up in New York because you'd won a bet. Or to go all the way to Switzerland to visit a dance studio.

When she asked Franco later about Monte Verità, he laughed.

"Have I heard of it? Who hasn't? They're all nudists and long-haired dreamers! But the people of Monte Verità aren't quite as pure as they profess to be. Everybody in my line of business has heard the stories about how the tavern keepers in Ascona never sold so much wine before those eccentrics arrived! The competitors in nearby towns are quite envious." When Marie looked baffled, he explained. "My dear, when nobody's watching, they come down from Monte

Verità to the village to have a square meal and a drink or two! Is it any surprise? A few glasses of red wine always help if you're seeking wisdom!"

17

She was in love and she was discovering new worlds of art. Despite all that, Marie kept her promise and told Wanda about Lauscha and her real father. Sometimes she just perched on the edge of Wanda's bed for a couple of minutes before rushing off to meet Franco and told a quick tale of village life, leaving Wanda impatient for more. She loved her aunt's stories, the more the better. "Didn't you say that it was time I heard *everything?*" she said whenever Marie tried to hurry these visits along.

And so Wanda learned that her father was a talented glassblower and that he still liked to drink, though he was no longer the wild lad he had been in his youth. He was hardly seen down at the village tavern anymore, for now he did the lion's share of the work for his family. When Wanda asked why that was the case, Marie held nothing back. Wanda deserved to hear the whole truth.

How her father's younger brother, Michel, got so drunk one night that he trapped his foot in the rails on the Sonneberg-Lauscha line as a train was approaching and couldn't get free in time. It was his bad luck that he lost his right leg, the leg that a glassblower uses to work the treadle on the bellows and control how much air mixes in with the gas flame. From that day on, there was one fewer glass-blower at work in the Heimer household.

"Michel used to make eyes at me—I think I was eighteen at the time—and we met up a few times. But I was only interested in spending time with him so that I could pick up a few tricks of the trade," Marie admitted, laughing.

Wanda's other uncle, Sebastian, had left Lauscha immediately when he found his wife Eva naked in bed with his father, Wanda's grandfather, and he never came back. Eva had stayed with Wilhelm, and they now lived together as man and wife. Wilhelm was an old man and in very poor health. Marie doubted he would survive the next winter.

Wanda was astonished. It was all so scandalous! She would never have believed that her relatives in the old country could get up to such mischief.

When she asked Ruth about Eva, her mother replied, "That Eva always was a snake in the grass. The only thing that surprises me is that it took her so long to start playing around behind Sebastian's back. I can well remember the way she flirted with the old man! Those two deserve one another!"

Wanda wanted to know more, but Ruth wouldn't go into detail. She didn't like the way Marie was dishing up old gossip, and she told her so straight out.

"Do you think you're doing Wanda any favors by telling her about that den of vipers?" she snapped at Marie. "None of them wanted anything to do with her—why should she care if the old man's taken to his bed with gout or arthritis?" Then she rounded on Wanda and accused her of caring more about a crowd of complete strangers than she did about her nearest and dearest. About her father, for instance.

Wanda knew that Steven was suffering. He took her sudden interest in Lauscha to mean that she no longer felt anything for him. Which was nonsense, of course. He was her daddy despite everything, surely he realized that! But she couldn't tell him herself, so none of them quite managed to say what they really meant. Ruth tried her best to act as though nothing had ever happened, Steven thought that he had lost his daughter, and Marie suffered terribly from having been the one to start the whole dreadful business. And Wanda? She didn't know which way to turn.

So Marie and Wanda continued their conversations up on the roof of the building. Nobody ever came up there except for a few scraggly pigeons, so the two women could talk without interruption.

Leaning up against the chimney, mostly with her eyes closed, Wanda listened while Marie told her about everyday life in Thuringia and the holidays they celebrated there. She told her about the carnival at the beginning of Lent and about the village dance on the first weekend of May every year. Marie's stories made life there seem good, and the villagers of Lauscha sounded like happy folk.

Once Wanda almost fell off the ladder backward in surprise as she climbed up to the rooftop and spotted a sumptuous picnic spread out on a cloth. There were even two bottles of beer. Marie was sitting in the middle of the whole arrangement, grinning broadly. She had bought a huge loaf of rye bread at a German bakery and some blood sausage and liverwurst from a German deli, along with pickled gherkins—although to her dismay they turned out to be salt pickled, not the vinegar pickles she liked. As the two of them tucked into their rooftop feast, Marie chatted away about how the glassblowers at home loved potato dishes of all sorts with a glass of beer alongside.

Wanda listened, chewing contentedly. At first she could hardly believe that many families only had one dish to eat from and that everyone around the table helped themselves with a spoon—or even with their fingers.

Marie giggled. "I can still remember very clearly the first day when we went to old Heimer's workshop as hired hands, your mother, Johanna, and I. Old Edeltraud, the maidservant, came out at lunchtime and put a great dish of potato salad and wurst in the middle of the table, and we were expected to eat from that like pigs at a trough. We were quite taken aback! But you can get used to anything . . . It wasn't an easy time for any of us, our father had really spoiled us in his way. We certainly weren't used to being ordered about the way your grandfather used to do. I'm telling you, we had to work our fingers to the bone for a few measly marks! But despite all that—there were good times too. Those brothers loved telling off-color jokes—and didn't seem to care who was listening. It took us quite some time to get used to their coarse jokes."

"Oh, Marie, it sounds like something from another world!" Wanda sighed. "I could listen to you talking about it for hours. But I still feel so cut off from it all. I keep asking myself what all these people have to do with me."

As chance would have it, a few days later on their way to dance class they passed a poster announcing that a well-known gallery would be holding an exhibition of Murano glass. This was Venetian glass, not Thuringian, but it was glass all the same. So Marie suggested they go see it. She knew that Ruth was a frequent visitor to the gallery and she wanted to ask her to join them. But Wanda talked her aunt out of it; talking to her mother about glass or anything connected to Lauscha these days was like waving a red flag at a bull. Wanda wanted to go just with Marie, but Franco came too.

Marie's detailed descriptions of Lauscha and the villagers had not prepared her for the sight of the exquisite glass pieces on display. Wanda was fascinated. Arm in arm with Marie, she walked from one showcase to the next, both of them exclaiming in delight.

"I can hardly believe that my father makes artwork like this too," Wanda said, shaking her head. "How do they put those spirals into the glass? And look how this one shimmers! It's iridescent! And look at the vase over here with thousands of tiny flowers melted into its sides. How in the world do they do these things? These glasses are amazing! You would hardly dare to drink water or wine from such a thing! They're magical . . ." She was at a loss for words. "It's such a cold material but it radiates such warmth . . . it's poetry!"

Marie smiled. "You're a glassmaker's daughter for certain!" she said, and Wanda felt a warm shiver run down her spine.

Marie did her best to explain the various techniques to Wanda, but some of what she saw was new to her as well. "I must admit that these Venetian glassblowers know a few tricks that leave our techniques in the shade! I'd love to sit down at the lamp and try out one or two of these ideas, though I don't know whether I'd manage!"

Franco had been listening to the women talk, his face impassive, but now he offered to find the two artists so that Marie could learn more about their techniques.

While he set off in search of them, Marie took Wanda aside.

"Don't misunderstand me; I don't want what I say now to spoil your good mood. But when it comes to your father's workshop . . ." she cleared her throat, embarrassed. "I don't want to give you the wrong impression."

"What is it, Aunt Marie?" Wanda said, though she was only partly listening. She had just spotted a glass that was tinted a delicate pink like cotton candy and so lovely that . . .

"Time was when the Heimer workshop was well-known for the quality of their wares and the range they could offer, but they've been in a bad way for a few years now. Don't ask me why!" Marie said, raising her hands in protest. "All I know is that Wilhelm would never hear any talk of getting into Christmas ornaments."

"But there are so many things they could make other than Christmas ornaments, aren't there? If . . . if Thomas Heimer is as good a glassblower as you claim, then he must get enough other work," Wanda replied. She couldn't bring herself to say "my father."

Marie laughed. "It's not that simple. You see, the orders don't come in these days the way that they used to. You have to go out and look for the work. Nowadays a glassblower has to have a streak of the salesman too, or he'll go under."

"Who goes out and gets the orders in your workshop?" Wanda asked, frowning.

"Johanna, of course! She takes care of the whole business side of things—I know nothing about any of that," Marie said. She waved to Franco, who was headed toward them with two men in tow. "Isn't he handsome, my proud Italian?"

Wanda rolled her eyes. There was no talking to Marie once she got that dreamy look on her face. She took a couple of steps and stood right in front of her aunt.

"Do you think I might ever become a glassblower?" she asked, feeling stupid as soon as the words were out of her mouth. "I only mean . . . since both of my parents are from famous glassblowing families. Sadly, though, I've never been terribly good with my hands. I can't do embroidery at all, for instance. Whenever I try to do fine needlework my fingers get all sweaty and cramp up—whatever I try ends up looking clumsy and ragged . . . Aunt Marie, you're not listening to me at all!"

"Could you blow glass? Well, we'd have to try and see . . ." Marie replied, her gaze still fixed on Franco.

Wanda held her breath. Should she go ahead and blurt out the crazy idea that had been buzzing around her head these past few days?

"What would you say to my coming to Lauscha to visit you sometime?" she asked, her voice trembling. "I could try my hand at glassblowing. Wouldn't that be wonderful? If Mother lets me, I could come with you when you go home."

Before Marie could answer, Franco gestured to the two Italian glassblowers to come forward.

"May I introduce Flavio Scarpa and Mateo di Pianino? They will be happy to answer any questions you have about their art, but you will have to put up with me doing the translation, since I'm afraid they can't speak English or German."

Marie and the two glassblowers launched immediately into a highly technical discussion of cameo technique, powder melts, layering applications, and a thousand other things that Wanda knew nothing about and didn't care about. Marie was absolutely in her element, though. She seemed to have forgotten not just Wanda but even her own handsome Italian, whose face grew ever darker.

I seem to have chosen the worst possible moment to share my idea, Wanda thought irritably as she wandered off among the showcases on her own.

18

After they had escorted Wanda home, Marie and Franco stopped by a little bar near Ruth's apartment building. The bar wasn't chic or especially cozy; it didn't have a fancy menu—in fact it only served sandwiches, and the regulars there were just ordinary folks. Despite all that—or perhaps precisely because of all that—Franco and Marie liked the place. When they sat at one of the little red oilcloth tables with a glass of beer or a whiskey in front of them, nobody intruded on their private little world. The other customers included neither artists wanting to talk with Marie nor Italian restaurateurs wanting to haggle with Franco for better terms. Marie occasionally spotted a neighbor from Ruth's building, but even then they exchanged nothing more than a quick nod of greeting. Marie loved the hubbub of Greenwich Village, but sometimes she just wanted a little peace and quiet.

"Oh, I'm tired!" she said as soon as she had sat down. "My feet feel about ready to fall off. But it was worth all that walking—it was a magnificent exhibition! Those pieces struck a chord that's still sounding inside me. And Wanda was so enthusiastic! She's like a child, don't you find? She can be a lot of hard work, though, can't she? Or . . . what is it, why are you looking so grim?" She frowned.

She realized now that Franco had been unusually quiet and introverted all day.

"We have to talk, *cara mia*."

"I hope you aren't jealous," Marie said, feigning anger. "Can I help it if Flavio kept on calling me *bella*? Or if Mateo insisted on taking hold of my hand so that I could understand his wound glass technique?" She smiled. In fact she liked it when Franco was jealous. It made her feel . . . desired. But of course she would never let him know that.

He looked at her. "I have to go back to Genoa next week."

Marie felt as though she'd been punched in the belly.

"What is it? Why don't you say anything?"

New York without Franco? She couldn't imagine it.

"A week, so soon . . . My ship doesn't leave until the end of September," she murmured.

He leaned across the table toward her.

"Marie, I beg you, come with me! I've never felt this way about any woman. Meeting like this, in this huge city, it can only have been fate! We belong together, you and I. I can't live without you!"

"Do you think I feel any different?" Marie cried out. "But this is all so sudden. I don't know what to say."

She looked into his eyes to see whether he understood.

"I could leave New York without thinking twice—the city's beginning to get to me anyway; I feel I can hardly relax. And Ruth certainly wouldn't care if I took an earlier ship, ever since I upset her little family idyll. But that isn't the only thing I have to consider. You and I . . . we haven't ever talked about . . . about the future. My family expects me to come home—there must be a mountain of work waiting for me. I have to prepare this year's catalog, I have work to do at the lamp, there are the rods as well . . . I can't just up and leave!"

Even though I want to, she added silently. She clung to Franco's arm. He took her hands between his.

"You wouldn't have to. There's still time to organize it all. You could send your family a telegram, for instance. And then write a longer letter later, explaining everything. Of course they'll be surprised by the news at first, but that would be true even if you had weeks to plan and prepare."

Marie gnawed at her lip. Franco was right.

"And as for your art . . . you can work in Genoa as well. I'll have a whole studio fitted out for you in the palazzo, and you can send your designs to Germany from there just as you do at the moment. Italy and Germany—they're hardly far apart! It's just a stone's throw. I'll work in the vineyards, and you'll have the days to yourself, but the nights will be ours to share! You'll love Italy, I swear! Just this afternoon you said that winter can be terrible back in your country."

Had she really said that? When Franco looked at her like that, Marie couldn't be sure of anything.

"Just imagine, *cara mia*: you look out the window and the sea gleams in every shade of blue, the houses are shining white in the sun . . ." He swept his hand around to underline his words.

"I can just imagine how a view like that would give me all sorts of ideas for Christmas decorations," Marie replied with a touch of mockery. She found it flattering that Franco had already thought of all this, but it riled her as well. It seemed that as far as he was concerned, everything was settled. She heaved a deep sigh. Why couldn't things stay as they were?

"Oh, Franco! It all sounds so lovely! But all the same your plans worry me a little. You don't even know whether your parents want me in their house. What if they don't like me? And then your idea of putting in a studio—that sort of building work costs money. There are so many unknown factors—"

"I know they'll like you!" Franco interrupted her. "And Mother will be glad if we find a use for one of the rooms, believe me! As for my Father—he'll love you! Marie, *mia cara*, there's only one decision you *can* make . . ."

He spoke so passionately that a few of the other customers turned to look at them. But Franco only had eyes for Marie.

Marie shuddered. At times like these she felt she wasn't ready for Franco's love.

"But my return voyage is already booked and paid for . . ."

Franco smiled triumphantly.

"If that's all it is . . . you can give the ticket away! We'll travel first class! I'll see that you're treated like a princess. And not just during the crossing. As soon as we arrive in Genoa, I'll buy you the finest tools to be had. And the most beautiful glass, the colored rods, everything you need . . ."

"I haven't said yes yet," Marie said, struggling to be stern with him. But she knew even as she tried that she couldn't be. Franco's offer was so tempting; it was as though he had spread out a picnic of all the finest delicacies in front of her. All she had to do was reach out and take one.

"But you will; I'm sure!" Franco replied as he waved the barman over. "A bottle of champagne for the most beautiful *signorina* in the world!"

"You're impossible!" Marie laughed. "My beautiful, impossible Italian!" But then she turned serious again. "Give me some time, at least a day or two—I have to ask that of you."

She breathed a sigh of relief when she saw him nod reluctantly. Then she cleared her throat.

"I want to talk to you about something else as well . . . If you don't mind, I want to drop by and see Sherlain. She was supposed to give a reading yesterday, but she never showed up. There were more than forty people there, all waiting for her in vain! Pandora and I wondered whether she had fallen ill—Sherlain's been even paler than usual lately, she looked very poorly to me—but when we went to look for her, she wasn't in her room. I know you think I exaggerate, but I'm worried about her." She was almost cross with him as she spoke.

Franco raised his hands in resignation. "As long as it's just a quick visit and you're not going to spend half the night playing nurse—no problem. I have other plans for the rest of the evening, though . . ." He took her hand and kissed her knuckles, one by one. "I am going to apply my own special form of persuasion . . ."

She found Sherlain down in the basement where she lived. And she wasn't alone. Coming down the stairs, Marie recognized Pandora's glowing red shawl.

"Are you here too? If I'd known I wouldn't have been quite so worried." Marie ducked her head and put her hand on the rickety railing as she came down the last few steps. Suddenly a terrible smell struck the back of her nose. She began to feel sick.

Then she saw Sherlain and had to stifle a scream.

The poet was lying in a huge pool of blood. Her dress, the gray bed sheets—everything was covered in reddish-brown blood, already dry in some places. Her brow was slick with sweat, and the whites of her eyes were as yellow as a jaundice patient's. Her eyes were wide open. When she spotted Marie, they fluttered a little.

Marie knelt down next to the filthy bed as though in a trance.

"Sherlain . . . what happened?" She shook her gently by the arm, which flopped back and forth like that of a doll. There was no answer, just groaning. A loud, persistent ringing erupted in Marie's ears.

Dear Father in Heaven, help!

"Pandora, tell me what's wrong!"

The dancer shook her head. Her eyes were rimmed with red and she looked wretched, exhausted. She dipped a dirty cloth into a bucket of brackish water, wrung it out, and put it to Sherlain's forehead.

"Stand up, Marie, we're leaving. This is no place for you!"

Marie looked up at Franco, who was standing on the last step, his features motionless.

"What are you talking about? I can't just leave! We have to get a doctor. You have to find a doctor; she's bleeding to death!" When he still didn't move she added, "Franco, don't make me plead with you! I'll wait here while you fetch a doctor."

"Leave it, Marie," Pandora said in a thin voice. "No doctor would treat her. But we've already had someone here, a nurse who took care of her. The worst is over now, she'll live."

"A nurse? But why is she still lying in . . . If it's a matter of money—I'll pay for everything!"

"Marie, calm down!" Pandora was almost shouting herself now. "Do I have to look after you as well now?"

Marie stepped back as though she'd been slapped in the face.

"How can you both be so . . . cold-blooded?" she sobbed, and shrank back when Franco put his hand out toward her. "Sherlain . . ."

What had happened to the proud poet? As a thousand thoughts coursed through Marie's head, she felt as though the world were crashing down around her ears. Suddenly Sherlain's bittersweet voice echoed in her head.

"I give you my blood, sweet lamb of mine, to still your thirst, to strengthen your spine . . ."

Other voices joined in.

"Don't you think it's interesting to see the dark side of the city once in a while . . ."

"In the end we women are the ones who are left with a bun in the oven . . . !"

"We have to talk . . . I have to go back to Genoa next week."
New York without Franco?
Alone.
Without the love of her life.

Marie screamed and put her hands over her ears. She clung to Franco's chest. Only when he held her in his arms did she realize that she had been holding her breath—and she finally dared to release it. The voices died away.

She didn't resist as Franco helped her up the stairs. Out of the corner of her eye she could see Pandora looking up at her, but she did not stop.

When they reached the street, Franco released her gently. He lifted her chin and wiped her tears away with his thumb.

"Everything has its price, *mia cara*. Sherlain must have known that a time would come when she had to pay it, but she went with all those men regardless." His voice was hard. "Or did somebody force her to behave like a whore?"

Not now. Not that.

"I don't want to talk about it," Marie said, tired.

He shrugged.

For a while they walked along in silence like two strangers. It had rained earlier and the streets were empty. The light from the streetlamps shimmered dully in the puddles, and rats scuttled across their path. Most nights the rats only ventured out of the shadowy walls of the buildings much later, and Marie screamed in alarm at the sight of them.

Franco spun around, but when he realized that there was no danger he walked on.

Marie tried to tell herself that she was happy he was leaving her alone. But they had only walked two blocks when she could no longer bear the distance between them. She swallowed hard to get rid of the lump in her throat. Then she grabbed his sleeve and turned him around to face her.

His gaze was cool.

"Franco, I don't want to argue with you. Please . . . I . . ." She screamed again as a rat ran over her right shoe. All of a sudden Marie found everything around her sickening—the streets, the trash on the sidewalks, the shadowy streets, the tall buildings hiding the moon. Ruth with accusation in her eyes. And Wanda, moping and feeling sorry for herself.

"It's this damned city! It's the city's fault that people here don't know what they're doing anymore!"

"Do you want me to leave you alone here next week, in this devil's kitchen?" Franco asked quietly.

"No." Marie was suddenly certain. "Take me away from here!"

He didn't answer right away, so she said again, "Take me away from New York."

PART TWO

The stars dance on your soul,
your heart shimmers in moonlight.
The sun your sister—
and as you go on your way
you feel that the truth,
if only for a moment,
is close by.

1

"How often do I have to repeat myself? I haven't the faintest idea!" Ruth shouted into the receiver. "At any rate she *won't* be going back to Lauscha at the end of September as planned. She's only told me what she told you in the letter, which is that she's gone off to Switzerland with this Franco . . . Of course she's in love with him—what kind of question is that? He's quite turned her head, this Italian of hers, and don't ask me how! It's the only way to explain her behavior, though."

Wanda tried for the umpteenth time to catch her mother's attention, but Ruth acted as though she hadn't seen her.

"Yes, there are two other women traveling with her. Friends of *mine?*" She gave a shrill laugh. "Great heavens above, no! I don't even know them. Well that's not quite true; I once had the dubious pleasure of meeting one of them, since she was Wanda's dance teacher!" This time she looked straight at Wanda, with disapproval in her eyes. "The other one is apparently a poet. *She* says they're her friends! Though if you ask me they're a pair of tramps! Back in Lauscha we'd have laughed at them in the street!"

"Ask Aunt Johanna whether . . ."

Ruth waved her away again. Her pale cheeks were flushed with hectic red spots and she had pursed her lips.

"My dear sister, I think you have got quite the wrong idea about how Marie behaved during her visit. She couldn't give a tinker's cuss what *I* had to say about anything—most of the time she was just out looking for fun."

A tinker's cuss? Wanda had hardly ever heard her mother use such language. Indeed her whole manner had changed, and she had become almost mean-spirited. Wanda sat down on the velvet chaise longue next to Ruth and kept her ears open for her next chance to bring the conversation around to her visit to Lauscha.

It was the first time since the sudden news of Marie's departure that Aunt Johanna had walked into town to use the telephone at the post office and call them. Mother had been urging Peter and Johanna to get their own phone line for as long as Wanda could remember, to no avail. Johanna stuck stubbornly to the old ways, writing letters that filled reams of paper and expecting them to write back in just as much detail. But the family back in Lauscha had suddenly leapt into action when Marie sent a telegram announcing that she would not be coming back as planned but would instead be traveling to Ascona with a man she had just met to spend the fall at some place called Monte Verità. All at once Johanna seemed to think that a letter simply wouldn't do in this case.

"*She's* not ill! It's one of those women with her; I told you that. It must be the poet, since Wanda tells me that her dance teacher was still in the pink of health last week . . . Oh, what does it matter!"

Ruth put her hand over the receiver for a moment.

"You see what Marie's gone and done now!" she hissed at Wanda. "She's put off poor Johanna with just a few lines, and now I'm supposed to explain her scandalous behavior! Just think, she never even wrote to Magnus; the poor soul had to hear secondhand that Marie has up and left with another man!"

Ruth turned back to the receiver.

"No, Johanna, I was just talking to Wanda. Yes, she's sitting right here next to me. She sends all her love."

Before Wanda could say a word, Ruth skewered her with another look.

"Franco de Lucca! Well of course he's Italian, you can tell that from his name! Why Switzerland?" Ruth rolled her eyes. "They're taking their sick poet off to a sanatorium! The Swiss know all about that sort of thing, or so I've heard. All the same I would have thought that a patient from New York might have gone to convalesce in New England somewhere. I mean, think how much the journey must cost! But apparently Franco's paying for everything, don't ask me why. Marie mentioned some nonsense about wanting to take her friend to a sanatorium that's run by artists—perhaps this woman thinks she'll recover sooner if she's surrounded by her own sort."

Johanna must have said something in reply, since Ruth frowned deeply.

Wanda ran her finger over the threads on one of the satin cushions, and her mother immediately put out a hand to stop her.

"Worried about Marie? To be honest, I don't see why you should be. She's made a very good catch with this Franco, let me tell you. You should have seen the tiara that he gave Marie as a present. A tiara!" she yelled. "Besides which, she's not worrying about you. Or do you think she cares how you're going to get through the next few weeks without her?" she said sharply. The tic under her right eye was back.

Wanda sighed. If Mother got a migraine now, she could forget all about asking permission to go off on travels of her own.

"Our little sister is only thinking about herself. She's out for a good time, believe you me. I know, I know, that doesn't sound like the old Marie at all!"

"Why don't you ask Aunt Johanna when I can come and visit?" Wanda asked, shaking her mother insistently by the arm.

"Will you be quiet?" Ruth hissed. And then she spoke into the receiver again. "I meant Wanda, not you. What does she want?" Ruth heaved a heartfelt sigh. "Well if I were to tell you everything she wants, you'd have nothing to eat next month because you'd have spent all your money on the telephone. I'll put it all in a letter, and more besides!" she announced ominously. "But I can tell you one thing for sure: after all that happened here, Marie needn't bother coming back anytime soon. She hit us harder than a hurricane just on this first visit!"

Half an hour later Wanda left the apartment. Rather than waiting for the elevator, she opened the heavy iron door at the end of the hallway and gathered up her skirts to climb the fire escape up to the roof.

Just as she had expected, her mother was now lying down with a migraine. Before she went to her room, though, she had left no doubt as to whom she blamed for her suffering.

"Ever since Marie arrived, it seems to have become the fashion for everyone in this family to look out only for themselves. Nobody ever asks how I feel! My nerves feel as fragile as glass," she lamented. "First Marie leaves town on a whim, and now you come along with this obsession about going to Germany! I told you last week that I think it's a terrible idea. Harold would certainly not welcome the thought of your leaving, and heaven knows that Johanna has enough to do right now, what with having to parcel all of Marie's work out to others!" Ruth spoke as though Wanda was to blame for all that Marie had done.

"She has one less glassblower in the workshop, so she doesn't have time for tourists. Quite apart from which, I haven't the faintest idea what you want to get out of going to Lauscha. If you imagine that the man who happens to be your father is eagerly awaiting your arrival, you're mistaken. He didn't even glance at you once the day you were born! He just went off to the tavern and got stinking drunk while I cried my eyes out back at home. That's how things were, missy!" Ruth became angrier with every sentence. "But nobody wants to hear about that, oh no. Anybody listening to you and Marie would think that I'm the villain here, that I stole you away from your *father*!" Her voice was bitter, as it always was when she spoke of Thomas Heimer.

Wanda knew exactly what would come next. As indeed it did.

"I only want what's best for you, child," Ruth said, her voice suddenly softer. "I can just imagine how Marie filled your head with all sorts of romantic nonsense about Thuringia, about the pine trees rustling in the forests and the brooks babbling over the rocks and birdsong everywhere. But the truth's quite different; cramped little homes that lose their roof tiles in winter, children who have to work alongside their parents from morning till night for a few moldy potatoes and maybe a scrap of ham to go with it. After our father died, we three girls didn't even know how we would afford the wood for the stove that winter! Oh, we were young and slim and pretty, but we didn't owe our trim figures to corsets or tailored dresses. Why do you think thousands of Germans emigrate every year? Why did Steven's family emigrate? Not because life in the old country is so wonderful! Forget Lauscha. You don't belong there any more than I do." She wanted to stroke Wanda's arm but her daughter pulled away.

"And so you want me to deny my roots, just the way you did?" she blazed back at her mother. "We speak a little German from time to time and that seems to be enough for you. Why do we never eat German food at home? And why do we celebrate Thanksgiving but never the harvest festival?"

Her mother was at a loss for words. Instead of even trying to answer she changed the subject just as she always did when she didn't like the turn a conversation was taking.

"What would you say to starting tennis lessons this fall? I hear that more and more young ladies are taking it up, and the white outfits are most attractive. Or if you like, you could go riding with your cousin Dorothy. She always says that a gallop through the park first thing in the morning is the finest pastime you can imagine."

Wanda waved the suggestions away. Tennis and riding—next her mother would suggest that she join a church choir.

Up on the roof she had to squint as the sun sank down behind the buildings across the avenue. It had been a cool day with heavy rain in the morning, and the evening was noticeably cold. Wanda shivered as she headed for her favorite spot by the chimney. It wouldn't be long before it got too windy and cold to come up here.

A pair of pigeons nesting by the chimney cooed curiously at her approach. Wanda shooed them away. There were no crumbs of dark rye bread for them today, no tales of the old German homeland. A tear ran down her cheek. She hadn't realized she was crying.

She missed Marie so much!

"What do I do now?" she whispered as the pigeons strutted off through a puddle.

"Everybody has a mission in life," Marie had told her. *"You just have to know what it is. And that's true for you too."* It had sounded so true when she said it.

Wanda ran her hand over the slab of cold stone where she sat. Only a week ago this stone had been warm, and Marie had been sitting there with her, a sketchpad on her knee. Despite Wanda's protests Marie had insisted on drawing her portrait. "Just like in the old days when you were only a babe in arms. You'd hardly started crawling. I drew so many pictures of you in those days that your mother could practically have wallpapered the place with them," Marie had said, laughing. Wanda also had laughed when she replied that Ruth probably wouldn't want to be reminded of that these days. It had been one of those moments when everything seemed easy and uncomplicated. Once Marie had finished the portrait, she shut her sketchpad so carefully that anyone would have thought the sheets were made of gold leaf. "This way I can take something of you with me," she whispered softly. And the carefree moment had passed.

It had been their last conversation before she left.

Wanda hadn't let Marie go so easily. She had burst into tears, and she had said some harsh words. She accused her aunt of leaving her in the lurch, and Marie had been visibly hurt by the charge, nearly in tears herself.

"I'm sorry if that's the way you see it," she had replied. "But there's nothing more I can do for you. Not even if I stayed a couple of weeks longer. You have to find out for yourself what you will do with your life." That was when she had told Wanda that everybody had a mission.

Wanda wanted so much to believe her, but instead she had replied, "What if I'm the sorry exception? What if the Lord made a completely useless human being when he made me? You have to admit that's how it looks."

Marie smiled. "How impatient you are! Perhaps the dear Lord decided he didn't want to make things quite so easy for you as he does for other women. Otherwise he'd have made Harold propose to you a while back, wouldn't he now? Then before you knew where you were, you'd be a married woman with a baby on your lap."

"It may not have happened yet, but there's still time," Wanda said stubbornly. Harold had been dropping clumsy hints lately about the changes that were about to happen in his life. Changes that would affect her too. Wanda had changed the subject every time. "And what if being a banker's wife is my mission in life?" The very idea was unbearable!

"Some women can fill up their whole life by loving a man. You may think they're few and far between, but your mother is one of them," Marie answered, grinning. "Personally, I couldn't imagine a life like that. As much as I love Franco, I don't think I'd be going with him if he hadn't promised me that I'd be able to carry on working. But he's very loving and generous as well. He's only going to Monte Verità because of me, can you imagine!"

Wanda frowned. "I thought that you were going to Switzerland because of Sherlain?" Pandora had said something about a chronic illness from which the poet had to convalesce.

Then Marie explained that the trip to Lake Maggiore was supposed to kill two—or even three—birds with one stone. First it would get Sherlain into healthier surroundings, far from the pernicious influences of the big city. Marie was also excited at the thought of meeting artists from all over Europe on Monte Verità—which had swayed Pandora into deciding to join them. Marie could hardly wait to find inspiration in Europe after all the ideas she'd come up with in America. Wanda wasn't quite sure how that was going to happen, given that Marie's sketchpad was already spilling over. Finally—and Marie hesitated a little here before she went on—a short stay in Ascona would put off the moment when she arrived in Genoa with Franco.

"I feel quite queasy at the thought of meeting Franco's father and the countess for the first time," she confessed to Wanda. "I can't imagine being apart from Franco even for a day, but sometimes I'm frightened of what the future may bring. And I haven't the first idea how I'm going to explain all this to Johanna . . ."

Wanda smiled. They were already in an uproar in Lauscha at the thought that Marie would be coming back home later than planned. She didn't even want to imagine what Johanna would say when she heard that Marie had followed her handsome Italian all the way to Genoa.

Wanda heaved a heartfelt sigh. Marie had such a colorful, exciting life. She had a wonderful job, she had Pandora for a friend, she had a handsome lover, and she had many exciting plans for the future.

She, Wanda, had nothing. She didn't even have a dance teacher anymore, let alone a passionate lover—when Harold embraced her, he did so like a big brother, and his kisses were just dry pecks on the cheek. And it looked as though she wouldn't be going to Germany anytime soon either. She had pleaded with her parents dozens of times to be allowed to go, but to no avail so far.

Wanda shut her eyes and took a deep breath. *What does the air smell like in Germany?* she wondered.

She tried again and again to imagine all the scenes that Marie had described to her. She remembered what her aunt had said about the weekly market in Sonneberg, the nearest big town. Did it smell sweet, like cotton candy? Or did it smell of fish, like down at the harbor? And the people: Wanda tried to imagine a group of women like her Aunt Johanna, doing their weekly shopping at the market. How were they dressed? Did they all know one another? Did they laugh at one another's jokes? Would Eva Heimer be there too?

Wanda opened her eyes. Come to think of it, was this Eva her aunt or her . . . grandmother? Since she had been married to Sebastian but lived with Wilhelm Heimer as his . . . She wondered what her father had had to say about it when the whole scandal took place.

What did he even look like? Wanda couldn't conjure a picture of the man in her mind's eye. Marie had described him in such vague terms that she could have been talking about almost any man. Wanda had looked through her mother's photograph albums in secret, but she hadn't found a single picture of Thomas Heimer.

There wasn't even a wedding portrait. If there had ever even been such a picture, her mother had certainly destroyed it long ago. She had covered her tracks, as they say. And now that Marie had gone it was near impossible to find out anything more about where she really came from. There would be no more German bread, no more stories.

That night Wanda lay awake for hours.

"*Everybody has a mission in life*"—Marie's words hammered in her brain like mischievous goblins, set on tormenting her. Gradually Wanda's sadness vanished, to be replaced by stubborn resentment. Ha! She wasn't going to give up just because she hadn't found her own mission yet! Everything had to happen right here, right now—at least that's how she had lived her life so far. Harold always said rather condescendingly that her spontaneous ideas were just castles in the air. Empty air. Meaningless air.

Shortly before midnight she sat up abruptly in bed.

Perhaps she had just been going about things the wrong way. What was so wrong with taking some time to stop and think?

She sprang nimbly out of bed and went to the window. She leaned her forehead against the cool glass and looked out into the night.

Over in Lauscha they would probably see the stars scattered across a clear sky tonight, but she saw the lights in hundreds and hundreds of windows. And that was something, wasn't it?

Wanda laughed softly.

How did the saying go? If Mohammed would not go to the mountain, then the mountain would have to come to Mohammed!

That was it!

Perhaps she couldn't go to Germany—not yet. But there was something else that she could do.

It wasn't quite eight o'clock in the morning when Wanda put her hand, trembling slightly, on the doorknob of a small bakery in a side street off Tenth Avenue. That was where Marie had bought the bread for their picnic, and she had been full of praise. "I've never had such good rye bread, not even back home! I can't understand why your mother doesn't have them send her bread every day."

A sturdy-looking woman, busy heaving loaves as big as cart wheels up onto the shelves, turned to look at Wanda as she came in.

"What can I do for you, Miss?"

Wanda cleared her throat. It was now or never. She made an effort to speak in her best German.

"Is there somewhere nearby where the Germans meet, where I can learn more about Germany and its customs?"

2

Marie screamed and sat bolt upright.

"Marie, *mia cara*, what's the matter?" Franco asked, sitting up in bed a moment later. He was wide awake in an instant, his eyes roaming the cabin, but nothing appeared to be wrong. He relaxed again.

"What happened?" He shook Marie's arm gently. "Did you have a bad dream?"

Marie nodded, her eyes still wide with shock, one hand to her mouth as though she had seen something dreadful.

"I don't feel well. I have such a knot in my stomach . . ."

There was sweat on her brow.

When Franco moved to put an arm around her shoulder, he felt her nightgown clinging to her back. "You're soaked through!"

He picked up a cardigan from the wooden chair that served as their bedside table and draped it around Marie's shoulders.

"Thank you." She took a deep breath. "I'm all right now . . . Good heavens, though, it was such a nasty dream! I was in the clearing over behind the sanatorium. It was flooded with light, like you get when the sun's shining down onto a white surface. There was a man . . . He had a great flowing beard and was dressed in a long robe. But it wasn't anybody from here, from the mountain," she added hastily when she saw the look on Franco's face. She pulled the cardigan closer around her.

Franco reached over to the chair and pulled out a cigarette, and Marie kept talking as he lit it.

"The man asked me to dance, but I didn't want to. His hand was ice-cold, and I tried to pull my hand away, but he wouldn't let go and kept on as though he hadn't heard me. We spun around in a circle and I felt quite sick. I didn't hear any music, though perhaps I just can't remember that part. There were other couples dancing there as well, some of them were women dancing with women and men dancing with men."

"And I—where was I?" *Why is she dreaming of other men?*

She shrugged. "'I have to go to Franco,' I kept telling the man, but he didn't look at me and acted as though he hadn't heard. 'Franco doesn't like it when I dance with other men,' I told him, but again he ignored me. He held me tight in his arms and we went round and round and round and didn't stop." She swallowed. "We danced right on past the other couples. 'We have to turn around; we're getting too close to the edge!' I shouted at him. I pulled at his arm and writhed like an eel, but he held me in a grip of iron. Suddenly the lake was coming closer and closer, not blue any longer; it had turned inky black like some vast chasm waiting to swallow us up. As we took the last step, he looked at me and laughed. Laughed like a madman. And his face was so horrible . . ." Marie began to tremble so violently that she couldn't go on.

"Marie, calm down! Everything's fine." Franco rocked her in his arms. "I know what it's like to have dreams like that: you fall and fall and fall . . ."

"Then there's nothing more below you, it's so awful! And then there's the fact that it was somebody else dragging me down!"

For a moment neither of them said a word. Then Marie sighed.

"Alois Sawatzky, the bookseller I told you about, would love to hear about a dream like that. He would interpret it and then speculate about its deeper meaning."

"I don't need any specialists to tell me what it's about," Franco said irritably. "It's because of this miserable wood cabin we're lodged in. So much for fresh air and nature's light! My father's hunting hounds have better accommodations. This is the last night we spend in this shack. We're moving to the Casa Semiramis tomorrow."

He looked around the room, still fuming. He had wanted to stay in the hotel from the very beginning, since it promised at least a little comfort. But during their first tour of the grounds he had let Marie talk him into staying in one of the wooden cabins that were scattered through the forest.

"How romantic!" she had exclaimed. How charming to wash on the front deck in the morning with just a bucket of water! Sherlain had been equally taken with the idea. Pandora, however, had been quite horrified at the idea of getting so close to Mother Nature.

"If it's so darn comfortable living in a chicken coop like that, why have Henri Oedenkoven and Ida Hoffmann built themselves a villa with electricity and running water?" she had asked. It was one of the curious features of the place that the owners of the commune lived in far greater luxury than the other members. In the end the two women had taken a room in the little hotel that stood at the edge of the estate, with its spectacular view of the lake. Pandora had read out loud from the hotel brochure. "Peace and quiet and freedom for those who are tired, who can gather new strength here." She decided that it was just the place for them.

Franco drew on his cigarette, furious. Why had he agreed to live in the forest like a savage?

Marie had had trouble sleeping even on their first night there—there were too many strange noises, rustlings in the undergrowth, small twigs cracking as though underfoot. She admitted to him the next morning that she had strained her ears at every sound, while he himself had slept like a log, since he'd taken a quick tour of the taverns down in Ascona that evening. She also told him that she always felt as though she were being watched. No wonder, given that there were no curtains in the cabin, or even shutters for the windows. "Now who on earth is going to watch us sleep in the middle of the night?" he had reassured her, then suggested that they move to the hotel. But she wouldn't hear of it. Then she should come down to Ascona with him in the evenings, he said; some wine would certainly help her sleep. But she hadn't agreed to that either. He asked whether she had converted to Monte Verità's creed of abstinence. At that Marie just laughed, unbuttoned her blouse and invited him to find out just how abstinent she had become. After that there had been no more talk of moving to the hotel.

He felt his desire reawaken now. He reached out and stroked her breast gently. Maybe he could get her to take her mind off things for a while.

But Marie wriggled out of his arms a moment later.

"That's enough feeling sorry for myself. I won't let one silly dream spoil my whole day. What I need right now is a cold shower," she declared with conviction in her voice. She pulled her nightgown over her head and walked outside, stark-naked, blowing him a teasing kiss first.

Franco watched her go. What was it about this woman that she could twist him around her little finger? Ever since he had met Marie he had been a different man—sometimes he barely recognized himself. He did things for her sake that he would never have dreamt of doing before. Such as this detour to Ascona. It had taken quite a lot of persuasion to talk his father into giving him these three weeks of leisure, and he had to promise to make up for lost work once he got back home. When the old count had grumbled that other men never let their love affairs get in the way of business, Franco had answered heatedly that this was more than just a love affair, that Marie was the woman he'd been waiting for all his life. His father had replied that he could hardly believe that some chance acquaintance he'd met on his travels in America was so much better than the many blue-blooded marchionesses and countesses his mother had presented to him over the years—any one of whom would have made a good match. Whereupon Franco had announced that he loved Marie. The old man spluttered with laughter and said that he loved his dogs.

After the heated exchange over the telephone in the Ascona post office, Franco decided it was probably best not to mention for now that he would be bringing Marie back with him. Clearly his parents needed time to get used to the idea that they would soon have to share their only son with a woman. But the time was drawing near when they would have to set out for Genoa.

Perhaps it would be a good idea to call his father today and fill him in on the details—after all, there were preparations to be made at the palazzo. *A glassblower's studio? Have you finally lost your mind?* He could just imagine what the old count would have to say about that. Franco took a deep breath, as though gathering strength for the coming duel of words. This time, he swore, he wouldn't let the old man's barbs get to him. There would be no repetition of the whole drama with Serena. He was no longer a boy whose father could break his will. He and Marie were strong together, and together, they could face down the count. He would follow her example and dedicate himself to his work in the vineyards, just as she let nothing distract her from her glass. And he would no longer serve as his father's errand boy. He was looking forward to the day when he would have nothing more to do with the smuggling. He had never let it show how revolting he found that part of their export trade, but it always hung over him like a dark cloud. Admittedly the cloud had thinned somewhat since Marie had come into his life; at least, it had become easier to bear. But everything would be so much better when it had vanished entirely. Oh yes, the old man would have to get used to the idea that from now on, his son had his own plans. And who knows, maybe at last his father would come to appreciate his efforts to renew the vine stock and breed new grape varieties?

Through the open door he could see Marie washing her breasts with a sponge. She dipped the sponge back into the bucket, careful not to lose a drop of water, then squeezed it out before rubbing it up and down her right leg. Wearing her nakedness like a simple, costly garment, she moved without a trace of self-consciousness. How beautiful she was, his princess!

He drew on his cigarette one last time and then stubbed it out.

From now on she would live in the lap of luxury; he would take care of that. As for his father . . . he didn't want to think about him right now.

3

After Franco had set off for the village, Marie walked over to one of the sunbathing areas, wearing nothing but a half slip. She met Pandora and Sherlain here every morning to lie in the sun. Sometimes Ida Hoffmann or Susanna, the partner of Pandora's New York friend Lukas Grauberg, joined them. Marie loved the hours they spent there. Ruth, who was always meeting her friends for lunch or afternoon tea, would probably have seen nothing special in such an arrangement, but for Marie it was the first time she had ever had a group of female friends. When she sat at the lamp back home, Peter, Johannes, and Magnus were always in the workshop; and as a woman doing a man's job she felt she had to play like a man to keep up with them.

When Marie turned the corner and saw Lake Maggiore and her friends all waiting for her, she forgot her nightmare. The naked female bodies were as white as the finest china against that azure background. She was almost overwhelmed by the wish to hold the moment forever. A wave of happiness washed over her.

"So, Franco finally let you get out of bed!" Pandora said, standing up. Grunting and groaning in a most unladylike manner, she walked past Marie and spread her sheet out on the mossy grass.

"Oh no, it was quite the other way around: *I* let *him* go, albeit reluctantly!" Marie replied, grinning. She squinted and watched Pandora head toward one of the big wooden bathtubs that stood at the end of the meadow.

"You don't seriously intend to climb into that fishpond!"

The first fallen leaves of the season were floating on the surface of the water, and hundreds of midges flew up from the tub as Pandora approached.

"Don't I indeed! Didn't you hear Ida's lecture about how water can magnify the sun's healing powers? Apart from which, I'm frightfully hot!" Pandora let the towel fall from her body and began to dance naked around the tub.

"*You have to dance to the music in your heart . . .*" she sang, then jumped into the tub with a raucous splash. Stagnant water dribbled down its mossy sides.

"It seems to me that there are others who can hear the music in your heart as well . . ." Susanna pointed uphill, where a group of men were practicing archery—though at the moment none of them were looking at the targets at all, for their eyes were fixed on Pandora's breasts.

"Let them stare. Maybe they'll be so . . . excited by what they see that there'll be something for us to look at as well," Pandora said, giggling. She stood up with exaggerated slowness and turned around once, then dove down into the water again. "Well, do you see anything moving?"

Marie and the others all giggled. They had already cracked a few jokes about the tiny loincloths that the archers wore.

Once she lay down in the sun, Marie realized that she was really quite tired. Her eyelids drooped. How nice to nod off for a while in the middle of the day! Whatever would Johanna say to such a change in her habits? She grinned.

"You look like the cat that got the cream," Sherlain said, as she sat up to untangle her red hair.

"That's how I feel," Marie said, stretching out on her towel. "I was just thinking how much my life has changed since I left Lauscha." She smiled. But she wasn't the only one to have blossomed with the change of scenery. Sherlain had recovered astonishingly fast after the botched abortion.

"It's just as I always say: you have to get out of your rut. If you only want it to be, life can be one huge adventure!" Pandora called over from her tub.

Marie rolled her eyes. Sometimes Pandora rubbed her the wrong way with that worldly manner of hers. But then again, she was often right . . .

There she was, Marie Steinmann, lying stark-naked on a mountainside in Ascona above Lake Maggiore with three other women, none of whom she had known for more than a few weeks. All around her, exotic plants were growing on the rock faces, and waterfalls were tumbling down in an Eden she had never even known existed before now. People were singing wordless melodies, strolling about with flowers in their hair, and moving in ways that even Pandora couldn't quite fathom. By now Marie and her friends had learned that this kind of dance was called eurhythmy, and Pandora was so carried away by it that she got up hours before her usual time to practice. She and the other dancers could be seen at daybreak, when tendrils of mist still veiled the lake, moving along the shore like a fairy cavalcade.

Everybody here—apart from a few oddballs—was friendly and smiling and loving. Many of them seemed to take "love thy neighbor" quite literally. Love was in the air, and people kissed and hugged and stroked and touched one another whenever they felt inclined to do so. It was a sensual and erotic backdrop for the playground of Monte Verità.

Once Marie had realized just how unconventional relationships were here on the mountain, she began to worry that Sherlain might simply pick up where she had left off in New York. And lo and behold: it took less than a week for Sherlain to go into raptures over Franz Hartmann, one of the founders of the commune, and his "powerful words," his "sacred devotion to principles," and his "gaze that drank in the starry skies." Marie and Franco laughed about the strange words people used here on Monte Verità, but Sherlain was quite intoxicated by the "honey wine of mountain poesy."

Marie snorted in derision at the idea that Sherlain had fallen for someone who preached morals morning, noon, and night. Just a couple of days before, Franz had walked past their cabin as Marie and Franco were having a pillow fight on the wooden deck. How he had looked down his nose at them!

"Are you off to bring your body and soul into harmony with nature, then, you loon?" Franco called out to him. Franz didn't react but walked on, his hands folded in prayer and his eyes turned to the sky, whereupon Franco giggled and whispered to Marie, "He's halfway to Heaven already!"

"Or he's taking his nourishment from the forest air," she answered. Then they raced into the cabin and made passionate love.

A shiver ran down Marie's spine. Even if all the Greek gods of Olympus came down and danced stark-naked, holding hands right here on Monte Verità, Franco was the only man for her. She would never have believed she could find such happiness in a man's arms. The way he . . .

Someone shook her arm, tearing her away from her daydreams. When she opened her eyes, Susanna was in front of her, an expectant look on her face.

"Sorry, I wasn't listening. What did you say?"

"I just asked whether you wanted to go and see Katharina von Oy later on."

"Mmm!" Marie said noncommittally and shut her eyes again. She suddenly felt sick. She opened her mouth and took several big gulps of air to fight the nausea. It seemed the nightmare had really upset her. She hadn't the least desire to get up from the soft mossy hillside where the sunshine warmed her skin. Quite apart from which, Susanna had already promised several times to take her to see the glassblower who lived up on the slopes above Ascona in a sort of hermitage, but nothing had come of it yet.

Katharina von Oy used to live in the commune with everybody else. However, once the sanatorium had opened up, and more and more visitors came to the mountain, she had left the hubbub and gone to live in a lonely forest shack. She made a living making pictures in glass, which were sold to tourists down in the village. Of course Marie was interested in what kind of glasswork people liked here, and she had not the first idea what pictures in glass might be. Did it mean stained-glass windows, like those found in churches?

"If you wait for my dance lesson to finish before you go for your walk, I'll come with you," Pandora muttered sleepily.

"You? Why do you want to go and visit a glass artist?" Marie asked in surprise. "Are you considering a career change?"

"Nonsense. I just want to see how she lives. Ask her a few questions. How she came to own the land. How much it cost, that sort of thing. Lukas tells me that after phylloxera killed off most of the vineyards hereabouts a lot of land was sold off for cheap. Who knows? Perhaps I can afford a little cabin here myself. I'm not going back to New York, that's for sure."

"You would stay here? Don't you think you'd miss the hustle and bustle of the city?"

Pandora stretched her right leg up into the air, admired it for a moment, and then crossed it gracefully over the left. "I won't miss anybody or anything. Quite the opposite. I've never been able to concentrate so completely on dance as I have here. I seem to feel the air vibrating around me. *You have to dance to the music in your heart . . .*" she sang again.

"Lukas and I knew this would happen," Susanna said triumphantly. The next moment, though, she frowned fiercely. "Pandora, darling—you're not lying right, again! How often do I have to show you how to sunbathe? This is how you have to do it, watch!" She lay down flat on her back with her arms and legs stretched wide, her back slightly arched, her face to the sun.

"I'll lie however I like," Pandora grumbled. "If I lay the way you told me to, I'd feel like I was on a rack."

Marie, who was lying on her belly, giggled. "I don't find it all that pleasant either, to tell the truth. You feel so defenseless . . ."

"That's right, isn't it?" Pandora said emphatically. "And I always worry that a bug will crawl in between my legs. Or even get into my bottom." She laughed merrily.

"The way you lot chatter away, it's worse than having to listen to the magpies cawing on the balcony," Sherlain grumbled.

The others looked over at her. Unlike the others, Sherlain had assumed the prescribed Monte Verità sunbathing position. Her hair lay spread out over the green moss like a ring of flame, making her look more than ever like a Celtic goddess.

The four women sunbathed in silence for a while, and Pandora even began to snore. Marie smiled to herself. She had never known her friend to be so relaxed.

In New York Sherlain and Pandora had been birds of paradise, praised and adored for their eccentricities—while here they were just two people among a whole crowd of self-appointed creative geniuses. Life on Monte Verità seemed to be doing both of them good. When she was honest with herself, Marie found the constant quest for wisdom rather silly. And it was almost shocking the way they thundered against alcohol here. Franz Hartmann stridently preached the message that wine and beer were only for the weak-willed, and many of the residents lapped it up, so to speak. Sherlain hadn't drunk a drop since she had arrived at Monte Verità, but Pandora wasn't quite so self-denying. The same held true with regard to meat. The hard-liners here talked of meat as carrion and held that it polluted both body and spirit. Marie rather liked the meals of sliced apple, grated carrot, and kohlrabi, but Franco refused to try being a vegetarian even for a short while.

"The whole of Ascona enjoys *la dolce vita* and I'm supposed to eat rabbit food?" he had said right at the start. He had since gone down to the village for at least one meal a day. Now and then Marie and Pandora joined him, but Marie always felt guilty after indulging in prosciutto and other meats. Besides, Italian food was bad for the figure. She had never been as plump as she was now.

Franco however had the time of his life strutting through the narrow streets of Ascona with Marie on his right arm and Pandora on his left. Whenever they sat down in a tavern, he insisted on picking up Pandora's check as well, which was beginning to get on Marie's nerves since the dancer didn't show the least sign of gratitude—quite the opposite in fact.

"How can you make so much money in the red wine trade when it sells for so cheap all over the world? Who knows what business you're really in?" she had teased him just the other evening, at which point Marie gave her a hard nudge in the ribs. Franco had once told her in no uncertain terms that aristocrats thought it very coarse to discuss business affairs, and that was the last time she had asked where all his money came from. All she had meant was that she didn't like the thought that he always paid for everything, but he had put on such dreadful airs that she had changed the subject . . . And maybe it wasn't so bad to let him spoil her.

Marie sighed contentedly. She seemed to have it all these days. The best lover in the world and . . .

"What do you think, Marie?" she heard all of a sudden in her right ear. "You're an artist yourself, wouldn't you like that? It would be like Greenwich Village on a mountainside."

"I'm sorry? What do I think of what now?" Marie blinked in the sunlight and looked up into Pandora's face.

"Admit it, you weren't even listening!"

Marie smiled ruefully. "I'm sorry; I must have been daydreaming."

"I don't think I need to ask what you were dreaming about! Are you so much in love that you're losing track?" Pandora said, peering at her irritably, and then turned back to Sherlain. "I'm sticking with what I said before—if nobody but artists came to live here, it would be just a ghetto and it would do art more harm than good!"

"Which is exactly where I disagree with you. You'd get something like the purest form of art, crystallizing from the very air."

Marie looked from Pandora to Sherlain and back again in confusion. What on earth were they talking about?

"Don't worry about it," Susanna said, her breath tickling her right ear. She came over so close that Marie could smell her body odor. "When I was in your condition, I couldn't concentrate on anything for half an hour at a time either. I felt so restless—and so sick every morning! It's the hormones, they say. Anyway I hear that there are doctors now who specialize in just this sort of thing."

Sherlain and Pandora turned their heads like bloodhounds picking up an interesting new scent.

"A doctor? My condition? What do you mean?" Marie frowned.

For a moment Susanna looked at her in astonishment; then a knowing grin spread across her sunburned face.

"Well really, Marie, you don't have to play the innocent with us! Here on Monte Verità we take a fairly relaxed view of that sort of thing as you know. Or are you really worried one of us might be shocked at the news?" Susanna seemed to be enjoying the moment enormously and glanced over at the others to be sure she had their attention. "How daft does she think we are?"

"Pardon me if I'm a little slow this morning, but I still don't know what you're talking about!"

Susanna's knowing remarks were beginning to get on Marie's nerves. The woman always seemed to have to let the whole world know how smart she was.

"Apart from having had a bad dream that left me feeling a little queasy, I'm perfectly all right. My hormones are certainly all in order," she said, and rolled over onto her stomach to show that the conversation was over.

"I see what it is now," Pandora said, groaning. "Oh no! Is it true? Marie, tell us—are you really . . . pregnant?"

4

Harold took his watch from his pocket for the umpteenth time and toyed with its gold chain. His heart gave a little leap of joy, as always, when he opened the lid and heard that satisfying click. As a little boy he had longed to have a pocket watch and now he had one—gilded, at that! He brushed away an imaginary wisp of lint from the watch glass and shut the lid. He would never indulge in this newfangled habit of wearing his watch on his wrist, the way some of his colleagues did!

He frowned and looked over at the door.

Where was Wanda? They were supposed to meet at eight o'clock, and now it was twenty past. *I should have insisted on picking her up at home,* he thought irritably. At least then he wouldn't have had to worry about whether she was all right.

The waiter in tails who had been hovering near Harold's table ever since he sat down took a step closer.

"Perhaps *monsieur* would like to choose a wine first? Or should I bring the menu?"

"No, thank you. I'm still waiting for someone."

"May I bring *monsieur* an aperitif?"

"No," Harold replied irritably. He hoped this restaurant wouldn't turn out to be the wrong choice—he wanted the setting to be just right, tonight of all nights. His right hand wandered involuntarily to the breast pocket of his jacket. The little leather case felt cool and smooth to the touch.

The waiter hesitated a moment longer, then stepped back and waited three paces away from Harold's table, his hands clasped behind his back.

Harold took a sip of his glass of water.

They could have met at Mickey's Brooklyn Bar, of course. Or at one of the Italian restaurants they both liked. But Harold wanted more than just beer or spaghetti on this occasion, and a fancy French restaurant seemed just the thing.

Besides, he knew that he wouldn't be confronted with German grilled wurst and potato dumplings here. He would hear no German conversation and no German songs. There were no German flags hanging on the wall and although the waiter was rather insistent, at least he wasn't wearing German folk costume. Thank goodness!

Harold kept an eye on the door as he tried to count up how many German clubs and patriotic societies Wanda had visited over the past three weeks. She had gone to the Black Forest Brotherhood, the Mecklenburg Ladies' League, the Hamburg Harmony Choir, and even to the Banat Swabian Society. And every time, she had given him a detailed account of each little clan's customs—in glowing terms. She told him all about the sense of community that bound them together. About the patriotism that shone through in every word and every action. She still didn't know which of the clubs she actually wanted to join. She liked the North Germans' songs best, but the Bavarians had the best food, and the Swabians had the most impressive rituals and ceremonies. At the moment, Wanda was most inclined to join the Banat Swabian Society. When Harold had arrived to take her out for a walk last weekend, he had found her bent over her needlework, embroidering a sentimental slogan about the waters of the Danube and the lush green fields along its banks. She showed him her work proudly, although frankly, she had made quite a mess even though she was barely past the first word. Her mother was visibly annoyed by the whole thing, but what influence had Ruth Miles ever had over her daughter's flights of fancy?

Harold smiled. Wanda! It was really something to watch her launch herself into her latest project, every single time.

Ever since Marie had left, she had been consumed by the idea of rediscovering her German roots. Wanda's obsessions reminded him of some of his Wall Street colleagues, who were never happy with their profits and always wondered what would have happened if they had invested just a little more money, held onto their stocks just a little longer. Some of them couldn't get such thoughts out of their heads and turned into virtual monomaniacs. Harold had long ago decided that although he enjoyed his job he never wanted to turn into one of them.

The latest bee in Wanda's bonnet had given him one thing to be grateful for: there was no more talk of her finding a job. Rather she spent her days browsing in German shops and reading books about Germany. Whenever they met, she wanted to tell him all about what she had been reading, in German of course. The fact that he only spoke a phrase or two didn't stop her at all. She offered to teach him German if he liked—it was her mother tongue after all, she said! Harold had refused as gracefully as he could.

He turned the glass of water around and around in his hands. He was looking forward to what might come next. If Wanda turned out to be just as enthusiastic about preparing for the wedding, and then keeping house afterward, there wouldn't be much left of his salary at the end of every month despite his recent raise. Well never mind that! It was high time Wanda found her "mission in life"— she'd been looking for one for as long as he'd known her.

A quarter of an hour later he finally spotted Wanda's distinctive blonde bob through the restaurant's full-length glass doors as she got out of a cab. She was wearing a simple black outfit that showed the lines of her trim figure to full advantage.

"Harry, you simply cannot imagine what I've just heard!"

Before Harold could even rise to pull out her chair, she had plunked down into her seat.

Her appearance had not gone unnoticed by the other guests. Wanda's effervescent manner made all heads turn as the diners looked up from their duck à l'orange, their truffled potatoes, and lobster bisque. The conversation at the next table suddenly seemed far more intriguing than whatever was on their plates.

"Do you have to make such a fuss?" Harold asked, fighting the wave of annoyance that washed over him. This was *his* evening. *He* wanted to be the one to set the tone!

"Just imagine: Marie's gotten married!" Wanda blurted out.

"Married?" he squawked. Then he cleared his throat and began again, dropping his voice. "Who has she married? And how do you know?" What a stupid question! She had married Franco, of course.

"That was exactly how I reacted when Mother told me that Marie and Franco had just up and married," Wanda said and passed a hand across her brow. Then she told him about the telephone call her mother had gotten from Johanna. Apparently Marie had decided that all she needed to do was send a telegram to Lauscha. There had been no further explanation, nor even any promise that she and her new husband would come and visit the family anytime soon. All she told them was that she planned to live and work in Genoa from then on.

As though Genoa were just next door! Harold thought that Marie had behaved scandalously.

"She'll be living in a real palace with a view of the sea. Mother's eyes almost popped out of her head when Johanna told her that part."

Wanda smiled and took the glass of water that the waiter had placed reverently on the table.

Harold watched her as she gulped down the water. That was typical Wanda, he thought fondly, then remembered why he had wanted to meet like this.

"So Marie has followed her heart in the end . . ." That wasn't such a bad way to begin, in fact.

"Yes, but she did it at the worst imaginable moment!" Wanda laughed, quite oblivious to his lovey-dovey tones. "Apparently they're right in the middle of preparing the new catalog back home in Lauscha—and the big question is how they'll ever get it ready by February without Marie to help. And as if that wasn't bad enough, my cousin Anna has just sprained her ankle so badly that she can't even walk, never mind work the bellows treadle. If I understand right, she not just one of the glassblowers, she also runs all the errands for the day-to-day business in the workshop. My mother tells me that Aunt Johanna is on the verge of a nervous breakdown. Marie's decision to move to Genoa is a catastrophe." Her cheeks were aglow with excitement.

"Wanda! Can you please forget your German relatives for a moment?" Harold leaned across the table insistently and took her hand. "I have some news too . . . good news!" He paused for effect. "You are sitting across the table, my dear, from a newly appointed bank manager."

"Harold!" Wanda squealed with delight. "I'm so happy for you!" She was already at his side of the table and leaning down to kiss him. "Congratulations! I'm quite sure they couldn't have picked anybody better for such an important job."

"There's a catch, though . . . I have to take over a branch down in New Mexico. I know, I know, it's a long way from New York. But I've asked around and apparently Albuquerque is a very nice city. They've got their own theater, lots of shops, and a well-tended park." He laughed. "I promise that you won't even miss New York. And it's only for two years. Mr. Robinson—he's in charge of deciding where managers are posted—he tells me that there's a good chance I'll . . ."

"Harold . . ."

He reached for Wanda's hand again and stroked it. "I know; it's all rather sudden. I hadn't expected myself that I would—"

"Harold!" she interrupted him again, this time more insistently. "I . . . can't . . . come to New Mexico with you."

He smiled. All of a sudden Wanda was showing herself to be the well-brought-up, levelheaded girl he knew and loved. At least her Aunt Marie's scandalous habits hadn't rubbed off on her!

"Of course you can," he said softly as she stared at him, perplexed. He decided not to leave her hanging any longer. In one smooth motion he took the little leather case from his pocket and flipped it open with his finger. Then he turned the case so that Wanda could see the diamond ring in its cushion of dark-blue velvet. "But you'll come as my wife. Which is why I'm asking you, here and now—Wanda, will you marry me?"

She looked down at the ring, then up at him. As though she couldn't quite believe what was happening.

Harold felt a wave of remorse. He knew how it could feel to wait an age for something and then finally get what you wanted; sometimes the joy at the achievement was mixed with a tinge of sourness, like milk left to stand too long.

He fumbled for words to set things right. This wasn't how he had imagined this moment.

If Ruth Miles had had any say in the matter he would have proposed to Wanda last year. But he had wanted to do everything right, damn it all! He hadn't wanted to ask Steven Miles for his daughter's hand in marriage when he was just a poor nobody himself—now at least he had a solid job title.

But why was Wanda behaving so oddly? She ought to be smiling again—she'd had time to get over the initial shock by now. He had expected her to spring to her feet and dance a waltz with him on the spot. Or at least order champagne. Or talk him into buying drinks for the whole restaurant—he had even put extra money in his wallet just to be on the safe side. That would have been his beloved Wanda! But he didn't recognize the girl who sat across from him now, her eyes wide and her chest quivering as though she'd just been shaken.

"Harold," she said for the third time. She took her hand away and passed it across her brow as though trying to clear her thoughts. "I . . ." She smiled helplessly.

He gave her an encouraging look, all the while fighting the dreadful feeling in the pit of his stomach that something terrible was about to happen.

"There's no way to say this gently." Wanda heaved a desolate sigh. "I can't marry you," she blurted out. "I have to go to Lauscha. I have a job to do there—my family needs me now."

5

Wanda was far from pleased to hear that her mother had chosen Yvonne Schwarzenberg and her daughter Wilma to chaperone her on her journey. Yvonne was the best friend of Monique Desmoines, who had broken off all contact with the Miles family after the debacle with the pigs' feet at Dittmer's. Although Ruth had initially been most annoyed about how Wanda had lost the job, she had been squarely on her daughter's side. "Monique acts like the uncrowned queen of New York!" she said angrily and then told Wanda, "It's just a shame you only managed to spoil *one* party for that snooty bitch."

Nonetheless, Ruth had picked up the telephone as soon as she heard that the Schwarzenbergs would soon be setting off to Hamburg to spend the winter there with Wilma's fiancé, a rubber wholesaler who had strong ties to Indonesia. Ruth found out the name of the ship and the date it would sail, and then she took the plunge. Would Yvonne be so kind as to take Wanda under her wing, just during the crossing? The answer was a hesitant yes, whereupon Ruth called the shipping line next thing and asked whether there was still a cabin free on the *Germania*, preferably on the same deck as Mrs. Schwarzenberg and her daughter. When she heard that there was indeed, Ruth finally agreed to Wanda's departure. She had been worn down by weeks of pleading.

"I won't stand in your way," Ruth declared and then sighed, adding, "Back when I left Lauscha it was a completely different situation of course, but to be honest . . . I wouldn't have let anyone or anything stop me then." She shrugged, almost defiantly. "And who knows? Perhaps you really will be able to make them forget their current troubles over in Lauscha."

So Wanda dutifully held back from making fun of the Schwarzenbergs—despite the fact that Wilma was such a gray little mouse and terribly dull. She had come to Pandora's dance classes once or twice but spent most of the time in the changing room, terrified of being asked to dance for the group. Pandora had to drag her into the studio by the hair. And then she just stood there, as stiff as a stuffed giraffe.

But if she had to, she could even put up with eight days of listening to Yvonne Schwarzenberg hold forth on what made a man a good match. Rubber—the very idea!

By now they had heard back from Johanna, in writing, that Wanda was quite welcome to visit. Wanda had read the letter over and over again until the pages were tattered, and she knew it practically by heart.

We are very much looking forward to having Wanda with us. I can hardly wait to see with my own eyes what a fine young lady that little blonde baby of yours has grown up to be. But I do have to add a word of warning: given the state of affairs here just at the moment, neither Peter nor I will have much time to show Wanda the old country. Of course I'll take her to Coburg one day and Sonneberg (that goes without saying). But we'll have to wait until spring for anything more adventurous.

*I'll be so relieved when we finally have our samples catalog off
to press!*

Then Johanna had spent a few lines lamenting that there were
still no viable designs from Genoa and that Magnus was so bro-
kenhearted that he had practically forgotten how to blow glass and
wasted valuable rods making items that they would have to sell as
seconds.

*Magnus still hasn't got over losing Marie. He's suffering like a
dog, and I feel guilty every time I remember doubting that he
really loved our sister!*

Johanna had found out in a recent telephone call from the
Sonneberg post office that her niece knew the truth about her father
by now, but to Wanda's great disappointment Johanna hadn't written a word about Thomas Heimer.

Wanda would set sail on October 15, which meant that she only
had two weeks to pick out her wardrobe, buy presents for all of
the Thuringian relatives, and go out to dinner with Harold one
last time. They exchanged promises throughout the meal, caught
between laughter and tears. Although Harold had been very upset
when Wanda had turned down his proposal for some unspecified
length of time, she sensed that once he had gotten over the shock,
he was actually a little relieved not to have to take up his demanding
new job with a wife in tow. Alas, he could not come to the farewell
party that her parents were hosting, since he would be setting out
for Albuquerque two days beforehand.

And then everything was packed, and all the farewells were
spoken.

On the morning of October 15, Wanda stood on the steps that led into the belly of the liner with a small valise in her hand—the rest of her luggage had already been stowed the previous day—and waved to her parents. She suddenly felt a lump in her throat. The people down there on the docks blurred together into little colored dots, and Wanda had trouble picking out her parents in the crowd.

Good-bye, New York!

Millions of people came here to make a new life.

Her mother had come here and found happiness.

Marie had come here and found happiness.

And now she, Wanda, was turning her back on the "capital of the world," as Steven called it.

It was a strange feeling to leave the city where she had grown up so that she could go back to the country where she had been born.

On the gangway she handed her papers over to a steward, her hands trembling. As he checked that all her documentation was complete and correctly filled in, she felt a growing urge to turn around and run back to her parents. What if the whole trip was a huge mistake?

"Welcome aboard!" The steward smiled as he handed her papers back.

Too late. There was no turning back now. And surely only cowards had second thoughts like this! All the same the thought of having a couple of familiar faces on board was tremendously comforting—even if they were just Yvonne and Wilma Schwarzenberg.

Apart from the Schwarzenbergs there were five other passengers at the table: an old married couple from Kentucky who bred horses and whose name Wanda didn't catch; Sorell and Solveig Lindström, two sisters in their midthirties traveling to Northern Germany to collect an inheritance; and Mr. Vaughan, a railway engineer.

The first course at lunch was beef broth with julienned vegetables, during which Sorell and Solveig regaled their traveling companions with an account of the letters their long-lost rich uncle had written them before his demise. The second course was poached salmon with parsley potatoes, accompanied by Mr. Vaughan's thoughts about a new type of railway engine that would apparently be faster and more comfortable than the current model. At that the Kentucky couple retorted that no technology in the world would ever replace horses. As the dessert was served, Wilma and her mother looked as though they were about to burst with their own news—how could an inheritance or technological advances compare to a rich husband? But before Wilma could even say the word "rubber," Solveig Lindström turned to Wanda.

"Pardon my curiosity, but what brings you to undertake an ocean crossing?"

Wanda put down her sorbet spoon. She had been expecting the question and had already prepared an answer some days ago.

"I'm on my way to Thuringia, where my mother's sister owns a large glass workshop. They've run into some trouble ever since several key members of the staff had to take time off work. I'm on my way to lend a hand in their time of need." She smiled around the table. "I only hope that I can be of some help to my family."

"You're their guardian angel! Now who would have thought it!" Solveig said.

Sorell nodded, impressed. "Just imagine: we had something much the same happen back home! There was a bakery that was a whisker away from having to shut down when the owner fell ill with a lung infection. Hardly surprising when you think he'd spent his whole life inhaling flour. But his brother and sister-in-law came all the way from Missouri to take over the bakery while Charles Klutzky got over his infection." Sorell nodded emphatically. "They worked day and night to make sure that all the customers got their bread fresh every morning."

"When you live in the country, you're even more dependent on your family for help," the horse breeder added. "One of our neighbors down south lost his wife to childbed fever, poor man, and was left with four little ones and the newborn. If his wife's only sister hadn't dropped everything and come to his aid, he'd never have coped. The work on the farm, the children, keeping house . . . Marjorie was just a young slip of a thing when she came to the farm but from the very first moment she set to work as though she'd never done anything else."

The engineer nodded. "People never know what they can do until they find they have to. I know of a similar case. Some friends of my parents . . ."

As they got up from the table, the gentleman from Kentucky clapped a hand on Wanda's shoulder. "If you don't mind, we'll drink to your health this evening."

"Oh indeed, we ought to recognize it when young people show themselves so willing to help," his wife chipped in, glancing at Wilma as she spoke. "Most young ladies seem to be seeking only to satisfy their own pleasure these days . . ." Wilma had finally gotten the chance to share the news of her engagement after all.

Wanda nodded softly, doing her best to look selfless.

She almost felt her shoulders drooping under the weight of her new responsibilities—not that she disliked the feeling. Quite the opposite.

Instead of going off to explore the ship, Wanda lay down on her bed and went over the table talk in her head.

Mrs. Kentucky had declared that the most important thing was to radiate confidence and keep her family's spirits up to help them through their troubles. She had to bring light and sunshine where all hope seemed gone. That was at least as important as the work itself. Solveig Lindström had nodded in agreement.

Wanda heaved a sigh. She would do her best!

She had already realized while her mother and Aunt Johanna talked on the telephone that her aunt was at her wit's end. Was that any surprise, though?

Even if it meant poring over the accounts books from morning till night, she would take some of the weight off Johanna's shoulders. Granted, she had never learned anything more advanced than basic bookkeeping at the young ladies' academy—the kind of thing the girls would need to manage a house later on—but she could learn how the business worked. Somebody would show her what had to be done, and once she'd gotten used to it, she would surely be able to satisfy everyone.

Wanda sat up and walked over to the porthole. She stared out, trying to recognize something, anything. But fine droplets of fog clung to the window and drenched everything in featureless gray.

Well, she didn't want to fritter the journey away in romantic reveries anyway. She turned away abruptly.

She would take care of Anna as well, who was probably angry at herself for having sprained her ankle while out dancing. The obvious question was why Anna had gone dancing at a time like this. But people sprained their ankle in all sorts of places, didn't they? Wanda decided that if Anna blamed herself, she would talk her out of it.

She would spread good cheer wherever she went—if nothing else, she was sure of that.

Then she frowned. Why was it that total strangers like the couple from Kentucky or the Lindström sisters had more faith in her than her own mother?

"For heaven's sake don't poke your nose in where you're not needed. Just take a moment to look and see how Johanna and Peter do things. And don't expect special treatment," her mother had said, before adding that the best thing would be for Wanda to do what she was asked and no more than that.

Wanda felt a pang of bitterness. Did Mother feel she had to be ashamed of her? After she'd spent a lifetime already telling Wanda how a young lady should behave and what was appropriate?

Wanda clenched her fists in a most unladylike manner.

Damn it all, she would behave just as she had been told, and more than that, she would show them all what else she was capable of!

6

By the time Johanna got to Coburg it was twenty of two. Wanda's train was due at two o'clock. Johanna muttered a hasty farewell in French to Monsieur Martin and flung open the door to his hansom cab before the cabbie could even climb down from the coachman's seat. As she hurried through the railway station's grand front door, she heaved a long pent-up sigh of relief. She'd made it!

That morning it hadn't looked as though she'd be able to meet Wanda's train. One of her most important clients, Monsieur Martin from Lyon, had turned up at the door quite without warning to place the Christmas orders for his chain of five department stores. By the time Johanna had gone through the whole catalog with him, there was no chance of catching the train to Coburg. Of course she had made contingency plans, and in her last letter to Wanda before her departure, she had explained in detail how to catch every train connection from Hamburg to Lauscha, changing at Braunschweig and again at Coburg. All Wanda needed to do for the last leg of the journey was ask for the train and then climb aboard. But Peter and Johanna had agreed that they ought to meet Ruth's daughter in Coburg if they possibly could manage it. Johanna felt that it was her duty. If one of her children were making such a long journey, she would be reassured by the idea that someone was waiting at the other end. So she was all the more upset when Monsieur Martin took half the morning to place his order. She had done her best not to let it show, but Martin had noticed that she was on edge. When he heard that she was due in Coburg, he insisted on giving her a lift in his carriage. Johanna hesitated at first; she still had trouble trusting strange men, no matter how honorable they appeared. But her desire to meet Wanda overcame her doubts. Once they were on the road, Monsieur Martin told the coachman to drive the horses as though the devil were after them. Johanna felt rather queasy throughout the breakneck journey, but at least they had got there on time.

In addition to her, there were two men in black coats standing on the platform, their collars turned up against the cold, while the other passengers had taken shelter in the waiting room. An icy wind blew the fallen leaves of a mighty chestnut tree across the tracks; although it was early afternoon, the dark seemed to be drawing in already. Johanna wished the weather were better for Wanda's arrival.

She drew her shawl tighter around her shoulders but stayed on the platform so that she could see the train pulling in.

Wanda! Little Wanda was coming back—Johanna still couldn't quite believe it. The only thing that would have made her happier would have been if Ruth were coming as well.

In the first few years after Ruth left, Johanna had missed her sister dreadfully. "Why don't you come and visit?" she has asked again and again in her letters. "Don't you miss Thuringia at all?" Of course she missed the old country, Ruth wrote in reply. But she had been traveling on forged papers, and it was impossible to come back. And later? Ruth had come up with all sorts of reasons not to undertake the journey. Johanna had eventually stopped asking, but she missed her sister dearly. Although they wrote letters, that wasn't the same.

As the cold crept up Johanna's legs, she began pacing up and down the platform. Then she remembered that she must have a pair of gloves somewhere in her coat pockets, left over from last winter. She put them on and the cold became a little easier to bear. And a good thing too, since Wanda's train was obviously delayed—it was now ten past two. But her excitement grew with every minute she waited. And besides, when did she ever have time to let her thoughts wander like this? It was good to have a few minutes to herself, even if it was an unfamiliar feeling. Johanna sighed happily and plunged back into the past.

It was odd, but she had always been able to talk to Ruth more easily than to Marie. Maybe it was because the age difference was less? Ruth had been nine years old and she had been eleven when their mother died, and they had taken care of seven-year-old Marie as well as they knew how. Ten years later, when their father had died and left them penniless, she and Ruth had been the ones to take charge. Or at least so they had imagined—in the end it was Marie who had gotten them back on their feet by teaching herself to blow glass. Even today Johanna was ashamed to remember how she had wallowed in self-pity while Ruth had marched off to Sonneberg with a few Christmas baubles in her basket to find a wholesaler. After her dreadful experience with Friedhelm Strobel, her employer at the time, she simply hadn't been herself. What luck that Marie had grabbed the opportunity when it came and . . . Johanna felt a pang in her heart as she remembered that Marie had now left the family business too. The worst part was the *way* she left! Couldn't she at least have come back to Lauscha to say good-bye? To tidy up loose ends, to collect some of her things, to explain?

And then there was Magnus.

Johanna heaved a sigh.

He and Marie had lived together for years like man and wife, and all of a sudden she didn't even think him worthy of a decent good-bye! She had sent no explanation and not a word of apology.

It wasn't as though Johanna saw Magnus as a brother. They had never had very much to say to one another, in good times or in bad. But that hardly meant that she didn't care about his feelings. Johanna felt desperately sorry for the poor man, who was obviously most upset. He had only heard about Marie's wedding from the telegram that she sent to them all as a family, and he didn't deserve such treatment.

Johanna put her hand to her brow and tucked back a lock of hair. She didn't want to think of Marie today. This was a happy day.

She stopped in front of one of the station windows and sneaked a look at her reflection. She was happy enough with what she saw. She still had the figure of a young woman, and her thick braid of heavy chestnut-brown hair had the same rich glow that had made all the other girls envy the Steinmann sisters when they were young. Though she now had a strand or two of gray at each temple—and no more than that—Peter insisted the gray made her look "distin-guished." Peter! As though she could trust a word he said in the matter . . . Johanna smiled. Whenever she complained to him that she found new wrinkles on her forehead every day, he just looked at her, baffled, and declared that she looked as lovely as ever. Well, that certainly wasn't true, but Johanna was nonetheless quite pleased with her looks. She glanced once more at her reflection. She had wanted to change into something more cheerful for Wanda's arrival, but their French visitor had put an end to that idea. In fact she always felt most comfortable in this dark-blue outfit, the one she called her "work clothes." She grinned. Ruth would probably fall over backward in shock if she knew that Johanna was still wearing exactly the same styles she had twenty years ago. But fashion was the last thing she needed in the workshop. What was most important was making a good impression with the clients.

Someone cleared his throat next to her, tearing her away from her thoughts.

"Pardon me, *madame*, but are you perhaps waiting for the Braunschweig train?"

"Yes, what about it?" Johanna stared in alarm at the railway official who stood next to her with a notebook open in his hand. For heaven's sake, had something happened to the train?

"It's running about two hours late, although I'm afraid I don't know why. I thought I should tell you just in case, so that you don't catch your death of cold out here. Do go into the waiting room; at least it's warm in there." He touched the brim of his cap, gave her a cheerful nod, and then went on his way to see who else was waiting for the train.

And she'd been in such a hurry! Johanna walked over to the waiting room, annoyed. She was just about to look around for a free seat when she spotted a sign through the station window: "Coburger Stadtcafé." She might as well enjoy a cup of coffee and a sweet pastry while she waited. She hardly broke her stride as she pushed open the wrought-iron station door. If she had to wait, she could at least pass the time pleasantly.

◆ ◆ ◆

The train screeched harshly as it lurched into motion. Not too many more miles and they would be in Lauscha.

"I can hardly believe that I'm finally here!" Wanda flung her arms around her aunt's neck, who sat next to her on the wooden bench. All of a sudden she felt so weepy that she had trouble holding back the tears that pricked at her eyelids. "Finally home," she added with a sigh.

230

Johanna looked at her, astonished.

"It's not far now, is it?" Wanda peered anxiously out the window but couldn't see much more than the forest. Her eyes stung and she rubbed at them quickly with both hands.

"No, it's not far now," Johanna assured her. "My poor girl! You must be dreadfully tired after the long journey." She stroked Wanda's head as though she were still a child.

"I'll be all right," Wanda said brightly. In fact she had to struggle not to burst into tears.

She had had to supervise the transfer of her baggage every time she changed trains, always with the nagging fear that one of the cases might get left behind on the platform or even stolen. Now she was exhausted, although happy to be with her family too.

"I'm a little cold, that's all. The train stopped in the middle of nowhere for two hours—nobody had any idea why—and it became rather chilly in our carriage." Then she sneezed hard, as if to add conviction to her words.

"Well, I do hope you don't fall ill," Johanna said, frowning in concern.

"Certainly not! I'm so much looking forward to exploring Lauscha, but first of course I'm looking forward to meeting all the others. Uncle Peter, Johannes, Anna, and Magnus! I had expected . . ." Then she broke off, shaking her head.

"What?" Johanna looked at her, smiling.

"Well, I . . ." Wanda was suddenly embarrassed. "I had thought perhaps that the others might be at the station as well . . ."

Johanna burst out laughing. A married couple sitting on the next bench looked at her disapprovingly.

"Oh, you're wonderful, my girl! And who did you think would do all the work meanwhile?"

Wanda blushed furiously. What kind of nonsense was she blathering here when she knew quite well how things were in the workshop?

"But I'm sure they couldn't concentrate on work today, because they can hardly wait for us to get home," Johanna added.

Johanna asked how she had spent her days on the ship, and Wanda told her about how Wilma had prided herself on having a rubber baron for a fiancé. That led of course to the subject of Marie and Franco, and Johanna wanted to know all about him. Wanda felt flattered that Johanna was talking to her like an adult, and she wanted to share one or two spicy details about Franco de Lucca, but all she really knew was that he was very good-looking. So she said, "Marie always calls him her *handsome Italian*."

Johanna laughed sadly. "I don't begrudge my dear sister her happiness . . . but it all happened so fast! Or maybe not, it depends how you look at it. Even in the months before she set out on her travels she was behaving so strangely that I hoped she didn't have some dreadful illness that was wearing her away from the inside. But it seems she just wasn't happy with her life anymore. All the same, though—who would have thought that one day Marie would simply leave Lauscha without a word of farewell, and all for love?" Johanna pursed her lips.

Wanda put a hand on her arm. She would have liked to offer her aunt some words of comfort but didn't know how to begin.

It wasn't so bad just to sit in silence. Wanda used the time to take a look at Johanna out of the corner of her eye. It was astonishing how much alike the three sisters looked. They all had the same regular features and the same big dark eyes that never gave too much away. Her aunt also still looked amazingly young—despite her old-fashioned outfit. She had appeared much older in the photograph Wanda had seen, rather like a strict schoolmarm, but the camera had clearly been lying. Wanda's mother always wore makeup to give her skin that pearly luster, but it looked as though Johanna was wearing none at all—either she thought that she didn't need it, or she regarded it as an unnecessary indulgence. Wanda began unconsciously to lick her lipstick off.

"So have you made any plans for your time in Thuringia?" Johanna asked, breaking the silence. "We'll have a great deal of work on our plate until the end of the year, but after that there will certainly be time for a few sightseeing trips if the weather plays along. If there's anything you particularly want to do you must be sure to let me know."

"I honestly don't want you to go to any trouble for me. Quite the opposite," Wanda replied earnestly. "I just want to . . . be there with you. Do what you all do. You know, Marie told me so much about the workshop . . ." All at once she found it hard to put her desires into words.

"And there is probably somebody else you particularly want to meet . . ." Johanna said, raising an eyebrow meaningfully.

"That's right," Wanda answered firmly. She hadn't thought that her aunt would broach the topic so soon. "I . . . does my . . . does my father know that I'm on my way?" Her heart hammered as she spoke, and she chided herself for being so nervous.

"I have no idea. Most likely he does. Everybody knows everybody else's business in Lauscha. Somebody will have told him that you're coming, although it wasn't one of us." Johanna looked thoughtful, as though she was trying to decide what to tell Wanda.

"We don't have much to do with the Heimers anymore; we each went our own ways a long time ago. Though that's mostly because we make Christmas tree decorations and they make housewares. We don't have anything in common, do you see?"

Wanda nodded, though she knew from Marie that that was only half the story. After Ruth had left, there had always been a certain . . . antipathy between the two families.

"It must have been something of a shock to you to find out about Thomas, wasn't it?" Johanna asked gently.

Wanda nodded again. There was a lump in her throat now, and she swallowed painfully. "Do you think he . . ." She stopped.

What had she wanted to say?

Do you think he'll meet me at the station? After everything Marie had told her about her biological father, she knew that he certainly wouldn't do that.

Or: *Do you think he'll come and visit?* Was he going to come and visit her at her relatives' house and talk to a family who had been his sworn enemies for almost two decades now? He wouldn't do that for the world.

Instead of pressing her, Johanna talked on, unwittingly repeating almost exactly what Marie had said on the roof of the apartment building several weeks earlier. "Thomas Heimer isn't a bad sort. But don't expect too much. He's not a straightforward man. He never was, and that certainly hasn't changed with age. He didn't grow up in a loving home; he and his brothers had to lend a hand with the work even when they were very little. Nobody ever asked how they felt or whether they missed their mother. More work than wurst, as we say hereabouts. When I think of how our father spoiled us, it was quite the opposite. Life's hard and you have to be hard yourself—I think that was an unwritten motto for the Heimers. They were an unloving, hard-hearted family, and that's what your mother found so hard to bear. But how could Thomas ever have learned to behave any differently? Especially when you think what *his* father's like! And nobody can help the way they're born, can they?" Johanna seemed almost surprised as she spoke, as though this were the first time she had allowed herself such thoughts.

"That rather sounds as though you're speaking in his defense," Wanda said. Although Johanna had only meant well, Wanda felt a heavy sadness in her breast. Somehow it had been easier to bear when her mother had raged bitterly about Thomas Heimer.

Johanna shrugged. "Now that you say it . . . perhaps I am. You know, I see some things differently these days. When I was younger I always used to laugh at him for being such a lout, and even despised him a little for being so much under his father's thumb. In Lauscha we're used to seeing a glassblower's son make his own way in life at some point. But the Heimer boys never did. Today I feel sorry for Thomas because of that. If you never look farther than the end of your nose, how will you ever get anywhere in life?"

Wanda frowned. What did Johanna mean by that remark?

It was just before eight o'clock when the train stopped in Lauscha. Since Wanda had so much luggage, Johanna suggested that they wait until the crowd had thinned before disembarking. She knew almost everybody who went by, and chatted a bit with some of them. Wanda watched, glassy-eyed, as dozens of women all carrying huge baskets on their backs vanished into the dimly lit station building and then into the foggy night air beyond.

When it was finally their turn to get off the train, Wanda had to cling tightly to the iron railing so as not to tumble down the steps. Her legs were trembling wildly all of a sudden. She was in Lauscha. She had followed her dreams all the way here.

A man waiting with a horse cart drove them home from the station.

"Mind your head!" Johanna called from outside the house— just as Wanda's forehead hit the door frame. She stood quite still for a moment, dazed, while Johanna told the driver where he should put Wanda's luggage. Two of the cases were placed next to her on the stairs, and the rest could spend the night in the storeroom. Then Wanda could decide in the morning what she needed most, as

Johanna said there was no way they would be able to fit everything into the wardrobe they had cleared out for her.

Wanda's eyes gradually adjusted to the dim gaslight in the hallway, whose faded wine-red carpet showed dirty footprints by the door.

So this was the house where Mother was born!

There was a smell of onions frying, and suddenly her nose began to run. Could it be that it was even colder inside the house than out?

"And this is your cousin, Anna."

Wanda had only just broken free of her uncle's bear hug, and now she held out her hand to her cousin. Anna's hand was rather cold, and she had a very firm handshake. For a moment Wanda thought that Anna might give her a clumsy hug as her brother Johannes had done, but she didn't.

"So you're the famous glassblower who spends all night long at the lamp! I've heard a lot about you. Marie is full of praise for your work, you know." Wanda spoke in glowing tones, or at least tried to. There was a persistent tickle in her nose, and she found it hard to breathe. Was she coming down with a cold, or was it just the smell of the workshop getting to her? Marie had warned her about the chemicals used to apply the decorations to the glass, but she hadn't expected everything to smell of rotten eggs this way . . .

Anna looked at her mother for a moment as though seeking permission to respond.

"I just do my job; that's all there is to it," she answered earnestly. "You are most welcome to Lauscha, cousin."

Oh my goodness, I'll have a hard time seeing eye to eye with this one, Wanda thought, and she was relieved when Magnus put out his hand to greet her a moment later.

236

7

Every morning when Marie woke up, the first thing she saw was the patch of sunshine across her bed. *How can the sun still be so warm this late in the year?* she wondered sleepily. Back in Lauscha it would be snowing in early November. She shifted out from under Franco's arm, which was lying heavily across her belly, until the sun was shining directly on her face. Just one more minute . . .

"*Mia cara*, come back here," Franco muttered, then scooted over to her side of the bed. "How is my princess?"

"Mmm-hmm."

"And how is our baby?"

"Hmm." She kissed his mouth. Don't say a word. Keep quiet and let the day come.

Marie loved this moment between sleep and wakefulness more than any other time of day. In bed with Franco, with a thin curtain between them and Genoa—close to the bustle of the city where the fishwives, housewives, tradesmen, and schoolchildren were all going about their business on the streets, but just out of earshot—she sometimes imagined she was back on Monte Verità, and she felt that same lightness and freedom that had flooded her there. At such moments, she was sure she must be in paradise.

She found daily life in the palazzo rather less heavenly. There was no freedom then—quite the opposite, in fact. There was a great long list of unwritten rules specifying what she could and could not do. It would have been quite impossible, for instance, for her to go and fetch a glass of water from the kitchen. First she had to ring for a maid, tell her what she wanted, and then wait for the order to be carried out. And nobody seemed to care if Marie was dying of thirst in the meantime! She had told Franco right at the start that she could air the bed linen herself. In fact she felt quite awkward when the maids came and did it for her. It was also most irritating to have the maids burst into the room when she was working and didn't want to be disturbed. Franco couldn't understand her concerns. "Just let them take care of everything while you enjoy life!" he had said. And that was that. When Marie suggested that she could prepare breakfast for herself and Franco, his mother, Countess Patrizia, couldn't have been more shocked if Marie had volunteered to scrub the toilets.

"Dolce far niente!" Franco stretched like a cat. "It wouldn't be such a bad thing just to lie in bed for a while, now would it?" He kissed Marie's nose.

"Can you read my mind?" she asked, burying her face in the hollow between his chin and throat. His rough stubble scratched her cheek, but she snuggled closer. "Back home in Lauscha they say it's work that makes life sweet, not lying about doing nothing."

"You Germans have no idea." Franco ran the index finger of his right hand gently around her breast. "Though I could perhaps be persuaded to go from lying around doing nothing to, well, lying around doing something." He had already pushed Marie's nightgown up and now closed his lips over her nipple. A thousand tiny sparks shot through her body.

"And what will your father say when we don't come down for breakfast again?" she murmured once she could finally breathe.

Without waiting for an answer, she sprinkled the back of his neck with kisses. But soon that wasn't enough and she dived down beneath the covers. She grasped Franco's manhood with both hands and began to stroke it, then smiled when he gasped impatiently.

"Slowly now, *mia cara*," she whispered. Two could play at that game after all.

"Are you going to have coffee with Mother today?" Franco asked with feigned indifference as he put on his socks.

Marie looked over at him from the bed. How handsome he was, her Italian! She stroked her belly, which was just beginning to grow round, with both hands.

"I don't think so," she said just as offhandedly. "As you know, I want to finally finish the *Four Elements*."

"She would be pleased if you did. You could have a chat, get to know one another a little better. Perhaps if you showed her your new glass pictures, drew her in a little, so to speak, she might be a little less confused about what it is you actually do . . ."

"Your mother is perfectly welcome to come by anytime she likes," Marie said, glancing over to the door that led to her glass studio. She knew perfectly well, however, that she could wait until she was blue in the face before the countess would ever deign to visit! She was astonished how little she cared that Franco's mother disliked her. Nothing could break through the cocoon of happiness that enveloped her and Franco and their child.

"Marie, why do you always have to be so hard on her?" Franco asked, coming over to the bed and kneeling down next to her.

"*I'm* hard on *her*?" Marie snorted. Who stared at her all the time as though she had just crawled out from under a stone? Who was it who barely spoke a word to her unless Franco was in the room? "You have no idea," she said quietly.

"It's not easy for Mother to get used to . . . how things have changed. And she was shocked to find that her daughter-in-law works with her hands. But once the child is born . . ."

"How's that going to change anything? Do you think I'll abandon my bench and lamp?" Marie asked, sitting bolt upright. "Remember what you promised me. I wouldn't have . . ."

"Of course, of course," Franco soothed her, then left the room, his hands held high, as though surrendering.

Marie frowned and watched him go. She would have liked a little quarrel just then—at least he would have stayed with her. What she didn't want was to have to make one more painful attempt to cozy up to Franco's parents. She lay sulkily back down in bed.

It wasn't that the count and countess treated her badly—at least not so anyone would notice. But they had other ways of showing her that they were anything but pleased with Franco's sudden, secret wedding. As she walked down the hallways, doors closed in front of her face as though by an invisible hand. Conversations were hastily broken off or reduced to whispers at her approach. The count treated her politely enough at mealtimes—he was almost friendly, albeit in a cool and distant way—but Patrizia acted as though Marie simply weren't there. Marie also sensed that her mother-in-law spoke deliberately fast to make it difficult for her to take part in a conversation. Patrizia had received the news of Marie's pregnancy with marked indifference—contrary to Franco's expectations. She had given Marie a rather startled look and then rattled away in Italian to Franco. Marie had only caught one word. *Vecchietta.* Old woman.

Marie grinned sourly and stroked her belly. Old, indeed! The word could never hurt her now. She felt younger than she ever had in her life!

Never mind all that. They could mutter in corners as much as they liked. The palazzo was big enough for them all to keep out of one another's way. For the time being at least.

Perhaps she would become closer to Franco's mother after the child was born. That always happened in the stories—a dear little baby was born and melted the mother-in-law's stony heart.

And if not? Marie saw no reason why they should live here forever, however big the palazzo was. There were other houses in Genoa.

Marie dawdled awhile rather than venture into the breakfast room and endure Patrizia's frosty glances. She had learned that the countess usually went out into the garden by ten o'clock. Marie decided to go down into the kitchen and ask the cook for a few slices of bread with a jar of honey and a glass of milk. She would have a quick breakfast at the kitchen table while the maid chopped herbs or jointed a hare or cleaned mussels at the table next to her. Marie probably could have asked to be served a late breakfast in the salon, but she didn't much care where she ate. Heaven knows she had wasted enough time with fine linen and tableware when she was staying with Ruth in New York. Here in her new home she wanted to use her time for what really mattered: her work.

It was nonetheless nearly eleven o'clock by the time Marie finally sat down at her workbench. In front of her lay the flat, square glass picture that she had begun a few days earlier, the last in a series of four depicting the elements. Earth, water, and air were already propped up on the windowsill, glowing in the November sunlight. Marie looked at the picture of air with a critical eye. Perhaps she should have used fewer shades of blue, and put in a shard or two of transparent glass here and there? There had been days on Monte Verità when the sky really had been one vast unbroken expanse of blue. But wasn't there more to air than just the sky? Wasn't wind a part of it too? Sweet tender breezes and fierce cold gusts alike? She should have thought of that before. It was too late to change it now, Marie thought irritably as she picked up the last of the four.

Glass was the hardest taskmaster of any material an artist could work with. It made no difference whether the work was glassblowing, glass painting, or another technique. An artist only ever had one chance to get it right, and even the smallest lapse meant starting all over again. Any slip would be visible forever after. That was precisely what had always drawn Marie to the work, though.

She looked at the element of fire and concentrated. She had chosen the image of a tree in the fall, its leaves glowing with bright autumnal colors on branches spread all the way across the picture. A little more crimson here. And perhaps just a touch of ocher, but no more than that. The picture already blazed with all the colors of a crackling log fire. *The tree of life,* she thought, and smiled. It was time to breathe life into the image now.

A deep, warm happiness spread inside her. How had she survived these past few months without her work?

Once she had put the pieces of red and ocher glass into place, she struck a match. But instead of lighting the glassworker's lamp as she used to whenever she sat down at her bench, she held the match tip to a soldering torch.

From glassblower to glass artist! Sometimes Marie couldn't quite believe that she had dared try out all these new techniques. But as she wound a length of wire around the edges of a leaf-shaped piece of glass and then soldered the ends together, she felt as though she had never done anything else.

It had all started on Monte Verità, during a visit to the glassmaker Katharina. After much idle talk, they had finally managed to seek her out. As soon as Marie and Pandora had opened the door of the modest-looking wood cabin, they found themselves in a wonderland of glass, where thousands of sparkling shards and mirrors glittered among artworks made with an array of materials ranging from feathers and silver wire to shells and pearls. And Katharina von Oy was the queen of this wonderland, cloaked like a sorceress in a silk garment in all the colors of the rainbow. When she heard that Marie worked with glass too, she was delighted to discuss the various techniques she used. Some of them were quite new to Marie—such as the way she combined glass with shells and pearls. Suddenly she was almost ashamed to think that it had never even occurred to her to combine glass with other materials. Glass and silver, glass and stone, glass and . . . the possibilities were endless. Some of the pieces fascinated her so much that she came back to them again and again, gazing, running her fingers over them. There were others that she felt didn't really work, such as the glass snake that wound its way around a carved wooden apple. The contrast between the rough wood and the sensuous glowing red snake was too great, Marie decided.

Nor had she cared for Katharina's painted glass pieces, at least at first. The figures were too flat and clumsy and the landscapes too one-dimensional, but she didn't say so, of course, since she didn't want to be rude. And she did like the way the pictures glowed when she held them up to the light so that Katharina's simple designs shone with a life of their own.

Though Marie had been deeply impressed by her visit to this wonderland, she had no intention of making anything of the sort herself. After all, she had promised Johanna that she would work on some new Christmas ornament designs once she got to Genoa. But then matters had taken their own course.

When they had arrived in Genoa, a little workshop was truly ready and waiting for her in the room next to their bedroom. It had a gas lamp and a burner, a bellows with which to mix in a stream of air to raise the temperature of the flame, some tongs, and a set of files—so far, so good. But whoever had chosen the glass clearly had no idea that glassblowers needed hollow rods to work with if they were to make anything like Christmas tree ornaments. Instead she found panes of colored glass in every conceivable shade. There was also a whole army of paint pots lined up behind the bench. Marie had looked at the supplies, half-amused and half-shocked. What in the world was she going to do with all this?

She hadn't gotten around to doing anything about it during their first few days, since she and Franco were out and about all the time—he wanted to show her every nook and cranny of the magnificent city he was so proud to call home.

After the first week had passed, though, Franco and his father regularly shut themselves away after breakfast in the ebony-paneled office in the front wing of the palazzo. Marie was happy to have her work so that she did not have to spend much time with the countess.

From the first moment, she felt right at home in her new workshop. It was on the ground floor, with windows all along one wall and double doors that led directly into the garden. At a right angle to the room was a large conservatory that Franco told her was called the orangery; evidently, the orange, fig, and lemon trees within bore fruit even during the winter months.

Inspired by the view, Marie had tried her hand at painting. She took a pane of pale-yellow glass and painted it with green foliage and orange fruit, but she was not happy with the clumsy and amateurish result. Next she tried breaking a pane into narrow strips. Perhaps she would be able to make her own rods? But that didn't work either.

It was Franco who finally gave her the answer.

"You needn't waste your time on this old rubbish. Throw it all away, and I'll order you the rods you need from Murano," he had said one evening when she had gone into the workshop again after supper and was sorting the shards of glass into boxes by color. He put his arms around her belly from behind and nestled close.

"You handle each little piece as though it were a precious stone!"

In bed that night, Franco's remark stuck in Marie's mind and wouldn't let her sleep. She had been too distracted to enjoy Franco's caresses to the full.

Precious stones?

Precious stones belonged in a setting.

Which meant . . .

The next morning Marie had asked Franco to find her a soldering torch and wire. The idea was simple; she would cut the panes of glass into the shapes she wanted with the tongs, then edge each piece with lead and solder them together. She hoped that the end result would be a kind of mosaic in glass, and her hopes were answered. She laughed when she had finished her first picture, two red hearts against a blue background with a light border around the whole thing. It was wonderful! How colorful, and how intense! Why had she never thought of it before? It was probably because the villagers back in Lauscha were not especially pious, for surely she would otherwise have noticed that churches and cathedrals were always built with stained-glass windows showing Biblical scenes to edify the congregation. But glass could be used for far more than the Virgin Mary with the Christ child in her arms. It could be used for any design an artist cared to create—and this idea was all her own!

Franco had been speechless when she showed him her work that evening. "Is that really your first attempt? It's nothing less than perfection! Flaming hearts—*mia cara*, it's the very image of love, captured for all time! It's beautiful. And you are even more beautiful," he said.

Marie did not make any more practice pieces, but instead started on her series of the four elements the very next day.

When she put down the picture of fire around noon, her fingertips were itching with excitement. She wanted to do more. She had so many ideas! Ruth's jewelry from Lalique and Gallé, all those dragonflies, butterflies, and lily flowers—couldn't she use her new technique for just such designs?

She had already picked up a pane of violet-colored glass and was holding it next to another one in pale, watery green, when she put both of them down with a sigh.

Drat it all! She was supposed to finish the designs for the new Christmas baubles today—Johanna was waiting for them and she must be in a fever of anticipation.

Unwillingly Marie hauled out her sketchpad with the first drafts of the designs. Every fiber of her being bristled at the idea of going back to old work when there were so many new possibilities to be discovered.

At first she had been very pleased with her idea of making Christmas baubles in the shape of good-luck charms. She was quite sure that people would like hanging shooting stars, horseshoes, or four-leaf clovers on their Christmas tree to bring good luck for the new year. But when she looked at the design for the shooting star now, she felt a twinge of skepticism—would old Strupp even be able to make a mold for such a complex design? And would Peter and the others be able to blow into it? Given the way Magnus moaned on whenever he had to blow one of the Santa Claus designs, she thought not.

Magnus . . . she wondered how he was doing. Marie still felt guilty whenever she thought of him. But she couldn't turn around and go back to him for that reason alone.

Lost in thought, Marie stroked her belly. If she was counting right, she was now in her third month, so the baby would be born sometime in May. She was going to have a child. It was a strange idea.

She still hadn't told her family back home about the pregnancy. She sensed that she mustn't overburden Johanna and the others with too much news at once. And after all, what was there to tell? She didn't feel ill and she wasn't suffering from mood swings the way some women did. She was perhaps a little more quarrelsome than usual, but otherwise, she had never felt so healthy in her life. Indeed she even suspected that the pregnancy was to thank for the boundless creativity that simply seemed to gush out of her these days.

No, her sisters could hear about the baby early next year, she decided.

Marie snapped her sketchpad shut.

Perhaps she should take a little time to think about the new designs in peace and quiet. A few days' delay wouldn't make much difference in the long run. The molds for the charm series would never be ready in time for the new catalog in February either way.

But she had no sooner sat down to her colored shards once more than she had another attack of guilt.

Even if she couldn't send Johanna some decent designs, she should write her a letter. A letter to her, and one to Wanda. And perhaps one to Magnus as well.

8

I'm finally here in Genoa. Dear Wanda, you can't imagine what a shock this city was for me. I thought I would find a romantic little fishing village, and then dear Franco led me through streets that were no less lively than New York! The harbor alone is enormous—Franco says it's the biggest in all Italy—and it lies in a cove surrounded by cliffs on all sides. Then the city climbs up the cliffs above it. The count's palazzo is halfway up, and when I sit up in bed in the morning, I can look out my window and see the sea. Can you imagine? The first time I went for a walk through Genoa I felt I was wandering through a museum of Renaissance art—there are marble palaces everywhere, and then churches, public fountains, and monasteries! I wouldn't be surprised if the art of sculpture had been invented here. The Italians call this city La Superba—Genoa the Proud. Franco says that art and life go hand in hand in Genoa—so I've ended up in just the right place, haven't I? I miss you all dreadfully, of course, but I figure there are worse places to wash up on the wilder shores of love . . .

I found it very hard to leave Monte Verità, though by now I'm glad that I have a little more calm and order in my life.

Yesterday when we walked across the square at Piazza Banchi, I was quite light-headed from the magnificence all around us, and I wished that Pandora or Sherlain could be here—especially Pandora. I can just imagine how she would go dancing through the streets like a Renaissance angel. Oh, I miss her too! Her, and the other women from Monte Verità. Their laughter and their lust for life. Just as I miss your laugh.

As expected, Franco's parents are not exactly thrilled to have a complete stranger as a daughter-in-law. Patrizia especially is most put out that Franco went and found a wife all by himself—she strikes me as a woman who likes to have the final say in matters. But I try to live my own life despite her.

As he promised, Franco has set me up with a workshop where I work away quite happily—much to my mother-in-law's disapproval. But we'll get used to one another in time so to be honest, I try not to think about it too much. Even though we live together under one roof, we don't have much to do with one another; I sit in my workshop all day (with a view of orange trees, believe it or not!), and Franco and his father sit in their dusty old office where they have dozens of visitors every day. I would never have thought that so many people were involved in the wine trade. You really ought to see how respectfully they approach Franco and the old count! It seems that a noble title really means something here.

At the moment I'm busy blazing new trails in glasswork. I'll write you more about that some other time. Unfortunately that means that I still haven't gotten very far with my designs for the next Steinmann-Maienbaum catalog. But I fully intend to return to them in the next few days.

I hope you had a pleasant journey and that you have found your feet in Lauscha by now. If I know you, you're fizzing over with new ideas and you have the whole village in a state of

excitement. I'm looking forward so much to hearing whether
you find the place just as I had described it to you. I know how
much this visit means to you, and my thoughts will be with
you when you walk up the main street for the first time to visit
your father's house. Or have you already done that by now?

Dearest Wanda, whatever you are doing now, I am sure
that you are blazing new trails just as I am.

Your Aunt Marie

PS: If you happen to go to Sonneberg, please be so good
as to visit Mr. Sawatzky and give him my very best regards.
Tell him that I finally managed to break my shackles—he will
know exactly what that means.

Blazing new trails . . .

"So much for that," Wanda said with a sob, which led straight
into another coughing fit. A fine spray of spittle landed on the unfamiliar coat of arms at the top of the sheet of creamy writing paper.

She had been confined to her bed since the end of October.
What had started out as a cold had turned into raging bronchitis
within just a few days. At night she was wracked by coughing fits
for hours on end and nothing seemed to help, neither the sage tea
that Johanna brewed for her not the bitter dark-brown herbal con-
coction the doctor gave her as a cough syrup when he looked in on
her every few days. All she had seen of Lauscha so far was the doctor's face with his bushy eyebrows and surprisingly sensuous, almost
womanly lips. He had muttered to Johanna as he left that her niece
needed to rest undisturbed and that he feared the worst if she tried
to leave her bed. Even without this warning, though, Wanda hardly
felt like going out to see the village, given that she could barely
make it as far as the outhouse. She spent her days in a sort of haze,
only dimly aware of what else was going on in the house. The front
doorbell seemed to ring all day long, and there were always visitors

coming and going—she could hear their footsteps in the hallway. Once Wanda thought she could hear snatches of English conversation. She decided to ask her aunt whether she had heard right, but by the time Johanna next looked in on her she had already forgotten the question.

The worst thing about getting sick wasn't that her chest felt like a bubbling volcano spitting gouts of lava as it burned her up from the inside, or the fever that had her sweating one moment and shivering the next. The worst thing was Anna's reaction. Wanda was staying in Anna's room, and Anna sighed in quiet exasperation when Wanda's coughing kept her awake at night. She cast glances of furious, silent recrimination at Wanda when she had to hobble downstairs to the workshop in the morning while Wanda stayed in bed and often slept through the morning without coughing once. Wanda offered again and again to sleep somewhere else—for all she cared they could make her up a bed in the attic—but Johanna wouldn't hear of it. Quite the opposite: she thought it was a good thing Anna was with Wanda at night in case her fever suddenly spiked or there was some other emergency.

Wanda remembered what a fool she had made of herself about the room when she first arrived, and she still blushed at the thought.

"And this is Anna's room," her aunt had said, opening the door with a flourish and putting one of Wanda's suitcases in the middle of the floor. Wanda had been a little surprised to see a second bed there, of course. But she had assumed it must have been left over from childhood days—perhaps the bed where the dolls had sat lined up in a row. So she had asked, "It's very nice, but where's my room?" Johanna had looked at her wide-eyed and probably thought the question was a joke.

Mother and daughter had spent weeks taking turns making poultices for Wanda's throat, boiling up onions with rock candy, which tasted horrible but soothed her cough for a while at least, and bringing her bowl after bowl of hot chicken soup. Wanda let them do whatever they liked. Her charm had quite collapsed in the face of the fever. She couldn't even manage a joke or a cheerful remark to draw the sting from the situation. Everything she had lived for in the weeks leading up to her journey had fallen apart. She had yearned to help her family and instead was nothing but a burden. Wanda wished she could just make herself invisible. Since she couldn't do that, she settled for keeping as quiet as she could.

Her cousin Johannes and her uncle Peter looked in on her twice a day—after lunch and at the end of the workday—and Magnus came by every few days. The men mostly shifted awkwardly from foot to foot for a few minutes and then left. What could they say to Wanda, really, to cheer her up? She was a complete stranger who had just happened to turn up in their house and then fall ill. They hadn't even had the chance to get to know one another. All the presents that Wanda had brought with her were still in the luggage, and she hadn't had the strength to do anything more than unpack the photographs and letters that her mother had given her for Johanna. She had expected that her aunt would look through them and then sit down on her bed for a chat about Ruth, New York, and Marie—but she hoped in vain. Johanna seemed to have time for many things but not for a conversation with her.

"The last few months of the year are always our busiest time. All our clients suddenly realize that they haven't ordered enough Christmas decorations," she had explained to Wanda once, when her niece hesitantly asked whether she could keep her company for a little while. "We have to cope with all these last-minute orders somehow and get everything produced and delivered!" Wanda had asked whether other workshops had the same trouble—maybe that was why her father still hadn't given any sign of knowing she was there. There had been no letter or even a message, never mind a visit. Johanna had looked at her rather oddly and explained that the workshops that dealt in Christmas wares were the ones most flooded with work; everyone else would be having an easier time of it. Wanda had tried to fight back her disappointment.

Her only contact with the outside world in all these weeks had been two letters from New York, in which Ruth ordered her to fit in and not to upset things.

And now there was this letter from Marie. It had arrived that morning, along with a letter for Johanna and a few more documents, in a thick envelope from Genoa.

Tears ran down Wanda's cheeks as she read Marie's words from Genoa, where "art and life go hand in hand" and she was "busy blazing new trails in glasswork." Why did other people have all the luck?

Four weeks to the day after she had arrived in Lauscha, the doctor finally declared that Wanda could leave her bed for a couple of hours every day. Johanna suggested that she spend the time sitting on the kitchen bench watching Lugiana cook, but Wanda said that she wanted to help in the workshop. Johanna was already immersed in lists and account books and wasn't even listening, while Anna rolled her eyes as if to say, *More fuss and bother for our American visitor.* Uncle Peter gently suggested that the chemical fumes wouldn't be good for Wanda in her current state of health. It was Johannes who asked his father, "Why don't we put Wanda at the packing table with the hired hands? They could use the help!"

Wanda shot her cousin a look of gratitude.

And so she spent the first afternoon folding cardboard boxes into shape and then packing them with Santa Claus figures and spires for the top of Christmas trees, all neatly wrapped in crepe paper. She was so worried that she would drop something or crack it by handling it too roughly that she moved no faster than a snail. While the other packers at the long table piled up their boxes in towering stacks, her side of the table was painfully empty, which Wanda felt was at least as bad as if she had rushed through the work and broken something. But by four o'clock, when the others stopped for a coffee break, she had hit her stride. She didn't want coffee or a slice of bread and jam, so she kept on working through the break. She even plucked up the confidence to look up from her work from time to time and glance around the workshop.

Everything was just as Marie had described it: the glassblowers' workbenches with the gas flame burning brightly, the hiss of the lamps, the silver bath hanging in its bottles on the wall—Anna could apply the silver to the inside of the globes despite her swollen ankle—then the decorations bench with its dozens of paint pots and jars of glitter and spools of gold and silver wire. Three more hired hands—young girls from the village—sat there. When Wanda came into the workshop at midday, they had stared across at her curiously, but none of them had spoken to her yet. Along with the women at the packing table, that made five hired hands in the workshop. Wanda soon learned that her aunt had many more people on her payroll; every Tuesday and Friday Paul Marzen came by with his horse cart to fetch dozens of boxes full of silvered globes, which he took all around the village to pieceworkers, who painted them at home.

Everybody in the workshop had a specific task, and Wanda saw that the whole production line was so perfectly planned that there were never any bottlenecks or idle moments. At the end of her first day in the workshop Wanda stared in disbelief at the number of cardboard boxes that had piled up, all full. Johanna smiled as she explained that the day's output had been relatively low, since the spires for the top of the trees were delicate work and took longer to make.

The brains behind the whole operation belonged not to Uncle Peter but to Johanna, who was called "the boss" by one and all. She was everywhere, saw and heard everything, at all times. When she made a suggestion, she did so in a quiet, friendly tone of voice, yet there was rarely any disagreement. In fact, everyone—even her husband—seemed happy to leave all the decisions to her. It was also Johanna who received the clients and negotiated contracts. While all the other workshops in the village sold their wares through the wholesalers in Sonneberg, the Steinmann-Maienbaum workshop dealt with their retail clients directly. This meant that the family got all the profits rather than having to hand a cut to the middlemen. Wanda didn't doubt for a moment that it was her aunt's impeccable business sense that had made the arrangement possible.

But she also found her aunt rather intimidating for just that reason. She would never have thought that a woman could drive just as hard a bargain as any man, but Johanna was a real businesswoman. Strange though it seemed, she made Wanda feel like a country bumpkin by comparison. She came from New York, the capital of the world, but she only knew women like her mother and Ruth's friends, none of whom ran anything larger than their own households. Or women like Marie and Pandora, who had their own responsibilities and made their own decisions, but unlike Aunt Johanna had only themselves to look after. There must be businesswomen like Johanna somewhere in New York—perhaps on the Lower East Side, where countless garment factories jostled for space—but Wanda had never met them.

She was very impressed by Johanna, and by the end of her first afternoon in the workshop had realized that her aunt, far from being thrown into a panic by Marie's desertion, was making the best of the new circumstances. She didn't even bat an eyelid at the news that Marie wouldn't be sending as many designs for the new catalog as she had promised. She simply called a quick staff meeting and told everybody in the workshop, in brief, clipped sentences, what Marie had written in her letter.

"Nothing will change for us in the grand scheme of things; we'll still be sending the catalog to press in February," she declared, then cast a sympathetic glance at Magnus, who was staring down at his bench, his shoulders hunched. Then she turned to Anna. "From now on, you'll have more say in the new designs—Marie writes that you've been ready for a while now. Now you can show us what you're made of."

And for the first time Wanda saw her cousin Anna beam with happiness.

"Did you see how Ursula Flein was giggling and gossiping with Kurt yesterday?" Anna asked as she turned the tap on the silvering flask and dripped solution into a globe. "All while her Siegfried is off on his journeyman travels in the Rhineland."

"That was perfectly harmless," her brother retorted. "If the two of them were going to get up to any mischief, we'd have seen it weeks ago at the Harvest Festival."

Wanda looked from brother to sister. The twins had gone out together the night before, as they did every Wednesday. Johannes had told her how the young people in the village met in an empty warehouse that had once belonged to the glass foundry. There was talk and laughter and jokes. Wanda decided that these meetings were probably much like she had seen back in New York at the various patriotic societies. Now that she had the chance to take part in German customs in their country of origin, she was confined to the house. But not for much longer, she swore to herself, doing her best to follow her cousins' conversation. It wasn't easy. To her dismay she had found that the people in Lauscha didn't speak anything like standard German but had their own peculiar dialect.

"Anyway, Siegfried and Ursula aren't married yet—they're not even engaged," Peter added once he had finished blowing another globe.

"What's that got to do with it? Either she's serious about him or she's not! I know that I would be in a right old rage if Richard were to flirt with someone else behind my back."

Richard? Who was Richard? Wanda pricked up her ears. Could it be that someone was courting her cousin, who always looked as stiff as if she had swallowed a broom?

"Not all the girls have your virtues," Johanna put in, without even looking up from her paperwork. "Ursula will learn what's important soon enough, once her reputation's ruined and no man wants anything more to do with her."

Anna looked at her brother triumphantly.

"And by the way"—Johanna looked up from her lists—"I ran into Fritz on the main road this morning. He says our new labels have arrived, which means that someone will have to go and collect them tomorrow morning."

Anna groaned. "Please don't ask me to do it. I want to see what I can do with that new bird-shaped mold. Besides, you know that I don't like calling on old Fritz. His hunchback gives me the shivers, and every time I go I'm afraid I'll find him lying stone dead among all the boxes!"

The others laughed.

"He's as old as the hills, our village box-maker," Johannes explained when Wanda looked at him inquiringly. "It's true, he won't last much longer . . . One of these days we'll have to carry him out of his workshop in one of his own crates!"

There was more laughter.

"That's quite enough!" Johanna scolded them. "What will your cousin think of you when you make such cruel jokes?"

Wanda cleared her throat. "If you tell me the way, I can go and fetch the labels myself. A bit of fresh air would do me good, and besides, it's time I saw a little more of Lauscha."

"That would be a fine thing, if the first place you saw in Lauscha was Fritz's dusty old warehouse! That would hardly give you the right impression of the place," Johanna said, dismissing her offer with a wave.

The others traded glances of amusement.

"I'd come with you, but we have that order from England, which can't wait, and . . . Peter can't leave the workshop either." Johanna tapped her pencil against the desk absentmindedly, as she always did when she was thinking something over. "No, we'll do it this way . . ."

Wanda waited patiently to see what plan her aunt would come up with. She was a little annoyed with herself for being so meek— she would never have put up with her parents deciding something like this for her.

Johanna looked affectionately at Wanda. "You won't go on your own, in any case. I want you to see the best that Lauscha has to offer, so that you know it's at least as lovely as Marie has described it to you. You've had to wait so long after all . . ."

"Do you mean eighteen years, or do you mean the weeks when she was ill?" Peter asked with a grin.

"Both!" Johanna laughed. "Now, listen to this: Paul Marzen can pick up the box of labels from Fritz when he does the rounds of the pieceworkers; that way none of us have to leave the house. Anna needs the time to work with the mold as she said, and she shouldn't walk far anyway. But if we all work a little longer this evening, Johannes can give Wanda a tour of Lauscha first thing tomorrow morning."

9

"Oh yes, and over there used to be the main foundry. My father was a master glassmaker there, but they shut the place nine years ago."

Johannes's breath hung in the air in the form of a white cloud while he spoke.

Wanda looked at the abandoned building and felt a twinge of sorrow. The wooden walls were black with soot, and all that was left of the windows were a few jagged glass shards, gnawing at the air. Somebody had torn the boards out along one side, leaving a gaping hole. Wanda had no desire to see what it was like inside.

When Marie had told her stories, the village foundry had been much more than just the place where the glass rods were made. It had been the center of village life, and the little square in front of the foundry was where the most important festivals happened, where everybody met at the end of the day's work before they went off to a tavern for a beer.

But that was all in the past.

Wanda pointed to the slender chimney that towered over all the buildings around them.

"Like a lonely giant . . . it's a sad sight."

Johannes hopped from foot to foot. "But when you remember that the other foundries shut their doors decades ago—there was Steeplejack here in the village, and a foundry up in Obermühle as well—you have to admit that our dear old foundry here did well to last as long as it did. With the modern glass factories that exist nowadays, an old-fashioned place like this was never going to be able to keep up. Well, that's the way of the world and nobody can hold back progress."

"The way of the world . . . you sound like an old man," Wanda teased him.

"You should hear what the old men say! My father and the other master glassmakers sit around their favorite table in the tavern and talk about how things are getting worse! *It was all so much better in the old days,*" Johannes said, imitating his father's voice.

On their walk through Lauscha, they had already passed at least five houses where Johannes told her that the family that lived there had no work and nowhere to turn for its next meal. Half of the villagers seemed to be on their last legs. And here was this tumble-down wreck, casting its shadow over the main square in the village.

Johannes cleared his throat uncertainly. "If you like, we can go to the museum next. You'll learn more about Lauscha there than you will anywhere else. And it's a little warmer in there as well."

"You're the guide," Wanda replied, though by now her feet were beginning to feel like blocks of ice too. Before they could cross the street, they had to stop to let a cart go past, clattering along the bumpy cobblestones with wares piled high in the back. As it passed, one of the horses lifted its tail and deposited a heap of steaming manure in front of Wanda and Johannes.

"Thank you very much!" Johannes called as the wagon went by.

Wanda laughed. "My mother tells me that years ago the women used to walk all the way to Sonneberg and beyond carrying glassware in baskets on their backs. She did that with Marie's first few globes. But that doesn't happen anymore, does it?"

"No, these days we just send our boxes to the railway station—in wagons like that—and then they go on by train." Johannes pointed up at the tips of the fir trees in the forest that climbed the steep hillsides to the left and right of the village. "I bet it's going to snow, no later than tonight. That white smear across the sky isn't fog; it's a sign that the clouds are ready to shed their snow."

"I do hope you're right. I can hardly wait to see the village all draped in snow," Wanda said with delight. Marie had vividly described the contrasts of light and dark when the gray shingled rooftops stood out against the snow.

They had hardly gone ten yards when a huge black dog leapt up behind a garden fence and began to bark furiously at them. Wanda jumped with fright.

"Here now, what are you *gowtzing* at like that?" Johannes called out. "We won't go near your *heppala*!" She could hear the sound of bleating from a low wooden hut at the end of the fence. "They're all in the *linny* there, freezing, the poor beasts!"

As always when her family slipped into the village dialect, Wanda didn't understand a word. She was just about to ask whether the *heppala* were supposed to be lambs or kid goats when a woman put her head out the cottage window and called out to the dog.

"Good day to you, Karline, how are the children?" Johannes called to her. "She's one of our painters," he whispered to Wanda.

"Up in the forest, the little scamps! They've left me with all the work!" She held up a paintbrush as she spoke to show what she meant, its tip covered in red paint. "You can tell your mother that the Santa Claus figures are ready." She scratched her head with the other end of the brush. "And that's the American girl! Are you . . . on your way up top?" The woman winked at Wanda knowingly.

Wanda smiled back, uncertain what Karline meant.

"No, we're off to the museum," Johannes called to the woman over his shoulder. "Our American visitor ought to see everything there is to know about our village and its history."

"And you're going to do that by showing her a few old scraps of glass?" The woman laughed and gave Wanda another knowing look. "Well then, have fun."

"What was all that about? Can you tell me why everyone stares at me like that? Have I grown a wart on my nose during the night?" Wanda asked once they had walked a little farther. "From what you all tell me, the villagers are used to having strangers come to visit by now, aren't they?" Even as she spoke she could feel more curious glances upon her, this time from two women across the street.

Johannes grinned. "Strangers, yes. But they're not used to having Thomas Heimer's daughter come to visit!"

"What?" Wanda stopped in her tracks abruptly. Her head began to spin. "You mean . . . they know that I . . . who my . . ."

Johannes seemed to enjoy her embarrassment. "We've got long memories here in Lauscha. Everybody still remembers what went on eighteen years ago. And then when your mother simply up and vanished like that . . . It's rare indeed that anyone leaves Lauscha for good; we're a lot of homebodies here. And then seeing as she was a married woman with a child . . ." He nudged Wanda gently in the side. "Don't look so downcast. They're just curious to see what you look like, that's all . . ." He shrugged apologetically.

"I . . . I don't know what to say!" Wanda had never considered the possibility that everybody here would know all about her.

"Your . . . your father's very well-liked in the village. And we don't tend to divorce often, either. And then when a missing child turns up all grown up exactly at the moment when the grandfather is on his deathbed and the inheritance is about to be settled . . . Well, people will *quassle*. Talk, that is. It's quite normal for folk to wonder what's going on. To be honest, even Anna and I thought about it at first . . . But then Mother told us that you didn't even know about your father until a little while ago. It's a crazy story!" He whistled softly.

Now Wanda was truly speechless.

When they went into the drawing school where the museum was located a few minutes later, Wanda was still shaken. People thought she was a fortune hunter? There was no way she could let them think that about her; she had to set them right!

She frowned as she listened to Johannes explaining the contents of the display cases arranged in an old classroom in the school building.

Johannes noticed the look of disappointment on her face. "I know, it's not much of a museum yet, but it's a start. The older pieces were first put on display thirteen years ago, when Lauscha celebrated its three hundredth anniversary. My parents helped organize it. These days everybody likes the idea of having the past on display like this. Here, look at these, some of the first glasses ever made in Lauscha." Johannes pointed to some beer and wine glasses made of light-green glass, painted with simple scenes of country life. Then he went past several cases full of Christmas decorations and stopped in front of a display with curious pipework and flasks.

"And this is the modern era! With only three hundred short years in between." He grinned when he saw the confusion on Wanda's face.

"What in the world are all those?"

"Technical glassware. There are quite a few glassblowers making laboratory equipment these days. It's a good business to be in, since there are more and more chemical factories springing up and they all need equipment. Anybody who works in technical glass will always have customers. Not like those who still make housewares and ornaments."

"Time was when the Heimer workshop was well-known for the quality of their wares and the range they could offer, but they've been in a bad way for a few years now." That was what Marie had told her.

"Marie mentioned that a lot of glassblowers are having trouble finding buyers for their wares, but she never said that half of Lauscha has been hit by the crisis."

"Aunt Marie!" Johannes laughed. "What does she know about life in the village?"

When he saw the question in Wanda's eyes, he took a deep breath and explained.

"Marie used to spend her days sitting at her workbench or with her sketchpad somewhere; she didn't get out and about much. She simply didn't care to. Whether it was carnival time or the May dance or our solstice celebrations—Magnus often used to complain that he could never persuade her to come out and see people. Her idea of a fun day out was to go and see that old bookworm over in Sonneberg."

"I don't believe it!" Wanda exclaimed. "You should have seen her in New York. My mother had trouble keeping her at home any night of the week. She was always going off to a gallery or a poetry recital—Marie was like a butterfly, flitting from flower to flower."

"Are you sure we're talking about the same Marie?"

Wanda giggled but quickly became serious. "All the same I still don't understand why the Lauscha glassblowers are going through such hard times. People need glass everywhere, don't they, all over the world?"

"They do indeed, but Lauscha isn't the only place that makes glass. Over ninety percent of the workforce in the Thuringian Forest region is in the glass business—at least that's what the fellows with the slide rules say. So there's an excess supply of goods and a labor surplus, and that affects us too, for good and ill. For instance if Mother isn't happy with one of our pieceworkers because the woman cuts corners in the painting or doesn't deliver the goods on time, she has no trouble finding someone else to take over. But if we can't deliver on an order, the client will drop us so fast we won't know what happened to us."

"People don't buy Christmas decorations all year round, though, do they?"

Johannes looked at her approvingly. "Quite right. Seasonal work is especially difficult, you see. And now that so many other suppliers have jumped on the bandwagon these past few years, prices have gone down rather than up. What helps our family is that we have good contacts abroad—thanks in no small part to your mother, who is always finding new clients for us."

Mother, broadening the client base? Wanda raised her eyebrows.

"And then the boss is always finding new ways to lower our production costs. Oh yes, and don't forget that we also make the prettiest baubles!"

"You're not shy about saying so, are you?" Wanda laughed. But she realized that everything Johannes said was quite true—the family business seemed to be on firm footing. She enjoyed talking to her cousin about business. It made her feel very grown-up.

Johannes had something to say about every item on display, and he seemed to have an excellent head for figures. Lauscha had been founded in 1597. The price of firewood went up in 1748, and then from 1753 onward the master glassmakers were excused from their obligation to supply glasses to the duke's court free of charge, although they had to pay more taxes instead. And so on and so forth. She found the way he explained everything most interesting, but all the same a dull sense of disappointment was creeping into the back of her mind. Lauscha was so different from how she had imagined it.

Where were all the families sitting by the fireside, painting globes together? Where were the glassblowers' lamps twinkling through the windows like glowworms to light up the long dark evenings? And where were the marbles men who made every child's favorite toy?

By the time they left the drawing school, it had begun to snow. Thick velvety snowflakes settled onto Wanda's hair, shoulders, and arms.

"It's snowing, it's snowing, it's snowing!" She danced with joy right there in the street.

Johannes had buried both of his hands deep in his pants pockets, and he grinned awkwardly. "Don't make such a fuss now, people are watching!"

"So what? This is the first snow I've seen in Germany! I'll never forget today as long as I live!" Wanda replied, sighing happily.

"The snow's late this year. But once everything's covered in white it will stay that way till spring, so you don't need to stand here in the street forever," Johannes said insistently. He suddenly seemed to be in a hurry to get back home.

Wanda grabbed her cousin by the sleeve. "Wait a moment . . . how can I even say this . . . ? There's something else I must do. Who knows when we'll get another chance . . ."

"If you think I'm going to go up the hill with you to the Heimer house, you're mistaken!" Johannes said, his face unreadable. "Wild horses couldn't drag me up there. Mother wouldn't like it one bit."

"That's not what I want," Wanda reassured him. "But there is something I'd like to do now."

10

"Oh dear, I do believe little Wanda is in love!" Marie chuckled. "Listen to this . . ." She ran her finger under the lines as she read aloud.

I'm so happy that Johannes finally agreed to my suggestion and took me along to meet some of his friends. To see how people live, and how they work in their own homes—that was always my dearest wish! And now I have seen real life in Lauscha. What an afternoon it was! Dear Marie, you can't imagine how kind they all were! Wherever we went, they offered me a cup of coffee. One of them—Hans Marbach—even poured me a glass of his herbal schnapps!!! The glassblowers of Lauscha really are the most wonderfully friendly people. Even the children were clinging to my skirts and wanting to show me what they had just been working on and painting.

Then we went to visit Richard Stämme in his workshop. Before we knocked at the door I joked to Johannes that I couldn't drink another cup of coffee, not with all the goodwill in the world, but Johannes simply said that Richard was not going to offer me any. Probably another old fellow like Moritz

*the marble-maker, I thought to myself—you know who I
mean, the poor soul who can hardly see a thing but still makes
the most wonderful marbles. He even gave me one as a present, with all the colors of the rainbow inside. And he let me sit
down at his bench and try my hand at . . .*

"Marie, *mia cara*—it's all very nice of course that Wanda tells you
everything in such detail, but do I have to listen to it all?" Franco
said, waving his hand impatiently. "Quite apart from which—how
does any of that tell you that Wanda is in love? She hasn't said a
word about it yet."

"The giveaway comes a little later, hold on . . ." Marie leafed
through the pages hectically. "Where is it now . . . ?"

Franco sighed. "I did promise Father that I would have these
papers ready by tomorrow." He pointed regretfully at the stack of
official-looking documents on his desk. "The ship will be setting sail
in three days, and it's not going to wait for our wares."

"If I'm boring you, I can leave." Marie gathered up the pages
of Wanda's letter and set off slowly for the door, waiting for him to
say something.

In vain. Franco was back at his ledgers again.

Marie turned to face him, her hand on the doorknob. "I
thought now that the wine harvest is done, you would have more
time for me!"

"*Mia cara . . .*"

Marie felt a lump in her throat as she walked toward the orangery.
There was always a pile of paperwork to be done! There was always
a constant stream of visitors, vintners, customers, all with some
request to make! There was always something more important than
her. More important than the studies they had planned.

How they had dreamt of that in the first weeks, when Franco's workday never seemed to end. They looked forward longingly to evenings spent together at the round walnut table in the library—Franco immersed in a book about wine-growing techniques and Marie looking through a thick volume about the history of art in Genoa. She had spent a whole day wandering the town before she finally found what she had been looking for in an antiquarian book dealer's shop. Franco had been as happy as a child when she came home and presented him with a book about the old grape varieties and how they could be improved.

Marie swallowed. To the best of her knowledge, Franco had leafed through that book once, the first time, and then never picked it up again.

Why couldn't he simply tell his father that enough was enough? The glass door shivered in Marie's hand as she yanked it open and walked through the palms and the citrus trees.

"I grew up in a family business as well. I know how your nearest and dearest can get their claws into you. If I hadn't insisted on having some time to myself I would probably never have designed a single new globe!" she had told him accusingly just the other night. He had spent the whole day down at the harbor, even though he had promised to help her look through a stack of children's fairytale books for designs to use in the nursery.

"That's different," Franco had retorted. "Father has nobody besides me he can completely trust. I can't put my own interests over those of the family."

Wasn't it in the family interest for him to take time to look after the vineyards?

Marie nodded to a gardener who was gathering up the fallen leaves from around a lemon tree. She headed straight for the white wicker chairs that were arranged in the middle of the orangery, under a vaulted dome. She sank down into a rocking chair.

The orangery had been the count's wedding present to his bride, since she loved gardening. The two of them had been terribly disappointed when they discovered that the countess always developed a piercing headache whenever she spent more than just a few minutes there. Nobody had ever figured out why, since she never suffered any ill effects when she was outside in the garden. Over the years the orangery had been demoted to a place where the gardening staff nurtured tender seedlings before planting them outside, and where the more sensitive plants were brought in for the winter. Marie was the only one who used it for its original purpose as a greenery-filled sitting room.

She put both hands on her belly and rocked gently back and forth, her eyes closed, surrounded by the scent of ripening citrus. Remembering the exercises they had taught her at Monte Verità, she held her stomach in as she breathed in and then relaxed it as she breathed out again. When her anger at Franco had finally ebbed, she picked up Wanda's letter and read on.

What I most admire about Richard's work is the self-con-fidence that shines through every piece. When I told him that I had seen some similar pieces in New York at an exhibition of Venetian glasswork, he just gave me a look! He told me that the similarity was quite intentional, and that he wanted to apply Lauscha's techniques to the Venetian style to create something quite new. Something all his own. To me he seems like a man rowing, who dips his blade deep in the water and pulls strongly at the oar, his eyes fixed on land, knowing exactly where he is headed . . .

How can someone so young know so precisely what he wants to do? You can't imagine how embarrassed I was when Richard asked me what I had studied or learned as a trade! I muttered something about having been to business college and

I hoped he would leave it at that. Should I have told him that my job is being a dutiful daughter? A man like him would just despise me for that. A man like that doesn't want a girl who's a china doll, he wants . . . I have no idea what he wants, perhaps I should ask my dear cousin Anna? When I found out at supper that day that Richard Stämme is 'Anna's Richard,' I almost dropped my spoon. If he's really courting her, then why does he never visit? After Harold and I were introduced, he was always turning up at our door and bringing me flowers or a box of chocolates. Don't they do that sort of thing in Lauscha? You understand of course that I don't want to intrude, but I would be interested to know just what the story is behind Richard's relationship with Anna. Perhaps you know a little more about this?

"Oh dear! Wanda, Wanda, you've fallen for him . . ." Marie muttered, smiling.

". . . *like a man rowing, who dips his blade deep in the water and pulls strongly at the oar . . .*" In all the weeks she had been in New York, she had never heard Wanda describe Harold in anything like such glowing terms. Rather, she talked of him almost disdainfully, as though she were laughing at the lengths he went to for her sake.

Richard Stämme—Marie wasn't in the least surprised that Wanda should take a shine to him. The young glassblower was not just confident and talented but also very good-looking—even though he could never afford fine clothes and his long hair was always badly cut. He was something of a lone wolf. People always wanted to spend more time in his company than he allowed. Marie knew from Magnus that the other glassblowers were always finding ways to invite him to come down to the tavern for an evening's drinking but that Richard preferred to stay at home and work on his designs. He made a living by working in larger workshops when they

271

needed extra help filling their commissions. Johanna had given him jobs from time to time when the Steinmann-Maienbaum workshop was at full capacity. That was how Anna and Richard had first met.

Marie suddenly felt slightly dizzy. She got up from the rocking chair and arranged some of the pink velvet cushions on the wicker chaise longue. Then she put her legs up, spread a blanket over herself, and resumed her train of thought.

Richard had once confided in Anna—and she was so much in love that she couldn't resist passing it on to Marie—that his dearest wish was to have a large workshop of his own. He lived in a shabby little house, and his burner wasn't even connected to the gas mains—it was all that his parents had left him, but that didn't stop him from dreaming. *"One day I want to have a workshop where high-society clients come to see my wares and buy them,"* he had told Anna. *"They'll place orders with me for the finest addresses in the world."* Marie was fairly sure that Richard would make his dream come true one day, and Anna agreed.

If he shared his dreams with her that way, did it mean that the two of them were already planning a life together? Marie didn't know, and she hadn't taken Anna's gushing reports all that seriously. But now that she thought about it, she couldn't imagine that they had ever kissed. Anna was still like a child, and she didn't know how to make the best of her admittedly meager womanly charms. But should she write as much to Wanda and encourage her? Or would it be better just to keep out of the whole thing? If Wanda really did have her eye on him, then she could only feel sorry for poor Anna.

Suddenly Marie missed her family so much that it hurt. She began to stroke her belly again, enjoying the closeness she felt to the child in her womb.

"Your mama's sentimental," she whispered up at the orange trees. "Instead of enjoying the Italian sunshine, she's pining for winter in Thuringia." For a moment she struggled with the impulse to fetch pencil and paper and write to ask Wanda why she had said nothing about any visit to her father. Had they really managed to avoid one another all this time? In Lauscha, that would have been difficult. Or had meeting Thomas Heimer been so bad that Wanda simply didn't want to write about it? Marie felt tears pricking at her eyes at the thought.

She decided not to write. If she composed a letter now, when she was so tearful, she might end up writing things that she didn't even mean and that her family would take the wrong way. Better to leave it a few days and think of the best way to tell them of her pregnancy. She would give them the news as a Christmas surprise, so to speak. Marie smiled. Wouldn't they be surprised to hear that there'd soon be a brand new member of the family!

She flung the blanket aside and stood up. "Never mind *dolce far niente*—work is the best medicine!" she said loudly, as though trying to convince herself.

A little while later she was sitting at her workbench, annoyed at herself. How could she have let half the day slip through her fingers when she had so much work to do! Her gaze fell on the mosaic that she had started the day before. Her fingers were quite literally itching to get back to work on it, since it would be one more step toward her greater, daringly ambitious plan to open her own gallery in Genoa's historic city center. She hadn't dared tell Franco about the idea yet. She still felt she had to protect her plans, nurture them like a young plant that needed plenty of water if it were ever to thrive and grow strong. But she wanted to share her vision with Franco in the new year. Perhaps he could help her look for suitable premises, so that she could begin outfitting the place after their child was born—if not earlier. White walls and plenty of glass, nothing that could distract the visitor from looking at the colorful pictures on show. Marie sighed.

The only thing that was missing here for her to work comfortably was the praise that Johanna's clients had always given her so unstintingly. Without someone to admire her work, it was like calling out into a void. She was used to hearing other voices echo her own—and though she knew that it was vain of her, an artist needed an echo, she decided. Which was why she could hardly wait to hear what Genoa's art lovers thought about her new masterpieces.

Instead of opening a jar and picking out the little green beads she would need for the picture in front of her, she got up and went over to the shelves where she kept the rods that Franco had ordered for her weeks ago. Marie had left them to gather dust—too immersed in her new technique of lead seams and mosaic images—but Christmas was creeping inexorably nearer.

Her first Christmas without her family.

Her first Christmas with Franco.

If she was to have her surprise ready for him in time, she had to work fast.

When she took the rod in her hand it felt smooth and cool, the old familiar feeling. A wave of happiness washed over her. Franco and his parents would be so astonished to see a tree full of shining new baubles standing in the dining room on Christmas Eve!

She had spent a long time pondering what the baubles should look like. In Germany the traditional Christmas colors were red, gold, and green, but those felt too heavy for the palazzo. She wanted to capture some of that Italian airy lightness, the glittering blue of the sea, the white of a marble balustrade, the pale winter sunshine. While she lit the gas flame, she tried to conjure an image of the finished product: silvered glass globes painted with delicate, featherlight strokes of the brush in pastel tones.

The flame hissed its old familiar song in her ear as Marie began to blow globes, each one exactly the same size.

11

"Are you sure you want to go? He could have come here to see you anytime he chose . . ." Johanna put her hands on Wanda's shoulders to lend her confidence. Her fingers were so cold from shoveling snow that Wanda could feel it right through her woolen dress. She could hear Magnus cursing from outside, where he had taken over the shoveling from Johanna. It had snowed a good eighteen inches during the night, and there were endless mounds of snow to be shoveled aside before anybody could get out of the house.

"He didn't, though," Wanda answered bluntly. "I don't mind taking the first step. And Christmas is a good time to do it, surely?" She pointed to the linen bag where she had stowed her presents for her father, Uncle Michel, Eva, and Wilhelm, who was sick in bed. There was nothing extravagant there, just little gifts—some handkerchiefs for the men and a bottle of schnapps each, which Uncle Peter had advised her to go and buy in the village store. Eva would get a silver locket that Wanda had bought at a silversmith's off Fifth Avenue. She was the kind of woman who was sure to like getting jewelry.

"I just don't want you to . . ." Johanna broke off rather helplessly.

"To be disappointed?" Wanda laughed dryly as she knotted her headscarf firmly under her chin. "I know quite well that Thomas

Heimer is not going to fling his arms around me and weep for joy. He probably won't be very happy to see me. But I don't care. I just want to meet the man whom I might, under other circumstances, have called father. Please don't worry about me." She was almost at the door when she turned around. "There is one thing, though . . ."

"Yes?"

Wanda felt her cheeks flush red. "How on earth should I talk to him? I mean . . . I don't want to sound like a snob by speaking standard German, but if I try to speak the local dialect I'll just make a fool of myself and he'll think I'm making fun of him."

Johanna laughed. "If that's your biggest problem then just calm down! Thomas Heimer won't feel you're looking down on him if you speak standard German. We may be from Lauscha but we know our own language, thank you."

The streets of Lauscha were busier than usual that day. People were out and about, though not because they were carrying glassware or materials to and fro. Rather someone in front of every house was shoveling a pathway to their front door; soon enough the snow was piled up like mounds of cotton candy on the narrow sidewalks and in the street. Wanda kept sinking ankle-deep into the snow. Then came the moment when the snow crept its way in over the top of Wanda's boots and was promptly melted by her body heat. A chill trickle of icy water ran down her ankles and soaked her socks.

By the time she got to the abandoned foundry, she was so exhausted that she toyed with the idea of turning around. She was worried she might get sick again, but she took off her headscarf all the same to wipe away the sweat that had pooled at the nape of her neck. Then she bundled the scarf up and stuffed it carelessly into her bag. She looked up the hill to the upper edge of the village. What if it was even worse up there? What if nobody had even started clearing the snow away in front of the Heimer house?

These were all excuses, she decided. This was no time for second thoughts. She had been born in Lauscha, for goodness' sake, and she wasn't going to let a little snow scare her. She marched on, her knees trembling.

Wanda had played through the moment a hundred times in her mind. Had tried to steel herself for the wave of emotion that she expected would break over her. She was quite convinced that it would affect her deeply; after all, didn't they say that blood was thicker than water? She had made up her mind on one thing, though: however this first meeting with her father played out, she wouldn't lose control of herself. She had made sure to consider every conceivable outcome, even the most terrible. Her father might slam the door in her face. He might swear at her. He might let her in and then treat her with cruel indifference. Or they might just end up sitting in painful silence for lack of having anything to talk about. Wanda had even prepared for that possibility, and had a little list of topics for conversation; first the weather, then what plans they had for Christmas, what she had seen of Lauscha so far . . . Perhaps she would even be able to steer the conversation around to the glassware that the Heimer workshop made—it would certainly help break the ice if she said a few words of praise. And if she really couldn't find anything else to talk about, she could ask after her sick grandfather.

Sometimes, when she was feeling especially softhearted, Wanda imagined that they would both burst into tears and fall into one another's arms.

There was only one thing she hadn't prepared herself for: that when she set eyes on Thomas Heimer she would feel nothing. Nothing at all.

The man who opened the door to her, dressed in a work smock and a faded old pair of pants that were going baggy at the knees, was a complete stranger. He was of middling height and pale with

gray stubble. His eyes flickered just once when he saw Wanda standing there, and then it was as though two doors slammed shut. His
expressionless gray eyes looked out at her from under bushy eyebrows that were creeping together to meet in the middle. There
were fine wrinkles in his thin face that made him look rather ill.
Nothing about this sickly, aging man even remotely resembled
Ruth's description of the good-looking youth she had fallen in
love with once upon a time, the broad-shouldered fellow with the
wicked laugh.

Wanda had recently read a novel about the American Civil War,
in which the heroine meets her father again after having believed
him dead for years. The author had described the moment by saying
she "felt as though she were looking at her own reflection." Wanda
waited in vain for any such feeling; try as she might, though, she
detected no familiar features in Thomas Heimer's face.

Was this even the right man, standing before her? Or was this
his brother Michel? She peered unobtrusively downward. This man
had both of his legs, so . . . She had to fight back a nervous giggle
when she realized how ridiculous the situation was.

"Why is your hair like that? Did you have lice, or what?"

Thomas Heimer jerked a hand toward Wanda's short hair. Then
he turned and shuffled back into the house, leaving the door open
as if to say, *Come in or stay outside, it's all the same to me.*

In a daze, Wanda followed him along a dark hallway, up some
stairs, and into the kitchen. So this was the house where she had
spent the first year of her life—the thought meant nothing to her.
She cleared her throat to get rid of the feeling that her vocal chords
were furring over.

"Thought you were never coming. You were ill, though."
Thomas Heimer sat down on the corner bench without offering her
a place. Then he reached over to the stove where a pot was clattering
its lid and pushed it aside.

"Eva!" he shouted, then said to Wanda in a normal voice, "What do you want?"

Wanda blinked. The air in the room was very stuffy, and there was an odd smell. She glanced over at the window involuntarily and saw that it was blocked by great drifts of snow that made it impossible to let in any fresh air.

"What do I want? I wanted to see you. Visit you, that is," she said in a little-girl voice. She scolded herself the next moment for using that tone—she sounded like a baby, not like a grown woman in search of her roots. Without thinking about it, she sat down opposite him.

"You seem to know all about me," she said in response to his last comment. "Yes, I was ill for a few weeks; otherwise I would have come earlier." Even as she spoke, she was thinking desperately about what she could say next. All of a sudden things were very different from any of the scenarios she'd imagined. She certainly wasn't going to blurt out that she'd only recently learned he was her father. She felt no desire at all to bare her soul to this man, with his chapped lips and rough manners. What she really wanted to do was get up and leave.

She had nothing to say to him, and he had nothing to say to her.

Coming here had been a hideous mistake—nothing more than that. Yet another of her silly ideas.

Just like the thought that she might be of some use to Johanna and her family—laughable!

"I know it doesn't matter to you whether you see me or not. There's no reason you should want to, so let's not bother pretending. Let's just keep it short." She got up. "Here are a few things I brought. Christmas presents. There's something there for the others too."

The presents, all neatly done up in shiny wrapping paper, looked out of place on the shabby wooden table. *Another mistake,*

Wanda thought with a sinking feeling. Her fingers were gripping the edge of the table so tightly that her knuckles had turned white.

Heimer was still sitting hunched over on the bench. Though his face was expressionless, he had a nervous air about him.

He looks like a stray dog, Wanda thought. He looks like nobody's taken care of him for so long that he's forgotten even the simplest rules for how to behave around people.

Her father.

A stranger. A man for whom she felt nothing, except a twinge of pity.

All at once her heart was almost bursting with love for the man who had taken Thomas Heimer's place eighteen years ago. She saw her stepfather vividly in her mind's eye—Steven in his elegant suits, Steven sitting at the wheel of his beloved new car, Steven surrounded by his business friends and rivals. Wanda's cheeks flushed with shame. Steven had always been there for her, had always forgiven her silly mistakes. How ungrateful she had been! Ever since she had found out when and where she was born, she had treated him like dirt, ignored his feelings . . . yes, almost laughed at him for feeling hurt—as though she were asking, *What right do you have to expect me to love you?*

There were loud steps on the stairs. Whoever was coming was panting and short of breath. Wanda suddenly found the thought of meeting another member of this family almost unbearable.

"I don't want to impose any longer. You must have plenty to do in the workshop . . ." She didn't wait for Heimer to reply but turned to go. Too late. A shadowy figure appeared in the hallway and a harsh female voice spoke up.

"Wilhelm's being quite impossible today, again! I've only got one pair of hands. I can't spend all my time at his beck and call! Michel's called for me three times already this morning as it is . . ."

Eva stopped in the doorway, rooted to the spot. Her eyes darted from Thomas to Wanda and back again.

"I thought I heard something!" She folded her arms in front of her, came closer, and looked at Wanda with a beady eye. "Well look at this, it's the American girl . . ."

"Hello, Eva." Wanda managed a thin smile despite the unfriendly stare. She wasn't going to let this haggard old woman get the best of her. Eva was as old as her mother but seemed worlds away from the provocative temptress in Ruth's tales. And what was she cooking in that pot?

Eva went to the stove and took the lid off. A cloud of steam shot up, accompanied by an odd smell. She took out something small and bony that Wanda could have sworn was a squirrel.

"I'll see myself out," Wanda gasped out as she tried not to breathe through her nose.

"Oh no you won't!" Thomas Heimer sat up straight. "You'll drink a cup of coffee with us now that you're here. Otherwise people will say we never offer our guests anything! Eva, put the kettle on. And bring some bread and something to go with it."

Now that she'd lost her chance to beat a hasty retreat, Wanda had no choice but to sit back down at the table with her father. Eva glowered as she thumped cups and plates down on the table, and Wanda tried to make conversation.

She mentioned how excited she was about all the snow. Was it going to stay like this all the way through till spring, she asked, although she knew the answer already.

Thomas Heimer asked how her journey had been and what she thought of Lauscha, then listened to Wanda's answers without any real interest while he drank his coffee. He seemed determined for her to notice how little he cared.

"Johannes took me to meet a few glassblowers so that I could see for myself how many different wares are made in Lauscha." She laughed, embarrassed. "To tell the truth I liked the marbles best of all. So many colors in one tiny piece of glass!"

"Old Marbles Moritz knows his work," was all Heimer said.

"And what's going on in your workshop?" Wanda asked. As she spoke she realized that the question really mattered to her. Perhaps if Thomas Heimer started to talk about his work, he might prove to be a little more like the man she had imagined he would be. So far the man sitting across the table had shown no signs of being the talented glassblower Marie had described with such admiration. Nor did he seem at all like the charming rogue her mother had talked about. Instead Thomas Heimer seemed fragile.

"Next to nothing, if you really want to know," Eva said, joining in the conversation for the first time. "We're just about keeping the wolf from the door, but not for much longer! If you and your mother think you can get your hands on anything worth having, she was wrong to send you here. She . . ."

"Eva, shut yer mouth! That's not why Wanda came," Heimer snapped at her.

Aha, what was going on here? Wanda looked at Heimer, and just for a moment their eyes met.

"You'll have heard by now that Michel's not much use any longer," Heimer said, nodding vaguely toward the hallway. "He has to lie down most of the time. Has what they call phantom pain. And Father hasn't left his bed for weeks now. Back in summer he still insisted on spending an hour or two in the workshop every day."

Was she expected to reply? Wanda decided the best thing to do was lend an open ear. She had just drunk the last sip of coffee when Eva snatched her cup away from her.

"Don't you pretend you miss having Wilhelm there while you work," she spat over her shoulder from where she stood at the sink.

"We haven't had any decent orders for three months—*that's* the trouble!"

"But how can that be? The Heimer workshop was always famous for its wares, wasn't it? Marie told me that you're one of the best in the whole village." Wanda saw Thomas Heimer's eyes light up briefly. Maybe she had improved his day a little with her visit after all.

A moment later, though, Heimer's eyes clouded over with sadness again. "What's the use now that nobody wants glass anymore? There are porcelain works springing up everywhere like mushrooms after rain—and they make vases and bowls and knickknacks so cheaply there's no way we can compete."

Other glassblowers seem to be able to, Wanda found herself thinking. She said aloud, "That's mass-production, though—handmade goods are always worth more, aren't they?"

Heimer shrugged. "You tell that to the buyers from the big department stores in Hamburg or Berlin. Customers there just want things cheap—they don't care what it looks like or if it's well-made."

"But you could . . . educate the customers' tastes." Wanda remembered when she had worked at Dittmer's. None of the customers there had ever complained about the high prices, but they certainly kicked up a fuss if they thought that the quality wasn't up to snuff!

"High-quality glass will always find a buyer. Maybe not in the department stores but in a gallery instead." Wanda wondered whether she should mention the exhibition of Venetian glass in New York. When she had visited again on the last day of the show, there had been a "sold" sticker on almost every piece.

Heimer shook his head. "I used to think so too. But you can't hold back time. Perhaps . . . if it had all happened differently . . . Three of us together might have been able to tackle the new fashions . . ."

He weighed every word as he spoke, as though he had thought it all over a thousand times but never dared speak it aloud until now.

"Oh, so now everything's my fault, is it? Even though I've spent my whole life cooking and cleaning for you men?" Eva said. "Don't you think that I wanted something else out of life too?" She slapped the damp dishcloth down into the sink and then ran out of the room without looking back.

Wanda found she had been holding her breath. Now she let it out again. Were the two of them always like this?

Thomas Heimer stared into the hallway.

"We Heimers just don't have any luck keeping our women happy," he said. "We don't have any luck. Not with anything."

Wanda was sorry for him, but she was horribly embarrassed as well. She stood up and pushed her chair back. "Now I really do have to go."

"Yes," he said.

As she went down the stairs, Eva blocked her way. "You don't want to leave without seeing your uncle and your grandfather, do you now!" She grabbed Wanda's hand and opened the door to a dim room with a bed standing in the middle.

"There's your Uncle Michel! He's asleep now, but he was up half the night whimpering like a child. Just like he does every night. We can hear it all through the house."

Wanda stared at the thin bedcovers, aghast, and could make out the human form beneath them. What a terrible way to live! She felt Eva looking at her scornfully and turned away. Before she could do or say anything, Eva had opened the next door.

"And here's your grandfather! Don't worry, he doesn't bite. Actually, he's in a good mood today. Not like usual."

"I . . . Wait a moment, Eva. I don't think that I . . ." Wanda struggled in vain against the hand pushing her into the room. What did this woman think she was doing, shoving her about like this?

"Eva? Who are you talking to there? I need my medicine! Eva! Come here!" It was a man's voice, but high and reedy with age.

"Visitor for you, Wilhelm!" And Eva gave Wanda one last push into the room. "You two make yourselves comfortable! I won't intrude."

As Eva shut the door, she laughed as though at a particularly good joke.

Wanda stared at the closed door, furious.

"Ruth?" Wilhelm Heimer was sitting up in bed, blinking incredulously. "Have you . . . come back?"

"I'm Wanda." She went hesitantly toward the bed.

So this was the fearsome Wilhelm Heimer. A shrunken old man, barely more than skin and bones, wrinkled and hunched.

"Wanda?" His rheumy eyes blinked quickly over and over as though this would help him see her. "I don't know anyone called . . ." The rest was lost in a fit of coughing. "Who are you? Get away from me! Why is Eva sending a strange woman in to see me? Eva! E-e-e-va!"

"You can't have forgotten about me, surely! I'm Ruth's daughter!" Wanda snapped at him. "And don't worry, I'm leaving anyway!" She turned abruptly for the door. Perhaps her grandfather no longer had all his wits about him, but he had to know that much, didn't he? Now she was really getting fed up. Her mother had warned her in no uncertain terms but nothing could have prepared her for the truth of what a ghastly family the Heimers were. A pack of ill-mannered louts. No wonder her mother had run away from them!

As she took hold of the doorknob, she heard the old man croak, "Ruth's daughter . . . Now that would be . . . a surprise. You're not lying to me, are you? Not you as well? Come over here, girl!"

Wanda pursed her lips and turned around again. *Be patient with him,* she told herself sternly, *he's an old man on his deathbed.*

"Ruth!" A secretive smile spread across Wilhelm's face.

Wanda didn't bother to repeat that she wasn't Ruth. She approached reluctantly as he beckoned her toward the bed.

On closer inspection the old fellow didn't look quite so deathly ill after all. For a moment she even thought she could see the stubborn lines of earlier days in his face; in the jutting chin and sharp cheekbones, she could see the fearsome old bully everyone had told her about. To her own amazement she even felt something like relief.

"Ruth's daughter, now who would have thought! Your mother . . ." He sat up straight. "Shall I tell you something about your mother?"

Wanda nodded—and was immediately angry at herself.

The old man's eyes lit up.

"Don't go telling anyone else, mind!"

He began to chuckle like a bleating goat, then relapsed into another coughing fit.

Wanda waited for him to recover.

"Ruth . . . back then, she had more moxie than all three of my sons put together." He shook his head sadly. "It was a long time ago. And nothing ever got better after that."

Wilhelm Heimer closed his eyes.

As she took hold of the doorknob again, Wanda fought against the lump in her throat. She knew that she had just heard the old man give the greatest compliment he was capable of.

"It's good that you came." The whisper from the bed was faint, but loud enough to hear even as she left.

12

The meal was everything that the occasion demanded: pâté with truffles, grilled red mullet that filled half the palazzo with the scent of rosemary, squab stuffed with porcini and saffron risotto. The table in the dining room was decorated as befitted the feast. The linen tablecloths were embroidered with the family coat of arms, the best china was brought out, and the silver was polished to a high shine. A bouquet of white lilies and yellow roses stood in the middle of the table, with two more at each end of the long main window. Despite the magnificence of the blooms, however, the overall effect was sterile, an impression that was only heightened by the fact that the flowers gave off no scent. Perhaps they were silk? Marie took a petal between her fingers when no one was looking: the flowers were real. She wondered if perhaps Patrizia had forbidden the flowers to spread any scent so that nothing could compete with her own strong perfume.

Marie waited impatiently for even a glimmer of holiday spirit. How long did she have to sit in this high-ceilinged room where every word echoed back from the walls, looking at the sour expression on her mother-in-law's face, while Franco and his father talked on and on about some winegrower and his sons? Marie tried to catch Franco's eye, but he was so absorbed in conversation that he didn't notice.

By the time the third course was served, Marie was full, but she began working her way through everything on the plate because it was unladylike enough to annoy Patrizia. And indeed the countess raised her eyebrows disapprovingly as she cut her own serving of pigeon breast into tiny little bites. A moment later she put her cutlery down.

"It will be eleven o'clock soon. I will go and make sure that Carla has cooled the champagne." Patrizia dabbed delicately at an imaginary drop of wine on her lips and then moved her chair back silently and stood up.

She was hardly out of the room before Marie surreptitiously unbuttoned the waistband of her skirt. She was sorry now that she had eaten so much.

For Franco's sake she wasn't wearing pants while she was pregnant. "It doesn't do the *bambino* any good to be buttoned up so tight," he had argued. Marie was fairly sure, though, that he was more worried about Patrizia's old-fashioned views. The countess had already declared that she was deeply shocked Marie did not wear a corset. Well, her dear mother-in-law would have to get used to the idea that Marie was not going to tie herself into a prickly wire cage, not even after she had given birth!

Marie tugged at Franco's sleeve. "Why don't we skip dessert and go for a walk?"

"A walk? It'll be time to go out onto the terrace soon," Franco said. "You've been looking forward to the fireworks for days, haven't you?"

He winked at her, and Marie felt a flush of resentment. Why was he treating her like a child just because she had never seen a fireworks display? Suddenly, she wasn't looking forward quite as much to the show.

"We can watch the fireworks from down in the harbor, can't we? Can't you hear how lively the crowds are out in the street?" She pointed toward the window and the distant sound of shouting and laughter. Sometimes the wind carried a snatch of music into the palazzo as well. "They seem to be really enjoying the festival out there!"

"They're drunk!" The count made a face.

"Father's right. Many people drink more than is good for them on a night like this. You wouldn't enjoy being shoved and elbowed in the crowd."

"Whether Marie would enjoy it or not is irrelevant. It is beneath the dignity of a de Lucca to go out into the streets with the mob," the count interrupted. "Listen to them shouting and roaring!" He shook his head, disgusted.

"What's the problem if the men have a little drink? It's the last night of the year! At least the folks down there have a bit of life in them!" Marie retorted. *Unlike you*, she wanted to add, but instead she clamped her lips together to suppress a groan. As always when she got herself worked up, there was a painful twinge in her womb, and it scared her. It was as though a hungry wolf were growling and snapping after the child. She reached over to Franco and gripped his arm tight.

"What's wrong? Aren't you well, *mia cara*? Perhaps you should lie down a little?" He drew back her chair without waiting for an answer and helped her to her feet, shooting an apologetic look at his father. Marie knew perfectly well what the look meant—*women and their moods*. All the same she let Franco take her up to their room.

She stopped in the hallway and put a hand to the side of her belly. *Breathe deeply now, it will be better soon . . .*

She could hear Patrizia's harsh voice from the dining room. Doubtless she was complaining about Marie's behavior again.

"What was all that about? Why do you always argue with Father?" Franco looked at Marie accusingly. "On New Year's Eve of all evenings."

"On New Year's Eve *especially*! The first one we've ever celebrated together! And we're sitting there with your parents as though we were old and gray ourselves!" she shot back without bothering to lower her voice. Let them all hear how angry she was! "And all this ridiculous self-importance! As though the de Luccas were the lords of the earth and everybody else just scum. Things are not what they seem, though I realized that long ago! You all think I don't see what's going on!"

"What do you mean?" There was a dangerous gleam in Franco's eyes now, but Marie didn't care.

"Oh, I see how stiff and anxious the visitors are when they come here," she told him bitterly. "They're happy to get out of the palazzo as quick as they can. I can't imagine you have many friends among 'the mob.' In fact I think your family is very unpopular! You should see how people behave when Peter or Johanna take a stroll through Lauscha! They can hardly go ten steps without stopping to shake someone's hand or share a few words!"

Instead of being angry as Marie had expected, Franco seemed almost relieved. He laughed. "If that's the worst of your worries! My father isn't the man of the people your brother-in-law seems to be, that's true. We do business on a much larger scale, you know, so we can hardly stay friends with everybody. But you must have gotten used to him and his ways by now. Surely you see he doesn't mean any harm."

Marie wasn't quite so sure about that, but she held her tongue. Her temper had vanished as quickly as it had flared up.

Franco put a hand to her chin and lifted her face fondly. "What's really wrong, *mia cara*? Aren't you looking forward to the year to come? To our child?"

Tears came to Marie's eyes. How could she tell him that she missed her family so much it hurt? Instead she sobbed, "Of course I'm looking forward to our child! And to 1911. But I thought that New Year's Eve would be different somehow—more Italian, more lively, more joyful—like the festival we went to in New York, on Mulberry Street!"

"Marie, please don't cry." Franco held her close.

"I can't help it," she sniffled. "I feel so alone." She missed Pandora and Sherlain and the other women from Monte Verità. She missed the conversations as they sunbathed. The childish pranks. Marie couldn't remember the last time she had enjoyed a good laugh.

Franco stroked her hair. "You still have me," he said hoarsely. When she didn't answer, he said, "I think everyone feels a little alone on the last night of the year."

Marie looked up, her eyes full of tears. There was something unfamiliar in his voice. Despair? Loneliness? Whatever it was, it didn't make her feel any safer, any less vulnerable.

"Just hold me tight," she said.

◆ ◆ ◆

After Marie had recovered from her fit of weeping, she enjoyed the fireworks after all. She even admitted that the uppermost terrace of the palazzo really did offer the best view of the harbor. She gasped in wonder at every whirl and burst of light. Her enthusiasm was infectious, and Franco felt as though he were watching the show for the first time. Even his father declared that the pyrotechnicians had done a particularly good job this year. When his mother raised her glass and proposed a toast to the next de Lucca heir, Franco felt light at heart. Everything was all right.

No sooner had the fireworks finished, though, than Marie whispered to him that she was tired, so they went to their room. They were in bed a little after one o'clock.

While Marie sighed gently in her dreams, Franco was filled with nagging doubts that kept sleep at bay.

"You all think I don't see what's going on!"—his heart had almost stopped beating at those words! For a moment he had believed that she knew all about the special shipments. Thank God she didn't! But her remark had shown him vividly, once again, how quickly the house of cards could collapse. The castle in the air he had built for himself and Marie. And if it did—what then?

Marie must never find out what all his bookkeeping and paperwork for the crossings was really about. Those records were so dangerous that he was the only one who could even look at them.

"Everything will be all right, *mia cara*. The new year belongs to us," he had whispered into his wife's ear shortly after midnight. How trustingly she had looked at him! It was up to him to make sure that her trust was not misplaced. And that meant no more people smuggling in the new year.

Marie spent too much time on her own and was lonely, he knew that. But how could he attend to his wife when he always had to listen to other people's tales of woe? Farmers' sons and poverty-stricken tradesmen came to him with their laments, all of them hoping to find their fortune across the sea in the promised land— and they ended up in a kitchen in Little Italy, enslaved by the same poverty they had fled in the old country. Meanwhile their parents back home lived on dry bread and rice because they had spent every last lira buying passage for their sons.

He knew too that Marie was disappointed that he still hadn't made a start on his plans to replant and reinvigorate the vineyards.

He would go to his father this very week. Perhaps he should ask for an appointment, so that the old man knew he meant business. Yes, that would be good. The tension in his body eased a little.

He grew vines and he sold wines—that was who he was. And that meant that the next time he went to New York, he would sell wine. Not sour rotgut that the restaurants only bought because they got cheap labor with every shipment of wine they took off him. De Lucca wines had once enjoyed a good reputation; their bouquet had taken homesick immigrants back to the Italian sunshine, if only for an hour or two. And it could happen again! If only he could make his father see things his way, their wine would be a force to reckon with once more.

Marie turned in her sleep and lifted her knees to her belly. Their child was growing in her womb. Inside her, in the dark, a tiny human being was waiting to see the light of day. Gently, so as not to wake her, Franco ran his hand over the bedcovers.

There was still plenty of time. By the time the child was born, he would be the man he wanted to be. Then the future could begin.

He liked the idea. He wanted to become a father without having to worry that a wine barrel might slip its moorings somewhere in the belly of a ship and crush a stowaway beneath its weight. He didn't want to live in fear because someone might block the airholes by loading the next piece of cargo and . . . enough of such thoughts!

Franco pressed both hands to his temples as though to chase the thoughts from his head.

Another ship had left Genoa two days earlier. In a week the *Firenze* would arrive in New York. If it were up to him, those twelve stowaways would be the last he ever smuggled out of the country.

If only it were over already.

293

13

New Year's supper at the Steinmann-Maienbaum family home was a low-key affair. Johanna had made a pot of potato soup and did no more to mark the occasion than add an extra sausage for each person, and there was bread with the meal, as always. But the food was merely incidental that evening. As soon as the dishes were empty, the men cleared all the tables and chairs to the side of the room. Their neighbor Klaus Obermann-Brauner balanced his accordion on his knee, and everybody stood in a circle. Wanda learned that Klaus and his wife, Hermine, celebrated New Year's Eve with the Steinmann-Maienbaum family every year, just like the rest of tonight's guests. Klaus began to play, and the dancing began. At first Wanda felt clumsy trying to follow the unfamiliar steps—there was much stamping of boots and kicking up of knees, nothing at all like the dances she knew from the ballrooms of New York—but she found the good cheer so infectious that she was soon whooping more loudly than any of them, leaping in the air and swinging her skirts with gusto. She could have hugged the whole world tonight! Instead she spun around, following the order of the dance, and held out both hands to the man behind her. Her laugh died on her lips.

Richard Stämme.

A shiver ran down her spine. She almost stumbled as she spun around once more.

As though to prove to herself that a strange man could never really have that effect on her, this time she looked him directly in the eye. Hundreds of butterflies fluttered in her tummy. She was almost glad when the next change of partner brought her face-to-face with Uncle Peter.

Goodness gracious, what had that been about?

When she had heard earlier that evening that *he* would be among the guests as well, she had gone quite dizzy for a moment at the thought that she would see him again.

Ever since Johannes had introduced her to the young glassblower, she had been racking her brain for some excuse to seek him out. Every time Johanna needed someone to run an errand, she had jumped at the chance, hoping to meet Richard somewhere in the village. But she didn't find him at the general store or the post office or the box-maker's shop. Then she had found herself making detours so that she could pass by his cottage, always returning in her thoughts to the afternoon when she and Johannes had visited Richard there. How his deep-blue eyes had sparkled when he talked about Murano and Venetian glass! His voice had changed as though he were describing a woman he loved—it was husky and incredibly tender, passionate and determined. At that moment Wanda wanted nothing more than to hear him talking about her like that. It was bewildering, astonishing . . . What a ridiculous thought!

And now she was dancing through Johanna's front parlor with him.

At about ten o'clock Klaus Obermann-Brauner packed up his accordion and called for a beer. The others were glad for the break in the dancing, and the table and chairs were pushed back into the middle of the room. Everyone sat down at the table, sweaty but full of good cheer, as Johanna brought in bread and butter and a tub of salt herring.

Once the fish had all been eaten, Johannes called out, "Now for the second-best bit!" He took a slice of bread and began to dip it greedily in the puddle of sour liquor that the herring had come in. When Peter asked Wanda whether she wanted to do the same, she declined, saying she was already full.

Once again she had to struggle to conceal her dismay at how modest her aunt's housekeeping was. It didn't make it any easier knowing that here in the village, the family was considered well-to-do. There was probably more than one family right here in the neighborhood that had nothing at all to eat tonight and that was sitting in an unheated room.

All the members of the Steinmann-Maienbaum family had even treated themselves to an extra little luxury that day: a hot bath. The men had taken turns since the crack of dawn keeping the old stove in the washhouse fed with firewood. Since Wanda was the guest, she had bathed first. Even though she otherwise firmly insisted that they mustn't make any exceptions for her, this time she was glad of the offer—she didn't much like the idea of climbing into the bath-water after Anna and Johannes had already had their turn. While the others were still at work, she guiltily climbed into the hot water, steaming and scented with lavender.

If her mother could see her now . . . after her first proper bath since she had arrived, wearing no makeup, dressed for the evening in her everyday clothes . . . Wanda grinned at the thought.

Johannes threw her a cheerful glance across the table. Ever since Wanda had been such a hit with all his friends on their little tour of Lauscha, he had become her greatest supporter—not that any-one outside the family would have realized it, given the way he was always teasing her.

"I have to wonder why we wait for New Year's Eve to turn the parlor into a dance floor," Richard said, chewing happily at a slice of bread. "A little bit of music and dancing and life seems very different all of a sudden, doesn't it?"

The others agreed that working life didn't leave enough time for fun and frolics. Anna was the only one who disagreed, saying, "Who would do the work if every day was a dancing day?"

Richard frowned briefly but didn't argue. Instead he passed the bread basket over to Wanda and asked, "Well? How do you like our Thuringian New Year's Eve?"

For a moment their fingers touched and his eyes held hers. She looked down.

My hand's shaking, she thought as she put the basket down in the middle of the table.

"I like it very well indeed. Marie told me so much about the festivities here before I came, but being here is different . . . I can't remember the last time I enjoyed myself so much," she answered truthfully. The dancing, Richard's friendly smile, the warmth in the parlor as the snow fell outside, her family, Richard's dark eyes, so intense, so . . . Without even realizing it, she had looked back at him so now she forced herself to turn away again.

"Christmas was just as lovely, with all the snow and the Christmas tree." She pointed to the corner of the room where the tree still stood, decorated with the first baubles Marie had ever made, following family tradition. "My first Christmas in Germany. And it was even more wonderful than the Germans in the New York clubs had told me to expect!"

Richard was still looking straight at her. She could feel his knee pressing up against her leg.

"But New Year's Eve is something else again, isn't it?" Wanda asked, struggling to keep her voice light and friendly.

His gaze became a little less intense and was softer now, some-how turned inward.

"Yes, the last day of the year is . . . an ending of sorts. The min-utes slip down through the hourglass . . . Suddenly everything that once was seems less important now, because we'll make a new start soon. Because anything can happen in the new year."

Wanda nodded. Richard had said exactly what she was feeling. She was even more bewildered now. His knee was pressing harder against her now, and she wondered whether she should move a little farther down the bench—for the good of her soul. She felt dizzier by the moment.

Richard gave her a knowing grin, then turned his eyes away. "We may not be such fine folks as they are in America, but we know how to have a good time, don't we, Peter?"

The spell was broken. Wanda took a deep breath.

Peter laughed and dipped his ladle into the pot of punch that was simmering gently away on the stove, then began pour-ing more into everybody's glasses. Somehow the pot never seemed to run empty. The others had all stopped to listen while Wanda and Richard talked, but as they picked up their own conversations again, Wanda saw that the expression on Anna's face had turned even grimmer than usual.

Wanda drank half her glass in one gulp.

A little while later they began to play cards, and the mood became even merrier.

Whenever Hermine had a good hand of cards, her husband, Klaus, began to grumble, and she did the same when he was in luck. The more the old couple bickered, the funnier everyone else found it. As some point Johannes and Richard began imitating the two of them and gales of laughter followed. Aunt Johanna giggled like a girl, and even Magnus was not his usual sorrowful self that evening.

Anna seemed to be the only one who didn't find it funny. When she laughed at all, the sound was strangulated.

Wanda looked around the room, her cheeks aglow as she held her right hand over her cards. This wasn't such a bad hand . . .

"Whose turn is it?" Why did her voice always have to go so squeaky when she was excited?

Johannes groaned. "Oh cousin, cousin, I think you still haven't quite got this game. It's my turn, of course."

"You watch out, she's just asking questions to make herself look harmless. These Americans are full of tricks!" Richard said, winking at Wanda.

She joined in the laughter, embarrassed. Look harmless indeed! How was she supposed to concentrate on the game with Richard sitting next to her, when she could feel the warmth of his body? How was she supposed to keep track of whose turn it was when his arm kept touching hers? She peered at him out of the corner of her eye. He was looking straight at her.

Wanda felt herself blush. Hastily she picked up her punch glass and took another mouthful, which only made her feel hotter.

Johanna glanced at her niece.

"It's eleven o'clock already, and we haven't cast the lead yet! Johannes, Anna—don't we want to know what the new year will bring? It always used to be your favorite part of the party. And while you're doing that, I'll go and fry the donuts!"

Johanna stood up slightly unsteadily and walked over to the pantry. Hermine followed her to lend a hand.

While Johannes went into the workshop to get everything ready for the fortune-telling, Anna stayed in her seat.

"Why don't you go and join Johannes? You're always turning up whenever you like the rest of the time," Anna said to Wanda.

Wanda couldn't have been more surprised if Anna had punched her in the stomach. She looked back at her cousin, mortified.

"I daresay the lead will just make lumpy blobs anyway, and we'll have to rack our brains to see any shapes that mean anything." Richard laughed as Johanna came back to the table with a dish of freshly fried donuts. "But casting the lead is all part of the fun at this time of year, isn't it?" Then he turned to Wanda. "Do you do that in America as well?"

She could feel his breath warm upon her cheek as he spoke. Anna's remark was quite forgotten.

"I . . . how can I explain . . . we . . ." She laughed, breathless. What had Uncle Peter put in that punch! She felt as though her head were stuffed with cotton wool.

"What kind of silly question is that?" Anna hissed at him. "Of course they know all about our customs; they were Germans as well once—even if most of them seem to have forgotten that."

"Anna!" Johanna frowned as she looked over at her daughter.

Anna stood up abruptly. "What do you mean, *Anna*? I think it's ridiculous what a fuss you're all making over Wanda just because she's come from America. As if it were heaven on earth!"

"We're happy to have Wanda here as our guest," her father answered softly. "And that has nothing to do with the fact that she's American, but rather because we've welcomed her into our lives."

"It seems to me that everybody has!" Anna spat, then ran out of the room.

Wanda stared down at the tabletop, mortified. Of course *that* was why Anna was so angry at her. Her cousin had been watching like a hawk all evening and hadn't blinked once as Richard and Wanda spoke or whenever they touched. Anna had tried to draw Richard into conversation more than once, but each time he had given her a short answer and turned straight back to Wanda.

Under different circumstances, Wanda might even have felt sorry for her. Instead she was worried that the others would notice how happy she was.

"I think I need a little fresh air," she murmured. Then she too left the room.

14

It was bitterly cold outside. Though it had stopped snowing, the sky was covered with low-hanging, pale-gray clouds. There was no sky sprinkled with stars, no shining moon.

Wanda stayed under the eaves where the ground was dry. The freshly fallen snow glittered in the light from the kitchen window like an evening gown strewn with rhinestones. *What's Mother wearing tonight?* Wanda suddenly found herself thinking. For a blissful moment she was distracted by memories of the splendid New Year's parties she had attended with her parents. Perhaps it would have been best if she had never left New York . . . *But then you would never have met Richard*, a voice inside her whispered.

What now? She sighed deeply, breaking the silence of the night.

It seemed impossible to go back inside and sit down at the table as though nothing had happened. On the other hand—what *had* happened? She was probably only imagining that Richard was interested in her. His behavior could easily be nothing more than the politeness shown to a guest, in which case Anna's jealousy was childish and unfounded.

The front door squeaked on its hinges, breaking her train of thought. Richard came outside.

She had known he would.

He came toward her carrying her coat over his arm. Gently, he helped her put it on. Then he knelt down and buttoned it up. When he was done, he drew Wanda to him as though it were the most natural thing in the world.

Wanda just stood there, her teeth chattering and her arms hanging down at her sides while the heat from his body warmed her. She was too afraid of her own feelings to return his embrace—her passion would surely get the better of her.

"Don't feel bad about Anna. It was bound to happen like this. It's best that she know the truth right from the start."

"What had to happen like this?" Wanda's face was so stiff with cold that she had to force each word out of her mouth. Her heart hammered as she wriggled free from his arms. She wanted to be able to look him in the eyes.

"I've fallen in love with you. As for your own feelings, well, you know better than I." He smiled.

Wanda didn't say a word. Should she tell him that nothing in the world mattered to her now except him? That she had never felt this way about anyone before? That she had never desired a man the way she did him? She didn't doubt his words for a moment, but she wasn't ready to answer them the same way. She was scared by these powerful new feelings.

"I don't know how I feel," she answered at last.

"It's New Year's. Anything is possible." Before she knew what was happening, he was kissing her, on the forehead, on both cheeks, but not on the mouth.

It was as though his kisses unlocked a door inside her. Suddenly she was calm. She stopped shivering. Richard was right. Anything was possible.

All the same she said, "I'm American. I'll be leaving at the end of April. I only came to Thuringia because I stupidly thought I would be able to help my family while Marie was away. And . . . then there was the whole story with my . . . my father. But I've even wondered whether I shouldn't take an earlier ship back. Because nothing is the least bit like I imagined it would be. As is always the case in my useless life."

Before she knew what was happening, there were tears in her eyes. Best that *he* knew the truth right from the start as well—she was of no use to anyone.

"And now Anna is upset with me. Johanna will say I've been abusing their hospitality. And Peter will . . ."

"Wanda! Stop blaming yourself. None of them will say anything of the sort."

Richard shook her shoulders gently. Then he wiped her tears away with his thumbs.

"There was never anything going on between Anna and me. We worked together a couple of times on special orders. She's a good glassblower, and I admire her work. But that's all. Perhaps I'm not entirely free of blame if she imagined it meant anything more. I should have told her long ago that I don't even see her as a woman. I didn't take her infatuation seriously, though. She's practically still a child!"

"I'm only two years older," Wanda said, sniffling. She wiped her nose.

"You're a woman," he told her firmly. He took her hands and kissed them. "When Johannes stopped by to visit me with you . . . I will never forget that moment. You standing there with your hair damp with snow, the snow melting and trickling down into your eyes. You were blinking like a scalded cat. *That's her!* I thought. It hit me like a thunderbolt."

Wanda wanted to burst out crying again. He sounded so certain! It was just like when he had talked about Venetian glass.

"Something like that only happens once in a lifetime. If that. Every day since then I've been going crazy trying to run into you again somehow." Richard laughed self-consciously. "Some days I went down to the general store three times hoping to find you there. Mrs. Huber looked at me as though I wasn't quite right in the head. I wanted to tell her that indeed I wasn't."

"But didn't that scare you?" Wanda asked breathlessly.

She glanced nervously at the door. How long was her family going to leave her alone out here with a man who was, after all, a total stranger to her?

His eyes gleamed. "I was only scared that you might leave for some reason before I saw you again."

Wanda giggled nervously. Then she admitted that she had been roaming Lauscha looking for him in much the same way.

Richard opened his arms and Wanda clung to him. She shut her eyes and turned her face up toward his, but all he did was stroke her hair and then kiss her on the top of her head, as though saving the rest for later.

How clever he was! Wanda leaned her head trustingly against his chest. She could hear nothing but her own heartbeat and her breathing. Any thought of what her mother might have to say about this vanished as she thought, with every fiber of her being, *I love this man!*

She would be able to explain to Ruth one way or another why she had to stay on in Lauscha.

Richard cleared his throat. "As for your departure . . . you can give the ticket away; you won't be needing it anymore now that you'll be staying in Lauscha."

"What?" Wanda tore herself abruptly from his arms. "How can you be so sure of that, we've only just—"

"I'm not talking about us," he interrupted her, as though all that were settled anyway. "I'm talking about your family. They need you more than you can imagine!"

Wanda laughed. "You're the only one who thinks so! I folded together a few cardboard boxes and packed some Santa Claus figures into them, but the other hired hands could do anything I do with their eyes shut. Especially since things will calm down in January, and then . . ."

"I wasn't talking about Johanna." Richard waved her words away. "You have to go up the hill. To the top of the village. To your other family."

"You're joking!" Wanda glared at him, furious. "That's just mean! I'm sure that everybody in the village has heard by now how 'overjoyed' my father was to see me."

Richard laughed. "But he was, believe me. You should have heard the way he sang your praises last time he came down to the tavern. He told everyone how pretty you are. How clever. Apparently your grandfather was saying exactly the same thing, going on about how nobody would mistake you for anyone but a Heimer. Thomas tells us that your visit gave the old fellow a new lease on life. Supposedly he even tried to get out of bed, though he was too weak for that. So there you have it!"

"I don't believe a word." Frowning, Wanda tried to clear the confusion in her mind.

"Why would I lie to you? What good would it do me?" Richard asked intently. "I know your father, and I know that he means what he says. He's not the friendliest of fellows, and when he's in a mood it's best just to leave him be. But he's honest through and through. If he sits there and tells the whole tavern what a fine girl you are, it really means something. Of course he would never tell you right out how happy he was that you came to see him. When he doesn't know how to behave, he turns surly. That's just the way he is. But one thing's for sure: your visit made him happier than anything has for a long time."

"Well, God knows I never saw any sign of that," Wanda said dryly. The way he had sat there staring down into his coffee cup as though he could hardly wait for her to leave. "And Eva was such a snake!"

"Eva's just a poor sinner." Richard lifted her face and fixed his gaze on her. "I know they say that blood is thicker than water, but you don't owe them anything for all that. That's clear. All the same . . ."

Wanda put her hand up to stop him. She was exhausted. There was so much going on that she couldn't think straight.

Richard grinned. "It's obvious, if you ask me. Your uncle and aunt can get along very well here even without you. But the Heimers are really in a bind. I don't know all the details, of course, but it seems that the last wholesaler who was taking wares from Thomas has just dropped him. He has nobody to blame for that but himself, the stubborn dog! Why does he always refuse to try anything new?"

Wanda wanted to ask him why he was so keen to help a glass-blower who was a competitor after all, but before she could speak Richard continued.

"Your father is still a damned good glassblower. I'd say he's even one of the best we have. His workshop might not have all the very latest equipment, but it's still very well furnished. I would be thrilled to have everything that Thomas has to work with. But the fact is that nobody wants to buy what he makes anymore—statues of stags and goblets with hunting scenes and the like."

"All that may be true," Wanda put in. "But what does any of it have to do with me? It's hardly as though we fell into one another's arms after all those years of separation. I don't even think he's a very nice man, for all that he's my father. I don't know him, I don't like that house, and I don't know the first thing about glassblowing!

How in the world did you get the idea that I might be able to help Thomas Heimer?"

Richard sighed. "It's obvious, I'm telling you. If he's not going to see his whole glassblowing business go down the drain, your father will have to move with the times."

He stopped. A crafty smile played at his lips.

"And who better to help him do that than his worldly daughter from America?"

15

Genoa, 7 January 1911

Dear Wanda,

How could you think of giving me such a shock! When the mailman came to our door with an express letter, for a moment I feared the worst—and you know where my imagination can lead me! I was all the more relieved then to read that everything is all right.

I can hardly begin to believe what you're telling me! Richard Stämme has told you that he's in love with you? Just like that? When you had almost given up hope? And you're going to help your father in his workshop? I have a thousand questions for you, and I don't know which to ask first. Your letter was so enthusiastic and so cheerful! And at last I recognized my own dear Wanda again, always full of ideas and get-up-and-go. I have to confess that for a while I feared you would lose heart, what with all the unlucky twists and turns your life has taken recently . . .

Oh, I'm writing such convoluted nonsense! All I want to say is that I'm happy for you, happy with all my heart!

Believe it or not, I knew from your very first letter that you had fallen for Richard. Of course I agree with you that he is an extraordinary man. And he's handsome too. I imagine that poor Anna wasn't the only girl in the village whose head he has turned. Are you quite sure, though, that you weren't exaggerating—even if only a little—about what happened on New Year's Eve in front of Johanna's house? I had always thought that Richard kept to himself. I would never have thought of him as a loving husband and father—although that hasn't happened yet anyway, thank heavens. Dear, dear Wanda, I'm so happy for you! All the same I am afraid as well, in case things happen too fast between you and Richard. I can hear you saying that your mother was already married by your age—and you're right, of course—but please consider that your mother was very unhappy in that first marriage. It would be rather silly to repeat the same mistake, wouldn't it?

Now I don't want to be comparing apples and oranges here, but all the same I will make one comparison: your mother left Lauscha for the sake of her great love, and you're planning to stay in Lauscha for the sake of your great love—isn't that odd?

What does your mother say to all this? The fact that you want to work side by side with Thomas must be something of a surprise to her, a shock even. (I do hope that you've written to her about this!) And what does Johanna say? She must have jumped when she heard it, I daresay. I can't imagine she's happy to see you head up the hill to your father's house every day. Ruth's phone must be ringing off the hook. And Anna? If looks could kill . . . am I right?

I'd love for you to tell me a little more, in your next letter, about how everyone around you reacted and less (even if it's just a little less) about Richard and his dark-blue eyes . . .

Franco has just looked in on me—I am sitting in the orangery, which is beautiful, and I am breathing in the scent of oranges . . . can you even imagine that where you are, deep in snow?—though only to say that he still has at least another two hours of work to get through with his father in the office! And it's almost six o'clock. Believe me, married life isn't all wonderful. There are days when I see the cook or the chambermaid more than I see Franco. This despite the fact that he solemnly promised that he would work less in the new year. Well, we shall see . . .

I have just decided not to go in to dinner this evening. When my mother-in-law is the only one at the table, I can't enjoy the food anyway. And so I have time to write a little more about your second piece of news.

You asked me for my opinion of Heimer and how things stand there. Dearest Wanda, I told you everything I know about his workshop back in New York. When I was still living in Lauscha, I never much troubled my head over other glassblowers and what they might be doing.

However, I was very surprised to hear that Thomas cannot even find customers for his glass hunting scenes. Even with all the goodwill in the world I cannot tell you how he should go about finding new commissions. Perhaps the simplest thing would be to go knocking on the doors of the wholesalers in Sonneberg to find out what sells. The job could be tailor-made for you!

You write that Thomas was very surprised by your offer to help and that he is still very reluctant to accept. Dear Wanda, that must be the understatement of the century, surely?! I can't imagine that stubborn old fool taking advice from anyone—even you. I do know that much about the Heimer men—they are muleheaded as can be and entirely convinced that they know best! The fact that you are still prepared to try your luck with them is proof of your kind and helpful nature, which I came to know so well in New York. Only time will tell, though, whether this is the mission that you have spent so long looking for. All I can do is advise you to take things slowly and not put all your heart and soul into it.

And please: write to your mother and try to explain to her why you have taken such drastic steps—Ruth loves you more than you know and the same goes for Steven.

Now I have some news for you in turn. (Please be so good as to pass on these pages of the letter to Johanna so that I do not have to write everything twice.)

I should have told you all long ago, but I thought that after all the trouble I had caused the best thing to do would be to let tempers cool for a while . . .

I am going to be a mother!

The little one is due in May—what do you say to that? I am most wonderfully happy as I am sure you can imagine. For years and years I thought that I was one of those women who was not destined to have children, and then a younger man comes my way and I am fertile after all! I already have a little bump and Franco says that if I carry on eating for two he will be able to roll me through the palazzo. Now and again I have cramps. Franco says that this is the child being cheeky with us. I have been wondering whether I should visit a doctor, but when I think how simple things were for Johanna even with the twins . . . She was on her feet in the workshop the very day she gave birth, and back at work not two weeks later. So of course that lifts my spirits whenever I feel a twinge in my back or a pain in my womb. Ah well, I'm not as young as I used to be, but I won't complain. I still sit at my workbench every day (although I never use the flame these days, I am working with a soldering torch instead). If only you could see the pictures that I finished yesterday! The rich glowing colors, the light that comes from the glass itself! I know it's not considered appropriate for an artist to praise her own work but my series In Vigneto *is really the best thing that I have ever done. In fact I had planned to give the pieces to Franco for Christmas, but I simply didn't have time to finish them. When I showed them to him yesterday, he was so touched that tears came to his eyes— my inspiration for the pictures came from the vineyards that he loves so much. He wants to hang them on the window in the office. Perhaps it would be a good idea to take advantage of his good mood and tell him of my latest plans . . . I have already written to you about how I want to open a little gallery this summer, but my new idea is to invite Sherlain and Pandora to the opening so that we can unite poetry, dance, and glass, so to speak. I am looking forward to hearing what Franco says about that.*

I have written till my fingers ache, so I will finish here and go and find my darling husband now, even though the office is at the other end of the palazzo. If only the hallways in this place were not so long!

Please give my love to everyone and tell them that I miss you all dreadfully!

With love, Marie

Marie put down her pen, exhausted. Her eyes fell on the pendant watch that hung on its long chain from around her neck. Ten o'clock already! Where had the time gone? The answer was right there in front of her: a letter, several pages long. She couldn't remember ever having written such a long letter before. Even though her stomach was beginning to grumble, she read everything through, adding a word or two here, crossing out there, putting little notes in the margin. When she was done, she hesitated for a moment. Wanda's own letter had been so insistent, so hopeful—and she had sent it express! But Marie could see in every line that her niece was uncertain of what she was doing and that she wanted nothing in the world so much as approval and forgiveness for her bold plans. Marie couldn't give her that, though—the news from Lauscha was too sudden, and she wasn't quite sure yet what to make of it all. For the time being, it would have to be enough that she wished Wanda well.

Marie smiled as she folded the pages together and put them into the envelope that she already had on the desk. She dipped her pen into the inkwell once more and wrote the address. It would go to the post office tomorrow.

As she straightened up she felt the bones in her neck crack. She was stiff from sitting for so long. She massaged the muscles a little, and a shiver ran down her spine.

It was pitch dark all around, and cold. Only one small lamp hanging above the garden furniture gave off any light. Though the orangery was warm and gloriously scented during the day, it felt cold and decidedly unwelcoming now. When the sun shone, she was surrounded by palms and lemon trees, but at night there were only vague looming shadows.

All of a sudden she felt an urgent need to get back inside where it was warm and light. She gathered her pen and paper hastily and stood up.

The lights were on in the hallway that led to the bedroom. Franco! Marie hastened her step. He was probably already waiting for her. With any luck he would be in a good mood and not too worn out. Otherwise there was a chance he would disapprove of her plan just because he was tired.

"Franco, darling! Have you already had supper? If not, we can . . ." Marie stopped dead with her hand on the doorknob. The smile froze on her face. She looked at the bed, freshly made up with the sheets turned down by the maids, and felt a surge of anger. How long was the old count going to keep his son sitting up tonight? In a rage, she slammed down her things on the side table, and was just about to loosen the ribbon in her hair when she stopped.

She had no desire to sit here and wait. She would end up falling asleep from sheer boredom and then her news would have to wait until morning—when Franco might not have time for her once again.

Marie threw a shawl over her shoulders and left the room. She took the letter to Wanda with her. If she put it on the hall table, the errand boy would take it to the post office the next morning.

When she got halfway down the long hallway, she was briefly overcome by a wave of dizziness, but she fought it off and marched toward the office.

16

As the oak door of the office came into view, Marie was still brooding over whether to let Franco know how upset she was or whether she should try to charm him away from his work. On the one hand it would certainly make sense for her to . . .

"Telefono . . . dodici uomini . . . Firenze . . ."

Franco's voice, loud behind the oak door, shouting, startled her back to her senses. She was just about to knock when Franco's voice reached her once more.

"Questo è colpa nostra!"

Marie stopped in front of the door, dismayed, her hand on the doorknob. She had never heard her husband shouting like this. She suddenly wondered whether it was a good idea to interrupt. Franco had mentioned that a ship called the *Firenze* was due to dock in New York any day now with a load of de Lucca wine in its cargo. What had happened? What was "our fault" here?

"Annegati?"

Drowned? The count's voice, raised in a question. One word like a whiplash.

"No, soffocati! . . . Firenze . . . una mancanza d'aria nel contenitore!"

Marie frowned. Who had suffocated? Not enough air in the shipping crate . . . what crate?

"*Una morte misera! . . . dodici uomini soffocati, capisci?!*"

A miserable death? Twelve men had . . . suffocated . . . on the crossing? Had she understood that properly or was her shaky knowledge of Italian letting her down? Oh God, something dreadful must have happened!

Marie swallowed. She felt a lump in her throat, felt disaster coming the way an animal smells danger on the wind. *Run back to your room as fast as you can,* shouted the voice in her head. Instead she stood rooted to the spot and went on listening.

"*Ci costerà una barca di soldi!*"

Wasn't it just typical that the old count should be thinking of how much this would cost—whatever 'this' was—while his son was on the edge of a nervous breakdown? Marie was amazed at how clearly she was thinking.

"*Una morte misera! . . . questo è colpa nostra!*" Franco shouted again. He had to be standing right by the door. His voice was loud and clear and, to her horror, she found she understood every word. "I curse the day I ever agreed to all this! How often did I beg you to make an end of it? Money, money, money! You would take any risk for money, however great. And now twelve men have met their deaths!"

Marie put a hand to her mouth automatically. Her head was buzzing, and she knew now with a terrible certainty that men had been shipped with the cargo of wine and that they had died on the crossing.

"*Siamo assassini!*" Franco shouted. *We are murderers . . .*

The door was thrown open—and Franco walked right into Marie.

"Marie!" He stared at her in horror.

317

He was as pale as could be, and his eyes were rimmed with red. His hair was plastered to his forehead by sweat.

At the sight of him, fear tightened its grip around Marie's heart. Wanda's letter fell to the floor as she wrapped her arms around her body and hoped that this sudden pain would not devour her. Smuggling people . . .

"I . . . was . . . looking for you," she said, staring into Franco's eyes, horrified, reading the guilt there. *We are murderers!* "I don't understand . . . Franco . . . Who has died? And what do you have to do with . . . smuggling people? Franco!" She clung to his arm. *This can't be true,* she thought in a panic. *It's a nightmare, I'll wake up soon.*

Franco looked down at the floor, his eyes wet with tears. He couldn't bring himself to answer. Behind him, the shadowy shape of his father drew closer.

"Have you been spying on us?" the count asked, his voice deadly quiet.

Marie glanced from one man to the other.

"I demand to know what is going on here!" Her voice was so shrill that she feared it might have startled the child in her womb.

"There's been an accident . . . but I'll take care of it . . . I'll make everything all right again and . . ." The words came out slurred, as though Franco had been drinking. "I can . . . explain everything . . ."

"You will explain nothing, not to her!" his father interrupted. Then he spoke to Marie. "What we were discussing has nothing to do with you. Aren't you ashamed to be listening at keyholes like a tattletale? Is that how you do things in Germany? Go to your room this instant! Franco and I are not done here. And don't you dare breathe a word about whatever you *imagine* you heard here." He put his hand roughly on her shoulder and was about to shove her away when Marie broke loose.

"Don't touch me!" she screamed. "If you think you can intimidate me, you're wrong! I've done nothing wrong, unlike you people!" She looked her father-in-law in the eye and saw how startled he was—the old man hadn't expected her to put up a fight. Disgusted, she looked away and turned to Franco. Why did he let his father treat her like this?

"So? How many more lies are you going to tell? Have you any more fine stories about your vineyards?" she asked coldly.

"Marie . . . I . . ." he stammered.

Her heartbeat was hammering all the way down to her womb. She was so furious that she was nearly ready to hit him. To beat her fists against his chest. To do anything she could to shake him out of his numb and helpless state. But she had to think of the child. She tried to take a deep breath. Her throat hurt.

"If you do not tell me the truth this instant, I will go to the police. They, and the emigration authorities, will certainly be very interested in whatever I *imagined* I heard. Especially since I can tell them the name of the ship that you used to . . ." She didn't need to finish the sentence.

It was a long night. Franco bolted the door of their bedroom so that the count could not disturb them, and then he confessed everything. He stuttered and stammered over the first two sentences, and then the whole story came pouring out.

It had all started five years ago when one of their neighbors had come with an unusual request: his son was involved in illegal gambling and had caught the eye of the police, so he had to hide out somewhere. Could Signor de Lucca perhaps help by getting the boy out of the country? It would be a shame for his whole life to be destroyed by one stupid, youthful mistake. And of course he would pay for their help. Times were hard and the winemakers from Venice, Friuli, and Tuscany were snapping at their heels; the Italian restaurant owners in New York could pick and choose from plenty of suppliers. Why not boost their difficult export trade with a little extra source of income? Franco's father agreed. The old count had told Franco that fate had smiled upon them, that it was a gift from Heaven.

And it went on from there. What had started as a one-time favor for a worried father developed into human trafficking on a grand scale. Young men who had run into trouble with the law, men who wanted to emigrate but had been refused an American visa because of their health—all of a sudden anyone could reach the promised land as part of the cargo of de Lucca wine. Of course it only worked if the customs men on either side of the Atlantic got their slice of the "fare." A family had to pay four hundred dollars a head for such an illegal crossing—and the ones who stayed behind often had to spend years working off their debt to the count. Twenty percent of the sum went to the "harbor fees" in Genoa and New York. One of Franco's tasks was to look for shipping clerks, customs officers, and longshoremen who could be relied upon to shut their eyes at the right moment—for a price.

But the crossing fees alone were not enough to wipe the slate clean for the stowaways. Once they got to New York, Franco made sure that they found jobs in Italian restaurants or building sky-scrapers—for wages that no legal immigrant would ever accept, of course. Which was why ordinarily the de Luccas only took men no older than forty. Anybody older would hardly have survived the hardship of the crossing and the backbreaking labor that followed.

"We worked out our system down to the last detail," Franco said, giving Marie a tired smile. Then he began to weep.

The fares for the crossing, the money he handed out at the docks, the cheap illegal labor—there was a code word for every-thing. Marie shuddered. She was leaning up against the headboard in bed with a blanket over her, but shivering all the same. She had no words of comfort to offer. Not to Franco, and not to herself. Franco dried his tears and went on.

There had been incidents and small problems of all kinds. Once a stowaway had almost died from a severe case of diarrhea. Another time a fight had started and one of the men had his arm broken. But in all these years, nobody's life had ever truly been in danger—until the crossing of the *Firenze*. Nobody knew what had happened. Twelve bodies had been found when the cargo was unloaded. All the evidence seemed to point to suffocation.

Marie did not stop asking questions until she knew every detail. Who the dead men were. Whether Franco knew their families. Whether the authorities in New York knew about what had happened. What was going to happen to the bodies. Every answer simply increased her torment, and Marie hated Franco for what he told her.

In the end she had to face the truth: She had married a liar. A slaver. And a murderer.

If anybody had asked her what she felt at that moment, she would not have known what to say. There was a gaping hole where her heart had been. Nothing mattered anymore, nothing was important in this life, nothing was as it should be. Marie felt a creeping fear that she might be going mad. She felt afraid for her child as well, wondering whether the little one was holding its hands over its ears in the womb to try to block out the dreadful truth.

"And now?" Franco's voice was tired. She looked up.

All her illusions had been shattered. She felt hatred, mixed with the painful knowledge that she had lost everything. She fought in vain against this certainty. *Why did you do this to me?* she shouted silently in her mind. Then she looked at Franco.

"Am I supposed to tell you what to do next?" She laughed bitterly. "All I know is that I was a stupid cow for believing anything you ever said about the honor of the de Luccas. About your traditions, about how much you love your wine. You were lying to me the whole time!" She buried her face in her hands. If only some magic would make everything right again! But when she looked up, Franco was still sitting there, silent, distraught. Suddenly she felt nothing but disgust for him.

"You must have been laughing up your sleeve when I gave you that book about vine selection! You and your father had a far easier way to make the money you wanted so much."

"Marie, please . . ."

"Oh, so suddenly the truth hurts?" It was only for the child's sake that she didn't fly at him with her fists. Instead she swung her legs over the side of the bed and put her feet in her slippers. Her gaze wandered around the room as though to get her bearings. Then she went to the wardrobe.

"What are you doing? Marie! What can I say? I'm so sorry, so dreadfully sorry! I didn't want any of this to happen! You wouldn't believe how much I was against the whole business! I tried a thousand times to show Father how wrong it was, believe me. But you know how stubborn he is. What choice did I have but to go along with it?"

His voice was tearful, which only made Marie angrier. *Now* he was upset? Of course he was! But what had he been doing all these months and years?

"So you were a coward, that's your excuse? What do you want me to do, Franco?" Her hands trembled as she grabbed a pile of blouses from the drawer. She would not stay in this house a moment longer. Even if she had to run through the streets of Genoa on her own in the middle of the night! Her marriage, her child's father, her love, her home, her workshop—she had lost them all. And Franco was a criminal.

"I know that you don't believe me now, but here's the truth," came a quiet voice from over by the bed. "I was going to put a stop to it after this crossing. I swore that to myself on New Year's Eve. I would give anything for this never to have happened."

Franco got up and tried to put his arms around Marie from behind.

"Please, Marie, don't go! Don't do this to me. Everything will be all right again, I promise you. Think of our child. Think of the gallery we wanted to open. I'll go to America and I'll make sure that . . ."

She shook him off. Her suitcase was in storage somewhere, and she knew Franco would never send a servant to fetch it for her, so she stuffed some underwear into one of the linen bags that was used to take dirty washing down to the laundry. She added the blouses in, then two skirts.

"Marie, I'm begging you! If you go, I won't survive that. Please, you can't leave me now. I need you . . ."

She looked at him, her eyes blank.

And I won't survive if I stay! she might have told him. But instead she said, "You've ruined everything."

17

Half carrying and half dragging two sacks of clothes, Marie stumbled through the palazzo's long hallways. She had to get out, away from there—she couldn't think of anything else.

From the opposite end of the hallway, she saw the count at the front door. Patrizia was at his side.

"You are not going anywhere."

Marie stared at her father-in-law, astonished. How self-righteous he looked! No "Marie, I'm so sorry." No "I repent of my sins."

"What are you going to do to stop me? Shut me away, like you did those poor men in your wine crates?" She spoke boldly but her words lacked conviction. Something crumbled inside her, and her strength ebbed away. *Please let me go so that I have time to think,* she pleaded silently.

"Marie, don't leave without me! Please, I'm begging you! If you must leave, then take me with you!" Franco had followed her and now he clung to her arm like a child clinging to his mother.

"*Ti amo,*" he whispered. And then, "I love you more than my own life."

A wave of pity broke over Marie. But she answered aloud, "That doesn't count for much, with a life as miserable as yours." It hurt her so much to say those words that she had to wrap her arms around her belly. She blinked against the pain and suddenly felt dizzy.

Franco flinched as though she had hit him.

"Marie, darling, be reasonable! We mustn't be too hasty; we have to sit down and help one another to deal with this tragedy. *Una famiglia, si?*" Patrizia said, putting her hand on Marie's arm with exaggerated concern. "In good times and in bad—isn't that what you promised my son in Ascona, when you were married? Didn't you tell us how happy you were on Monte Verità? That was a very good time for you and now the bad time has come, but it doesn't have to stay this way, don't you see? Everything can be good again, just as it used to be."

Her voice was soothing, cajoling—almost a chant, as though she were driving out evil spirits.

Ascona, the wedding . . . Marie's head was buzzing. What did Monte Verità have to do with all this? The mountain of truth, freedom, and love . . . How dare Patrizia mention it in the same breath as the terror and suffering that . . . Marie's eyelids fluttered but the veil that clouded her vision grew thicker. If only she weren't so dizzy . . . She raised a hand to her temples to brush the dizziness away, but it was becoming harder and harder to think.

What had she done wrong? All she had wanted to do was tell Franco about her idea of inviting Sherlain and Pandora here to Genoa! To help open her gallery. And then she had heard it. *We are murderers.*

The drawstrings of the laundry bag were pulling at her hand. So heavy. Everything was so heavy . . .

Just to lie down for a moment, then . . . Suddenly a lance of pain stabbed into her skull.

Marie fainted.

◆ ◆ ◆

"What's this?" Patrizia said in a tone of disgust. She reached out and picked up the letter from the floor where Marie had dropped it.

Her husband looked thoughtfully in the direction of the bedroom where Franco had carried Marie after she fainted.

"Send it," he said absentmindedly.

"Are you sure?" The countess rarely intruded upon her husband's affairs, but they could not afford any false steps now.

"Of course I am!" he snapped. "She knew nothing of all this as she was writing it."

He took the letter from Patrizia's hand and inspected it.

"It's to her American niece, as always. Meaningless gossip, that's all." He put the letter down onto the hall table with the rest of the outgoing mail and then turned to go back to his office. "I have to prepare everything for Franco's departure. What luck that there is a ship leaving tomorrow!"

Patrizia followed him. "Are you really going to send Franco to New York? Into the lion's den?" Her voice shook.

Though her face was usually calm and composed, fear had left its mark on her. There were wrinkles at the corners of her mouth, and her lips twitched. Her eyes were wide with shock. She looked like an old woman. "Isn't that dangerous for him?"

The count shook his head. "It would be more dangerous if we do nothing. At the moment nobody can connect us to the dead men; their bodies washed up farther north along the Hudson. Franco has to make sure that it stays that way. It will cost us a great deal of money, but what can you do?" He threw up his hands in resignation.

The countess bit back a reply. Instead she asked, "And what are you going to do about Marie? Do you think she'll just calmly accept the fact that Franco has left? You've seen how foolish she can be. She's a danger to us all! What if she goes to the police? And what will she tell her family in her next letter? Do you want to let her ruin us?" Though Patrizia was whispering, her voice was shrill.

The count looked up only briefly from his pile of papers. "There will be no next letter."

◆ ◆ ◆

It was still dark outside when Marie woke up the next morning. The left side of her head was throbbing. The terrors of last night came flooding back to her, shrouding her in darkness.

Without even looking over at the other side of the bed she knew she was alone—Franco was bound to be with his father again, in the office.

Feeling drained, she was just about to sit up when she noticed something on the pillow next to her.

A letter from Franco.

Her hand trembling, she picked up the sheet of paper.

Mia cara, *by the time you read these words, I will already be on my way to New York. In the name of all those who died, I have to try to set this tragedy right, even though I wonder if this is even possible. I know that it is the worst possible moment for such a journey, but there is nothing else I can do. Please do not do anything rash while I am away—if not for my sake then for that of our child. I beg you to wait for me. I will make sure that you have everything you need while I am away.* Please stay! *Give me this one chance. If you leave me after I come back, I will not stop you. In everlasting love, Your husband Franco.*

Marie put down the note. An attempt to save what could not be saved. How could he leave her on her own, at this time of all times?

In good times and in bad . . . but how much did she still owe Franco after all this?

Pale winter sunlight streamed into the room. Marie looked outside, her gaze vacant. The palms, the laurel bushes, the neatly trimmed box trees—everything looked just as it had before. The thought that she had not even said good-bye to Franco only added to her misery.

Air! She had to get out of bed and go out for some fresh air. Perhaps that would calm the tumult in her head a little.

She walked barefoot through the workshop and tried to open the double door that led into the garden, but it was stuck. She twisted the handle and shook it hard, but the door wouldn't budge. That was odd, as the gardener had oiled the hinges and the lock at her request only last week—it used to squeak with every little puff of air.

Well then, not out into the garden. What then? Should she pack up a few things and sneak out of the house?

Perhaps Franco was still there? It was only seven o'clock after all. If she saw him again, perhaps that would help her to understand. She could tell him *why* she had to go—she owed him that much, at least. Marie rushed to put on her robe. Suddenly she was in a hurry. But when she went to open the door to the hallway, that didn't open either.

Marie frowned. Was she being especially clumsy today? She rattled in vain at the doorknob, but to no avail. This couldn't be happening!

She leaned against the door and pushed with her whole weight. Nothing happened. What could it possibly mean?

"Franco!" she shouted. "Franco, open the door!"

Panic rose inside Marie, stretching its tentacles like an unfurling octopus.

"Damn it all, what is this? Can't anybody hear me?"

Nothing happened.

Marie was a prisoner.

18

"Great God in Heaven, Wanda! I'm a glassblower, not a factory worker! You and your ideas!" Thomas Heimer's fist crashed down on the kitchen table. He shook his head, enraged. "When you said you wanted to help in the workshop, I thought you were talking about the dusting, or doing the spring cleaning when the time comes. You never mentioned that you wanted to turn the whole place upside down!"

Wanda was speechless for a moment. She pressed her lips together angrily.

"I certainly never said anything about *dusting*! Do you think Mother would ever have agreed if she knew that I were just here as your cleaning woman?" she said once she recovered a little.

Only two days before, a letter had arrived from New York, five pages long, in which Ruth had expressed in no uncertain terms her disapproval of Wanda's sudden wish to help her father. Wanda had been racking her brain over the best way to phrase a reply that would calm her mother down—although so far she had come up with nothing.

"Oh yes, the young lady's much too good to do the dirty work! Just like her dear mama, back then!" Eva spat from where she stood by the stove.

"Don't you think I'd have switched over to technical glass long ago if I had seen any point in it?" Heimer answered with forced patience. He lifted his beer glass and signaled to Eva that he wanted more.

"Reaction flasks and test tubes—what's any of that got to do with the glassblower's art?" Eva asked, slamming a new bottle of beer down on the table in front of Thomas. Then she went back to the stove and gave one of her nameless soups a stir. "Quite apart from which there are already plenty of glassblowers who earn their living that way."

"All I ever hear about is your art! But the fact is that however artistic your work may be, it doesn't put food on the table. Isn't that right? So what's the logical next step? Look for something that does earn you a crust of bread! That's all I'm trying to do, and I'd be grateful if the two of you could at least try to make an effort instead of knocking down every idea I come up with. And please, Eva, if you're not going to put a lid on that pot, then at least open the window! The steam's making me quite queasy," Wanda snapped. This whole undertaking was just getting to be too much for her!

She had quickly noticed that nobody in the Heimer household treated anyone else with kid gloves. Nobody took much trouble to be polite or consider anyone's feelings or speak a kind word. Everybody said exactly what was going through their minds— Wanda included—and said it plain. All the same she still felt a pang of frustration every time Thomas knocked down yet another of her suggestions—one or two of which were quite good ideas! Of course she was no expert on how to run a business, but she was nonetheless astonished at just how much she had learned about Lauscha and the glass industry in the last few weeks. Once she had even sat down at the lamp and tried her hand at blowing a glass, under Thomas's guidance. She hadn't done very well, however, and she remembered how much she had hated craft lessons back in New York.

Eva slammed a lid onto the pot and then slammed the door behind her. A moment later, she stuck her head back into the kitchen.

"Nobody invited you here, don't you forget that! You come here and you imagine we've just been sitting waiting for you and your daft ideas! If Wilhelm could hear you, he'd be a lot less pleased to have you in the house!"

Then the door slammed again.

Silence filled the room.

Thomas Heimer was the first to speak. "Technical glassware, glass buttons, spun glass—we can't just switch production over from one day to the next; there are specialists in all those areas. And that wild idea of yours of putting a display case on the front of the house . . . None of this is as easy as you imagine, Wanda." He spoke gently, as though ashamed of his earlier outburst.

"I never said that it would be easy, did I?" Wanda said. "But even you have to see that something must be done."

"Perhaps. Perhaps not. Good times give way to bad times and then the other way around. You have to be able to sit it out without turning the whole workshop upside down in the meantime. That's just a law of nature; it's always been that way." Heimer sighed. "But what does a city girl like you know about these things?"

"You and your laws of nature! I'd be interested to know why these laws don't affect all the glassblowers equally but only the ones who refuse to move with the times. Fashions don't come back around again all that soon once they're passed, because people have simply had enough of looking at them. I'm a city girl; I know what I'm talking about when about it comes to trends! Isn't most Lauscha glassware sold in towns? People want something new! Modern products that make life that little bit easier. Pretty new things to decorate their homes. And all those factories that are stealing work from under your nose, they're not going to disappear either!" Wanda leaned back in her chair, worn out. How many times did she have to explain it all to him? She was beginning to feel like one of her mother's phonograph records, skipping over a crack and repeating the same thing over and over again.

Neither of them said a word. Stubborn silence reigned.

They simply couldn't find any common ground. Her father refused to even consider any of her ideas. But she trudged up the hill to the Heimer house every day anyway.

The way he sat there, sulking like an overgrown schoolboy! When he did that, he had the same stubborn lines around his mouth as her grandfather when he refused to eat what Eva tried to feed him. If she came out now with her idea about the colored marbles, he would undoubtedly say that wouldn't work either.

Wanda stood up. "I'm going. I promised Richard I would say hello."

Heimer looked down into his empty beer glass.

After she left, Wanda stuck her head back into the kitchen, just like Eva had done before. "Sometimes I think you only agreed to have me come up here because you know it annoys Eva."

"You did *what?*" Richard put down the piece of glass he was working on and looked at Wanda in dismay.

"I suggested that he put a display case on the front of the house and have some of his pieces on show there. And a sign inviting people to come into the workshop to watch him work. Anybody who has never seen how glass is blown is bound to find it interesting. Something like that will bring the customers in, I'm sure of it. But he refuses to even consider the idea. *I'm not an animal in a zoo!*'

was all he said. Shouted, even." Wanda smoothed down the hair at the back of her head. Her hackles rose just at the memory!

Richard laughed. Then he beckoned her over. "Come here so I can kiss you!" he called out, still laughing.

"I'd like to know what you find so funny," Wanda answered, staying where she was. Her glance fell on the frost flowers that covered the inside of the windowpanes. How could Richard work in this cold all day long? "The shops in town would be quite lost without showcases and window displays. There has to be something to tempt people inside!"

"Well yes, but not here in the village. Wanda—we're at the back of beyond here! Don't you know what the city folk used to call us? Hillbillies with bellows!"

Wanda blinked back tears. "Now you're against me as well!"

Richard's flame flickered and died. His stool scraped across the floorboards and he walked over to Wanda. He took her hands and kissed each palm.

Wanda felt a shiver run down her spine and went weak at the knees.

"Who's going to come looking at shopwindows? You can count on two hands the number of visitors who find their way to Lauscha. We make a living from our contacts in the outside world." There was a faint note of impatience in Richard's voice.

"I know all that," Wanda grumbled. She was stung by the thought that she had made herself sound ridiculous. "And contacts are exactly what my father doesn't have. Not anymore. He's had one lousy commission these last few weeks. Fifty bowls, with stem and foot—what riches! He's stone broke and the workshop is finished, but do you think he understands that?"

She heaved a sigh.

"He's so fatalistic! How can I persuade him that he has to make things happen himself? You can do anything you want in this

PETRA DURST-BENNING

world! Though first of course you have to know *what* it is that you want . . ." Her anger died down a bit and she turned thoughtful. "I feel like a fisherman casting my rod into a murky pond without really knowing what kind of catch I'm after. Whatever I suggest to my father—he's against it. The whole thing's turning into a staring match. At least that's something we're both good at!"

She broke off abruptly.

"Why did I ever open myself up to this?" she choked out finally, weeping. *And why doesn't Richard take me in his arms in that way he has and stroke me . . .*

"Please don't take this the wrong way, but somehow I thought that you would be a bit more . . . organized about the whole thing." Richard looked at her with a faint gleam of amusement.

"I beg your pardon?" Wanda's sobbing subsided and gave way to a surge of fierce anger. "What ever made you think that I have all the answers? *You're* the one who got me into this fix in the first place!" Even though he had been so rude to her, she still desperately wanted to grab hold of him and kiss him, which only made her angrier.

He grinned. "What you said just now about being a fisherman wasn't bad, but I see it slightly differently: you're an American and you've been trained in business, so there's no doubt you'll be able to land a big fish. It's just that maybe you've been using the wrong rod. Or been casting in the wrong place. But you can change all that."

Wanda felt the fluttering in her stomach intensify. *Trained in business, my foot*—how could she have known that he would believe every word she told him!

What would Steven say to all this? The answer was obvious. He would say that Richard was right. "Without organization and strategic planning, business is just a waste of time and effort!" How often had she and Mother heard him deliver little speeches like that at the dinner table? Mostly when yet another of his competitors had gone bankrupt. Perhaps she should draw up a plan? With a list of items to work through one after another? There was something comforting about the thought.

Richard nudged up next to her on the narrow bench. "Stop worrying now. Tomorrow is another day. Everything will be all right, believe me." He kissed her on the crown of her head several times, which scattered her thoughts again.

For a few wonderful minutes Wanda surrendered to Richard's caresses, but then she broke free. She couldn't just switch off that way.

She nodded toward his bench and lamp and asked, "How do *you* make a living, in fact?"

The words puffed out and hung in the cold air as little white clouds.

Richard frowned at the sudden change of mood.

"I blow Venetian-style glass, you know that."

"That's all very well, but who buys the glasswork from you?" She knew that it wasn't appropriate to talk about business so directly—it wasn't considered ladylike, but ladylike behavior wasn't getting her anywhere.

"I've been lucky. A little while ago I got to know a gallery owner over in Weimar. Gotthilf Täuber. Rather an odd fellow. He thinks he's the only one in the world who knows anything about art, and he's not shy about saying so in the most highfalutin terms. You'll never hear him say 'I like this one, but I don't like that one.' No, he goes on about all those isms. You know, Realism, Impressionism . . ."

Wanda grinned. "Naturalism, Symbolism—oh my, you don't have to tell me about those! The New York art world juggles those terms like balls. Marie was always caught up in those conversations; she could spend hours going on about all the different schools of art. But continue: How do the two of you work together?" It could hardly be a very lucrative connection, Wanda thought, or Richard wouldn't be scrambling for every little commission that Johanna gave him. If it made him any real money, surely he'd be able to afford enough firewood to heat the place at least for an hour or two a day . . .

"Well, he buys one or two things off me every now and again—and he pays well too. Either he comes to Lauscha or I go to Weimar if I have something special to show him. The last time I visited he even gave me a present, the catalog of an exhibition in Venice. Have a look at that!" Richard snatched the catalog off a shelf and held it up in the air like a trophy.

Biennale, Wanda read on the binding. It was old and shabby by now but still impressive.

"Täuber says he'd like to help me make my way as an artist. If I manage to find my own way of using Venetian techniques, he says there's a good chance he can give me a solo exhibition. In his gallery, do you understand? All my own work!" His voice glowed with passion as he spoke. He jumped up and picked up a glass from his bench. "He said that people are crazy for the Italian style. Look, this is one I've just finished. The Italians call this technique *aurato*. We take gold leaf and apply it to the hot bubble of glass. The gold doesn't expand along with the glass as we keep blowing, so it rips and tears as it goes. That's the effect we're after. Not bad, is it?"

"It's splendid!" Wanda took the glass reverently by its stem and turned it in the light. The flecks of gold glittered strangely as though thousands of tiny sunbeams were shooting up from the stem into the sides of the glass.

Richard took the glass away and handed her a tall goblet. "What do you think of that?"

It was of transparent glass, blown very thin. Streaks of colored glass covered the entire surface, creating the effect of a delicate net. Every shade of blue was there, fading into purple, and light green alternating with darker shades, all of it shot through with pink.

"I've never seen anything like this, not even at the New York exhibition I told you about," Wanda said, shaking her head. She had known right from the start that Richard knew his craft. The glasses that he had shown her the first time she came to visit were something special in their own right. But the pieces standing on the table in front of her now were of an entirely different caliber. She looked lovingly at Richard. He was an artist! She told him as much.

Pride shone in his eyes. "This technique's called *pennelate*, and the glass has to be hot for this as well. We make these delicate streaks by drawing a rod of colored glass over the surface very gently." Richard's face darkened suddenly. "I'm happy enough with what I can do with hot glass now. But I just can't make any headway with the cold-work techniques. It's not just that I don't have the right tools. Täuber tells me that etching is the next big thing and that I have to find someone who knows his way around chemistry. He said he'd help me there—in fact he's already written to a gallery owner he knows in Venice. We'll see what comes of that . . ."

Wanda nodded. This man Täuber seemed to be serious about Richard's future. She picked up the gleaming golden glass once more. "When I think of Heimer's glasses and the leaping deer he puts on everything . . ."

"Don't underestimate your father's handiwork! I may be the only one in the village who knows that gold-leaf technique, but I've already found some of our own techniques in the Venetian glasses Gotthilf Täuber has shown me. Cameo work, threadwork, cut glass—we've been doing all that for centuries. Murano glass is all very beautiful, but most of it is done in some kind of neo-this or neo-that technique. It's an old hat with a new ribbon, so to speak. It took me a while to realize that, but it convinced me that you can make something very special, something unique, by mixing old and new." Richard's eyes gleamed. "And I'm also convinced that a fellow can make money that way."

Wanda had to laugh at his enthusiasm. "Then at least one of us has something to believe in!" she said dryly, then kissed him passionately on the lips.

Although it was already after eight o'clock by the time Wanda finally said a fond good-bye to Richard, she could see the gas flames still flickering in the Steinmann-Maienbaum workshop as she approached. Indeed, that morning Johanna had announced there would be a great deal to do that day. Wanda was thankful that the house was so quiet as it gave her a chance to think. All the same the first thing she did was look in the kitchen to see whether she could lend a hand there. When she saw that there was a pot of soup simmering away on the stove and that the bread had already been sliced, she sat down at the kitchen table and opened the drawer. She took out the notepad that Johanna always used for her various lists, then, with a smile on her face, she picked up a pencil and began to write:

Business Plan for the Heimer Workshop

She looked at the title and nodded. That was the way to do it! The next few sentences almost seemed to write themselves.

1. *What can we do to get more commissions?*
   - *Find out what the wholesalers in Sonneberg are after, as Marie suggested in letter. Visit to Sonneberg urgently needed!*
   - *Perhaps find new clients in other nearby towns? For example Coburg, Meiningen, Suhl, Bayreuth, and Kulmbach? Discuss idea with Richard.*

> - *List techniques Father knows. Sit down with him and talk about whether he can make something new from old skills the way Richard has.*

With every item she added to the list, Wanda's confidence grew. "*Somehow I thought that you would be a bit more . . . organized about the whole thing*"—Richard's rebuke had somehow given her new energy. She may not have trained as a bookkeeper or gone to secretarial college or learned any of the other skills needed in the business world, but she had grown up in a business household. She had ingested business thinking with her mother's milk, so to speak. She only needed to remember that day when Pandora had sat in the courtyard of her tenement block surrounded by all her worldly goods—hadn't she come up with a plan on the spot? She had smoothed things over with Pandora's surly landlord and arranged a dance performance in her mother's house. *You can do anything you want in this world!*—her own words came back to her.

Everything was suddenly clear as day: she would not be able to fix this mess on her own. She needed people on her side. Her pencil flew across the coarse paper.

> 2. *Who can help me get all this done?*
>   - *What can Michel do? Write lists and letters? I have to talk to him right away.*
>   - *What can Eva do? How can I win her over so that she helps too?*
>   - *I have to try to get Grandfather on my side here.*

The next thought struck her like a bolt of lightning. She wrote:

> - *Richard! Is there any way he and Father could work together?*

Richard was always complaining about not having enough equipment in his workshop after all—if he joined forces with her father, he could use all the Heimer family tools. Wanda was practically overjoyed at the thought. This was the argument she could use to lure Thomas Heimer in. Why had she never thought of it before? Her father would no longer be the only glassblower in the house, and there would be two of them to tackle every task. The wholesalers would certainly see greater production capacity as an advantage, and they might place more orders for that reason alone. New scenes formed in her mind's eye, so wonderful, so promising that she was almost a little scared. Richard and Thomas blowing glass, Eva and Michel packing the wares, herself with a notepad in hand making sure every order went to the right client—the Heimer workshop bustling with life just as it had back in the day, just as Marie had described. Hope—more than hope, confidence—flared up in Wanda like the flame of a gas lamp.

When her family came into the kitchen, tired and hungry, an hour later, she had written down four pages of ideas. Wanda felt happier than she had for a long time—this despite the fact that Anna was looking daggers at her again. She knew exactly what she had to do in the next few days.

19

"This has to be the dumbest idea I have ever let anyone talk me into!" Eva muttered from the depths of the scarf she had wound round and round her head against the cold. "Walking to Sonneberg! In the middle of winter! Not even the gypsies do that; they've got the good sense to sit up on the wagons and let the horses pull them."

Eva jerked her chin toward the little caravan of shabby-looking wagons that was just passing them. Then she kicked at a shaggy dog that was trotting alongside the carts.

"Can't you see how dangerous it is to be out and about on foot these days? There are even wild beasts roaming the roads."

Wanda frowned. "Oh, really, Eva. The poor dog wasn't doing anything to you!"

"Only because I defended myself!"

"Do stop grumbling," Wanda said, summoning unsuspected reserves of patience. "You know quite well why I wanted to go on foot. This landscape might not be anything special for you, but do try to remember that until now I've lived all my life in the city! This is the first time I get to see winter this way." She swept her hand around to point at the steep mountainside with the fir and pine trees all covered in snow. Then she stopped for a moment as if to take a closer look at the landscape. Even though they were walking along the main road where the wagons had already flattened the snow for them, the walk was tougher than she had expected. The sweat was running down her arms and trickling between her breasts too. Wanda had wanted to look as grown-up and capable as she could, so she had gone to her suitcases out in the warehouse and gotten out a black jacket with fur trim on the collar and sleeves. If she had known that the sun would be so strong when they were out from the shadows of the trees, she would certainly have chosen something lighter. "Besides, I want to know how my mother felt back then, when she set off to Sonneberg with Marie's baubles to find Mr. Woolworth."

Eva hopped from one leg to another. "What nonsense! If I remember right it was the height of summer. If Ruth was feeling anything, it was sunburn! And unlike her we don't have any baskets full of wares on our backs. We're empty-handed—we look like beggars! Just so that we get one thing clear—I'll show you where the wholesalers are, but I'm not coming in with you. I'd rather stand outside and freeze to death than grovel to one of those cutthroats."

Wanda sighed and walked on. She was beginning to think it hadn't been such a good idea to insist that Eva come with her.

"You know all the wholesalers in Sonneberg; you would be a great help to me," she had wheedled, and when Eva hadn't agreed immediately, she mentioned the idea to Wilhelm, adding, "If two of us go in, it makes a much better impression than I would all on my own, given how young I am!"

When Wilhelm ordered Eva to go, Wanda congratulated herself on a masterstroke; for one thing she had shown Wilhelm how much she valued his opinion, and for another she had gotten Eva on her side . . .

For a moment they walked along in silence, each deep in thought.

Thomas and Wilhelm Heimer had both approved of the idea that Wanda should call on the wholesalers to find out what kind of glassware was in demand—and Wanda had thought it best not to mention that the idea had originally been Marie's.

Marie . . . Wanda found her thoughts wandering. She wondered whether her aunt liked the baby things that she and Johanna had packed and sent to Genoa the day after the letter had arrived. They had made a special trip into Sonneberg to buy the presents, even though Johanna was working hard to meet a big order. They had chosen the very finest the shops had to offer: a baby gown of Plauen lace, a silver teething ring, and a rattle of snow-white horn. Wanda had thought that Marie would write back as soon as the package arrived.

Wanda forced herself to think about her business plan instead and about why she was going into Sonneberg. Item one, item two, she counted them silently in time with her steps.

Thankfully, she could tick off another item on her list: she had talked to Michel.

She had to pluck up her nerve before going to visit her uncle in his stuffy little room—she always felt so sorry for his disability that she could hardly say a word. First she had beaten around the bush and asked him how he was feeling. She listened to a litany of aches and pains before she finally interrupted.

"Yes indeed, losing a leg is a dreadful thing to happen to anyone. And the pain you describe must be awful," she said. "But all the same you're going to have to pull yourself together. I need your help!" She didn't feel anywhere near as confident as she sounded. *How can this poor man help me, really?* she thought as she kept her eyes fixed on Michel. It didn't help that he was so startled by the whole situation that he suddenly felt the call of nature and shouted for Eva to bring the chamber pot—Wanda had to rush out of the room. How embarrassing! She was so taken aback that she went down to the kitchen, where Eva was waiting for her with a face like thunder.

Wanda was still trying to decide whether to go back into Michel's room when they heard a dragging, thumping footstep in the hall. When Michel appeared in the kitchen doorway a little while later, leaning on two crutches, neither she nor Eva could quite believe their eyes. Eva was just about to make some remark—most probably a pointed one—when Wanda glanced at her imploringly and managed to stop her from speaking.

His arms trembling, Michel clumsily sat down across the table from Wanda. His voice trembled too as he asked her how a cripple like him could help. Just then, of course, Thomas chose to come clomping upstairs from his workshop. When he saw his brother, the first thing he did was take the schnapps bottle from the cupboard. A moment later all four of them raised a glass and drank a toast together. It burned Wanda's throat terribly on the way down but it gave her a warm glow in her belly, and she told Michel that he could help her by making a 'skills inventory.' As she had expected, the others were most impressed by the high-sounding phrase. Wanda seized the moment and told Michel she needed a list of all of Thomas's glasswork techniques. They should also dig out all the sample pieces that had been made in the workshop over the decades, whatever was gathering dust in a drawer or a cupboard somewhere—taking stock, so to speak. When Eva offered to do that part herself because she knew where everything was, Wanda's heart leapt. A first success!

Before her father could come out with one of his pessimistic remarks and nip this new hope in the bud, Wanda told them what Richard had said about the Lauscha techniques being just as good as anything they knew how to do in Venice. If they wanted to make new items, the very best thing they could do was to use their old techniques. Even as she spoke, Eva slipped out of the kitchen and then came back with the first few pieces. A goblet of frosted glass painted in enamel, dated 1900. A deep bowl of clear glass laced with colorful threadwork, from the same year. A much older bowl with great thick knobs on the surface like the warts on a toad.

Wanda didn't like every piece she saw, but she did her best to seem delighted by all of them. Her enthusiasm was infectious: suddenly Thomas remembered some pieces he had made years ago for a hotel over in Suhl. He ran down to the workshop and came back a few minutes later with an elaborate table decoration made up of several smaller parts—a pair of kneeling angels supporting a fruit bowl on their heads and the tips of their wings. And this time Wanda truly was impressed; she said that it was glasswork of the first order, admired the detail in the feathers and the robes, and the two brothers beamed with pride. Suddenly each of them wanted to outdo the other, and Eva and Thomas scurried from the kitchen and back again repeatedly, bringing a new treasure each time until the kitchen table was covered with glassware of every kind. Wanda was so happy she could have cried.

"If only I knew where those perfume bottles are that we made for the Frenchman that time!" Thomas muttered, and then told Wanda that her mother had liked them very much.

That evening Wanda was so late getting back home that Johanna had told her off mercilessly, threatening to complain to Ruth in New York. "We're not running a hotel here where you can come and go as you please," she scolded. Wanda looked into her aunt's eyes and saw how tired she was from sitting up waiting for her, and she felt a hot flush of guilt. She resolved never to be so inconsiderate again.

All the same the evening at her father's house had been worth Johanna's complaints. For the first time in ages, there was a sense of purpose in the Heimer household, and even old Wilhelm had done his bit. "You'd do well to listen to your daughter now and again," he told Thomas between two coughing fits. "The girl's got the sharp wits all we Heimers have, and she's got Ruth's nose for a deal as well! She's a godsend to us, and we're lucky to have her back here with us!" Wanda had been out in the hallway, buttoning up her jacket, so she hadn't caught whatever her father had said in reply.

She'd done the right thing, she decided now, not to spoil the family atmosphere by bringing up the idea of working together with Richard. As she and Eva turned a corner on the road, Wanda saw houses around the next bend. They had gotten as far as Steinach, thank goodness!

"Maybe we could take the railway the rest of the way after all." Even the thought of somewhere warm to sit put a spring in Wanda's step, although her knees were trembling.

Eva laughed briefly. "Go all that extra way to the station now, and then have to wait for the next train to come along? No, I don't fancy that at all." She put her head down and plodded on past Wanda. "Let's keep going, quick as we can. I don't want to run into any of my brothers and sisters and have to tell them why we're on foot. They'll decide right away that we don't even have the money for a train ticket these days." She drew her scarf farther up around her ears.

Wanda had no choice but to follow Eva. She didn't say a word, but she took the opportunity to peer around at the village where Eva had been born. Several dozen houses were all jostled up together in a narrow valley. The roofs were tiled with slate, and slate was visible everywhere else as well, in every shade of light and dark, glittering silver gray on the house walls in the sunlight.

"How beautiful," Wanda said, pointing to a house with a particularly lovely mosaic pattern of tiles on the front. Then she saw a head pop up in one of the windows and she looked away quickly. Only a few yards on, though, she exclaimed again: there on a house wall was a spray of flowers framed by a pattern of diamond shapes.

The natural colors of the slate had been used so cleverly that the whole design looked almost three-dimensional.

"It all looks so . . . cozy and cheerful!" It seemed that the villagers of Lauscha were not the only people with a gift for the decorative arts. Wanda resolved to visit Steinach with Richard once the snows had melted.

They had hardly passed the last few houses in the village when Eva straightened up. *"Cozy and cheerful!"* she spat, imitating Wanda. She tore the scarf from her head. "The only reason you think so is because you've never been cold or hungry in your life! Believe you me, if you'd had the childhood I had . . ." She clamped her mouth shut and looked grimmer than ever.

Wanda felt dreadfully naive. She linked arms with Eva, who stiffened and left Wanda in no doubt that the gesture was unwelcome, though she pretended she hadn't noticed. Eva's scarf was about to slip off her shoulders and Wanda put it back in place with her free hand.

"Why don't you tell me how it was back then?" she asked gently.

"So that you can have a good laugh at me?" Eva glanced at her mistrustfully.

"I won't, I swear it!"

But Eva simply pursed her lips even tighter and they walked on in silence.

A few minutes later, when Wanda had already given up on the conversation, Eva began to talk. She told Wanda about being one of eight children and about her father, who worked in the slate mine like most men in the village. She talked about the thousands of slate pencils that they made and packed into boxes in their little house, week in and week out. "Day after day and late into every night. We were hardly home from school before it was time to sit down at the table and work. Oh, how my back ached, even after just a couple of hours of sitting there! But Father never listened to our complaints;

he just cursed if any of us dared to start crying from the pain. Even today I get the shivers whenever I hear a grinding wheel whir!" She shook herself. "There was slate dust everywhere—in our hair, on our skin, in the rags we wore instead of clothes. Everything was so horribly dirty! And it was no good at all for our health!" In a flat tone, Eva told Wanda about her brothers and sisters who had died because the dust had settled into their lungs, tearing them to shreds. "'*For every one born, there's one who dies*'—that's what my mother used to say. But our house was always full of children, and I was the one who had to look after them, wiping their little butts." Eva laughed harshly. "Then when I got married, I never had even one child of my own."

Not knowing what to say, Wanda kept silent. Marie had already told her how much Eva had suffered from not having children of her own.

"All the same—I wouldn't want to swap places with any of my sisters. I was lucky Sebastian came my way!" Eva grinned wryly. "Love is blind; you say that in America too, don't you?"

Wanda nodded so emphatically that both of them burst out laughing.

20

By the time they got to Sonneberg, Wanda was so exhausted that she insisted they stop at one of the taverns first thing. She ordered a grilled sausage and Eva persuaded her to have a beer with it, then they discussed their plans: Eva would begin by taking her to the wholesalers who had dealt with the Heimers in the past. Then, if Wanda wanted to meet with some more, Eva would take her to others. Even though they had gotten a little closer during the walk, Eva could still not be persuaded to go in with Wanda on her visits. So Wanda put on fresh lipstick, squared her shoulders, and set off to be of some help to her family.

It took a while before she found anyone who seemed likely to help.

"Of course I am aware that I am almost the only one left who thinks so—in an age where the slogan of 'Art for All' seems to be on everyone's lips. And they make money with it too . . ." Karl-Heinz Brauninger folded his hands and stretched his arms out as though he felt a twinge of rheumatism. "All the same I am not ready to jump on the bandwagon of mass production just so that anyone can fill his living room with all sorts of ornaments that will simply gather dust! Others are quite welcome to sell figurines of ladies dancing—I will have no such gewgaws in my catalog!" His expression indicated his distaste.

"So what do you have in your samples books?" Wanda asked curiously.

"Samples books—now there is another symptom of the mass-production mania. Believe me, if I showed any such thing to my clients, they would jump like a scalded cat! My wares are all one of a kind. They are poems in glass; they are delicate and fragile works, and each one reflects the feelings of the artist who made it. Every glass is a cornucopia of inspiration; every bowl is an expression of humanity's infinite creative potential and boundless soul! These pieces are the very essence of one moment in the artist's life—and who can ever repeat such a moment?"

Wanda heaved a sigh of genuine agreement. "You have no idea how pleased I am to hear you say so. So far my market survey has only turned up wholesalers who want cheap wares at rock-bottom prices—which is exactly what we wish to set ourselves apart from, in our workshop."

Wanda treated Brauninger to one of the smiles that had always gotten her another drink in Mickey's bar in Brooklyn no matter how deep the crowds. She sat forward on her chair and spoke to him in hushed tones.

"Do you know what I simply don't understand? That these wholesalers put on airs and proclaim that their products are the very peak of the modern artistic style! When really, let's be honest, they're just production-line goods, aren't they?" Wanda watched for the gleam of agreement in the man's eyes and congratulated herself silently as it appeared. Perhaps she'd come to the right place?

If Eva had had any say in the matter, Wanda wouldn't even be visiting Brauninger; the Heimers had never dealt with him directly, though they had done some work for his father years ago. After that, there hadn't been any more commissions. "The old man was an arrogant pig, and his son won't be any better!" Eva had said. But Wanda hadn't budged from her plan—she didn't want to go back home feeling that she had left even a single stone unturned. And it seemed her stubbornness had not been entirely in vain.

"Their dishonesty is precisely what I hate so much, my dear young lady!" Brauninger replied. "They call themselves revolutionaries, friends of the proletariat, and they take money from the poor worker's pocket for gimcrack that has no real value! Whereas I come straight out and say that I sell art, and that not everyone will be able to afford it."

Where many people would have been put off by such arrogance, Wanda felt that this was her chance . . . now she just had to take it!

She cocked her head and said, "Did you know that such a forthright approach is a very American way of doing business? I mean that as a compliment," she added hastily.

"Well now, I can't really be the judge of that, but if you say so, young lady, then . . ." He was blushing! Although Wanda hadn't asked for it, he poured some water into a tall, elegant glass for her.

Wanda batted her eyelids demurely and thanked him. As she did, thoughts raced around in her head. Karl-Heinz Brauninger's dislike of mass production could be just the chance she was looking for. The only question was how to start doing business with him. Wanda took a sip of water.

She need not have worried so much—her elegant outfit and the fact that she was from America had ensured that wherever she went, she was welcomed most civilly and politely. She had always made quite sure to say that she was not there to represent Miles Enterprises, rather she was inquiring on behalf of a new and very modern glass workshop that was just setting up in Lauscha. The wholesalers offered her a seat and listened to what she had to say about a market survey to find out what the customers wanted these days. However what they told her was anything but encouraging. Most of the wholesalers got their goods from factories, and the rest already had plenty of pieceworkers under contract.

"Is it fair to assume that most of your clients are galleries?" Wanda asked once she had drunk half the water.

"It's true that I have a handful of gallery owners who buy from me, but even they seem to pay more attention to price than to originality or quality these days." Brauninger waved his hand. "I do most of my business at the large art fairs. I know that my esteemed colleagues here in town find that rather ludicrous; they think that I am nothing more than a common salesman. But what do they know? Paris, Madrid, Oslo—there are art lovers all over the world who are ready to pay money for luxury goods. Indian maharajas, opera singers, bankers: the crème de la crème buy from me, and—" Brauninger broke off as he suddenly realized that he had said a great deal more than he intended.

Wanda swallowed. Maharajas and opera singers—she could hardly imagine that they would want Heimer's warty glass bowls, or the goblets with pictures of deer . . .

"My dear Mr. Brauninger, you have not merely impressed me; I might almost say you have dismayed me," she confessed with a disarming smile. "The workshop I represent in my market survey has some artistic items to offer, it's true, but . . ." She paused for effect. "If you will allow me an indiscreet question: Who do you buy from? Or to ask a little less directly, do you have any glassblowers from Lauscha among your suppliers?"

"You will understand of course that I cannot name names," Brauninger said in a rush, as though regretting having given away so much already. "But, yes there are one or two Lauscha glassblowers who work for me. Our working relationship, however, is . . . how shall I put this . . . difficult."

Wanda frowned. "Are they not able to meet your high standards?"

"Quite the opposite. They really know their glass up there!" He nodded vaguely in the direction of Lauscha. "But they're such a tight-lipped crowd! Whenever I ask them what they were thinking of as they made this or that piece, it's like pulling teeth! Just recently one of them brought me a set of four bowls in blue glass. Excellent work, that goes without saying! I realized immediately that if I nest the four bowls one inside the other, the whole assembly looks like a forget-me-not flower. The viewer is drawn into the blossom the way a bee is drawn to nectar. The effect is all the more powerful because the bottoms of the bowls are a pale yellow."

Wanda nodded, delighted. "I can just see it! An allegory, a description in glass of how we were tempted in Eden!" *Monique Desmoines and all those well-heeled customers at Dittmer's would be blown away by the idea,* she thought mischievously. She would never have imagined that she would have cause to be grateful to New York's high society.

Brauninger nodded, impressed. "A splendid comparison, dear lady! What do you imagine the artist told me when I asked what had been his inspiration as he worked? He told me that it was very practical to be able to stack the bowls one inside the other so that they took up less room in the cupboard!"

Wanda had to laugh. Her father could quite easily have said that very thing!

Brauninger joined in her laughter. Then he said, "How much more sensuous the French artists are! They understand the emotions so well! Perhaps you know the name Émile Gallé?"

Wanda nodded. "My mother admires the French glassworkers enormously. Being a New Yorker, she likes Tiffany as well, of course," she added, to show him again that she knew a thing or two about art. "And what opinion do you have of Venetian glasswork?" she asked as innocently as she could manage.

Brauninger smirked. "I know that the whole world raves about Murano, but to be perfectly honest the work they do there is a little . . . insincere for my tastes." He flapped his hand dismissively.

Wanda nodded wisely. "The backward-looking style, I know." She waved her hand as well, as though to suggest that she had considered the question of Murano glass closely and come to precisely the same conclusion.

Brauninger cleared his throat. "I do not wish to be impolite, my dear lady . . . But sadly I have an appointment in a few minutes." He blinked in embarrassment. "And though I have found our conversation most pleasant, I am not really sure how I can help you."

Wanda gathered her skirts. "You have already helped me far more than you will ever know, my dear Mr. Brauninger," she said as she rose to her feet. Then she opened her eyes a fraction wider and said, "Now that I know there are still connoisseur dealers such as yourself, I am all the more determined to make Lauscha glass a byword for the most refined achievements of the glassblower's art. You might easily say that you have restored my faith in mankind!"

Brauninger frowned, and she realized that she had gone a bit too far. She did her best to look businesslike. She put out her hand and took a deep breath.

"If it should happen that in the next few weeks or months I am shown a piece of glass that I feel might satisfy your high standards— may I bring it to show you?"

Karl-Heinz Brauninger beamed. "Anytime, dear lady, anytime! I am already looking forward to our first transaction."

Dusk was falling by the time Wanda went back out onto the street. The snow was glittering in the twilight—a sure sign that it would be another ice-cold night.

"There you are at last! I was beginning to think you'd decided to spend the night in there!" Eva's shadow detached itself from a doorway across the street. "If we don't hurry, we'll miss the last train back to Lauscha!"

"I'm sorry. I never even noticed the time passing," Wanda answered guiltily as they hurried off to the railway station.

Eva peered over at her. "You've got such a look on your face . . . Was it worth my freezing my backside off out there? Go on, tell me, do we have a contract?" Eva's eyes shone as if she were a young girl again.

Wanda put her arm through hers and this time met no resistance. "Not yet, but I've got something much more valuable, and it's going to change our whole future!"

The light in Eva's eyes died away. Wanda was twinkling like a Christmas tree, however. She stopped and turned to face Eva. Wanda was shivering from head to toe—she wasn't sure whether from the cold or excitement.

"These days it isn't enough just to make beautiful glass. There are too many people doing exactly that. If you want to be a success, you have to do something else as well."

"And what may that be, if you please?" Eva's face was blue with cold and deeply skeptical.

Wanda shut her eyes and enjoyed the moment. When she spoke, the words melted like cotton candy on her tongue. "The real art is in selling stories!"

21

The first few days were the worst. The hole that had opened up in Marie's life gaped so wide that she didn't know how she would ever be able to close it again.

Franco was in America, and she was a prisoner in the house. It was all very simple, but even after several weeks had passed, her mind simply refused to accept the facts. So most of the time she thought of nothing at all. That was the only way she could bear it all. The silence. The loneliness. The confinement. The dagger in her heart.

Marie stood at the glass door, leaning her forehead against the glass. The door was still firmly bolted. A gentle breeze ruffled the blossoms on the almond trees, and the petals drifted down like pink snow, scattering across the garden and the paths. That was the only thing that told her that spring had come—that, and the height of the sun in the sky. The seasons flowed together in Patrizia's garden like dabs of watercolor paint on damp paper.

Lauscha was still firmly in the grip of winter, she was sure— the thought was there before Marie had a chance to chase it away. Perhaps the villagers could occasionally hear the birds of spring and draw strength from their song, but otherwise every day would be spent just as all the days had been for months now: shoveling snow, scattering ashes on the icy paths, and waiting. And waiting.

A hot tear ran down Marie's face and splashed on the floor.

Snow. Would she ever feel the crunch of frozen snow under her feet again?

She rubbed at her face so vigorously that it hurt. She mustn't cry. She mustn't startle the child. She had to hold on; it couldn't last much longer now. She was expecting Franco back any day now. And then . . .

Then she wouldn't stay here a minute longer!

She had made her decision. It was her lifeline, leading her to what came next: she would leave Franco and take her child with her.

No more discussion, no more asking why. There could be no answer to that. And no more feelings for Franco. Whatever she still felt for him was banished to the furthest corner of her mind, and she had forbidden herself to look there. Didn't they say that time heals all wounds?

It no longer even mattered to her whether he knew that they were keeping her under lock and key like a criminal. Maybe he had no idea. She had read his farewell note a thousand times, weighing every word. *I beg you to wait for me*—he wouldn't have written that if he knew she was to be a prisoner, would he? *I will make sure that you have everything you need while I am away*—then again, perhaps he did know. Patrizia told her nothing at all. Whenever Marie asked anything, she always received the same answer. "Franco is in America, and you are here." Somehow Marie had come to accept it. Just as she had accepted that there was no chance of escape. There was no need for bars on this prison; all it needed was locked doors, locked windows, and prying eyes and ears everywhere.

"Soon it will be over, soon, soon . . ." she prayed over and over. If only Patrizia would tell her which ship Franco would be coming back on . . .

Her hand drifted down to her swollen belly. If it weren't for the child in her womb, she would have gone mad long ago. The baby was the only reason Marie could stand the passing of time, even when the days crept by as slowly as a snail through dry grass, leaving nothing in their wake but a trail of dull slime.

"Soon it will be over, soon, soon . . ." Marie turned away from the glass door and sat down at the dainty little desk that hardly had room for a single sheet of paper.

She had begun to write in a little notebook. That helped too. Eventually, she would give her child this diary to read. At first she had found it painful to write. It had been hard to look back and remember the young girl who had begun to blow glass in the dead of night. But that was when her story really began, after all. So Marie began the diary back then.

It hurt to have nobody here to talk to, nobody who could help her remember times past. How she and her sisters had built up the workshop together. And then her great journey to New York. Seeing Ruth again, so elegant, so different but still a sister whom she adored. Then the grand new feelings when she met Franco! The memories were mingled with pain, with the knowledge that she was now more alone that she had ever been—but the pain told Marie that even here in prison she had not lost her ability to feel.

Once all the old stories were in the pages of the notebook, Marie slowed down a little. It was enough to write a line or two every day for her unborn child. She didn't write about how she was, how she felt. Her child must never learn how unhappy she had been during the pregnancy. Instead she wrote about the new beginning that they would make together as soon as Franco was back, once he had let her out of this prison.

She and her child. A new beginning, like a sheet of blank paper. She didn't know where yet. Perhaps she would settle on Monte

Verità for a while. And then? It didn't matter . . . as long as it was away from here.

Marie sighed and hid the book under her bedstead again. Then she looked at the pendant watch that hung around her neck. Four o'clock in the afternoon.

She went into the workshop. Just that morning the glowing colors of her work had granted her a few hours of blessed relief from prison. She felt better when her head was filled with colorful images. The mosaic pictures that she had made over the past few weeks were propped up all around the walls—bizarre, almost abstract compositions that not even Marie herself could explain. It was as though the pictures had created themselves. Now she ran her fingers through the bowls where she kept the pieces of colored glass and felt nothing. Just so that she had something to do, she began to arrange pieces of glass in various shades of green, putting them together to make leaves.

These afternoon hours were the worst. When her strength from the morning had left her but she had not yet grown tired with the approach of night. As the weeks had gone by, something like a routine had developed, a semblance of normality that lent shape to her days. She got up around nine o'clock when Carla came in with breakfast—it was always Carla, never one of the other maids. Two slices of white bread, butter, honey and some fruit. Then Marie washed. Carla took the pitcher and basin away along with the breakfast tray around ten o'clock. Marie had been very pleased to discover on her arrival that there were five toilets with running water scattered throughout the palazzo, but now Patrizia wouldn't even let her leave her room to use the toilet. "It's not good for you to walk so far," she said primly. "You have to save your strength for the *bambino*." What hypocrisy!

Marie spent the rest of the morning in her workshop until the door opened again around one o'clock. Sometimes Patrizia brought lunch and stayed for a few minutes. Marie was so lonely that she began to look forward to these moments despite the hatred she felt—after all, Patrizia was her only connection to the outside world. Most of the time it was Carla who brought lunch, though, and she simply stared at Marie as though she were scared of her. Marie had no idea what Patrizia had told the girl—probably that their guest had some infectious disease. Or that she was mad. More likely that, since Carla never responded when Marie begged desperately for help. She just flinched and turned away.

After she ate, she took a nap. How she would have loved to lie down on the wicker chaise longue in the orangery! To smell the scents, to hear the palm leaves rustling around her as they waved in the breeze from the open panes in the roof . . . But Patrizia ignored all her pleas and refused to open the door to the orangery—she was probably afraid that Marie would smash one of the windows and run as fast as her legs would carry her! She would certainly have tried. The panes weren't as thick in the conservatory as they were in her room or in the workshop, and there were no bars. She would have run like the wind. Away from this prison.

In the first few days she had thought of nothing but escape. Once she had shoved Carla aside, lunch tray and all, and run to the front door of the palazzo as fast as she could—only to discover that this too was locked tight. She had collapsed in floods of tears. How humiliating it had been when Patrizia and the count had led her back to her room like a criminal! Patrizia had cried as they went, acting as though Marie had devised some dreadful insult for her.

She could have simply stopped living, refused to eat even a bite—but for the child in her womb.

Fetch help from outside? No such hope. Whenever the gardeners came past the window, Marie hammered like a madwoman on the glass and tried to show them that she was being held against her will, but not a single one of them reacted. What had Patrizia told them?

Marie swept her hand across her workbench in a rage. Hundreds of tiny pieces of glass flew off the worktop and scattered over the floor like colorful raindrops. They lay there, almost mocking her, beautiful and utterly indifferent to her plight. Marie screamed in pain. For as long as she could remember, glass had been the only material she wanted to work with. Glass revealed even the smallest mistake; glass showed every weakness in the maker's hand—which was precisely what she found so fascinating. It was a sensitive material. More than once it had driven her into a fury and then brought her back to her senses; it had taught her patience and humility and then urged her on to new heights of ambition. Marie would never have imagined that glass would one day become her enemy.

At five o'clock sharp the key turned in the lock. Marie was sitting on the bed. She noticed with astonishment that Patrizia had brought the tray today, with a cup of mocha coffee and a slice of cake. She certainly hadn't been expecting *her*, though at lunchtime she had begged her mother-in-law to call a doctor for her backache.

"I swear to you I won't tell him anything!" she had pleaded, and she had meant every word. Where was she going to run to with her huge belly? If she hadn't been pregnant, she would have spent all day every day looking for a chance to escape, but she had to think of her unborn child. So she had said, "It worries me that I'm in such pain! What if there's something wrong . . ." But the discussion ended as it always did, with Patrizia leaving the room, her back ramrod straight and her lips pursed. She usually punished Marie for such outbursts by not coming to see her for a few days.

Perhaps she had found out that it was Marie's birthday?

Without looking at Marie, Patrizia put down the tray on the little table by the bed. Her hands were trembling, and her eyes were rimmed with red as though she had been crying.

"Can you ask Carla to heat some water for the bath?" Marie asked, pointing toward the tub that Patrizia had had brought into her room on the first day. "Perhaps the warm water will do my back some good," she added.

Patrizia nodded wordlessly. She was already halfway out the door when she turned around and stopped where she was. Then she cleared her throat, almost inaudibly.

"What is it? Have you heard from Franco at last?" The spark of hope leapt up before Marie could smother it. They had been waiting for weeks for him to call.

Patrizia shook her head. "There's been a problem in New York . . ." Her haughty expression crumbled and she whimpered. Quickly she put a hand to her mouth.

Marie felt as though she had been punched in the gut. She leapt to her feet. "And? Tell me!"

"One of the customs agents who knew what was going on has talked." Patrizia's lower lip quivered. "They've arrested Franco."

22

The thaw set in from one day to the next. First the snow in the streets melted, then it slipped down off the rooftops, then the trees on the mountain slopes all around began to show their branches. By the end of March the landscape was shaggy and patchy like a dog shedding his winter coat, and Wanda had to get used to seeing colors other than white. Rivulets and streams ran down the slopes wherever she looked; the meadows down in the valley became quagmires, and the water in the streets pooled into great puddles. It was no easier to walk the streets than it had been when the snow was knee-deep. Everyone got wet feet one way or another, but they never complained as they went about their business—rather they seemed to welcome the melt. After all, it meant that the landscape was finally struggling free from its cocoon of snow and that spring was near.

Though Wanda's head was brimming over with plans and ideas, she noticed that everyone around her was growing restless. Suddenly everybody was on the move: a neighbor set off for Neuhaus to fetch two piglets from his brother-in-law. Anna and Johannes were planning a trip to Coburg—without asking Wanda if she wanted to come along. Lugiana, the Italian maid, sang Roman songs from morning till night and cast longing glances at Magnus, who didn't notice a thing.

Wanda felt the same restless urges—among other symptoms, she wanted to kiss Richard whenever the chance arose. She was more than a little scared by the strength of her physical desire for him, and she was glad that Richard kept a cool head when it seemed she might lose control of herself.

Lauscha woke up from hibernation with regard to business matters too. A great many more wagons were slipping through the last of the snow now than in months gone by, and visitors were seen among the old familiar faces. Richard's patron, the gallery owner Gotthilf Täuber, came to visit and bought everything Richard had made. After that Richard grew even more dedicated to his work than before; whenever Wanda came by his workshop, he was either hard at work on a piece or studying the most recent catalog that Täuber had brought.

There was a new sense of purpose in the Steinmann-Maienbaum house as well: Johanna sent off gold-edged letters to all their customers, inviting them to a show of the new collection in the spring. Wanda was impressed all over again by her aunt's flair for business.

But nothing could compare to how Wanda felt about the new mood in her father's house. Karl-Heinz Brauninger had begun to contract with the Heimer workshop. He had already bought a whole series of artistic pieces, and he had told them he was interested in more.

By curious chance, the seeds for these new and promising developments had been sown back at carnival time when Wanda and Richard hadn't missed a single dance or party or costume parade. Wanda had never seen anything like the weird and wonderful costumes and colorful grotesque masks people wore for Mardi Gras in the Thuringian Forest. She loved every minute of it and got swept up in the locals' good cheer. And then it was all over on Ash

Wednesday. *How fine it would be if there were only some way to bottle some of this festive spirit for the rest of the year,* she had thought, her head buzzing. Bottle . . . Wasn't Lauscha a glassblowing village? She got the idea for a series of glass pieces called *Carnival* on the spot. As Wanda had expected, her father was deeply skeptical about her suggestion, arguing that the kind of detail she was describing took far too much time to create. Eventually, however, he gave in, and the result was a series of bowls and drinking glasses in various sizes. There was also a centerpiece and a set of glass napkin rings, which were Wanda's idea. The whole series was blown from transparent glass and then decorated with thousands upon thousands of bright colorful flecks like confetti. In the end even Thomas had to admit that it had been worth the effort: every piece sparkled with good cheer, awakening visions of elegant banquet tables, tinkling glasses, and merry diners drinking to one another's health. Karl-Heinz Brauninger was also delighted with the result and offered a higher price than Wanda had been planning to ask. They'd gotten off to a good start—now she had to keep the ball rolling!

"Please, Aunt Johanna, let's not call New York until next week! If you like we can go to the post office in Sonneberg first thing on Monday, but not today," Wanda pleaded urgently, glancing nervously at Johanna across the kitchen table.

Everybody else was already toiling away in the workshop, and Wanda would usually be on her way up the hill to the Heimer house by this time, but she had asked Johanna to talk with her for a moment.

Johanna shook her head. "I really don't see what you hope to gain by that. There are only four weeks until you're supposed to leave. You know that you're very welcome here, despite . . . despite everything. But if you really do intend to stay in Lauscha for longer than planned, you have to at least ask your parents' permission! Or don't you think they have any say in the matter?" Johanna frowned angrily. "Quite apart from which, you're making things very difficult for me too." She sighed. "Every time your mother writes or calls, she asks me to take better care of you, instead of letting you run off to your father every day."

"But I've written to her to explain why I—"

Johanna waved the interruption away. "And then there's the question of your affections . . . I really ought not to let you see Richard every day. Even if you do swear your most solemn oath that the two of you are behaving appropriately."

"Oh, Aunt Johanna!" Wanda felt a pang of guilt. "I know that I'm not making things easy for you. But Richard is such an honorable soul that you really needn't worry about my . . . about my innocence. And as for my father . . ." She threw up her hands helplessly. "Please try to see things my way. For the first time in my life I feel that I'm doing something really useful! I know that Mother only wants what's best for me, but can I help it that I'm just not the sort of girl who enjoys a life of cocktail receptions and tennis games? I do so much like to see how things can really get better when you put your mind to it! I'm sure that *you* understand that. You and Mother and Marie—you never let anything change your mind. You each followed your own path!"

Even as she uttered the words, Wanda realized that it had been a mistake to mention Marie.

And indeed Johanna's face darkened.

"Don't even mention Marie! I've got a bone to pick with her, never mind that she's pregnant!" she snorted. "Heaven knows I'm not expecting her to write at any great length, but is it too much to ask that she drops us a line every now and again just to let us know that she's well?"

Wanda said nothing. She had no explanation for Marie's behavior. Her aunt hadn't replied to any of her last three letters, not even to the one telling her all about the *Carnival* series and what a success it had been—she would have thought that surely would have interested her.

"Perhaps she's not well . . ." Wanda muttered, shifting back and forth uncomfortably on the bench. She didn't have time to talk about Marie, not now.

"Don't say such things!" Johanna gasped and her eyes glazed over. "Sometimes I can't even sleep at night, I'm so worried about her. I imagine her lying in an Italian hospital somewhere, and I find myself wondering whether she's lost the child . . ." She sighed. Anger had given way to despair. "She must be terribly unhappy in that palazzo."

Wanda reached across the table and took Johanna's hand. "I can't believe such a thing could have happened—she would have told us by now! Marie knows what she wants, that's all. It's much more likely that being pregnant has given her a new burst of creativity and she works every hour God gives her. Then in the evenings she's too tired to write."

Johanna looked skeptical.

Wanda leapt to her feet and hugged her aunt. "Don't worry! I'm sure Marie is happy and healthy! And I'll call Mother on Monday, I promise you I will."

Before Johanna could open her mouth to protest, Wanda was in the hallway, putting on her coat and scarf, and she was soon on her way up the hill.

Her heart was beating fast, though she couldn't have said whether this was because she was walking quickly or because she was bubbling over with excitement. Though there was no way that Johanna could have known, today was a special day—Thomas and Richard would be working together for the first time. It had taken all her powers of persuasion to make it happen. At first Thomas had flat-out refused even to consider working with another glassblower.

"It's bound to fail," he said gloomily, adding, "just look what happened when they tried to set up a crafts cooperative! They spent all their time arguing about their plans and designs and were never able to agree on anything!" It was only when Richard himself came calling that Thomas had finally agreed to give it a try; Richard pointed out that by working together they could try their hand at much more elaborate pieces. And Richard had chosen a particularly daring and difficult project.

I do hope it all works out, Wanda thought nervously. She wasn't even halfway up the hill when she let out a sudden cry of dismay; water was seeping into her shoes, soaking her stockings. She lifted the hem of her skirt but it was too late, that too was dripping wet.

"Well, young lady, weren't watching where you were going? You've probably never seen a thaw like this in America."

Wanda turned around and recognized the apothecary's wife.

"Not in New York, that's for sure," she sighed, looking down at her ruined shoes. "And it had to happen today, when Richard and my father are expecting the supplies I ordered from your husband! I can't even go back home and change into a dry pair of shoes. I do hope that everything's arrived by now?" She couldn't help the note of impatience that crept into her voice—they had been expecting the silver leaf last week, along with all the other chemicals whose names she could never remember.

"The delivery man brought your order yesterday," the woman said. "All the same you mustn't ignore wet feet. You're no good to your father if you get ill, you know," she scolded gently as the two of them went on up the hill together.

"You should tell him that!" Wanda said, grinning. "He says that I'm more of a nuisance than a help. Only yesterday he told me that I was worse than having a herd of cattle charge through the shop!" she admitted. By now she was used to the things Thomas Heimer said and she didn't take them much to heart.

The apothecary's wife clicked her tongue disapprovingly. "That silly man. He should be glad to have you! Glad!"

Wanda just laughed.

23

There wasn't a sound in the workshop aside from the humming of Thomas's gas lamp. He was heating part of a hollow glass rod in the flame.

"Little bit more," Richard muttered, standing next to Thomas, ready to apply the aventurine, which glittered just like real gold. Then he called out, "Stop! That's enough."

When Thomas held the vase out to him, Richard sprinkled the grains of golden aventurine over the heated portion of the rod. Thomas rotated it slowly this way and that at Richard's command and the grains sparkled in the light. Then Thomas put the end of the rod back into the flame and closed it up. He put the hollow end to his lips and blew.

Wanda watched, spellbound, as the slender glass rod swelled up and became a thick-walled bubble. Just as she feared that the glass would burst, Thomas stopped blowing and turned the bubble with a pair of large tongs. Then he warmed the closed end and attached a stem at the bottom. As soon as it was firmly attached, he turned the piece around again, held the open end to the flame, and picked up a set of pliers. He worked his way deftly around the rim, crimping and curving, and gradually the vase took shape.

Eva had been passing through the workshop on her way to the kitchen and hadn't really intended to stop. But now she tiptoed up to the workbench. When she saw what the men were doing, she grabbed Wanda's sleeve as though she had never before seen glass being blown.

"That's it!" Thomas said. He put the vase back into the flame and picked up the tongs, working at the crimps in the lip, teasing them out and giving them shape. The aventurine began to split apart, stretching itself out along hairbreadth cracks.

Great God in Heaven, let everything work out well! Wanda prayed silently, holding her breath, while the aventurine glowed brighter in spots. In some places, it looked just like real gold.

Thomas's brow was beaded with sweat. He put down the tongs and waved the vase gently from side to side to cool it. For the first time since sitting down at the bench, he looked up. "We did it!"

Wanda finally allowed herself to breathe again.

"Thank God!" Eva called out. "At least we didn't spend all that money for nothing." She snorted and left the workshop.

"So what do you think? Not bad for a first try, is it?" The pride in Thomas's voice was unmistakable.

Wanda had to swallow the lump in her throat before she could speak.

"It's absolutely beautiful!" she said decisively. "The way it glitters . . . just like a thousand dewdrops on a white lily, catching the morning sun!" She looked from Richard to her father, her eyes shining.

She had known it would work! She had known right from the start that the two of them could do good work together once they set their minds to it.

Richard picked up the vase and held it up to the faint light of the oil lantern, squinting. "The balance of glass to quartz could be better. Next time I'll try to get the grains to sink in a little bit deeper.

371

I wanted to do that right away, but I was worried they wouldn't go into the furrows. That would have spoiled everything."

"Oh, you're always finding fault!" Wanda scolded him.

Thomas, however, nodded. "It was a risk." He gnawed his lower lip. "And you're sure we put the acid on now? Isn't the vase lovely enough as it is?"

Richard laughed. "Have you lost your nerve? Come on now, let's experiment! That's the whole point of the exercise! Why else did we buy the stuff? It cost a pretty penny after all!"

"Now you two wait a moment!" Wanda grabbed her notebook and shoved her way between them. "Before you start the etching, I'd like to know what you were both feeling just now." She held her pencil ready and looked from one to the other. These notes would be important when the time came to describe the new series to Karl-Heinz Brauninger. It had been easy enough with the *Carnival* series, since she could describe her own thoughts and feelings in that case. But this was different.

The two men stared at her. Richard scratched the back of his head, embarrassed. "You really should ask the fellow who blew the glass . . ."

Thomas snorted stubbornly. "If you really want to know, I felt my bladder almost bursting. I had to pee the whole time."

They both laughed. Then Thomas went outside.

Wanda watched him go. She felt as though someone had just poured a bucket of cold water over her head.

"That . . ." She was at a loss for words for a moment. Just when she thought she had got used to his rough ways, he came out with something like this. She swallowed hard and started again. "That beast!"

Richard muttered something along the lines of "don't take it all so seriously" and "we'll do the etching tomorrow," then kissed Wanda hastily on the lips and left.

She stared miserably at the vase as she waited for Thomas to come back inside.

"You're still here then," Thomas said as he came in. "I thought you'd be off with Richard."

"And I thought we were going to work together. It seems I was wrong, though!" she answered bitterly.

Thomas groaned and folded his arms. "What do you want now then? You can really drive a fellow out of his wits. Just like your mother!" he snapped.

"And you can't do anything but grumble!" Wanda shouted, jumping to her feet. He was her *father*—how could he be so hurtful? She walked right up to him until her face was just a few inches from his. "Was I asking so much of you? I only wanted you to tell me your feelings!" To her horror she realized that she was crying. She turned away before Thomas could see her tears.

For a moment there was silence. Thomas sat down at his workbench again.

"How I feel . . . nobody's ever asked me that before," he said at last. He stared down at the wooden worktop, blackened by years of flame. The furrow between his deep-set eyes was even more pronounced than usual. "Ever since I can remember, I've sat in this workshop, at this bench. Every day. Earlier, when there were three of us and Father brought in the orders, we worked from morning till night—whether we were blowing a thousand bowls or hundreds of perfume bottles. Sometimes I thought I would go mad if I ever had to blow one more blessed bowl. Always the same thing, over and over again. I had my own ideas; I was never short of those— I filled a whole sketchbook of ideas over time—but nobody ever cared."

He looked up, but Wanda was still turned away from him, staring out the window.

"Father didn't want to hear any of that. He didn't even look at my designs, just said I shouldn't go wasting time when we could hardly keep up with the work anyway. The other lads in the village never got that: sooner or later they got to make their own things, not like my brothers and me. And then Marie came along with her sketches, and the old man was all smiles and praise!" Thomas sounded as though he still couldn't believe it. "I almost burst from envy, let me tell you. But did anyone care?" He laughed mirthlessly. "Ah well, those funny ideas of hers didn't impress him for long; the old stubbornness came back soon enough. *We* put up with all that but Marie didn't. She went out and made something of herself! Not like us."

Wanda found it hard to listen. She had never seen her father like this. She didn't dare turn around for fear that he would stop talking. At the same time she felt a bit queasy when she heard Marie's name. *If only I knew that there was really nothing to worry about,* she thought.

"And when Sebastian left, Michel and I had to do the work of three. And even then nobody asked me how I felt when I could finally get up from my bench after working for fourteen hours straight! After Michel had his accident, I was all on my own, but there was work to be done if we were to put bread on the table. If I've learned one thing in all these years, it's that it's best not to think about things too deeply. Don't dwell on the past. Just do what has to be done."

He got up from his stool, walked over to join Wanda at the window, and looked out as well. She suddenly felt that they were much closer—and not just because he was standing next to her.

"And then you come along and ask a question like that," he said softly.

"Times change. Believe it or not, sometimes they change for the better," she murmured hoarsely.

"It felt . . . beautiful," he said, so softly that for a moment Wanda thought she was imagining it. Her heart began to hammer wildly. *Go on. Please go on.*

"I'd almost forgotten how glass can stretch that way. But today—today I felt it again. That glass has no limits, really. It's just us, the glassblowers, who have limits." He laughed awkwardly. "What rubbish I'm talking!"

"No!" Wanda cried out. She turned to him and said, "I was so worried the glass would burst!"

He smiled, almost tenderly. "That's the whole trick of it, you see. Knowing when enough is enough." He stroked her arm clumsily and left the workshop.

24

"She hasn't been in touch with your mother either," Johanna said to Wanda as soon as they left the post office. She shook her head. "I just don't understand it! Never mind that we haven't had any new designs from her for months now, but she must know that we're worried about her."

Johanna stopped dead in the street.

"And that Franco's no better, if you ask me! It's no way to behave. What is it, are you even listening to me?" She plucked at Wanda's sleeve as she walked on.

"What were you saying?" Wanda gave a start. She tried to blink away the tears in her eyes.

"Look at you!" Johanna exclaimed. "What are you crying about?" She put her arm around Wanda's shoulders tenderly, though, which drew some of the sting from her words.

Wanda burst into tears. "How can she do this to me? Mother's so cruel!"

She had chosen her words so carefully when she told her mother that she wanted to stay in Lauscha forever. She had lain awake at nights pondering how to break the news and anticipating her mother's reaction, but what she heard first was the crackle on the line and silence from Ruth's end. She had been ready for almost anything but silence. After a few moments, Ruth began stammering helplessly. Wanda had never heard her mother like this, though Ruth recovered herself after a couple of minutes. And when she did, there was no use pleading. Ruth was implacable: Wanda could stay for another four weeks, but after that she had to come straight back to New York. After all, she could hardly stay on and be a burden to Johanna any longer!

When she said that, Wanda had turned her back on Johanna, who was standing next to her, and dropped her voice to say that Thomas Heimer would have no objection if she moved in with him. Ruth answered icily that it would not come to that. If Wanda was really thinking of staying on and living in Thuringia—and Ruth objected strongly to the idea—then at least they would make the necessary arrangements. And they would make them from New York—after calm reflection—and with Wanda there to discuss the matter.

It was probably just a cheap trick to get her to come back home, Wanda thought. Mother very likely believed that once Wanda was back there, her fascination with Lauscha would vanish like smoke up the chimney. But she was wrong. All right, maybe she had once been a bit of a scatterbrain. But this time nothing and nobody could change her mind! The thought comforted her somewhat.

"And just when things have begun going so well," she sniffled, then had to leap aside to avoid being knocked down by a wagon.

"If you fall under those wheels, it won't matter how things are going," Johanna answered. Then she led Wanda into the nearest café, quite unprompted. She ordered them a cup of coffee and a slice of tart each.

"Come on, give us a smile! As I understand it, your mother isn't entirely against the idea of your living in Thuringia. But this kind of thing needs planning, I agree with Ruth there. For instance what about this Harold, who your mother says is your fiancé? Doesn't he have a right to know what you intend to do with your life?" There was no mistaking the note of reproach in Johanna's voice.

"Harold!" Wanda said scornfully. "There was never anything official, that *engagement* of ours was more like a private joke. Do you know I've only had two letters from him since he was appointed bank manager? Out of sight, out of mind—you say that in Germany too, don't you?" She sighed. "But you're right about one thing. It's about what *I* intend to do with *my* life! I don't owe Harold any apology and Mother shouldn't imagine that she can make me feel guilty about him."

Johanna drew a deep breath as if she were about to deliver a strong response, but Wanda watched her fall silent when she saw the waitress coming over. The scent of freshly roasted coffee beans rose up to them and after the first sip Wanda decided that Johanna was right to call coffee the elixir of life. She already felt a little better . . .

Johanna looked up from her tart. "If I can come back to our conversation . . . Whether or not it was an official engagement, I do feel that you should tell him the truth straight out. Or do you want to just wriggle out of things, the way Marie did with poor Magnus?"

No, she didn't want to do that, Wanda admitted silently. She always felt sad when she saw Magnus suffering in silence, with that look in his eyes that said he still didn't understand how the love of his life could simply vanish like that. Not that she believed Harold would suffer the same way—he seemed to have adjusted quite nicely to life without her. All the same, she was ready to make a clean break. But that didn't mean she had to go back to America, did it?

"And then there are financial considerations. Even banal details like handling your own household budget need thinking about, you know. Please don't misunderstand me, you're welcome to stay as long as you like," Johanna said. "But you won't be able to live out of a suitcase forever. And you must have things back home that you miss."

"I have everything I need," Wanda answered huffily. For all she cared, her mother could give all her possessions away to charity—what need would she have here for a ball gown or pearl-encrusted strappy sandals? "Mother only had a suitcase when she left here, and she never even told you she was going. And Marie left everything behind when she went to live with Franco in Genoa. It seems I'm the only one who has to do what everyone says."

She thrust out her lower lip petulantly. What if she just stayed here?

"Oh, Wanda . . . Why are you so dead set on repeating the mistakes of the older generation?" Johanna sighed, looking tired all of a sudden. "Wouldn't it make sense to at least *try* to do a little better?"

"Why didn't you tell your mother that we're getting married?" Richard asked, frowning. "I'm sure that would have changed her mind."

"Married?" Wanda squealed. "We've never even talked about that . . ."

"Why are you blinking like a startled deer? It was clear from the very first that we'd stay together. Which means it's just as clear that we'll get married one day. Actually I wanted to wait until . . . well, until I had more to offer you." He waved his hand vaguely about the room. "But if we have to, then I'll go up to your father this very evening and ask for your hand in marriage. Whether it happens sooner or later—what difference does it make?" He shrugged as though everything were decided. "Would the future Mrs. Stämme like to give her bridegroom a kiss?" He reached out to Wanda with a twinkle in his eye.

Mrs. Stämme . . . She was extremely tempted to snuggle up in his arms and enjoy the warm glow that his words had kindled within her. Instead she shrank back. She knew her heart should be beating wildly, but she felt a surge of anger.

"Actually I had pictured a proposal of marriage a bit differently . . ." she said in a haughty tone.

He could spend hours talking about a new glasswork technique or telling her everything that Gotthilf Täuber had said on his last visit, but he hadn't bothered using more than a few words to address something as important as their wedding! And he hadn't even *asked* her. Besides, Wanda didn't believe that her mother would be at all keen if she told her she wanted to marry. Quite the opposite: she would probably do all she could to stop her daughter from marrying a glassblower! Wanda said as much to Richard.

For a moment they were both silent. Finally, hesitantly, Richard began to speak.

"I can see that your parents might have objections to . . . well, to me. I'm not too sure of myself either. So . . . I mean . . ." He ran his hand through his hair, and it stuck out in all directions. "I'm sure that I love you, of course, but everything else . . ." He waved his hand helplessly. "Perhaps the reason I'm rushing at it like a bull at a gate is that otherwise I feel my head will explode. What can a man like me offer a girl like you? The question haunts me in the middle of the night, first thing in the morning, even when I'm at work. It's like a great dark monster and I can hardly fight it off. A . . . clever girl like you, with all your book learning and worldliness. A New York lady, staying here in Lauscha for the rest of her life—"

"But I . . ." Wanda interrupted him, but Richard carried on. "Of course you like it here now, when everything's new to you. But there'll be another winter next year, that's for sure. And then another after that. How are you going to cope with the fact that sometimes Lauscha is completely cut off by snow? Will you be so bored you start to hate me? And how will you like life in a glass workshop day in and day out? Do I even dare do that to you?" He sighed. "Sometimes the monster's stronger than I am, and then I think we'll never be together. But now that I've told you that's what I want, I'm so relieved! Wanda, love—we can make it work! I know that we can, and I'll do everything I can to make you happy!"

There was a note of stubborn certainty in his voice that didn't agree at all with the doubt in his eyes. Wanda had never seen him look so vulnerable. Her heart was brimming over with love for this man, who always did what he had to do and said what he had to say, no matter what. She took his hand and looked at him earnestly.

"I'm a little scared by all that too. But it's just as you say—we have to fight the black monster. Doubt is a dragon, but we can slay it! Doesn't love conquer all?" she said.

He blinked skeptically. "Was that a yes or a no?"

Wanda grinned. "It was a yes, you big dumb ox! Yes, yes, yes!"

This time she let him take her in his arms. He picked her up and swung her around the room as if she were as light as a feather, whooping with joy. "She's going to marry me! Hurrah!"

Wanda laughed happily. She kissed Richard on the lips, on his ears, on the back of his neck under the fringe of hair.

He eventually let go of her gently and raised his brows as he looked her straight in the eyes.

"There's just one little problem—apart from the fact that we have to get your parents to agree. An organizational problem. Nothing we can't sort out." He went to the cupboard and came back with a letter in his hand. "From Täuber," he said. "We can't get married until June at the earliest. In the second and third weeks of May—"

"We haven't even started talking about the date," Wanda interrupted. She might have said yes but that didn't mean she had no say in the matter! And they still had to talk about her trip to New York.

"I'll be in Venice. Do you remember the art fair that I told you about? This is my invitation. Gotthilf Täuber wants to introduce me to some of the glassworkers there. And he'll pay for my trip too. He says I can use the chance to learn as much as I can from the Italians and—"

"You're leaving?" Wanda's voice was faint. "Why didn't you tell me?"

"I'm telling you now," Richard replied. "Anyway, it's only for two weeks. Täuber says I should . . ."

"Two weeks! We have even less time than I thought, then!" Wanda grumbled. If she ended up having to go back to New York, then she would have left Lauscha by the time he got back. And what if he fell in love with a beautiful Italian girl on his trip? Just the way Marie had fallen in love with her handsome Italian? Then she'd be left all on her own in New York and . . .

She flung herself into Richard's arms and held him tight. "Please don't go!"

Her fear of losing Richard was suddenly stronger than anything in the world. Perhaps she should ignore what her parents wanted and stay in Lauscha?

For a moment the only sound was the monotonous drip-drip-drip of snow melting into the brimming rainwater barrel behind the house.

"Why don't you just come with me to Italy?" Richard suddenly murmured into Wanda's hair. "The art fair might be useful for the Heimer workshop as well. They say a lot of business gets done there. That's the other reason I want to go—though I'd never say as much to Täuber. But I'd like to have more than just one customer, do you see what I mean?"

Wanda nodded, still leaning her head on his chest. She knew just what he meant. She worried that so far she had only managed to interest Karl-Heinz Brauninger in her father's wares. Finding more buyers was right at the top of her list. But how should she go about it? That had always been the question.

"The two of us in Venice . . ." Wanda heaved a heartfelt sigh. But before she could fall too much in love with the images this conjured up, she pushed herself away from him. "But there's no way in the world that Aunt Johanna would allow that! Not any more than my parents would!" She didn't say whether she meant Ruth and Steven, or Ruth and Thomas Heimer.

Richard gnawed at his lip. "And I can understand them too. We're not married yet, or things would look different of course . . ."

The image of gondolas in the pale glittering sunlight was fading away when another thought struck Wanda. "How far is Venice from Genoa, though?"

Richard shrugged. "I have no idea. Why?"

"Do you have an atlas where we could look it up?" Wanda asked, though she knew that he didn't.

"An atlas—me? Where would I get something like that? But your aunt has one, Anna brought it over one time. We wanted to see how far it is to the Bavarian Forest and the Black Forest, there are a lot of glassblowers down there as well. We would have liked to visit . . ." He waved the idea away. "You get ideas like that on the long winter evenings. But tell me, why do you ask?"

Wanda fought back the twinge of envy she had felt at Richard's words.

"Well, if I remember right, then Marie will give birth sometime in May. And I'm wondering . . . what if I used the time I have left to go visit her? Nobody can object to that, can they? I'm family after all."

In fact, Johanna objected a great deal, as did Ruth and Steven. Even Thomas Heimer scowled more than he usually did when Wanda told him her plan. They all said the same thing: that it was not proper for an unmarried girl of her age to travel with a man, even if they would part company as soon as they'd crossed the Italian border. Wanda thought it best not even to mention that she planned to follow Richard to Venice once she'd been to see Marie. Even she felt rather alarmed at the thought of catching the train from Genoa to Venice all on her own. Nor did they mention anything about getting married. Wanda had persuaded Richard that this was not the time to say anything. Wanda was quite sure that her parents would be even more worried about their daughter's virtue if they knew that she and Richard were planning a wedding. So instead she repeated that she was almost frantic with worry for Marie. It was some comfort to think that that wasn't even a lie.

The calls flew back and forth between the post office in Sonneberg and Ruth's apartment in New York. Since she couldn't make any headway with her mother, Wanda even called Steven at his office. As soon as she heard his voice, she burst into tears. Then she told him at length how sorry she was to have hurt him with her childish behavior before she left New York. Steven did his best to calm her down. At last he managed to bring her around to why she had really called, and she asked whether he could put in a good word for her. There was nothing she wanted so much, she said, as to see Marie again. Steven answered that he understood that Wanda was worried about her aunt, of course, but he wasn't really sure that he would be acting in her best interests if he let her take this trip.

Whereupon Wanda burst into floods of tears again.

A few days later the postman came to the Steinmann-Maienbaum workshop with a telegram for Wanda. When he didn't find her there, he cursed under his breath and then climbed the hill all the way to the Heimer workshop.

Wanda's hands trembled as she took the telegram from him. She held her breath as she opened it. She scanned the lines quickly and only then did she let herself breathe out.

Her cry of joy rang through the whole house.

Despite their reservations, Ruth and Steven had given their permission for Wanda to go to Italy "for Marie's sake." They had also sent her a money order for a considerable sum.

25

"The doctor says that your backache could be early contractions," Patrizia said, smoothing the covers down over Marie. Then she tucked them in at the sides of the bed so tightly that Marie could hardly move. Although Patrizia had pulled the curtains closed, it was still bright in the room and very warm.

Marie blinked in shock. *Early contractions?*

"What does that mean?" She looked over at her mother-in-law and then at the doctor, who was standing a discreet distance away from the bed. She was worried. The doctor had examined her by palpating her stomach and then her back through her nightgown— the whole thing hadn't lasted more than two minutes. Then he had rattled away at Patrizia in Italian from under his mustache, speaking so fast that Marie couldn't follow him. The only word she caught was *complicazione*.

"What kind of complications is he talking about?" Marie asked when Patrizia didn't reply.

"He isn't; you must have misunderstood," Patrizia answered. She didn't mention that the doctor was concerned because of Marie's age. "But Dottore di Tempesta recommends strict bed rest from now on. Otherwise there's a danger that the child may be born prematurely."

"But I—"

"No buts!" Patrizia interrupted sternly and then nodded to the doctor that his consultation was over.

Marie watched helplessly as the man snapped his medical bag shut and turned to leave the room. She still had so many questions! The baby was due at the end of May. But what if it came earlier? Would there be problems? And wouldn't it be best to have a doctor present for the birth? After all, he had mentioned complications.

Although Franco's mother had become a little more approachable in the last few weeks, she still refused to accommodate any such request. "The women of the de Lucca family have given birth without help for centuries. If a birth was difficult we brought in a midwife, but that's all." Marie was tired of hearing this little speech every time she mentioned her concerns. Patrizia clearly thought that Marie was lily-livered. All the same she had finally given in to her pleas and called the doctor for a consultation, though not before Marie had sworn on her mother's grave that she wouldn't say anything "silly" while he was there. Marie was so grateful that at that moment she would have sworn anything at all. Now, however, she was so worried that something might be wrong that a promise meant nothing. She tore the sheets away and sat up in bed.

"Dottore, uno momento!" she cried out when the doctor was already halfway out the door.

Patrizia cast her a warning glance.

The doctor turned around. *"Si . . . ?"*

"Is my child well?" Marie asked softly.

He hesitated, just for a moment. Then he nodded energetically and vanished into the dark hallway outside.

Marie watched him go. *Thank God!*

That was all she had wanted to know. Only that.

"Was that really necessary?" Patrizia asked when she came back into the room. "Hadn't we agreed that you would keep quiet?" She put a pitcher of milk and a glass on the bedside table.

The sight of it made Marie feel queasy. "You know that milk makes me feel sick these days. I would much rather have a cool glass of lemonade." She sighed. "And I'd like to go for a walk. It's so stuffy in here you could cut the air with a knife. If the heat's this bad already, I hate to think how hot it gets in the summer."

Patrizia pretended not to have heard that last remark. "Milk never did anybody any harm. It would do the *bambino* good for you to drink it. After all, you'll have to make your own milk starting in a couple of weeks." She held the half-full glass out to Marie, urging her to drink.

Marie forced herself to take a sip and tried to fight back the nausea. In the end she needed to stay on Patrizia's good side if things were not to get any worse in this prison.

"Is there any news?" Marie asked. Patrizia raised her eyebrows and she realized she must have a milk mustache. She wiped her mouth hastily with the back of her hand.

Patrizia shook her head. "Nothing. Nothing at all. I spend every day waiting for the lawyer to call and tell us whether he's managed to make any progress. But so far . . . nothing." Her voice failed her. She took a starched handkerchief from her sleeve and dabbed at invisible drops of sweat on her brow. When she was able to speak again, there was a note of bitterness in her voice. "That man has been taking fat legal fees from us for decades now, but heaven forbid we should ask him to actually go to court!"

"I don't understand! How can they put Franco in jail when there's no proof at all that he had anything to do with it?" Marie was genuinely upset. As long as Franco was a prisoner in New York, she was a prisoner here in the palazzo. She had felt a surge of hope when Patrizia told her that the family had sent one of the best lawyers in

Italy to America, but that hope was long gone now. Either this lawyer couldn't make any headway against the American legal system,
or there was more evidence against Franco than the testimony of
one bribe taker.

Or . . . perhaps both were the case.

"If Franco doesn't come back soon . . ." Marie whispered, her
voice choked with tears. Even though she was lying down again her
back began to ache. She moaned softly.

Patrizia was following her own train of thought.

"He'll be back for the birth of his child," she said. She saw the
doubt on Marie's face and gave her hand a squeeze. "We just have
to stick together. *Una famiglia, si?* As I always say."

Marie didn't answer.

Patrizia whispered, "We should pray. For our beloved son, for
your husband."

26

After fourteen days of hectic preparation for the journey, the moment had finally come. Richard and Wanda bid their farewells to Lauscha as everyone who was staying behind showered them with words of advice, best wishes for the journey, and even a tear or two. Johannes gazed at his cousin with undisguised envy, having taken her aside earlier to admit that he had always wanted to travel abroad. Anna simply shook Wanda's hand and muttered something about having a lot of work to do, then turned and fled without saying good-bye to Richard at all.

It showed plainly on Johanna's face that she still wasn't convinced about the propriety of letting them travel together, but she forced a smile all the same. Peter hugged Wanda, then Richard, then stuffed some money into Richard's pocket and told them both to drink a glass of Bavarian beer on him that evening. "Just the one, though!" he chuckled, wagging his finger.

Thomas Heimer had insisted on coming to see them off at Paul Marzen's house, where they were loading their luggage onto Paul's horse cart for the trip to Coburg. He shook Wanda's hand over and over again and then handed her a packet of food that Eva had packed for their journey. Although she could smell the unappetizing scents of Heimer home cooking through the waxed paper, Wanda was so touched by the gesture she could have cried. And then Thomas turned to Johanna and said, "Whoever would have thought we'd be here together, both of us worried silly?"

At that, Wanda couldn't hold back her tears any longer. Her only consolation was that while she was away Thomas would be kept busy with a large order from Brauninger; an American collector had come to see the dealer and had ordered several dozen vases, each of which involved using a different technique. "A cross section of everything Thuringian glassblowers can do!"—so Brauninger had declared. That was just the thing for Father, Wanda decided happily. At first Thomas hadn't believed it and had accused Wanda of making a bad joke, but then he had set to work with a vengeance. He was so carried away by the task that Wanda hardly recognized him; he seemed to have become a young man again overnight.

Wanda wanted to set about finding more clients when she got back. Secretly of course she was hoping she could make new contacts for the Heimer workshop in Venice as well.

It was so hard to say good-bye to Lauscha!

"Hey, Wanda, are you planning to stay here after all?" Richard asked, reaching out to her impatiently.

Wanda sighed and then let him pull her up onto the hard wooden bench of the cart.

"It's only for two weeks," Richard whispered in her ear when he saw how miserable she looked. She nodded.

They were off.

When they arrived at the railway station in Coburg, their train had already pulled up to the platform. As soon as Richard spotted it, he began to run, worried that they wouldn't be able to board. Wanda giggled and pointed out that the stokers were still shoveling coal into the tender up front—the train wouldn't be leaving quite yet!

The train was to take them from Coburg via Nuremberg to Munich, where they would spend the night in a boarding house near the station. The next day they would cross the Austrian border to Bozen, and there they would part ways.

Although Wanda had bought her own ticket at the Lauscha station, Richard's had been issued in Weimar—Gotthilf Täuber had sent it to him along with his reservation for a *pensione* in Venice and a ticket for the art fair. At the sight of the Weimar-issued ticket, the conductor raised his bushy eyebrows and looked long and hard, paying no attention to the murmuring queue of passengers that was forming behind Richard and Wanda. When he finally let them board, they found that they were in luck; the compartment was only half full so they were able to sit down and have a free bench across from them. Wanda put some of her luggage there, even though it ought to have traveled in the luggage compartment. She had a whole suitcase full of things for Marie's baby and presents for Marie herself. Richard had brought his own suitcase into the compartment as well, which looked pitiful next to Wanda's elegant luggage. Richard seemed to notice the discrepancy, and he draped his jacket over the case as though to hide it.

It was a bright sunny day, and the spring air blew in through the train windows as a pleasant breeze. The whole world seemed to be in bloom outside. Wherever they looked, they saw the gleaming white of apple and cherry blossoms.

At first Wanda took Richard's hand and savored the idea that this journey was a dream come true for her. Even two weeks ago she would never have believed it could happen. But with every curve of the tracks, reality became more wonderful than any dream. There was something new to look at every few minutes, and Wanda simply couldn't sit still. She waved her hands in excitement, pointing first at dark forests, then at orchards stretching up the hillsides, then at the little villages with their red-tiled rooftops—she hadn't seen slate since they left Thuringia. They also passed several lakes where the water gleamed a rich dark-sapphire blue.

It took Wanda some time to notice that Richard did not share her excitement but was instead staring ahead, lost in thought. When she asked him what the matter was, he said, "Did you notice how it was only my ticket the conductor checked? He didn't even ask the other passengers to show theirs."

At first Wanda didn't understand what Richard was driving at. She had long forgotten their little delay in boarding.

"It's typical, though!" Richard went on. "People think they can treat us hillbillies any way they like. If that's the way it's going to be, then I've already had enough!"

And with every mile they traveled away from Lauscha, he grew more and more taciturn. Wanda knew that Richard's bad mood had nothing to do with her, that he was simply feeling nervous. Secretly she was even a little amused that her own dear Richard had lost his self-assurance as soon as he left Lauscha behind . . . She decided to leave him alone, however, and instead buried herself in the guidebook on Italy that she had bought a few days before from Marie's friend Alois Sawatzky.

Richard didn't relax until that afternoon, but then he was happy to talk. And by the time their train reached Munich toward evening, he was almost his old self again.

The boarding house by the Munich railway station was modest but well kept. Once Wanda and Richard had taken their luggage up to their rooms, Richard would have been quite content to stay in and order the dish of the day in the dining room—a lentil soup with sausages—but Wanda rolled her eyes. The sun was still shining golden outside and the streets were still full of people out enjoying life. So she persuaded Richard to come out with her and take a walk along the famous Maximilianstrasse, which she had heard about even in New York. The shops were all closed at this hour, but they could still enjoy window-shopping. Wanda put her hand on Richard's arm, then laughed as she spotted their reflection in a shopwindow. All they needed was a walking stick for him and a parasol for her and they would look like an old married couple. It was only when the streetlamps came on and their feet began aching from walking that they finally decided they'd had enough.

Instead of going back to their boarding house to eat, they ended up at a restaurant in the Schwabing district where two fiddlers were playing lively tunes. Richard kept glancing curiously over at the other diners as though they were from another planet. He pointed discreetly at the man at the next table, who was wearing a black tailcoat and a fiery red scarf, and then at another man whose scalp was shaved completely bald but who had a great bushy beard down to his chest. Then he pointed to two young women who were kissing one another on the lips in front of the whole restaurant. Soon Richard was so embarrassed that he didn't know where to look next.

Wanda felt right at home however. The atmosphere reminded her of the many evenings she had spent with Marie and Pandora in Greenwich Village.

"They're artists," she whispered to Richard, then told him that he had best get used to such eccentric characters since there would be droves of them in Venice. When she saw one of the diners being served a plate of spaghetti, she suggested that they order the same thing—they were headed for Italy after all!

"Women kissing, men whose hair has slipped down to their beards, spaghetti here in Bavaria—well, why not!" Richard commented dryly. At that Wanda kissed him on the lips.

As the evening wore on, the mood among the customers grew ever more cheerful. The music was so loud that it was hard to engage in conversation, but Wanda and Richard were content simply to gaze into one another's eyes and sway gently in time with the melody.

At last the musicians sat down with a jug of wine and it became a little quieter—aside from the heated political arguments at some of the other tables.

Wanda and Richard could talk now, and as always their conversation roamed far and wide. There was so much they had to say to one another!

Wanda eventually told him about the evening when Marie had let slip that Steven wasn't her real father.

"All through my childhood I somehow felt that I . . . that I didn't quite belong. Neither fish nor fowl nor good red meat, do you understand? And that's only changed recently, in these past few weeks. Now I know that Steven is part of my life just as much as Thomas. It feels as though I'm gradually finding my feet in the world." She looked at Richard, who was listening intently, absorbing all she said.

Wanda went on. "Part of me will always be American, but I'm more and more of a glassblower's daughter with every passing day! It's crazy, isn't it?" Suddenly all the doubts and anxiety she used to feel in the old days were back, so close at hand that Wanda shivered. How many times had she started a new project full of hope, only to see it fail miserably later! She took a generous gulp of wine.

Richard looked at her thoughtfully. "Everything was so much simpler for me. I've known ever since I was little that I'm the son of a glassblower. My father was one of the best. My parents made it quite plain to me from the start that they expected me to follow in his footsteps. Or rather, that they expected me to do even more. It's just a shame that they're not here to see their wish come true. Father wouldn't like the idea of my going off to Murano, mind you, but apart from that . . ." He reached across the table and took Wanda's hand. "They would be proud to see me marry Heimer's daughter!"

She didn't quite understand what he meant by that remark at first, but then she realized that in Richard's eyes that was what she was, first and foremost—a glassblower's daughter. He couldn't see the contradiction that had split her childhood in two, or didn't want to see it. For him, she wasn't the little rich girl from Fifth Avenue with a head full of whimsical dreams that needed getting rid of. Richard saw her as a woman who knew how to get things done and who would stand at his side as he made his way in the world. A warm wave of happiness washed over her.

Her eyes sparkled with love as she lifted her glass and drank to their future together.

"And I'm proud to marry a glassblower. How does the saying go? Marry a glassblower and your cup will never run dry!" Marie had told her that once, or something of the sort.

Richard frowned quizzically. "I think the saying is a little bit different, but I like your version too!"

27

The second day of the journey was just as wonderful as the first. With every mile, the landscape became more and more like the pictures in the books that Johanna used to send to her in America: there were the snowcapped peaks of the Alps, the deep-blue sky with its white cotton-candy clouds, the light-brown cows with their great dark eyes. Waterfalls along the side of the train tracks splashed down the steep mountainsides to the left and right. Wanda felt that the closer they came to Brenner Pass, the closer they came to Heaven itself, and she was overjoyed. Their fellow passengers were amused to hear Wanda break out into new raptures every five minutes or so.

Richard had his own way of appreciating the magnificent landscape outside. He glanced out the window, then down at his sketchpad, then back again. Later he told Wanda that he hadn't expected the journey itself to be such a source of inspiration. She told him that since it was, they should plan to travel regularly in their future life together.

The other passengers had already decided they must be newly-weds, and smiled at them indulgently or wistfully. To be so young, and so much in love . . .

The hotel in Bozen was more elegant than the boarding house the night before and had a much grander dining room where almost all the tables were taken. This time, it was Richard who insisted that they go and explore the town. Once they had found their rooms and freshened up a little, they walked hand in hand through the narrow streets. It was a warm evening, and it seemed that everyone in Bozen wanted to spend it out on the street: children were playing, women in aprons were sitting together scrubbing vegetables, and men were chatting animatedly on street corners, the smoke from their cigarettes wafting through the air. Wanda and Richard sometimes found it hard to make their way through the crush. Though winter had only just ended in Lauscha, it already felt like early summer here.

"This is just how I imagined the south would be!" Wanda pointed to a long row of flowerpots bursting with bloodred geraniums, and a black cat sitting in front of them grooming himself. "The smell of summer in the air and the deep-blue sea!"

Richard laughed. "I can't see the sea from here."

"Spoilsport!" Wanda nudged him in the side. "You have no imagination."

A moment later they came upon a piazza, and whatever answer Richard might have been about to give died on his lips. In front of them was the most beautiful fountain either of them had ever seen. Within a broad sandstone basin, countless cherubs cavorted in various poses, each holding a cornucopia from which the water poured out.

"Have you ever seen anything so beautiful?" Wanda asked, amazed. She put a hand in front of her mouth. "That must be hundreds of years old, don't you think?"

"I think it must be from the Renaissance," Richard answered. He sounded just as impressed.

When they got closer, they saw that coins filled the bottom of the basin.

"It's a custom here. You throw a coin into the fountain, shut your eyes, and make a wish. Then the wish comes true. Drat it all, I must have some small change somewhere . . ." Wanda said, and began scrabbling around in her purse.

Richard took her hand and drew her toward him. "My wish came true long ago," he murmured and kissed the palm of her hand.

Later they ate roast squab with garlic potatoes in a little trattoria. They drank a Chianti wine that warmed them from the inside. They laughed, they talked, they touched hands across the table, and every movement meant more than it ever had before; every twinkle in their eyes was a message meant for the other alone; every gesture was a secret that shut out the rest of the world.

He is my man, Wanda thought all the while, almost bursting with pride and happiness.

They left the trattoria with the last of the other customers, and then, finally, they were standing in front of their rooms, each with a key in hand. When Richard kissed Wanda good-night, she clung to him with all her strength. *Don't leave!* She didn't want to be alone—she wanted to be with him, to feel him with her as never before.

The air between them was almost sparking with desire. It would be so simple to spend the next few hours together! But they had made a promise back home in Lauscha. And besides, they had to leave early the next morning; Richard's train to Venice and Wanda's train to Milan both left shortly after seven. They ought to get a few hours' sleep. More embraces and more kisses followed, and then Wanda and Richard parted, their hearts heavy.

Wanda sat in her camisole at the old-fashioned dressing table that took up almost the whole wall in her little room and stared forlornly at her image in the mirror. She couldn't summon the will to open her suitcase and look for her nightgown. Even though Richard was just on the other side of the wall, she missed him already!

Ever since he had told her how he felt on New Year's Eve, so suddenly and with so much certainty, they hadn't been apart for even a day. His trust in her, his good humor and tender caresses—how empty the days to come would be! Lost in thought, she ran her hand over her bosom but felt nothing. When Richard touched her there she shivered all over. When would she be back in his arms again—and happy? Richard . . .

Perhaps her longing would not be so bad tomorrow when she could look forward to seeing Marie again, but tonight, the idea of being without him for even a day or two was more than Wanda could bear.

She stood up so suddenly that the shellacked stool tipped over backward. She cringed, knowing that a noise like that at such a late hour would annoy the other guests. Then she went to the glass doors that led out onto the balcony and opened them. Just to get a breath of fresh air. To gather her thoughts.

Just that.

She wasn't the least bit surprised to see Richard standing on the balcony next door. All the same her eyes widened when she saw what he was doing.

"You're smoking?" She pointed at the glowing cigarette in his hand, astonished. He was one of the very few glassblowers in Lauscha who did not smoke. Whenever one of his friends offered him a cigarette in the tavern or on the street, he replied that he didn't care for tobacco.

Now he grinned wryly. "You won't go telling anyone, will you?" He took one last puff, then threw it to the floor and ground it out with his foot.

Wanda nodded and said nothing.

For a moment they stood there, silent, each leaning against the balcony railing, staring fixedly out at the houses opposite. There was a sharp smell in the air, perhaps rising to their balcony from the hotel kitchen. The tension between Wanda and Richard grew and grew.

Wanda swallowed. Then she said slowly, "I won't tell anyone." Her heart was hammering like crazy. A moment later she heard herself say, "I'll keep your secret if you'll keep mine."

After that everything happened quite naturally. Without even thinking about it she opened the door for Richard. Tonight she wanted to be his woman. She'd never wanted anything so much.

When they were facing one another, she lifted her arms and pulled her camisole over her head. It fluttered to the floor and lay there. Then she reached behind her back. It took her a moment to open the hooks on her brassiere, her hands were trembling so, but it soon lay beside the camisole. Then she took off her panties. Unhurried and unashamed. The tension was thrilling, these moments of waiting so sweet!

She knew that she was beautiful. Ever since she had grown into womanhood a few years ago, men had looked at her admiringly—and women enviously. She knew the reason why. But she had never felt so beautiful as she did now, the first time Richard saw her naked.

He looked her up and down with awe in his eyes, more reverently even than he looked at his beloved glassworks. Without being asked, she turned round in front of him like a dancer on a music box. He drank in her nakedness like wine, and she in turn grew drunk on his admiration. Now she could hardly wait for his touch. Her skin was growing warm just from his gaze, and she felt hot flushes ripple across her body. Wanda wrapped her arms around Richard, nestling into his shirt, but he pushed her away gently but firmly. Without taking his eyes off her, he began to undress.

Involuntarily she wondered whether she was the first woman he had ever undressed for. Once, early on, she had asked him whether he had ever courted another girl—apart from poor Anna—but he had never answered. She didn't doubt, however, that—unlike her—he was experienced in matters of love; he had always been so certain in his caresses, had never lost control, and he was a fantastic kisser.

Wanda passed her tongue over her lips expectantly as Richard knelt down and untied his shoes. Her thighs were trembling almost unbearably, so she had to sit down on the bed. Richard unbuckled his belt briskly, and his pants fell to the floor.

A sigh escaped from Wanda's throat. Was it acceptable to tell a man how beautiful he was? She didn't dare. He was just as muscular as she had imagined he would be, without being bulky. With his broad chest that tapered down to a narrow waist, he had a physique like those of the male ballet dancers in New York. Wanda glanced downward. Without his pants, his legs were more sturdy than she had expected.

Once he was quite naked she found herself to be a little afraid after all. Afraid not of the unfamiliar sight of a naked man, but rather of her own desire for Richard, which almost smothered her. She wanted to pull him down on top of her, put his hands on her breasts; she wanted to . . . she blinked hastily to dispel the seductive visions.

"You're so . . . manly," she whispered hoarsely.

Richard had seen what she was looking at and grinned. "All the muscles are from the hard work at the bench and lamp."

"And where's . . . that from?" Wanda's eyes were half-closed as she pointed at his erection, which was straining upward, pulsing with strength. The brazenness of her question made her blush. What must Richard think of her!

"That's your doing. All you," Richard murmured, his voice choked.

A moment later, his arms were around her and his lips were upon hers. His lips roamed to her ears. She bowed her head. His tongue lapped at the hollow between her shoulders and back up to her neck where his warm breath stirred the small soft hairs.

Wanda was breathing faster with every kiss. She could not hold herself back any longer but ran her hands over his body and kissed him, tasting the salt on his skin and breathing in his scent. By now they were lying together on the narrow bed. It groaned reproachfully under their weight and they laughed.

With every kiss, every caress they spun a cocoon of passion more tightly around themselves. Nothing outside that cocoon mattered. The nearness of their breath, velvet skin, gentle moans, their hearts beating together, her soft curves and his strong arms around her, the pleasure and the pain . . .

Wanda surrendered herself entirely, felt the cresting waves of passion lift her higher and higher, washing away the pain and leaving nothing but this joyous appetite.

Any thought of the other guests in the hotel was long banished from Wanda's mind as she screamed from the depths of her soul, "Hold me tight! Forever . . ."

◆ ◆ ◆

"Help me . . . I can't take it anymore!"

Marie's scream ripped through the room. Her torso bucked and thrashed, the searing pain in her abdomen ripping through her even worse than before. Whatever was happening couldn't be right. It was too painful. She was being torn in two. She . . .

"You have to keep still! Eleonore *is* helping you! The *bambino* will be here, soon, soon!" Patrizia's face was dripping with sweat; her face was set in rigid lines as though she shared in Marie's pain.

She looked impatiently at the midwife who was standing between Marie's legs. What was taking so long?

The midwife's right hand was hidden inside Marie. She was concentrating, feeling for the child who refused to be born.

"Send her away! I don't want this. It hurts so much . . ." Hot tears ran down Marie's face. Then she howled as another wave of pain ripped through her before she had recovered from the last.

The young midwife had only ever delivered four babies before now. She drew back her hand, covered in blood, and Marie's groans diminished a little. Eleonore's face showed clearly how helpless she felt as she took a damp cloth and dabbed at Marie's forehead.

Theoretically she knew exactly how to take hold of the child and turn it so that the head was in the right place. But the textbook hadn't told her anything about what to do when the mother was thrashing like a mad thing! Whenever she had hold of the head, Marie bucked and twisted and the head slipped out of her grasp. When she had studied with the *matrona*, all the women had stayed calm and done what the old midwife had told them. "Let them scream as much as they like," the *matrona* always told her. "Screaming helps." Well, this German woman was screaming until it seemed her throat might burst, but it didn't seem to be making the birth one bit easier.

If only it weren't so hot! Eleonore tried to loosen her blouse a little, which was drenched with sweat. Then her glance fell on the clock on the wall and she gave a start. So late already!

Six hours had passed, and the child had hardly changed position at all.

For the first time Eleonore felt a touch of panic. She had to do something, or else the child's life would not be the only one in danger.

"What is it, how long are you going to flap that wet cloth around in her face?" the countess snapped at the young woman.

"Can't you see that she's almost lost consciousness? Her pulse is getting weaker . . ." She let go of Marie's wrist. The arm fell onto the bed as if Marie were a lifeless puppet.

Eleonore took a deep breath.

"If she won't lie still I can't take hold of the baby's head." She tried to put a note of authority into her voice. Neither of the other women would like what she was going to say next. "We will have to tie the *signora* down."

28

The next morning everything happened so fast that there was no time for painful farewells. Richard was terribly nervous, which he tried to explain away by saying that there was a lot at stake for him at the art fair. Wanda knew, however, that he didn't like the idea of traveling the last leg of the journey on his own.

After one last kiss on the platform, they promised to meet the following Sunday at Richard's hotel—and then Wanda had to urge him off, waving good-bye.

Unlike the first part of the journey, she hardly noticed anything on her train ride from Bozen to Milan and then on to Genoa. The orchards gradually gave way to vast wheat fields, which were still tinged with green at this time of year. The light in her eyes was caused not by the beauties of the Italian landscape but by the passion of the previous night, which still glowed within her.

"Now you are really mine," Richard had whispered to her as they lay next to one another, sated. And then he added, "Let's get married as soon as we get back from Italy."

She had nodded without saying a word. The hot tears made it impossible to speak. It didn't matter. She could never have found the words for how happy she felt at that moment.

She knew one thing for certain: not for an instant did she regret last night, even though she had broken every promise she had made to Johanna and her parents.

Richard . . . her man . . . What was he doing at this moment?

Suddenly she was terribly tired. Soon she would be able to tell Marie everything, woman to woman. That was Wanda's last thought as she fell fast asleep, leaning against the window, utterly exhausted.

Despite her fears, Wanda found it easy enough to ask her way to the de Lucca family home in Genoa. When she hailed a cab in front of the railway station and gave the driver the address, the driver shook his head sullenly before she could even climb in. He gestured as he talked, and she understood enough to realize that Marie's home was only two streets away, so it was not worth his while to take her fare. Wanda pointed to her luggage and insisted. The driver grumbled but took her all the same. A few minutes later they stopped in front of a vast rectangular pile with a discreet brass plate on the door that read "Palazzo Delizioso."

So this was a building by the famous Italian architect Palladio! Marie had written pages and pages about him and the dozens of splendid villas he had built so Wanda was surprised to see how plain the exterior was here. Certainly the Palladian style was impressive, but it was also unusually severe. She wasn't here to study Italian architecture, though. Wanda tugged the bell pull to the right of the door.

"*Scusi, signorina*, but Countess Marie . . . is unfortunately . . . unavailable today!" explained the maid who opened the door. Then she curtsied briefly without moving aside.

Unavailable? What was that supposed to mean? Wanda frowned. Had the girl even understood that she had come all the way from Germany to visit Marie? She glanced around at the building's huge façade as though she expected to see Marie's head pop up in one of the countless windows.

Wanda tried again, speaking slowly and clearly. "Please . . . tell . . . my aunt that . . . Wanda is here. Wanda! Tell her that, can you?" Perhaps Marie didn't want to see any strangers when she was so heavily pregnant, but that couldn't apply to her niece.

The maid twisted her fingers in her starched apron.

"That . . . won't be possible . . ." she answered in broken German.

Up until that moment Wanda had been holding her luggage in her hands. Now she dropped it with a thump.

"What does that mean? Has Marie gone out? If she has, then she'll come back sometime, won't she?" she asked indignantly. Was this how the Italians treated their guests, simply leaving her standing on the doorstep after she'd come all this way? She stepped aside to get out of the sunshine that was beating down on her back. She wouldn't mind a chance to cool down somewhere and drink a glass of lemonade after her long journey. She suddenly wondered whether the telegram she had sent ahead to announce her arrival might have been lost. Did Marie even know that she was on her way?

The maid looked back over her shoulder as though hoping that someone would come and help her get rid of Wanda. When no help came, she stepped a little closer to Wanda.

"She is . . . very weak after the birth of her daughter yesterday," she whispered, peering back into the palazzo again as she spoke. She made no move to let Wanda in.

"Marie has a daughter? The baby's already here?" Wanda asked incredulously. The maid nodded vaguely.

Yesterday . . . Marie had given birth to a little girl while she, Wanda, had been sitting on the train! It took her a moment to digest the news. Then all at once her heart was brimming over with happiness. Marie had a daughter! She wanted to shove the maid out of the way and run into the house. She had to see Marie right away! And the baby.

Instead she took a deep breath. "Of course my aunt needs peace and quiet today, I understand," she said, smiling at the maid, who looked greatly relieved.

"Where is Franco?" Only now did Wanda think to ask after him. Why hadn't she thought to do that immediately? The least she could do was congratulate the father on the birth of his daughter. And Franco, of course, would insist that she be given a room in the palazzo rather than having to go and find a hotel while she waited for Marie to recover from the birth. She would take a look at the little one, just quickly, say hello to Marie, and then . . .

"Signor de Lucca . . . not here. And his mother, Countess Patrizia, also not. Tomorrow they come back!" Carla answered stiffly and then shut the door before Wanda could react.

Wanda stared in astonishment at the elaborately carved wooden door. It was all well and good that the servants should ensure the new mother had some peace and quiet, but this was going too far! There was only one way Wanda could explain it to herself: the staff had not been told that she was coming. And there were only two ways to explain that: either the household had been in such an uproar at the birth that it had simply been overlooked, or the telegram had gotten lost somewhere.

Perplexed, she picked up her luggage and turned on her heel. The marble chips on the pathway crunched as she walked, and her feet were painfully swollen from the long train journey. Wanda turned around at the gate to the courtyard. The palazzo was certainly large and magnificent—but the people who lived in it had some very strange manners!

She could just about believe that Franco would be in town having a drink with some friends in a bar to celebrate the birth of his daughter, but the idea that his mother had left the house as well . . . If Marie really was that tired out by the birth, one might expect that her mother-in-law would stay with her. What would Johanna say when she heard that? A tinge of foreboding mixed with Wanda's outrage, but she was too upset to really think about it.

She came to a crossroads and stopped to get her bearings. The city was indeed beautiful and its buildings magnificent, but she didn't care about that at the moment. She decided to head down to the harbor, since she figured she might find the hotels there.

Her luggage became heavier with every step she took, and she was annoyed that she hadn't thought to leave the case full of presents for Marie and the baby at the palazzo. Now she would have to cart it around with her.

Tomorrow, she decided, she would hire a cab to take her from the hotel to the palazzo.

29

The sun hangs low in the sky, shining through beneath the trees. Their long shadows stretch out like grasping fingers, reaching out to . . .

Let me go!

Marie ducks away, beneath the branches. She has to get out of this darkness! But the shadows are faster than she is; they slip ahead and are lying in wait wherever she steps. I'm here already, you cannot get away . . .

A game that Johanna's twins used to play. The pictures flash through her mind's eye . . . chalk circles on paving stones, skirts swinging, and children's songs . . . one, two, hop! and the shadow eats the words before she can remember any more.

"Marie, come on, get undressed! You have to be naked if you're going to sunbathe." Sherlain's voice, chiding her as she always did for not following Monte Verità's rules. Hands pluck at her clothes now, and a cloth slaps at her face; she's gasping for air, but she can't breathe. It's so cramped in here, so narrow and tight; she's scared but . . .

"No, don't undress me! No . . . ! The man with the beard! He's coming for me . . ." The thought blurs at the edges like ink on wet paper. What man?

"Quiet now, Marie! Nobody wants to undress you." A hand pushed her back down into bed. "Let me put that cloth back on your brow. We have to drive this fever away."

Marie sat up, soaked with sweat. "Fever . . ."

For a moment she didn't know who the woman was, dipping the white cloth into a china bowl, wringing it out. Then the memory slowly came back to her: the birth, the terrible pain, then at last, from one moment to the next, merciful oblivion in which she felt nothing and nothing hurt anymore . . .

The man with the beard . . . there he is again, hiding in the forest, hiding in among the blue and green and . . . He waves to her, she can see him clearly . . .

She remembered something. Something so important that she struggled to sit up again so that she could think clearly. She fought with all her strength against the dizziness that threatened to overcome her. These moments of wakefulness were a rare gift; she had to use each one to the fullest.

"My baby. Where is my baby?"

How could she have forgotten her daughter? She had to look after her. Her Sylvie.

Soothing words reached her ears as though through cotton, calming the panic that rose within her.

"Your baby . . . is well . . . She's well."

Marie's eyes drooped closed. There was nothing she could do to stop them.

Sylvie, like Marie. A short name. Her baby didn't need anything more than that. A good name. Sylvie Steinmann . . . The dizziness was there again, stronger than before, her head was so heavy . . .

Something is sparkling behind her eyelids, like droplets after spring rain. But they are not drops of water; rather they are polished prisms of glass that catch the sunlight and refract it in a burst of color.

Georgie is at Marie's bedside. She's holding up a necklace of glass beads in front of her face. "You see, the shadow's gone away!" She laughs and her skin shines in all the colors of the rainbow.

"Now we can have some fun . . ." She swings the necklace back and forth, the prisms melt and flow together, growing rounder and rounder until they become a globe.

"That's the paradise of glass . . ." Marie murmured.

◆　◆　◆

"Please believe me, Signorina Miles, this really is the worst possible time for you to visit your aunt! The birth was unusually hard on her, since the baby was not in position. We had to take . . . certain measures to save the life of both mother and baby."

What measures? Wanda frowned in concern. She couldn't imagine what the word meant but it sounded awful. Or perhaps the countess had picked the wrong word? Her English was rather broken.

"And how are the mother and the baby now?" she asked, sick at heart. Why was the countess so tight-lipped? How could she sit there so calmly on that dainty little chair and not even tell Wanda what Marie's daughter was named?

Patrizia shrugged noncommittally. "The doctor was here this morning and examined Marie and the *bambino*. The child is very well, and a wet nurse is taking care of her. Thank heavens that we found her—she lives just a couple of houses away, and she is quite willing to nurse Sylvie alongside her own child."

Sylvie. So that was what Marie's daughter was called. "And what about Marie?" Wanda asked urgently.

Patrizia heaved a great sigh. "She has an infection and a high fever. She sees things in her sleep; it seems that she is having hallucinations. The doctor says that the most important thing now is for her to rest."

"She has childbed fever? That can be fatal, can't it?" With every word she spoke, Wanda's heart pounded harder with fear. Her mother had often told her about the women she saw in the New York hospitals' indigent wards. They gave birth in insanitary conditions and then died of childbed fever soon after they were brought to the hospital.

A shiver ran down Wanda's spine. "I have to see her, now, just for a little while!"

Patrizia took Wanda's hand. Her fingers were cool. "Believe me, we are doing everything we can for Marie. But she must not become unnecessarily excited by visitors. The doctor says if she does not have complete rest . . ."

Wanda drew her hand away. She had rarely felt such horror at another person's touch. *If not—then what?*

A moment later the countess was on her feet, and her posture clearly conveyed that she considered the conversation over. She didn't say a word about when Wanda could come again. And she certainly wasn't going to invite Wanda to live in the palazzo until Marie was better.

What now? Wanda felt as though she were acting in a play in which the director had forgotten to give the actors their script. The whole situation was so absurd that it frightened her. She had come all the way from Germany to visit Marie, and gotten no farther than this ghastly anteroom. And now Marie's mother-in-law wanted to put her off with vague excuses. She said that Franco was away on urgent business—and then nothing more about her son's absence.

Something was wrong. Very wrong.

To buy herself a little time, Wanda teased a handkerchief from her pocket while she watched Marie's mother-in-law from under hooded lids. The countess was already standing in the doorway. The way she held her back ramrod straight as she gazed into the middle distance with a forced smile on her lips reminded Wanda of her mother, who always struck that pose when she had to be polite to people she couldn't stand. It was a mask behind which anything at all might be hiding.

What does the countess have to hide? Wanda wondered as she dabbed at nonexistent drops of sweat with her handkerchief. She tried desperately to order her thoughts a little and not to let this cold-eyed woman intimidate her.

Was something wrong with the baby? The idea was so dreadful that Wanda could hardly think what it might mean. Or was there a greater danger to Marie's health that the countess had not told her about? If there was, then wasn't it even more urgent that Wanda be allowed to visit her now?

At that moment she wished for nothing in the world so much as to have Johanna there at her side. Or her mother.

But she was on her own, and Marie needed her. Needed her more than anyone.

At last she rose to her feet and went toward the door, stopping only when she was standing face-to-face with Patrizia. How stern the woman looked! Wanda could well imagine that most people would bow their heads and turn away from the look in Patrizia's eyes, forget their request, and leave without further ado. But not Wanda Miles! Anyone who had run the gauntlet of the Sonneberg wholesalers had nothing to fear from an Italian countess. Without even the faintest note of hesitation in her voice, she said, "I would like to be taken to Marie this instant. If not, then . . ."

She hoped that the implication was enough of a threat in itself. Since she had not the least idea how she could have finished the sentence.

◆ ◆ ◆

The hissing of the flame grows louder. Soon it will be the right tempera-ture to blow a glass globe. A large one. A glittering globe, with all the colors of a soap bubble. Like the soap bubbles that Father used to . . .

"Aunt Marie, are you awake?"

Marie groaned. *Don't shake me! The soap bubbles will burst.*

"Aunt Marie, can you hear me? I . . . can wait till you've had some more rest."

Pop! Pop! Pop! and they burst, one by one.

"Wanda?" Marie's arm trembled as she tried to sit up. She blinked in the darkness of the room. "Is that really you?"

"Yes, it's me," Wanda answered.

Such a soft voice . . . like an angel's . . . not like Wanda, always so lively and excited . . .

Marie struggled to concentrate. To see clearly. Was Wanda really standing there by her bed or did she only exist in her head, like all the others? And then—a hand on her hand, soft and warm. It must really be Wanda.

"You . . . came. All this way. How did you know that . . ." All at once Marie didn't know which question to ask first. She began to cry. *How did you get here? Are you well? And how's Johanna?* Her head was so full. A tangle of thoughts from which she could not tease out what was important from what was not.

"I have to tell you something . . ." Marie began softly. "I—"

"Shhh, lie still. We'll talk later. We have plenty of time . . ." Wanda murmured. She put her arms around Marie and rocked her back and forth like a baby.

Marie never wanted to leave this loving embrace. She was so happy and yet she had to cry. Soon Wanda's shoulder was wet with tears.

"You see, she's already becoming overexcited!" Patrizia hissed from over by the door.

"She's crying because she's happy!" Wanda answered. Then she let go and gently urged Marie back down onto the pillows. "Your mother-in-law says that you must rest. I'm not allowed to agitate you or she'll throw me out," she said and gave Marie a conspiratorial wink.

Patrizia immediately stepped closer. She hadn't understood what Wanda had said to Marie in German, but she knew that it had been about her.

Wanda, here—this is a gift from God! Dear Lord, thank you! I have to use this time. The dizziness might come back at any moment. All these voices in my head, the . . . Marie blinked away her tears.

"I . . . I'm well. I'm just a little weak still." She tried to smile. It was good to have her head clear again. She was filled with the hope that everything would be all right. "Have you seen my daughter? Sylvie? Isn't she beautiful?"

"And she's so strong! The wet nurse says she's as big as a boy. No wonder the birth left you feeling tired."

Make Patrizia leave us alone, Marie pleaded silently. *There's so much I have to tell you. But I can't when she's looking at me with those sharp eyes of hers.*

"Sylvie de Lucca—what a beautiful name! Wait till you see all the things Johanna bought for the baby!" Wanda laughed, just a shade too merrily. "There are some little dresses in case she turned out to be a girl. And we bought pants for a boy . . ."

Not de Lucca, Steinmann, Marie screamed inside. How was she going to explain all this to Wanda with Patrizia in the room? She shut her eyes. She would rest for a moment, then . . .

Not de Lucca. Not anymore. Sylvie Steinmann, that's what she'll be called.

When Marie woke up Wanda was still sitting by her bed. She was holding Sylvie in her arms. The picture was so wonderful that Marie began crying again.

"Doesn't she look just like a Steinmann?" she whispered through her tears. "She has the same blonde hair that my mother had. And that you had when you were a baby . . ."

"Do you think so?" Wanda asked, smiling. "Franco won't be very pleased when you tell him that the baby looks more like our family than his . . ." She pointed vaguely over to the door, where Patrizia was standing watch.

Marie laughed and then immediately wished she hadn't. She suddenly felt so dizzy that she had to grasp the side of the bed. She moaned softly.

Don't faint. I have to tell Wanda everything; I have to get Sylvie to safety . . .

"Can't you see that your visit is harming the patient?" Patrizia hissed. "I am sorry, Signorina Miles, but if you cannot see for yourself that you must go, I shall have to fetch my husband."

"No! Let Wanda stay. I don't want to be alone!" Marie cried, gripping Wanda's hand. "You can't throw her out! This is my home as well!" she screamed hysterically at the doorway.

Wanda was startled. Looking at Marie, she saw that her aunt's eyes were wide with fear. She made soothing sounds such as she would use to comfort a frightened child.

"Don't worry. I'll stay here until you're quite healthy again. And nobody is going to throw me out," she said, glancing at Patrizia.

Marie shut her eyes again. Oh, but she was afraid. Afraid that her time would run out.

30

The next few days were the worst in Wanda's life. Whenever she thought back on that time with Marie, she saw a kaleidoscope of hope, fear, and dreadful despair turning and turning in her mind's eye.

Once she saw how ill Marie was, Wanda refused to leave the room except to go to the bathroom. She toyed with the idea of sending a telegram to Johanna to tell her about Marie's poor health, but to do that, she would have to leave the palazzo. So Wanda decided against it. What good would it do Marie if Johanna worried herself sick? It was better not to get in touch with Lauscha until there was good news.

Wanda sat by Marie's bed day and night. When Marie was asleep, she snatched a little sleep for herself in an armchair that she pulled over to the bedside. But when Marie was feverish and delirious, Wanda forced herself to stay awake. It was frightening to see Marie in such a state. She talked to people who weren't there and sometimes she cried out, but Wanda couldn't understand anything other than a couple of names and some scraps of words. It was during these hours by Marie's bedside that she first understood how many kinds of laughter there were: sometimes Marie giggled like a little girl, sometimes she gave a full-throated laugh of merriment, sometimes she cackled like an old woman who had lost her wits. At such moments, she was in a world where nobody could follow her. It was especially bad when she lay there with a forlorn smile on her face. She looked so lonely then that Wanda felt compelled to hold her in her arms and caress her, never wanting to let her go.

Wanda managed to persuade the countess to bring Sylvie's cradle into the room. At first Patrizia protested loudly, saying that the baby's crying would disturb the patient. And the wet nurse's milk might dry up if she had to sit in a sickroom. And if she refused to come to the palazzo anymore, what would they do then? Of course Wanda didn't want to risk that, but she nonetheless insisted, hoping that Marie would recover more quickly if Sylvie were nearby.

It turned out that the new arrangement worked for everyone. The wet nurse didn't mind putting the baby to her breast in the mother's room, and her milk came just as it had before. Sylvie slept most of the time, and Marie held her when she was feeling strong enough. Those were the best moments, when Wanda could rest and gather her strength, hoping that everything would be all right.

At first Patrizia stood by the door all the time like a watchdog, her eyes never leaving the sickbed. Only when Wanda told her directly that she was not leaving until Marie was well again did Patrizia begin to leave them alone, at least while Marie was asleep or hallucinating. Every time the countess left, Wanda felt she could breathe more freely.

Patrizia's behavior was extremely odd. At first glance she really seemed to be a worried mother-in-law, full of concern for her granddaughter and the baby's mother. But Wanda soon got the impression that the countess was trying to control Marie's every waking moment; whenever her daughter-in-law woke up and wanted to talk to Wanda, Patrizia would come into the room as though she had been listening at the door or had sent the servants to spy on them. She always brought something for Marie—a pitcher of lemonade, or fresh water and washcloths to make the cold compresses, or a clean gown—but she never brought anything for Wanda. It was as though she were trying to force her out to the kitchen to grab a bite to eat. Wanda rarely went there, though; she was so worried about Marie that her appetite had quite gone.

More than once she sensed that Marie was urgently trying to tell her something. But the impression vanished as soon as Patrizia came into the room. Then there was simply a look of need in Marie's eyes. But Wanda could hardly throw Patrizia out of the room, here in her own house! So she had no choice but to wait for their chance to talk unobserved and to save up all the questions that were burning inside her.

Why haven't you written for months? Did our first parcel with the baby gifts even arrive? Why does your father-in-law look at us the way a hungry snake studies a rabbit every time he comes into the room? And why on earth isn't your husband here? All your mother-in-law has told me is that he's in New York. In New York? While you give birth to your first child?

But whenever Wanda even tentatively tried to broach one of these subjects and Marie began to speak, Patrizia stopped her.

"Speaking is too much of an exertion for you, remember what the doctor said!" And to Wanda, "You are irresponsible, asking Marie questions like this when she has a fever! Can't you see that she's hallucinating?"

Wanda didn't think that was true at all. It was easy to tell the difference between those moments when Marie was off in a world of her own and those when she could think clearly. She thought that Patrizia was a dragon guarding the cave where Marie was held prisoner.

She grew to dislike Marie's mother-in-law more with every passing hour. If the dragon had actually mistreated Marie or neglected her, then Wanda would at least have been able to say why she disliked her so. But there was fresh bed linen every morning; light, nourishing meals were served at regular intervals; the pot of herbal tea at her bedside was always full—Patrizia did everything by the book. She also made sure that the doctor came twice a day. Wanda had to leave the room during these visits. She would have liked to talk to him, but he spoke neither German nor English and she had only a very few words of Italian. But Wanda learned all she needed to know when she saw how grave his face was when he left the room. Her aunt's life was in danger. Every time Wanda asked Patrizia what the doctor had said, the countess replied that the fever was the greatest risk. Marie had suffered a tear during the birth and had to have stitches. Although they had done all they could to keep the wound clean, it had become infected. The fever showed no signs of abating.

At these moments, standing outside Marie's room in the hallway, Wanda and Patrizia were united in their fears.

◆　◆　◆

A flame, bright yellow, flickering, right there in front of her eyes. But somehow blurred, as though seen through a window on a foggy night in Lauscha. She goes closer to the flame. Or is the flame coming closer to her? It's all the same . . . Strange, it's not as hot as it looks . . . The core of the flame is pale. Marie puckers her lips to blow air into the flame. "You have to blow hard to make the flame sing!" That's Father's voice! Marie smiles. She can hear him, but where is he? She's so happy that for a moment she forgets the flame, forgets to blow. The flame dies. And Papa says, "You see, it's gone out now. Gone out forever."

When Marie awoke, her nightgown was drenched with sweat. She had been dreaming, as so often during her illness. She tried to remember. She *had* to remember, it was important!

Marie drank some tea, but it tasted flat and dull.

She could hear Wanda's voice from next door. She seemed to be speaking to Sylvie, or perhaps to the wet nurse. Not to Patrizia. She never used such warm tones with her. Marie had to smile. Dear Wanda. Faithful Wanda. Blood really was thicker than water. All of a sudden she remembered.

It hadn't been one of those dreams where so many different people danced past her eyes that her head spun trying to follow them. No. This time it had been a very simple dream. She had seen her father. And a flame that went out. Not any old flame from a glassworker's lamp—this was the flame of her life. The insight struck her so hard it knocked the breath clean out of her.

Why me? I don't want to die now!

She pulled the covers over her head so that nobody could hear her whimpering. Tears ran down her cheeks.

There was so much she still wanted to do in her life! Her life was like a mosaic in which the most important pieces were still missing.

Johanna and Ruth . . . will I never see them again? They had always stuck together. Everyone in the village always called them the Steinmann sisters, as though they were one entity . . . and then she left without even once looking back. Forgive me, Johanna, forgive me!

What will happen to my baby if I die? Who will take care of Sylvie? Who will tell her that she can do anything she wants to in this life? That even a woman can make her own way? But that everything has a price. Will her father tell her that?

The thought of leaving Sylvie alone was more than Marie could bear. She tossed and turned like a wounded animal, whimpering softly.

I can't die . . . I'm too young . . . there's so much I have to do . . . who will do all that, if not me?

Helplessly, she put her hands together in prayer. She wondered what she ought to say at such a moment.

Neither she nor her sisters had ever been particularly religious. They believed in God, of course, and in Heaven, but the good Lord had never played any great part in their lives.

"Dear God, I implore you, make me healthy again. For Sylvie's sake." Marie's voice was thick with tears and sounded strange in her ears. The whole prayer sounded strange. All the same she went on, "But if You must call me to You, then at least tell me what I can do for my child!"

◆　◆　◆

It had been three days since Wanda arrived. She had just finished quickly washing up after another night spent at Marie's bedside. The previous evening she had persuaded Patrizia to send Carla to fetch some of her luggage from the hotel, so she finally had some clean things to wear. *Perhaps it would have been best to bring all of it,* Wanda mused as she turned the handle to go into Marie's room. But since Patrizia still hadn't actually invited her to stay, she had decided to make do with the little traveling bag she had packed with those few things she needed for the journey itself.

"Marie! You're awake!"

The sight of Marie sitting up in bed flooded Wanda with happiness. Perhaps the fever would break today; perhaps this was going to be the day they had all been waiting for . . .

Marie put a finger to her lips. Her eyes were wide open but they were clear and focused.

"I have something here that I want to give you before she comes back. Quick, take this, hide it." She was holding a tattered little notebook in her hand. Her gaze darted nervously toward the door, as though she had stolen all the silver in the palazzo and was handing it over to Wanda.

"What is it?" Wanda whispered. Before she even had a chance to look at the book, Marie gestured to her to hide it. She only relaxed a little once Wanda had shoved the book down between her bodice and the top of her dress. Her unease was infectious, for now Wanda found herself glancing again and again at the door. At any moment the dragon might come in with the breakfast tray. It was almost a miracle that she hadn't appeared yet.

"It's my diary," Marie whispered. "I've been writing it ever since January. Ever since they locked me away in here."

"Locked you away?" Wanda frowned. Was Marie hallucinating again?

Marie raised a hand to stop any more questions. "I know that it sounds crazy. What you're about to read is even worse than that. But it's the truth." She was speaking quickly, not even pausing for breath. "I want so much to tell you everything myself! But I've been talking such a lot of nonsense that you wouldn't know what to believe. Perhaps it's better if you just read it. Then you can ask me questions. Everything in that book is true, every word of it!" Marie's voice became louder with the last few words and her chest was rising and falling as though she'd been running hard.

Wanda felt once again that this was all too much for her. It wasn't good for Marie to get agitated this way; the fever would never break if she did. Where in the world was she supposed to go to read this diary? If she didn't want to wait for nightfall, then she had no choice but to shut herself away in the bathroom.

Marie gave a tired smile. "I feel so dizzy again . . ." Her gaze roamed around the room, and she was having trouble concentrating on Wanda. "When you've read what's in there, you'll understand what I must ask you to do." Her lower lip began to tremble as she spoke.

"What do you want me to do?" With every word Marie spoke, Wanda felt more sick at heart. This was a nightmare. She was trapped in a nightmare. *This water is too deep for me!* screamed a voice inside her. *I can't swim!*

"You have to take Sylvie with you. Back to Lauscha. She mustn't stay here, not for anything. Do you hear me? Not for anything! Don't let anyone stop you from taking her!"

Had she heard right? "But how . . ." Wanda began.

Just then, the door flew open. When Patrizia saw Marie so agitated, she became furious and began hurling reproaches at Wanda. But Wanda paid no attention to the dragon, not any more than Marie did. They looked into one another's eyes, each trying to read what they saw there.

"Do you promise me?" Marie asked again, urgently.

Wanda nodded. How could she have refused?

The next time Marie fell asleep and Patrizia left the room, Wanda teased the notebook out from her bodice. Her body heat had warmed it right through, and for a moment she was worried that the ink may have blurred. But when she opened the first page, she saw Marie's unmistakable handwriting with its deep loops and slightly oversized capital letters.

Saturday, 14th January. A week ago today I was driven from Paradise. A week ago today I discovered that my husband, my "beloved," is not a man of honor but a murderer.

Wanda froze.

Next came a detailed description of all that Marie had heard that night at the office door. A few pages later she had written:

I still cannot believe it. Every part of me fights against the knowledge. Night after night I lay in bed next to a murderer, I delighted in his caresses. Perhaps he already had deaths on his conscience when I fell in love with him? The idea almost drives me mad.

How could I have been so mistaken about him? Again and again I remember our time together in New York. What did he say and when? And how did I answer? I feel like a surgeon, placing my scalpel to the chosen spot . . .

The pain in those words! Wanda could hardly bear it. She lowered the diary and looked at Marie for a few minutes as she lay there asleep. What demons was she fighting when she thrashed about and moaned? Wanda could not imagine. She did not doubt for a moment the truth of what she had read. All the same she was unable to make the connection between the words in this book and the people she knew. She began to read once more.

Perhaps . . . if I had listened more closely at the time, I would have realized that light and dark are very closely mixed in Franco. But I was so much in love that I did not want to see what I was looking at, to listen to what I heard! Otherwise I would have realized that the Italians, the restaurant owners, treated him with a mixture of fear and contempt. I was a silly cow to believe that they were showing deference, that they respected his noble name! And why did I never wonder why he did not ever want me to go to the harbor with him? When he was otherwise so jealous of every minute I spent with others?

There was more such self-recrimination. Wanda felt shocked, but also enraged and deeply, deeply sad. What had Marie done to herself during all those weeks when she was imprisoned? None of this was her fault! Nobody had seen through Franco; he and his family had put up such a fine show that nobody would have suspected their evil deeds!

When she read about how Marie had tried to escape, her heart almost broke. The count and countess were monsters!

> . . . *after that Patrizia did not come to see me for a few days. She sent that dreadful Carla instead. It's crazy, I know, but now I actually feel guilty that I tried to escape.*

The old witch! It wasn't enough that she kept Marie under lock and key, but she had been playing mind games with her as well! Wanda looked toward the door, filled with hatred. If only Patrizia should dare show herself now! She frowned and read on.

> *And I can shout and rage as much as I like—Patrizia doesn't see that she has done anything wrong. She is convinced that she is only acting in the family's best interests and she says that I will simply have to put up with a few "inconveniences" for that reason. What an elegant way to describe this prison they have put me in! Una famiglia—how often must I hear those words! Nevertheless, if there is ever another chance I will try it again. But only if I do not put the baby at risk. Patrizia may put the family above all—but for me, my baby is more important than anything else. They can take my freedom, but they cannot take my child!*

Wanda smiled sadly at all this useless bravery.

> *Tuesday, 14th February. Today I was startled to discover that I had spent all morning staring at a tiny rip in the wallpaper. I have to take care that I do not truly go mad. If only I could pull myself together and sit at my workbench! Patrizia has offered to buy me some more glass. She probably believes that she can keep me quiet this way . . .*

"So? Have you read it all?"

Wanda gave a start. She hadn't noticed Marie wake up.

"No," she choked out. "But I have read enough! It's a good thing you wrote everything down. What do you think the police would say if I showed them this?"

Marie shook her head weakly. "No, not the police."

"But why ever not? They can't go killing people and locking you up here and—"

Wanda stopped when she felt Marie's cold hand on her arm.

"Please don't, I'm begging you! You have to think of Sylvie. You have to use what you know to help her . . ."

"What do you mean? Surely it would help Sylvie if all of this was known and investigated?" Wanda asked, frowning. But Marie's eyes closed once more. Her moments of wakefulness were getting ever shorter—the realization struck Wanda like a thunderbolt. She had to face the truth. Marie was not going to get better. She had been fooling herself.

Marie slept. Her breath came and went in gasps, and she tossed and turned restlessly.

The doctor had looked even more worried after his last visit. He had stood in the hallway, talking urgently to Patrizia. A little while later Patrizia had come into the room and taken Sylvie's cradle away. Then she put a candle on the bedside table. Not long after that a black-clad priest arrived. He was very old. He read a passage from the Bible aloud to Marie in Latin. Soon the sickroom was filled with the scent of incense.

Wanda stood at the foot of Marie's bed together with the count and Patrizia. Although she had never witnessed such a ceremony before now, she knew what was going on. This was the Extreme Unction. The priest anointed Marie with blessed oil as she lay dying to bring her closer to God, and he was saying a prayer for her comfort. As she lay dying . . . every fiber of Wanda's being recoiled at the knowledge.

"Marie, darling Marie, you mustn't die," she whispered after the priest had left the room with Patrizia and the count. Her heart clenched with fear. "Stay with us, please. We love you. And we need you. I . . . don't know that I'm as strong as you think I am."

She stroked Marie's cheek. As she leaned forward, the diary hidden inside her bodice pushed at her belly. She had only been able to forget for the briefest moment how Marie had suffered, how she had been mistreated.

How sanctimonious Patrizia had been, standing there next to the priest . . . Wanda had to struggle to stay calm. She had to think of Marie. And of what Marie had told her: she had to use what she knew to help Sylvie. By now Wanda knew what that meant, though everything within her struggled against it.

Marie opened her eyes. A strange light shone in them that Wanda had never seen before. It was as though they were glowing from within.

"Wanda, dearest . . . I still have so much I want to say to you. But . . . too weak. You must . . . take Sylvie back to Lauscha. You promised. My daughter must grow up among glassblowers, not among . . . murderers."

"She'll grow up with you!" Wanda called out in desperation. "You'll be well again soon; the fever just has to leave you."

Marie shook her head almost imperceptibly. "The fever won't leave. I shall."

And she shut her eyes for the last time.

31

The funeral took place the very next day. That was the way things were done in Italy, the countess explained. Wanda was tearful and devastated.

There was no time to tell Lauscha. No time for Johanna and Peter and Magnus to come and see Marie buried. No time even to get used to the idea that she was dead. Beautiful Marie. Marie with the sparkle in her eyes.

Only a few people gathered for the burial: the count and his wife, Carla and another chambermaid, and Wanda. Sylvie was with the wet nurse, and Franco was in prison in America. Nobody had even told him yet that his wife was dead.

The cemetery was not like the ones Wanda knew in New York. Nor was it like the one in Lauscha. Wanda watched, her eyes blank, as Marie's coffin was placed in a niche in a huge stone wall. One niche among many, with a hastily chiseled inscription. All around, on either side, above and below, were more niches with their own dead bodies. No flowers, no crosses, no "Ashes to ashes, dust to dust," no return to the bosom of Mother Earth. The ground here was too stony to receive the dead.

It wasn't good for Marie to be buried here—she belonged in Lauscha. The thought stirred somewhere at the back of Wanda's mind, but it was all happening in such a hurry that it never quite became conscious. Perhaps . . . if Mother had been there with her, or Johanna—they would never have allowed . . . But there was nobody else here, and Marie's body was deposited in the stone wall.

Wanda's departure was quick and dramatic. The count and countess shook Wanda's hand stiffly. To her astonishment, the count had even ordered a coach to bring her to the station with her luggage and the baby—she would never have imagined that he would be so "considerate." He even rode along with her. At the station he helped her find the right train. Wanda took her seat with Sylvie in the compartment where the count had reserved two places.

She stared out the window, her eyes blank. Although the train moved very slowly, she noticed nothing of the grandeur of the Alps passing by. After the exertions of the last few days she was more tired than she had ever been in her life. Every thought was an effort, yet the dreadful feeling that she had done something wrong never left her.

How could she have allowed them to bury Marie in Genoa? Shouldn't she have insisted that Marie be cremated, so that she could take her ashes back to Lauscha? It would certainly be very complicated to try to arrange that from Germany. Wanda expected yet more recriminations from the others when she got home, for she had not even been able to telegraph and tell them that Marie was dead. But how could she have put such a terrible event into a few short words? The whole thing was so dreadful that she hadn't even sent a telegram to Richard.

And then there was another worry that was much more pressing.

A few minutes earlier, the conductor had come by to tell the passengers that they were approaching the Italian-Austrian border.

What if the border patrol saw something wrong with Sylvie's papers? What if everything she had done in the last few days ended in failure because some stubborn official's suspicions were aroused when he saw a young woman with a baby in her arms?

Wanda glanced at the baby, asleep on the seat next to her in a bassinet. How she clenched her little fists as though to fight against the whole wicked world! Yet no force in the world could protect her against fate . . .

Beautiful, stubborn Marie was dead.

Wanda shut her eyes and waited for the pain to pass. If she grieved for Marie now, she would never stop crying. She had to pull herself together, put off her grief, or she at least had to try. She took a deep breath. She just had to do her best to keep Sylvie safe. That was all she could do.

Should she wake Sylvie when the officers came into the compartment? Men didn't like crying babies so perhaps the passport inspection would be over more quickly? But perhaps it would draw the officers' attention to the young mother with her child. Wanda tried to look at her reflection in the mirror, but the morning sunlight made it difficult. She knew, however, that even with makeup and a more grown-up outfit, she still wouldn't look much older. An older woman traveling with a child might not be so conspicuous. But she was traveling on her own, without family or a servant, and her passport would soon reveal that she was unmarried . . .

Wanda bent over and looked into the bassinet every few minutes. The little one was asleep. Everything seemed to be all right; her cheeks were rosy pink but not too flushed. There were tiny crescents of shadow beneath her eyes cast by her eyelashes, which were astonishingly thick for a newborn—Marie's daughter was an exceptionally beautiful baby.

So far she had been the perfect traveling companion; she had fallen asleep almost as soon as the train got moving. When she woke up, Wanda gave her a bottle of the milk that the wet nurse had expressed for her and changed her diaper just as the wet nurse had shown her. But she didn't know whether she would be able to make the baby hush if she began to cry.

She mustn't think so much. One thing at a time. Everything had been all right so far.

Her hand trembled as she took her own passport from the bag along with Sylvie's papers. How she had had to bluster and threaten to get her hands on those papers!

All she had wanted to do after the burial was sit in a corner and cry until she could cry no more. Instead she had threatened the count that she would make Marie's discoveries public until, at last, he had given way to her demands. Secretly she was rather surprised. Why didn't he try to get the book from her? Why didn't he try to buy Wanda's silence some other way? She didn't like to think what else he might have tried . . . In the end she suspected that the count was already in so much trouble that he didn't want to be burdened with a motherless newborn baby girl on top of everything else.

He had grumbled that she could take Sylvie with her if she must and the two of them could go to the Devil together. Then he had suggested a trade: Sylvie, for Marie's diary. Wanda had agreed and the count had set out to twist the arm of one of his corrupt contacts in Genoa's city hall. Perhaps it hadn't even required that much pressure—Marie's notes revealed that there were plenty of corrupt officials to choose from. However it had happened, Wanda now held a birth certificate proclaiming that Sylvie was her daughter, born while she was visiting the de Lucca family. She would have to take this to the authorities in Lauscha. Or would she have to go into Sonneberg for that? She didn't know. And then? What name would Sylvie have growing up? Who would . . . She shook her head in irritation, as though trying to shake off a fly. She mustn't think too much.

Wanda didn't care whether the doctor, the priest, or the servants knew about the deception—perhaps the old man had paid them to keep quiet as well. The de Luccas were living in a web of lies and would entangle themselves in it ever deeper—*she* had only done what she had to.

One thing at a time. First she had to get the baby to Lauscha. And there was nobody who could help her do that.

Though Wanda longed for Richard, she couldn't let herself think of him—and of his broad shoulders that she could lean on if he were here. He would probably be worried when she didn't show up in Venice as planned. But she mustn't think of that either. She would tell Richard everything when he got back to Lauscha.

The immigration officials were in the next compartment. Wanda could hear their clipped tones. Her heart was beating like a drum. She had to stay calm, had to think of something else.

Would the count have given way to her threats if the baby had been a boy? Perhaps he would not have let go of a young heir to the title so quickly. As it was, he had simply insisted that Wanda sign a declaration that Sylvie had no claim on the de Lucca family. Wanda had signed. It was only when the ink began to dry that she wondered whether she had given in too easily. Her signature had robbed Sylvie of any rights to a share of the de Lucca family fortune. Wanda wondered nervously what they would say to that in Lauscha. Probably that Wanda had let Franco's father swindle her. But it was done now. And the others hadn't been there when Marie begged her to take Sylvie, Wanda decided stubbornly. Marie had said very clearly that she didn't want her daughter to grow up having anything to do with the de Luccas. That meant financially as well, didn't it?

Patrizia had put up more of a fight, pleading with Wanda to leave Sylvie with her. How was she to explain to Franco when he got back that his daughter would grow up in a foreign country? He would never forgive her for that, or for her failure to tell him when Marie died.

What a dreadful woman! She hadn't felt the least bit guilty, not even after Marie's death.

"If Marie had stood by her husband the way a wife should, we need never have taken such drastic measures. But she wanted to leave Franco at the very moment when he most needed her support," the countess had declared, her voice quivering. Wanda sensed that she still hadn't forgiven Marie.

I feel sorry for Franco, Wanda thought as she opened her passport. Franco was a victim of that web of lies. But no, he was guilty as well; there was no way around that. How could they all have been so wrong about him? Her handsome Italian, Marie had called him.

"Good day, miss. Your papers, please!" A uniformed official was standing in front of Wanda with his hand out. When he spotted the baby in her bassinet, he frowned.

"Good day." Wanda handed over the papers with a smile. *Don't tremble, look cool and collected but not condescending, breathe calmly,* she told herself silently as though this were a class in finishing school.

The man studied Wanda's American passport. He seemed especially interested in her entry stamp.

A vein in Wanda's neck began to throb. Surely he could find nothing wrong with her passport! She fought against rising panic. How disdainfully he looked at her! She cleared her throat. He must have seen her as a fallen maiden who somehow had the money to travel across Europe with her illegitimate baby. Perhaps he thought her family had disowned her. That she was on the run—and he wouldn't be far wrong. Wanda was almost cheered by the thought.

At last the official handed her documents back. "Did you know that my colleagues in Germany put their stamp in the wrong place?" The man tore the passport abruptly from her hands and pointed. "That's supposed to be where the American exit visa goes!"

He waved it impatiently in front of Wanda's face. "If everybody went on this way, we would never find our way around a passport!"

"Oh . . . I see, I see. Yes, that was very careless of them . . ."

Thank you, God. Thank you a thousand times.

Once the border official had gone, the trembling started. First her right hand began to tremble. Then her left. When she looked down, she saw that her knees were jiggling up and down as well. She glanced around the compartment. Had anybody noticed? But nobody was looking at her, just as nobody had sat down next to her.

Suddenly it was all too much for Wanda. The last few days by Marie's sickbed with hardly any sleep, the burial service at the dusty, rocky cemetery, the struggle to save Sylvie . . . Tears flowed uncontrollably down her cheeks, and she sobbed loudly. Her nose swelled up and she could barely breathe.

Marie was dead. Shut away where no gleam of light could reach her, no shine of silver or glitter of glass.

It was so unfair! Marie had never done anything to harm anyone. All her life she had never done anything but work; she had never even wanted to do anything else. And then, the first and only time she wanted to escape from that life, fate had not allowed it.

Why?

Try as she might, Wanda could see no sense in Marie's death. She buried her face in her coat.

How could somebody with such an appetite for life just die? How could that happen?

Old people died—or not, like Wilhelm Heimer, clinging to life with every fiber of his withered old body. Why had Marie not been strong enough?

Fever . . . that damned fever. Why hadn't it broken? If it had just ebbed a little, day by day, Marie would be healthy again. But to

just shut her eyes like that and say, "The fever won't leave. I shall."
She couldn't understand it.

Wanda blew her nose, her fingers trembling, and then she spotted a movement out of the corner of her eye. Sylvie was waving her little hands in the air as though beckoning to her. Her blue eyes under their long lashes were looking aimlessly around.

"Come here, you little thing!" Wanda lifted the baby carefully out of her bassinet. Luckily the trembling had stopped, and she could put her arms around the warm little body.

Wanda held Sylvie so her head was nestled against her shoulder. The baby would have to grow up without a mother.

"We'll all of us miss your mama. We'll miss her terribly."

32

Wanda arrived in Bozen early that evening, and the train to Munich did not depart until the next day. Over the course of the day a mountain of clouds had appeared and hidden the sun, and the heat was almost unbearable. The birds had stopped singing—an unmistakable sign that bad weather was brewing.

Wanda looked up at the sky, concerned. A storm was the last thing she needed. Her fingers were damp as she shifted the bassinet from her right arm to her left, then shouldered her bag and picked up her suitcase again. After just a few paces she felt her strength failing once more. She couldn't go on like this; she had to rest. She spotted a little patch of grass across the street in the shade of two huge chestnut trees. Wanda staggered to the lawn, where a marble monument and a bench stood. She put down the suitcase and her bag, then put the bassinet on the bench and sat next to it. She stared ahead, her eyes blank.

Only a week ago she had strolled through these streets with Richard as though they had all the time in the world, happy beyond measure. They had gone to dinner nearby and they had kissed in front of that fountain with the chubby cherubs. And then later that night . . .

Wanda's feet burned as though she had been walking over hot coals. Her mouth and her lips were dry, and her stomach was so empty that she was dizzy with hunger. It was just a matter of time before Sylvie started to protest at being carried around town in this heat. But none of these challenges were her biggest problem.

She had trudged around town for more than two hours looking for a place to spend the night. She had been to three hotels and two smaller boarding houses, and every one of them had turned her away. Was it because she was so young, or because she looked rather bedraggled after the long train journey? Was it because she didn't have a husband or her parents with her, or was it all because of the baby in her bassinet? She didn't know. All she knew was that she'd had the same answer everywhere: they had no free rooms.

She had never missed her mother so much in her life. And Aunt Johanna too. Both of them were always so sure of themselves! Their problems seemed to solve themselves on their own. They wouldn't end up sitting here like a sniveling heap of misery. No, they would . . . What would they do? Wanda had no idea. She would so much have liked to follow some example.

Her arms were tired as she lifted Sylvie from the bassinet and gave her the last bottle of milk that she had. The baby began to suckle at the rubber nipple. Her red cheeks pumped in and out and a little furrow of concentration appeared on her brow. Wanda smiled. Was she imagining things or had Marie's daughter really grown in the last two days? The sight of the hungry little girl filled her with new strength.

She couldn't just sit here! She had to find a pharmacy and buy some powdered milk for Sylvie. And she had to find a room for the night.

While she fed Sylvie she went over an inventory in her head of what she was carrying in her luggage. The travel bag was full of the presents she had brought from Lauscha—mostly baby things. She would be able to do without most of those, especially the clothes that were too big at the moment, but she would need all the diapers.

When Sylvie was full and back in her bassinet, Wanda got to work. She didn't care that the passersby stared as she sorted methodically through her luggage, discarding everything that she did not need on the journey. Once she was finished, her traveling bag was almost bursting but she could leave the suitcase behind. Perhaps somebody would come by who needed it more than she did. She set out, her load lightened and her feet a little rested.

When she found a pharmacy after only five minutes, she could have almost cried with relief. Her voice shook as she asked, half in German, half in Italian, for something her baby could eat.

"I will have to go into the stockroom. If the young lady would be good enough to wait . . ." the pharmacist answered in a melodious Austrian accent. Then he vanished through a door.

He came back with three cans, various glass flasks marked with white lines, and some bottles with rubber nipples. He arranged everything carefully on the counter and explained to Wanda how to prepare the milk.

A weight fell from Wanda's heart. She had been worried that she wouldn't be able to buy powdered milk in a little town like Bozen. Ever since she boarded the train in Genoa that morning, she had been scolding herself about not having bought milk for the journey. When the pharmacist asked if there was anything else he could do for her, Wanda felt another surge of panic. What else did a baby need? He was the first person she had met on her journey who had been friendly and polite, but she could hardly ask him for childcare advice. So she bought a little box of peppermints and thanked him for his help, then left.

The shop bell was still tinkling behind her as she opened the box and shoved one of the peppermints greedily into her mouth. Right away the cool taste of mint quenched the worst of her thirst.

A moment later, she had the idea.

It was such a simple idea—and it was wonderful.

It was exactly what her mother would do instead of tramping around the streets like a beggar. Wanda picked up her pace. Why hadn't she thought of it sooner?

Wanda and Sylvie reached the entrance of the Grand Park Hotel just as the first raindrops started to fall. At reception she paid the wickedly high price for a room, and as she took the key she silently thanked her parents for their generosity, which allowed her to spend the night at such a fancy place. All manner of well-heeled and worldly guests came and went here, and the receptionist was far too discreet to ask how a woman happened to be traveling alone with a baby. It was house policy to welcome any guest who was ready and willing to pay the outrageous cost for the night.

A bellhop took Wanda's bag and showed her to the room. Once he had unlocked the door, she asked him to bring her a pitcher of lemonade. He asked whether she would like him to bring something to eat as well or whether she would prefer to dine in the hotel's restaurant, the Belle Époque. As soon as he asked, Wanda's belly began to rumble in a most unladylike manner. She ordered the dish of the day and waved away his description of what the chef had prepared.

No sooner had the young man shut the door behind him than Wanda took Sylvie out of the bassinet. The baby began to wave her arms and legs immediately. Wanda spoke gently to the little one as she went into the bathroom, where she was pleased to find hot and cold running water. She ran lukewarm water into the elegant washbasin and added a pinch of the pink bath salts as well. If they were good enough for high-society ladies, they were good enough for her little princess!

"I think you already know just what you like, don't you!" Wanda said as she washed the baby rather clumsily. "We'll have to heat the stove every day in winter so that our little princess can have a bath! My word, that'll take a lot of firewood! Richard will have to sell a few more glasses."

Richard . . . the thought of him was like an arrow to her heart. She was supposed to meet him at the Hotel Riviera today. She could already see him in her mind's eye, pacing impatiently up and down and looking at a clock on the wall every few minutes.

A knock roused her from her thoughts. She wrapped Sylvie up in a thick towel and opened the door.

"*Madame*, your supper! Veal schnitzel in a lemon sauce, with butter noodles and . . ."

As soon as Wanda saw the bellhop, she knew just what she had to do. She hastily pulled him into the room complete with the tray. Then she stood in front of the door, blocking his way.

"It smells wonderful—but all of a sudden I'm not hungry anymore. What a pity . . ." She shrugged apologetically. "Perhaps you should eat it so that it doesn't go to waste?"

"Me? But . . ." The young man looked at her in astonishment.

"No buts! Sit down here at this table, right now, and have a good meal! I have something very important I have to do in the meantime. It's a matter of life and death, so to speak," Wanda pleaded. "And I need your help, or else all is lost!"

"But . . ."

She pushed him farther into the room. She fumbled in her bag for money and said, "Nobody but us needs to know what happened here, that goes without saying. If your boss tries to tell you off for staying away from your post, just blame me! Tell him . . . oh, tell him anything you like! And while you eat, will you please keep an eye on my daughter? She's just fallen asleep, and I'm sure she'll be no trouble. I'll be right back."

"But . . ."

"Please! Stay here and watch over my child, will you do that for me?" Without waiting to hear his objections, Wanda pushed some money into his hand. Then she ran from the room.

"It's an emergency. I swear to you that it is!" she pleaded at the reception desk a few minutes later. "I need a connection to the Hotel Riviera in Venice, whatever it costs!"

"It is not a matter of cost, dear lady, rather it's a technical problem," the receptionist told her for the second time. "Even if you happened to know the number of the hotel—which clearly you don't—I still couldn't call it directly. We would need an operator to put us through. And the telephone exchanges are hardly ever manned at this time of night."

Wanda wrung her hands. "But couldn't you at least try? Perhaps . . . if luck's on our side . . . please!"

She summoned the charming smile that she had worn so easily in a previous life.

The receptionist gave a resigned shrug, picked up the receiver, and began to dial.

33

"Wanda! I've been waiting for you for hours! I didn't leave the hotel all afternoon because I thought perhaps you might arrive earlier than we planned . . . Where are you? At the station? Should I come and meet you? That would be no problem, I know Venice like the back of my hand by now, even if all these canals . . ."

It was so good to hear his voice! Wanda's hand began to tremble as she held the receiver. She was close to tears.

"Richard, be quiet for a moment and listen! I'm not in Venice. I'm in Bozen."

"You're where? This connection . . . I don't think I heard you right."

Wanda smiled sadly.

"I'm in Bozen," she repeated. "On my way back to Lauscha." And before he could reply, she burst out with all the essential details. That Marie was dead. That she, Wanda, was traveling back to Lauscha with Marie's newborn baby. She said as little as she could about Franco, and about Marie's confinement. How she longed to be able to tell him all these dreadful things! But she didn't feel comfortable explaining it all over the telephone. She also had to blow her nose, since she could hardly breathe through the tears.

For a moment Wanda heard nothing but the crackle of the line. Then Richard said, "I . . . I don't know what to say. Wanda, my darling Wanda, it must have been dreadful for you! I can hardly believe that Marie . . . I'm so terribly sorry—"

Richard fell silent. But his honest sympathy said more to comfort her than a thousand words.

Then he seemed to pull himself together. He asked how Wanda was holding up. And how Sylvie was. She noticed gratefully that he had remembered Sylvie's name without prompting.

"I'll pack my things tonight. Then I'll catch the first train to Bozen in the morning. You stay right where you are, and we'll go back to Lauscha together. I'll take care of everything from now on. You needn't worry about anything, all right? We'll make it."

It was so tempting! It would be so easy, so simple. Wanda took a deep breath.

"No, Richard, I want you to stay in Venice. It's important for you. I've made it this far; I can go the rest of the way as well," she answered with more confidence in her voice than she truly felt.

"Forget the exhibition! I've already made a few useful contacts. And the whole thing's happening again in two years anyway. But you need me *now*! Great heavens, when I think that you are on your own there with Sylvie—" He stopped abruptly, then started again hesitantly. "It's just that . . . tomorrow's not the best time to leave, but I can certainly come the day after tomorrow. No later than that. And then we—"

"No!" Wanda broke in. "Please don't say another word. I miss you dreadfully, of course I do! But right now all I want is to get back to Lauscha as fast as I can. That's where Johanna and Eva are, and they'll help me. Don't you understand? I'm not entirely comfortable looking after her on my own. What do I know about babies, after all?" She laughed awkwardly.

Richard took a while to digest what she had said. Then he heaved a deep sigh.

"Well . . . to tell the truth I do have some appointments over the next few days; there are some people who want to look at my work. And now that there are three of us, we'll need every penny I can earn, won't we?"

"We will indeed!" Wanda said through her tears.

"But I won't stay all the way through till Sunday, that's for sure. I'll leave as soon as I can. I . . . I miss you so much! Poor Wanda . . . I want to be with you and hold you tight. Forever."

Which was just what she wanted too. "I love you," she whispered into the receiver.

"And I love you too," his voice came back over the crackling line.

The next morning Wanda's eyes were rimmed red and sore with weeping. Talking to Richard had unleashed the tears all over again. But this time she found that it did her good to cry, that it washed away the pain, and afterward she felt exhausted but healed. It was as though the worst of her grief had been blunted.

Richard would be there for her. His love would heal her pain; she knew that now. As the Tyrolean landscape sped by outside the train window, she thanked whatever fates had smiled upon her last night and allowed a telephone connection. However, she was still dreading having to break the terrible news to Johanna and the others. At least *she* had had the chance to say good-bye to Marie, difficult though it had been. Wouldn't the others find it almost impossible to accept their loss? Nevertheless, she had to tell them and the sooner the better. And tell her mother as well. Perhaps she would be able to call New York tonight from Munich.

Richard had said that they would look after Sylvie just as if they were her own father and mother. Father and mother—it sounded strange coming from him. *Would every man be so quick to take in the child of strangers?* Wanda wondered. *How would Harold have reacted?* She had no doubt that he would have hesitated, that he would have had a thousand questions. But what had Richard said, in that practical way of his? *"Now that there are three of us, we'll need every penny I can earn, won't we?"* Wanda smiled. She suddenly felt that she could face her future with confidence.

Confidence. Wanda thought for a while about what that word meant. It might be the best name for the tiny, warming flame that she felt deep within her, the flame that had not been there yesterday.

After Wanda had made sure that Sylvie was sleeping peacefully in her bassinet, she shut her own eyes too. The rhythmic rattle of the train along the tracks lulled her into a half sleep. When she awoke a little while later, the first thing she did was look at Sylvie. Everything was all right.

When they arrived in Munich, Wanda hailed a cab to take them to the best hotel in the city. She had just enough money left to pay for one night in a luxurious suite. Her last night away from home, Wanda told herself with relief as she followed the bellhop into the room. She eyed the heavy silk curtains, the vast bed with its royal-blue linens where a whole family could easily have slept, the magnificent Persian carpets on the gleaming parquet flooring. But there was no time to enjoy her surroundings. She unpacked hastily and counted her money. Then she washed Sylvie and fed her. Once the baby was lying happily in the middle of the bed with a light towel over her, Wanda rang for the concierge. She was surprised to see how young the woman was. She explained what she needed, and a few minutes later an older chambermaid appeared at the door. Reassured that she was leaving Sylvie in good hands rather than with a surprised and nervous bellhop, Wanda set out to find the nearest post office. As she walked through the crowded streets, she counted time zones in her head; it was nine o'clock in the morning in New York. If she were lucky, her mother was still sitting at breakfast, having a second cup of coffee.

It was not difficult to get a connection to America, though the clerk did insist on being paid for five minutes in advance, explaining that if he could not put her through she would, of course, get her money back.

Five minutes . . . What could she tell her mother in such a short time? Wanda wondered as the clerk plugged and unplugged cables, threw switches, and tested the connection several times through his headphones. Where should she even begin?

"Miss, your connection."

Wanda's hand trembled as she took the receiver. The line crackled and hissed; then she heard, "Hello, Mrs. Steven Miles here." That cool, familiar voice!

"Mother!" Wanda blinked rapidly so that she did not cry. Five minutes was so little time . . .

"Wanda?" her mother asked incredulously. "Are you already back from Italy? I thought that today was—"

"Mother, I have dreadful news!" Wanda broke in breathlessly. Her heart was in her throat. And before Ruth could say anything, she went on, "Marie is dead. She died after she gave birth to her daughter. I held her hand. She wasn't alone, do you understand me? She was buried two days ago, it was awful." She heard her mother take a breath at the other end of the line. Then she heard a soft moaning. Wanda didn't want to imagine the blow she had dealt her mother with her words.

"Sylvie, that's her daughter, is well. Marie's last wish was that I should take her back to Lauscha. That's what I'm doing now. I'm in Munich . . ."

All at once she didn't know what else to say.

"Mother?" she whispered when the silence at the other end of the line stretched on and on. "Are you still there?"

"Yes. I . . . pardon me, please, I . . ." There was a sound as though Ruth was blowing her nose, and then she said, "I can't believe it. It's . . . did she suffer very much?"

Wanda bit her lip. Should she tell the truth—or . . . ?

"No. She wasn't in any pain," she answered. "She had a fever, do you see?"

"Fever . . . Does Johanna know yet . . . ?"

Wanda shook her head. Then she remembered that her mother couldn't see her. "No. How could I even have told her? It will be a dreadful shock for them when I get home tomorrow with the baby in a bassinet . . ."

"Have I heard you right? You have Marie's daughter there with you? You're traveling alone with a newborn baby, such a long way . . . How . . . how did Franco even agree to let you take his daughter away?"

"Franco? I didn't even see him, but that's another story. Mother, don't worry about me, I'll manage. I'll call again when I get back to Lauscha. And I'll write as well!" Wanda felt a surge of love and tenderness. She would have given anything to ease her mother's pain!

At last Ruth recovered her voice.

"Believe it or not, I had such a . . . strange feeling these last few weeks whenever I thought of Marie. When Johanna told me that she hadn't been in touch for such a long time . . . My Marie . . . all the same . . . after the birth . . . I can hardly believe that she . . ." she sobbed. "I'm glad that she wasn't alone when it happened. It must have been such a comfort to her to have you there at her side. I'm proud of you," she whispered.

"Oh, Mother, the things that happened in Genoa . . . I can't tell you about them, not yet! But I did everything I could, and I—"

Wanda took a deep breath. This was no time to lose track of her thoughts.

"But there's one thing I have to tell you now—I promised Marie I would look after her daughter. Richard and I will do that. Sylvie needs me. She's such a sweet little thing! Marie said she looks like your mother . . . Mother, please understand, I can't come back to New York, not now!" Wanda held her breath.

"Yes, I . . . understand that," Ruth said in a hollow voice. The next moment a crackle drowned out her words. ". . . can't come . . . journey . . ."

How could that happen now, of all times! "What did you say, Mother? The connection . . . Mother, I have to go soon," Wanda yelled into the receiver.

"I said if you can't come, then I'll just have to make the journey myself!"

Wanda couldn't believe her ears. Mother wanted to come to Lauscha—after all these years?

"As soon as we hang up, I'll call and reserve a cabin on the next ship out. Perhaps . . . Steven will come with me. If not, then I'll come on my own." Ruth's voice was much stronger now, decisive. "We Steinmann girls have to stick together, don't we?"

34

There was not a soul to be seen on the single platform in the provincial station. So why weren't they pulling out? Wanda's gaze fell on the round clock on the platform. Two o'clock already! If this went on, she wouldn't get back home before nightfall.

Finally the train departed, snorting and shaking. Wanda very nearly felt like climbing out to help push it herself.

They had stopped at least five times since leaving Munich. Every single time the harsh squeal of the brakes had woken Sylvie, who had promptly begun to cry. Wanda found it hard to put her back to sleep. And every single time the smell of burning coal made its way into their compartment, irritating their eyes and noses. Wanda's handkerchief was already sooty, and she felt as though she'd spent the night in a coal mine.

She watched with relief as the station dwindled away behind them and vanished from view.

At last. She wanted nothing more than to be home.

A little while later the open landscape gave way to forests, which grew gradually thicker. There were no longer any roses and lilies blooming by the side of the tracks; instead, strange grasses nodded their heads gracefully in the wind. Wanda was gazing out the window, lost in thought, when suddenly she was amazed to recognize two huge spruce trees wound around one another.

The Siamese twins!

Richard had pointed out these two trees to her not long after they set out from Coburg! He had told her that their love should be just as deeply rooted as these trees, as closely knit together as their branches. A smile flitted across her face.

What on earth would her mother say about Richard? When she got to know him a little better, surely she would forgive the fact that he was a glassblower . . .

Mother in Lauscha. Wanda still couldn't quite imagine it. Perhaps Ruth had been so shocked that she just blurted it out without really thinking? Perhaps she had already changed her mind? From the sound of her voice, though, her mind was really made up.

Sylvie began to whimper softly. Wanda put a blanket over her arm and picked up the baby. She gently smoothed the fine hairs at the nape of Sylvie's neck, which were matted and sweaty.

"Dear, dear Sylvie," Wanda murmured. "We'll be home soon, very soon . . ." The little one calmed down and turned her head toward Wanda.

Wanda's thoughts flitted to her mother—and the way Ruth had spoken to her. As though to a grown-up. Not at all like before. "I'm proud of you," she had said. It had felt so good to hear those words!

"Poor little baby, you still don't know anything about your mother, and maybe it's for the best . . ."

The realization struck Wanda so suddenly that she almost jumped. Wasn't she in almost exactly the same situation as her mother all those years ago? There she was, traveling halfway across Europe with Marie's baby in her arms, a de Lucca who was going to grow up in Lauscha. Back then Steven had arranged forged papers for her and for Ruth, while this time it had been Franco's father.

Back then her mother had decided that it would be best if Wanda knew nothing about where she came from. And now it was up to *her* to make sure that Sylvie never found out what dreadful things her father had been involved in.

Wanda sobbed.

"Everything will be all right, my little princess," she whispered, her voice nearly choked.

Johanna's words came back to her as if from nowhere. *"Why are you so dead set on repeating the mistakes of the older generation?"* And *"Wouldn't it make sense to at least try to do a little better?"*

Wanda couldn't remember quite when or why her aunt had said those words. All that seemed so long ago.

But she would be home soon. With Johanna.

And her mother would be there as well, soon. It had taken a terrible tragedy to bring Ruth back home to where she had been born—what an irony of fate! Wanda shook her head. They would mourn Marie together. All the Steinmann girls. And she was one of them.

All at once she felt the flame called confidence burning brighter inside her. It grew with every mile, growing stronger as the train made its way through the valleys, between the pine forests on the mountainsides.

Everything would be all right.

She would move into her father's house with Sylvie until the wedding. That way her mother could stay with Johanna. Eva would be happy to have a baby in the house and she could help Wanda with Sylvie—she certainly had enough experience from looking after her own brothers and sisters. A grin flitted across Wanda's face—the first in a long time. Woe betide Eva and Ruth if they slipped back into their old quarrels! If that ever happened, she would tell them exactly what she thought of them.

It would also be very strange for all concerned when her mother and her father met again for the first time after so many years. All the same Wanda firmly believed that Ruth's visit would go without a hitch.

The baby girl in her arms squirmed.

She would give Sylvie all the love there was in the world. She would tell her stories every evening about her beautiful and proud mother, the woman who had made the glassblowers of Lauscha quake in their boots! Stories of glitter powder and glass baubles . . . Richard would take Sylvie on his lap so that she could watch him work. Perhaps she had inherited Marie's talent?

And when the time was right, Wanda would tell Sylvie about her father.

ACKNOWLEDGMENTS

I owe my warmest thanks to all who shared their knowledge with me, especially the glassblowers of Lauscha, among whom I can name only a few here: Lothar Birth, Michael and Angelika Haberland, Sabine Wagner, Peter Müller-Schloß and Thomas Müller-Litz. Their help was invaluable, and any mistakes that I have made in the descriptions of glasswork techniques are mine and mine alone.

I would also like to thank my friend Gisela for reading the draft of this novel with such care and attention and helping to polish the final version.

The little Tyrolean town of Bozen is now known as Bolzano and is part of Italy. In 1911 Tyrol was still part of the Austro-Hungarian Empire.

ABOUT THE AUTHOR

© Privat

Petra Durst-Benning lives near Stuttgart, Germany, with her husband, Bertram, and their dog, Eric. Before writing her first novel she worked as an import/export translator and edited a magazine for dog owners. All this changed with the publication of *The Silver Thistle*, which was set against the background of the peasant uprising in Germany in 1514. Her next dozen books take place in times ranging from the sixteenth century to the nineteenth century, and are set in Germany, France, Russia, and America. They bring tales of historical times, love and family, and happiness and hardship to an ever-growing readership. *The American Lady* is the second book in *The Glassblower Trilogy*.

ABOUT THE TRANSLATOR

© Maria Pakucs 2013

Samuel Willcocks is originally from Brighton on the south coast of England, but he now lives with his family in the historic city of Cluj, Transylvania, where he spends as much time in the cafés as he does in the libraries. A keen reader in many genres including science fiction and historical novels, he studied languages and literature in Britain, Berlin, and Philadelphia before winning the German Embassy Award (London) for translation in 2010. He has been a full-time translator from Czech, German, Romanian, and Slovene ever since. When not overindulging in cakes or dictionaries, he can be found at book festivals and other literary events, sharing his enthusiasm for Central European books and writers.